INTERRUPTIONS

SUSAN FROETSCHEL

W⊕RLDWIDE®

TORONTO • NEW YORK • LONDON
AMSTERDAM • PARIS • SYDNEY • HAMBURG
STOCKHOLM • ATHENS • TOKYO • MILAN
MADRID • WARSAW • BUDAPEST • AUCKLAND

For parents—Joe and Pat, Roy and Rory

INTERRUPTIONS

A Worldwide Mystery/July 2007

First published by Five Star.

ISBN-13: 978-0-373-26606-7
ISBN-10:   0-373-26606-5

Acknowledgments

First and foremost to editor Deborah Brod for her careful editing, as well as the entire team at Five Star Publishing for believing in this book. Thank you to John Helfers, Mary P. Smith, Tiffany Schofield and Feroze Mohammed.

For assistance with research and encouragement, I extend gratitude to Herman Leonard of Harvard's John F. Kennedy School of Government who first introduced me to the lack of accountability associated with development bonds; the librarians with Yale's Sterling Library, and public libraries in Henrico County, Virginia, and New Haven and Guilford, Connecticut; and Douglas Olsen of the Yale School of Nursing and Lawrence Strauss for critiquing the manuscript. Any mistakes are mine, not theirs.

Lasting gratitude goes to Thad and Sandy Poulson, editors of *The Daily Sentinel* in Sitka, who trusted a young reporter and taught her about the nuances and ethics of writing, as well as to the fishermen of Sitka who provided so much inspiration.

The great enemy of truth is very often not the lie—
deliberate, contrived and dishonest—but the myth,
persistent, persuasive and unrealistic.

—John F. Kennedy

ONE

MARCY JAMES HAD JUST STEPPED into the school from the pouring rain, in a skirt that was too long and a sweater that was too big. She was clearly at a disadvantage in any argument with the school principal, a perfect woman who sat behind her desk, with hands folded primly.

"Our only concern is helping Gavan," said Henrietta Cordola. Despite the late afternoon hour, the principal showed no signs of battle fatigue. Her black hair was pulled into a chignon, not one hair astray, and her navy suit still looked crisp and expensive.

Marcy paused and looked at her twelve-year-old son, trying to be objective. She simply saw a typical little boy: his head was down, but his back was straight and stiff. His hair, a tad straggly, was uncombed, and his jeans were worn but comfortable. "Of course, that's my only concern, too," Marcy replied, feeling defensive. "But we don't agree on a solution."

"Perhaps Gavan should leave the room while we talk?" the principal said, with a bright smile.

Gavan's head snapped toward his mother, his eyes alert and wary. "No," Marcy said, politely. "He should hear what you have to say."

The principal spoke slowly, patiently, as though Marcy were one of her young charges. "Many children in the school are on Ritalin, many whose problems are less severe than

Gavan's. His most recent stunt was inconsiderate. Mr. Fenlow finds Gavan to be completely unmanageable."

"Can't you consider changing his teacher?" Marcy pleaded. "I think Gavan is bored. If he were challenged, his behavior would improve."

The principal shook her head, the smile remaining stiffly in place. "That's not a solution. Students have to learn to deal with all types of teachers. Mr. Fenlow is one of our finest."

Marcy wanted to retort that she knew Thomas Fenlow better than Henrietta Cordola, new to town from Virginia. But she liked to think of herself as a tolerant person. She also was weary of arguing with the principal and getting nowhere. "Gavan's behavior is fine at home," Marcy explained. "And his grades were good last year with Ken Jabard."

"But he's in junior high," Mrs. Cordola countered pleasantly. "Every year, there are new demands. He needs help with self-control. The medication will help put Gavan back on track. I advise that you talk to his pediatrician again. And his father. We always appreciate meeting with both parents." With that subtle barb, the principal ended the meeting and stood near the door. As Gavan passed, she lightly placed her hand on his shoulder. The boy flinched, and quickly left the room.

Marcy hurried to the pickup and put the keys in the ignition, then turned to Gavan. "I'm glad you didn't talk a lot in there and make excuses," she began. "But couldn't you have at least said good-bye to her? Apologized? Promised that it won't happen again?"

Gavan shrugged. "Mr. Fenlow hates me, Mom. And I hate him. The class is torture."

"But you're stuck with him for now," Marcy said. "You don't have to like him. Just stop antagonizing him. Why would you want to snatch his notes from his desk? Making a teacher look foolish doesn't made the subject more interesting."

"I wanted to prove that he repeats himself year after year,"

Gavan said. "He can't think without his notebook. Why should we have to memorize so many names and dates?"

"Look, I don't want to put you on a drug to do well at school," Marcy said. "Your father and I think you can do well without it. Your behavior in school can either prove me right or prove me wrong."

Her son looked out the window as if he were trapped. "I don't want any drugs either. Thanks, Mom, for trusting me."

"No more dumb pranks, okay?" she stressed.

He nodded slowly, almost with a hint of a smile. Marcy started the pickup and headed away from the school parking lot. She felt guilty, wondering how she could help out more at the school. But Mrs. Cordola was right—junior high was not elementary school. Parents were less involved, and teachers who worked with adolescents had to be more cynical. "This isn't funny," Marcy said simply. "They're angry with you."

"Because we won't take their advice about the Ritalin," Gavan explained."'Tim's on it now, too."

"But why?" She started to make a U-turn, remembering she wanted to stop by the grocery store. "He does well at school."

"Mrs. Cordola told his father that it would make him a better student. The people at that school don't really want us to think. They want robots."

"Hmm," Marcy said. Her son had a talent for debate that could infuriate his parents. But sometimes Gavan was right. "You understand why Dad couldn't be at the meeting today. But we're there for you. Please come to us if there are problems."

He nodded again.

"For now, your job is to stay out of trouble. I know I've been busy lately and I'm not at home much in the evening. I just want to get through that last meeting tomorrow night and end any talk of a road crossing this island once and for all. In the meantime, do your best at school."

Gavan turned his head, staring out the side window at scenery they passed every day. Marcy wished she could read his thoughts. As a little boy, he had shared all his secrets with her. Maybe if she spent more time with him, he'd get into less trouble. She thought about trying to point out to her child the reality of living in a rural Alaskan town with less than ten thousand people. The school was labeling her child, and in a small town, those labels were impossible to shed.

But Gavan was stubborn and wouldn't care, so she remained quiet, and her thoughts returned to her long fight against the cross-island road—one more day and the fight would be over. And then she could spend more time with her son.

TWO

Friday, September 18

SWEET RAIN AND PALE afternoon light swept over Baranof Island, offering a soft illusion of perfection. The forest could have been an image detailed by a watercolor brush, except for the panic in the eyes of a fawn, wandering among the trees in search of his mother.

With very sound, the fawn felt a surge of hope, followed by lingering disappointment hen the doe did not appear. The fawn drifted toward a stream that his mother frequented at twilight. Distracted by the rhythm of swaying branches and tumbling water, the fawn did not pause to test the air before emerging from the stand of spruce. He bowed his head to drink.

A flash of golden brown charged and the fawn's legs crumpled. An old brown bear pressed one paw against the fawn's flank and lowered her head. The fawn died, eyes open, without a sound.

FROM NOW ON, ONLY cunning, intelligent pranks, Gavan promised himself after the session with the principal and his mother. Tim and Gavan hâd a plan to stop the island's biggest development project, and no one in town would ever know what really put an end to the cross-island road.

Gavan had listened closely to his mother's complaints about the road plans and how she didn't trust the engineer in town who was supposed to consult on environmental issues.

Gavan did not have to work hard to talk Tim into skipping school to follow the engineer, Dennis Kovach, into the woods. Skipping school was easy, especially with Mr. Fenlow, the teacher for their homeroom and most of the important subjects, out ill. "Sean will hand our homework in, and the substitute will never miss us," Gavan promised.

"She'll miss you," Tim noted.

Gavan smiled. Tim was well-behaved, accustomed to decent grades and steady doses of success. Oddly enough, Gavan charmed substitutes, who were unaware of his inconsistent performance. All week, while other kids fooled around and ignored the substitute teacher, Gavan kept limp discussions alive, impressing the nervous young woman with his ability to analyze conflicts leading to the Civil War.

"You do your best at school when it doesn't count," Tim pressed, as they hid the boat in some brush along the shore of Silver Bay. "Why?"

"All that matters is what I know, not what the teachers think I know," Gavan said.

THE ENGINEER HIKED farther than they had anticipated. Early on, the boys kept a careful distance. Both seventh-graders wore black jeans and dark sweatshirts. Gavan sported a floppy camouflage hat and Tim wore an oversized camouflage jacket. Cautious, the boys stayed back, hiding behind clumps of devil's club and other large plants, observing the engineer. Kovach hid his pack among the trees, occasionally returning for small packages in brown paper. With a bone-handled pocketknife, he sliced away brown paper, careful about the contents and placing all the scraps of paper inside his vest pocket. The boys kept their eyes on the pack, which the engineer never left alone for more than fifteen minutes at a time.

Just before noon, the boys stared through binoculars as the engineer stretched out near a log and lit a joint.

"That would not go over big at tonight's town meeting," Tim said with a giggle.

"But how can we prove it?" Gavan said wryly. Then he mimicked the engineer—taking a deep breath and leaning backward slowly, pretending to exhale. Tim burst into laughter. Holding his mouth and backing away, the boy tripped and landed with a thump. Gavan laughed harder, and the stream rushing over the rocks no longer disguised the tenor of merriment. Boots splashed through the stream, then tore through the brush, as the engineer approached. "Damn, he heard," Gavan said, standing still.

"I can't get caught," Tim whispered, scrambling for cover and shoving their makeshift lunch into his pack. "Let's run!"

"He'll catch us," Gavan hissed. "Get behind those bushes and freeze. I'll handle—" He cut the sentence off, sat on the ground, and broke out into a raucous cackle.

Tim's eyes widened, as heavy boots pounded nearer. Gavan sternly pointed to the brush, then turned the other way just before Kovach pushed his way through a mess of salmonberry bushes, the thorny branches snapping.

Tossing a small rock high into the air, Gavan did not look the engineer's way. The rock caught momentarily in the branches of a cedar tree, and Gavan laughed at the sky.

"What the hell are you doing?" Kovach growled angrily.

Gavan turned and didn't have to pretend fear. The engineer held a pistol. When Gavan didn't answer, the man grabbed Gavan's collar with his other hand and yanked upward. Choking, Gavan tried to pull away. The guy was strong. "I asked you something, boy."

Gavan squirmed, reaching for his neck and staring at the gun aiming somewhere above his left eye. "Don't," he gasped. Kovach gripped tighter. "I promise! I didn't hit it."

Kovach loosened his hold on Gavan's shirt. His eyes were

dilated and tired, and his cheek had a long scratch, beaded with blood. "What are you talking about?"

"The raven. I didn't hurt it. Honest!" Gavan kept his eyes wide, knowing that adults appreciated steady eye contact.

"Were you watching me?"

"I didn't expect to find a game warden out here," Gavan protested. "My uncle brought me out here a long time ago. I'm trying to find a cave we found."

Kovach gave the boy a shove. Gavan landed sprawled on the ground about eight feet away. He considered running, but the lunatic engineer was tall. Besides, Gavan couldn't outrun a bullet. "Who's out here with you?" the engineer asked harshly.

"No one." Gavan backed away. "Don't hurt me, mister. Please."

"I'm not going to hurt you," Kovach said, returning the pistol to a holster inside his vest. "Why didn't you come with your uncle?"

Gavan looked down, the ache in his voice real. "He's dead. And I can't find the cave."

Kovach's voice softened. "What's your name?"

"Jimmy Gromdin," Gavan lied instantly.

"Why aren't you in school?" Kovach asked.

Gavan shrugged. "I have more fun out here."

"I understand that." Kovach sighed. "But I'm working for the state and don't need a kid messing up the results. Take my word, there's no caves around here. I won't report you this time, but if I find you out here again..."

"I didn't know you were here," Gavan replied forlornly, collecting his pack. He gave Kovach a lopsided smile, one that had not worked on his parents in months. "I won't bother you."

"Don't come out here alone," Kovach warned. "It's dangerous."

Mumbling some thanks, Gavan immediately felt annoyed

with himself and took off fast in a direction not taken by Tim. He moved noisily through the trees, not looking back. After a hundred yards, he abruptly cut the noise and paused, making sure that Kovach hadn't followed. Then he circled back toward the stream and Tim's hiding place. But Tim had vanished.

Alone, nervous, Gavan stealthily approached the engineer, close enough to see the man remove wrappers from small packs of Oreo cookies. Stretched along the ground, Gavan made a point of moving only when the engineer moved. The man finished lunch quickly, and then stood, looking around and listening before stepping behind a stand of trees. Gavan held his breath until Kovach emerged without the large orange frame pack. He looked around in all directions, before moving among the trees, in and out of Gavan's sight, about fifty feet away, engaged in an odd but methodical task: first, he removed a brown paper package from his vest and sprinkled some contents in his gloved hand. Then he knelt along the edge of the stream and rubbed his hand back and forth across the gravel bed, almost as though scrubbing a floor. After a minute of scrubbing, he retrieved a handful of the debris along the edge of the stream and studied the sample before tossing it back with a splash. Then he walked upstream and repeated the process. Kovach was intent on the work, but cautious as well. Pulling a half-frozen juice box from his own pack, Gavan tired to think about what this work had to do with the cross-island road. Soft ice cooled his throat and fear.

Suddenly, a hand tapped his shoulder. Starting, Gavan twisted his neck around and saw Tim grinning and slowly waving the engineer's orange pack back and forth. "I don't believe you!" Gavan whispered, sputtering with laughter. "You really want to torment this guy!"

"I had to do something after you took his heat."

"Did you hear? The jerk thinks he owns the Tongass. The largest forest in the country, and there isn't enough room for a kid."

"He's hiding something!" Tim said.

Gavan's eyes sparkled with glee, taking the pack. "Maybe the answer's in here."

Dirty fingers emptied the pack. Gavan quickly ate two granola bars while Tim examined the camera, removing the lens cap and the cover. "Twenty-one photos taken," Tim said.

"I wish we knew what he was throwing in the stream. Maybe one of these small rocks in here?"

Tim kept toying with the camera. "How do we know what's evidence if we don't know the crime?"

"He got awfully mad. That's when people make mistakes."

"Let's take the pack and make him even madder!" Tim said. "Committing a little crime might stop a big one."

"I wonder how much trouble we'd get in?" Gavan mused, pocketing the rock.

"None, if we don't get caught!" said Tim.

"He'll know it's me," Gavan said, warily.

"Sorry, Gav." The excitement faded from Tim's voice and guilt swept over his face.

Gavan snorted softly and kept his voice low. "Stop. Besides, the jerk doesn't know my real name. He's from Juneau. Do you really think he'll want to drag the police to school and put all the kids in a line-up?"

"All right! Hey, I'll take a shot of those gravel beds." Tim crept closer to the stream and photographed the fan patterns along the banks. Before nightfall, southeast rains would obliterate any sign of the engineer's work.

Gavan followed and dipped his hand into the water. "Damn! That's cold!" Shivering, he held a handful of gravel. Both boys combed their fingers through the rocks, but found nothing unusual. "I wonder what he's adding."

"Nobody will listen to two kids." Tim shoved away wisps of brown hair caught in his eyelashes. "Fighting this road shouldn't be hard, but adults give up too easy! Except for your parents..."

Gavan kicked a large rotting mushroom, scattering pieces. "My old man's no better than yours, Tim. He might be a fisherman who doesn't go to an office. But he's the first to say there won't be fish left to catch ten years from now. Parents are all the same. They want us to go to college and be like that goofy engineer."

"That guy, our parents, they're screwing up the world and they don't know how to stop," Tim said.

"Nothing will be left when we grow up, and that's the biggest crime of all!" Gavan stuffed more granola into his mouth, remembering a book by Chris van Allsburg. In the story, the boy falls asleep and dreams of a forest destroyed for a toothpick factory, a hotel on Mount Everest. Gavan had long outgrown picture books, but he still stopped by the shelf in the library and turned the pages of the books by van Allsburg, wistfully hoping to change the world.

"Hey, look at this." Tim waved a small bag of marijuana. "We could take this to the police."

Gavan sniffed the contents and arched his eyebrows. "Not before we figure out what he's putting in the stream." He looked around and scowled. "We better get out of here before he comes back after his pack." The two boys shoved papers, the camera, back inside the pack. "We can check this stuff out at home." A smaller, worn piece of paper slipped from the pile—a map, meticulously hand-drawn, fell. Gavan studied the map with squiggly lines and notations in minute block print about gravel banks, trace mineral deposits, erosion and currents and then added it to his jacket pocket along with the marijuana.

Massive clouds glided across the sky, wind swept through the hemlock branches and crystal water tumbled toward the ocean. Gavan looked around at the forest that compelled him to fight the cross-island road, to stop this part of the world from changing.

Gavan carried the engineer's pack and Tim carried the smaller backpacks belonging to the two boys. They did not talk as they walked quickly away from the stream and back toward Silver Bay. Approaching the bay and the hiding place for Tim's tiny red skiff, they followed a narrow trail and Gavan almost stepped on the scattered bones of a fawn. Shuddering, he put his arm out to stop Tim.

"We interrupted someone's dinner," Tim said.

LATER THAT NIGHT, Marcy James paused in the doorway to the Centennial Building, the site for Sitka's largest meetings. She detested crowded rooms, always feeling a bit more nervous and less significant as extra people shared her space. At the special town meeting, she decided to sit toward the front, better to avoid all the faces and reactions of Sitkans who had a strong opinion, one way or another, on the cross-island road. As seven o'clock approached, the seats filled quickly and Marcy grimaced when Thomas Fenlow, a timid environmentalist and her son's seventh-grade teacher, sat next to her. Like her, he opposed the road. But she detested him more than any of the road's supporters.

"How are you feeling?" Marcy asked, knowing that he'd been sick from school all week. She was still annoyed that the teacher had complained about Gavan's behavior and then missed the meeting with the principal. "Are you sure you should be here?"

"I wouldn't miss this if I were on my deathbed," he replied. "Too bad I didn't make our last meeting. The committee letter is not as strong as I'd hoped."

"But would you sign a stronger letter?" Marcy asked.

"You know I can't sign any letter!" The teacher's spine stiffened. "I'm a public employee. Teachers can't take positions on these issues!"

Another teacher, Ken Jabard, paused near their chairs and

put his hand on Marcy's shoulder. "How's one of my favorite students doing this year?" Fenlow rolled his eyes and coughed.

"Gavan misses you for science, Ken," Marcy said, smiling up at the teacher who was so easygoing, in and out of the classroom. "I wish you'd move along with him every year."

"He'd outpace me, I'm afraid," Jabard said with a smile, before heading off for the coffee table.

"Thanks for signing the letter, Ken," Marcy called out.

"Humph," Fenlow said defensively. "He wouldn't think so highly of Gavan if he had to teach junior high history."

She twisted in her seat to face Fenlow directly. "I can't believe that history's a problem."

"Gavan reads a lot," Fenlow admitted. "But does he absorb? Not as much as you think. His work habits are deplorable. He refuses to follow directions or complete assignments. If he's not daydreaming, he acts silly, anything to get other children laughing. He stole my notes and he lied. All symptoms of attention deficit disorder."

"Since that new principal arrived from Virginia, every child in this town has attention deficit disorder," Marcy scoffed.

"The new principal understands the challenges of modern teachers. Chaotic homes. Chemicals in the environment. Mothers who don't have time for their children—"

"That's not me!" Marcy protested in exasperation.

"I understand," he said soothingly. "Look, it doesn't matter why Gavan suffers from the disorder. There are medications that smooth the rough edges. Plenty of parents are trying them. Six boys in Gavan's class, including his friend Tim."

"I'm not giving my son a drug to make your job easier," Marcy hissed. She remembered Gavan's entrance home that afternoon of the meeting. Tired and quiet, he had headed to his bedroom, piling textbooks on his desk and diligently starting homework. She had delivered lemonade to his room and asked about the large frame pack on the bed. Gavan had explained that he had borrowed it from Tim.

"Make school less boring, and Gavan won't be a problem," Marcy snapped. "And Tom, maybe I'm hyper, too. If you haven't noticed, that's the kind of person gets work done. Now excuse me, I want to discuss some last-minute strategy with people who are willing to testify." And she walked a way from her seat, joining some fishermen standing in the aisle.

Minutes later, Mayor John Perni started the meeting with an angry rap of his gavel. The room felt heavy with tension, maybe because rain from the Pacific slashed at the windows; it was the kind of autumn night that made an impatient audience long to return to woodstoves and families. Special meetings of the assembly, the town's governing board, were unusual. But Mayor Perni had extended the favor to Tim's father, Jeremy Bander, who was in a hurry to sell bonds and start construction of a winding road across Baranof Island.

The audience and the assembly who represented Sitka voters were almost evenly divided over the cross-island road. Everyone in the room knew Perni had the deciding vote. His office, on Lincoln Street, was a neighbor to merchants who relied on tourists for survival. But the thin accountant-turned-politician had bucked the tourism industry before, as well as every other special interest in Sitka at one time or another. That's why the majority of Sitka voters repeatedly returned the independent thinker to the mayor's office. The bond issue, while not the most expensive issue to come before the assembly during Perni's twelve years in office, was among the most contentious.

The debate lasted two hours.

Baranof Island, larger than Delaware, was a massive hunk of national forest. Any road would cut through some of the most stunning temperate rain forest left in the world. Sitka's environmentalists and fishermen despised development. On the other hand, the merchants who depended on an abbreviated summer tourist season—limited by weather, tides and waning daylight—constantly sought more attractions to prevent visitors from bypassing Sitka. The city had a rich history, once an Indian village and capital of Russian America, but it was also the only one in the Alexander Archipelago that directly confronted the harsh north Pacific. Any ship stopping in Sitka had to detour away from the Inside Passage and maneuver intricate waterways like Peril Straits.

The merchants demanded that construction begin immediately for a thirty-mile scenic route that would cut the island in two, between Sitka and Baranof Warm Springs. That road, to the south of Sitka, would nestle against inland lakes and ridges where the most frequent visitors were brown bear, Sitka deer and bald eagles. Cruise ships and ferries could remain in protected waters along the island's eastern shore, and tourists would take day trips to Sitka, viewing rugged wilderness through the windows of a bus.

The South Road, desired by the tourism community, would be scenic but expensive—more than one hundred million dollars. The North Road was proposed by Katmai Shee Corporation, based in Sitka and one of more than two hundred native corporations created to settle native land claims after oil was discovered in the Arctic. That road would be shorter and constructed in phases—initially costing twelve million dollars. The federal government made it clear it would contribute funds to a single road.

Observing the heated testimony, Marcy was certain that the assembly would refuse to approve a road through the heart of the island that would be the beginning of the island's destruction. Her side had worked on the research and coached everyone well.

The natives of Sitka argued heatedly for the compromise road. "We recommend phased construction," said Jane

McBride, who represented the native corporation. "Sitka has about eight thousand people. On the opposite side of the island, Baranof Warm Springs has less than fifty who don't want their town to expand overnight. Gradual construction would give both communities time to plan. Our proposal costs less and causes less environmental damage than the South Road supported by the tourism industry."

A shareholder of Katmai Shee spoke next. "We want to reach our property," the gray-haired man said simply, clutching his worn cap from his job at the local seafood plant. "Tourist trappers only dreamed up the South Road after we began plans to access our property. If we can't reach our property, we can't create jobs. Fishing quotas are locked up. The mills will close. I have a son in high school who wants to stay in Sitka, but there's no steady work." Such sentimental testimony ordinarily did not move Perni, who had long boasted that he based decisions on facts and numbers. But everyone knew that Perni's oldest son had gone to college in California and dropped out. Perni had not seen the boy since.

Dennis Kovach identified himself as an engineer and environmental specialist from Juneau, hired by the city to report on project feasibility and cost/benefit analysis of the alternatives. The man apologized for his lack of maps and other documents, sheepishly explaining that his pack, containing his work, had been stolen. Perni, who detested excuses for incompetence, cut the man off.

"Enough talk on these two roads," Perni announced and reviewed the options. "We can approve the North Road, South Road or no road. But not both. Do I hear a motion?"

"I move that we approve six million in bonds for the North Road, pending matching federal highway funds," said Lois Henry, the only assembly member who could claim native heritage.

"Okay, we vote on the North Road, the road to be constructed by Katmai Shee," Perni said.

The clerk called out the names of the assembly members. When called, the mayor responded gruffly: "Aye." Several gasps came from the audience. "Four in favor, three opposed," the mayor concluded. "The assembly recommends construction of the North Road, in phases." He slammed the gavel. "Meeting's adjourned." Men and women in worn jeans and flannel shirts, fishermen and natives who had not expected to win, burst into cheers. Those sitting next to Marcy hugged and congratulated her.

"Hold on!" ordered Jeremy Bander, director of Southeast Alaska Tourism Council, who stood in the aisle, surrounded by glum men in business suits. The crowd quieted. "It's unfortunate that so many want to keep Sitka a private playground for a handful of people. Mrs. James has led many to believe that stopping the road will protect the wilderness. The simple truth, ladies and gentlemen, is that the wilderness does not belong to you. It's federal property, and as such, belongs to all citizens of the United States. How do we protect this state if we refuse to share our treasures? Sitka has only a few thousand residents, with tens of thousands more visitors each year who are tired of your artificial limits. Citizens throughout the nation, not just in Sitka, have a right to decide on how federal land should be enjoyed.

"Tonight, the assembly threw away an opportunity. But that doesn't stop our road. And next week, the board of directors of the Alaska Development Authority will vote on our project.

"By coincidence, the national convention of cruise directors is meeting in Anchorage. More than a thousand cruise directors, travel agents, travel writers promise support for this vital project. Thank you." The room went into an uproar, but not before Marcy heard him mutter to his partner: "...lazy bunch who don't want progress..."

"Anyone can use the forest now!" Marcy shouted, in fury. "There are no limits!"

"Open the meeting back up!" a man roared. Perni shook his head, expressing his regret. The public meeting had been formally closed. Reporters and road opponents made plans to reserve seats on jets bound for Anchorage the following week.

Marcy walked slowly away from the meeting room with Beth Roberts, her friend and lawyer. "Those comments from Bander," Marcy said, her shoulders slumped. "I feel like he slapped me in the face."

"Politics," Beth said, sympathetically, placing her thin arm lightly around Marcy.

"Can he do it, Beth? Is that road financially possible?"

"Only if nothing goes wrong," Beth said. "And when has that ever happened with public construction?"

Then she said, "Where's Davy?"

"He stayed home with Gavan," Marcy said, heading for the door. "That reminds me, I have to talk with that engineer."

"His report doesn't help your cause," Beth warned.

"It's nothing to do with the road," Marcy called back. She hurried away from the angry crowd and caught up with the engineer in the parking lot. "Excuse me, Mr. Kovach?" Marcy called, pulling her jacket close around her neck as she spoke. "I wanted to ask about your pack."

"Yes?" He turned, alert. Marcy approached his car and waited for a few people from the meeting to pass, all in a hurry to escape the stabbing cold rain.

"It's orange, large?"

"Yeah, but…" He hesitated.

"Could you have misplaced it?" Marcy asked, crossing her arms for warmth. "I might know someone who found a pack like that."

Kovach tossed his briefcase into the back of a Buick and

leaned against the open door. "Mrs. James, do you have a son, about so high, with dark hair? About ten?"

"He's twelve," Marcy said, nervously.

"Go home and pat your boy on the back," Kovach said, with a bitter laugh. "He succeeded in making me look like a total ass."

"Wait, but Gavan was in school today," she said, desperately. "I did see a pack in his room, but I'm not even sure if it's yours."

Kovach shook his head with disgust and climbed into the car. "I doubt Gavan went to school, Mrs. James. I met him in the middle of the Tongass early this afternoon. If you don't mind, I want my pack, contents intact. Tonight. Then I'll decide whether to press charges. Katmai Shee Hotel. Room 214." He slammed the car door and roared away. Shaken, Marcy wandered the lot, trying to remember where she had parked.

MARCY STORMED THROUGH the side door of her home. Gavan and her husband, Davy, were stretched out on the family-room sofa, both reading. The fire was hot, and the old yellow tabby nestled between their legs.

She pointed her finger at her son. "You're in big trouble," Marcy promised, before stomping to Gavan's room where she found the pack propped behind his bed. Hefting the pack to her shoulder, she returned downstairs, continuing her tirade, "I argue at school for you. I tell teachers, 'He understand the concepts, he works hard, he can pay attention, he doesn't need medication.'"

"Marcy!" Davy implored. "What happened at that meeting?"

"We won," she snapped. "But Bander knows how to worm his way through the bureaucratic system."

Gavan bit his lip as he stared at the pack.

"Why are you so angry at Gavan all of a sudden?" Davy asked, bewildered.

"He knows," she said, her anger transforming into weariness. "A day after meeting with the principal, he has to go and validate everything the people at school say about him."

"What happened?" Davy asked.

"I skipped school today," Gavan admitted quietly.

"And he stole the pack that belongs to the consulting engineer!"

"What?" Angry now, Davy joined Marcy, taking the heavy pack from her hands. The cat slunk into the nearest closet.

"I was trying to help stop the cross-island road," Gavan protested sullenly.

"Oh, Gavan," Marcy said, her voice low with disappointment. "Why couldn't you talk to me? Winning doesn't count when you don't play by the rules. And then worst of all, you lied. You said that pack belonged to Tim."

"You're returning that pack tomorrow," Davy said sternly. "And you're grounded until further notice."

"No," said Marcy, reaching for the pack and awkwardly clutching it to her chest. "The engineer is livid, and he wants it back tonight."

"I can take it back," Davy volunteered.

Marcy shook her head. "I better go. I don't want him to think that I had anything to do with this."

"Wait, Mom, Dad, can't we look inside first?" Gavan pleaded. "The engineer has papers in there—about the cross-island road! We could find out his real plans."

"You're saying that you didn't already search through this pack?" Marcy asked.

"Not enough," Gavan admitted. "It was a long day of hiking and I was waiting for Tim or someone else to help. Maybe even you."

"Absolutely not!" Then she softened. Maybe her son had not caused too much damage. "We don't need to cheat or steal to fight this road, Gavan. Maybe I can explain to the engineer somehow. I'm hoping that I can talk him out of calling the police." She sighed. "Close that book and go to bed, and we'll talk more about this tomorrow."

SHE DROVE FAST TO THE HOTEL, with the pack sitting beside her like a mute passenger. Halfway there, she thought about turning around and letting Davy return the pack. The engineer only wanted the pack back and probably wouldn't care. But she pressed the accelerator harder. Marcy was one of the leaders in the fight against the cross-island road and was probably the only one who could convince the man that she was not the instigator behind the theft. Maybe her sincerity would convince him not to call the police and press charges against Gavan. Charges against a juvenile were supposed to be confidential, but she found herself wondering if school officials were an exception to that rule. Marcy could just imagine Henrietta Cordola gloating over this predicament.

Determined to convince Kovach to forgive her son, Marcy lugged the pack and held her head high, an effort to hide the fact that she was five-feet-one in her heels. Instead of calling from the desk, she headed directly for the hotel room and knocked firmly on the door of Room 214. She still wore the soft black sweater and matching skirt from the meeting. Kovach immediately swung the door open, and she held out the pack. "Here, my son said that everything's in here."

She waited by the door, while he zipped it open and quickly checked. "Everything looks intact," he said, finally. "I thought I'd never see this stuff again."

"Honestly, Gavan never did anything like this before," she said. "And if I had known this afternoon, I would have called you. Immediately." She held her hands out helplessly.

"He's a kid," Kovach said with a laugh that was both wry and friendly. "Boys are crazy at that age. Secret plans. Impulsive. I miss feeling that way." After a pause, he added, "Well, maybe only a little."

"I assure you, Mr. Kovach, he'll be punished for this."

"Call me Denny," the engineer urged. He reached his hand toward her shoulder, not actually touching. "And if you have a few minutes, I'd like to talk to you about Gavan." After tossing his pack onto the bed, he stepped into the hallway and closed the door to his room. "Let's head down to the bar."

His tone was so friendly that a wave of relief soared through her. She nodded and followed him to a lonely table in the back, away from the music. "I'm sorry that I snapped in the parking lot," he began. "I should have known that you didn't put Gavan up to pulling that prank."

"Please, you have no need to apologize," she said, knowing that he could have easily used the word "theft" rather than "prank." "Gavan told us he was trying to help, and I guess I'm at fault, too. As you know, I detest that road. I just can't imagine that it will ever happen, a highway across the island." She gestured toward the window at Mount Verstovia and the Sisters, hazy shapes in the rainy night. "I still think that it's too expensive, impossible. As an engineer, you must realize that."

"Nothing's impossible to an engineer. People despised other roads and bridges. The Brooklyn Bridge. For that matter, the bridge to Japonski Island." Kovach pointed to the graceful cable bridge covered in bright lights, crossing from downtown Sitka to a nearby chain of islands. "The development will happen anyway. In the 1950s the government built the hospital, airport, Coast Guard air station. Ideas never go away and the bridge was an afterthought. Bander needs to bait more people into that trip of a lifetime. But I promise, after a while, the road will seem less radical."

"Jeremy Bander's a calculating bastard," she said.

"But he's right about one thing—the state is the appropriate authority to decide such a road," Kovach explained. "I don't know why he bothered trying the city first."

"It's no secret how I feel. That road will destroy Sitka."

"That's what people said about cars and computers," Kovach countered.

"This is different," Marcy said. "This road promotes tourism. Tourism is not about progress. It freezes a town and forces a town to grow the way outsiders want to see it. Sitka has done a lot for tourism, but this road's too damn much."

"Maybe you're right." Kovach looked toward the window. Marcy couldn't be sure whether he studied puddles glittering with streetlight or the reflection of his face. "Don't be hard on your son. It's good that he believes in something."

Marcy was less sure and pushed her glass of beer aside. "I can't finish this."

"Have coffee," Kovach suggested. Without waiting, he called the waitress.

Marcy crossed her arms and leaned over the table. "Gavan knows we hate the cross-island road. Any development ruins the streams. Every salmon caught by a tourist cuts into the overall quota. But we'd never encourage stealing."

"I'm surprised he didn't throw it in a Dumpster. He didn't hide it?"

"You have to know Gavan," Marcy said, looking out the window, toward Crescent Harbor and the odd shapes of more than a hundred fishing vessels, including her husband's. She sipped the hot coffee slowly, holding on to the cup to warm her hands. "He gets absorbed in something and nothing else matters. My son inherited all my husband's and my own worst traits. I was a precocious tomboy, and my husband was a daydreamer who walked away from school one spring to sign on with a fishing crew."

"But that's why you love him," Kovach commented. "He takes risks. Makes decisions."

Marcy flashed a smile. "You're right," she agreed. "There's a good side to those traits, and I should know better than anyone else. Gavan is young. But in the meantime, if I can help make up for any damage that Gavan may have caused for you after tonight. Can I write a letter to Bander or help some other way?"

He sighed. "No, I'm just relieved to have the data for the state meetings. But I'd like to talk to Gavan. Ease his fears about the road and show him the work involved. Is he busy tomorrow? He could come along and help with some of the fieldwork."

Marcy hesitated, wondering how to warn the engineer that Gavan could be a handful.

"If he doesn't have other plans," Kovach continued, sounding awkward, probably a man who was unaccustomed to teenagers. "And I promise he'll be safe with me."

"It's the least he can do," Marcy replied. "I only hope he's not a bother."

Kovach smiled. "I'll pick him up at seven."

She jotted her address on a napkin for Kovach. Then she checked her watch. After midnight. "Then I better go," she said, standing. "Again, I can't thank you enough."

Denny nodded, and reached out for her hand to say farewell.

KOVACH FELT DREADFULLY lonely, missing Marcy James as soon as she walked away. He stayed in the dark Katmai Shee bar, ordered another beer that he really didn't want and stopped the waitress when she started to collect Marcy's unfinished beer and coffee. He reached for her crumpled napkin, touching the edges and smoothing the wrinkles.

He chided himself for being silly. Her eyes never revealed a hint of desire. All she cared about was the road and her kid. Shame, women his age always came with crazy children. He sighed as he thought about Gavan, only slightly regretting his rough confrontation with the boy. That kid had played him for a fool, deliberately following him and then lying. Kovach detested the kid, but he also had to get Gavan alone and find out how much he knew. Kovach wondered how long the kid had watched, how much he realized about the entire operation. All Kovach knew at this point was that the kid had told his mother nothing. If he had, she would never have agreed to letting Gavan accompany Kovach.

A dark-haired man from the bar, carrying a beer, disrupted the engineer's thoughts. "What the hell's going on?" The man's teeth were crooked and dirty. A chill went through Kovach. This job was getting too complicated, and he didn't like being watched. He was supposed to get the job done and talk to as few Sitkans as possible. Meeting Marcy in the bar, talking to Gavan out in the forest, were definitely not part of the plan. Instinctively, Kovach knew that he had to protect Marcy and Gavan.

"And who are you?" Kovach asked, glaring.

"We have the same employer." The man introduced himself as Ray Roland. "And we're not supposed to be talking about this project with anyone in town."

"You have the wrong man, buddy," Kovach said calmly. "I'm self-employed."

"You know what I mean. The cross-island road. Why did that woman have your pack? Where was it at tonight's meeting?"

Kovach sat back and stared at the other man. So, the client did not trust him. "You've never made an excuse to meet a woman?"

The man lifted his eyebrows and chuckled.

"There's nothing in that pack," Kovach said dryly. "And tonight's vote didn't hurt the project one bit." With that, he waved the waitress and ordered two more beers. He remained silent as the woman cleared away Marcy's place, and then tucked her napkin away into his pocket.

THREE

Saturday, September 19

GAVAN WAS IN THE PANTRY, searching for granola bars, fruit, anything that would make do for lunch, when he was surprised to hear the alarm clock ring upstairs. Moments later, his mother wandered into the kitchen and announced her own agenda for Gavan that day. "But I have other plans." Gavan groaned in protest, slouching against the wall.

"You *had* other plans." Marcy spoke sharply, fumbling to pour water into the coffeepot. "I'm too exhausted to argue, and you're grounded anyway! Mr. Kovach will be here in thirty minutes. You'd better hurry if you want to grab some breakfast."

"Mom, you don't know this guy," Gavan confided, changing both his tone and strategy. The boy dropped his voice to a low whisper. "He's mean. He's violent."

Marcy stood by the coffee pot. "Yes, Gavan, people tend to act that way after having their belongings stolen."

"I'm afraid of him," Gavan said, softly.

His mother shook her head firmly. "I met Mr. Kovach last night. He's a nice man and he's counting on your help today…" She didn't wait for the coffee to finish, whipping the pot off its burner, and filled her cup halfway. Water sizzled on the burner. She cleaned the area with a paper towel and returned the pot to the burner, before leaning back and sipping.

No wonder the school called him hyper, Gavan thought.

His mother couldn't wait a few minutes for coffee to brew. "Tim was counting on spending the day with me," Gavan went on. "How do you expect me to be reliable if I can't keep commitments? Please, Mom."

She waved her hand in irritation, ending the argument, and ran upstairs to change.

Gavan immediately phoned Tim. "I can't believe I have to go out with that guy! He'll probably shoot me! Or worse give me a big lecture the whole time about why a road isn't that bad for Sitka. How does he know what's good for this town? And I'll have to smile and pretend I'm grateful because he didn't bust my ass in jail."

"That's awful, man. Did my name come up?"

"Not a word," Gavan whispered. "No one's guessed that you were out there. Kovach doesn't know his nose from a banana— and my parents assume I'm the only troublemaker in town."

"Thanks, Gav. My dad would kill me. He's already in a foul mood after that meeting last night. What did your mom say about the meeting?"

"Not much. She hasn't talked about anything except the pack," Gavan said. "I don't want to spend the day with that guy."

"Hey, you can talk with him, maybe find evidence against the road."

"He's not going to do anything with me standing right there."

"You never know what could happen if you act dumb."

"Maybe." Gavan's spirits picked up. He was a spy. Spies never gave up.

"And I'll cover for you!" Tim exclaimed, his voice a low whisper.

"What do you mean?"

"Let's see if he's stupid twice."

"Tim, that's not a hot idea." Gavan felt uncomfortable telling Tim what to do.

"Why not?" Tim protested. "Are you planning on getting high with him or something?"

"Watch your beak, birdbrain! Thank God, I moved the dope to my jacket, so my mother didn't find it. She's mad about school and my lying about the pack. But she'd go ballistic over drugs. No, when I do drugs the first time, Tim, it will be with you and not the enemy." Gavan had been toying with the idea of trying some of Tim's Ritalin, to see if the drug really worked. But something in his mother's fury held him back. "But I still don't think you should go out there. You could get hurt."

"You sound like a parent," Tim said, sadly. "Man, I'm in focus. My dad made me take the Ritalin today. I tried to argue, so he stood there in the kitchen and watched."

"Practice tucking it in your cheek." Gavan knew plenty of older kids who saved their Ritalin and sold it to high school kids: the poor kid's cocaine. "How do you feel?"

"The same as always," Tim said. "Look, I want to keep an eye on you."

Gavan sighed. To be truthful, he didn't want to be alone with Kovach. Besides, if Tim had been caught, Gavan wouldn't mind following the pair. "All right," he conceded. "I'll call you tonight and let you know how good you are." He heard a pickup truck pull into the driveway and swore, checking the clock. The man was ten minutes early. "I've got to go. Hey, Tim, be careful." He hung up, grabbed his jacket, his pack and a box of cereal and ran outside.

DENNIS KOVACH HAD almost called Gavan to cancel. But he wanted to check the kid out, learn what he really saw, without raising suspicion.

His employers could not find out about Kovach entering the Tongass with anyone, especially the kid of a road opponent. So, Kovach took precautions. He left the hotel before dawn, almost three hours before his usual starting time. Ignoring his own skiff and rental car, he headed for ANB harbor. A few fishermen had engines started. It didn't take much to borrow another guy's pickup and skiff—only a bag of the best dope and a promise not to go far. The exchange made, hands shaken, Kovach took a nap in the parking lot. He set his watch alarm and didn't stop for his usual cup of coffee. Irritable, he pulled up the Shore Road home and grudgingly admired the gray and white home nestled among trees, the porch with a sweeping view of the sea. It was a picture of security and happiness—a life that Kovach would never know.

Gavan climbed into the pickup, and nonchalantly slid the ounce bag across the seat. Dennis frowned and pulled out of the driveway. "I wondered if I'd ever see that again," he murmured. "You and I both have our little vices. You steal. I smoke an illegal substance. So, we're even."

"If we're even, stop and let me out of the car," Gavan said. "I had plans for today."

"I'm not letting you off that easily."

Gavan didn't answer, maintaining his distance.

Kovach took an extra spin around a few blocks and checked the rear-view mirror before heading south along a road that ended near a secluded cove. No one followed. Kovach could not risk being seen with Gavan. The client had insisted that Kovach work in secrecy. And if anything happened to the boy, Marcy would hate him forever.

Certain that no one had seen him with Gavan, Kovach took off down the city access road and parked at the end. Without waiting for directions, Gavan leaped out, helping to unhitch the skiff.

The boat ride was brief, and both Gavan and Kovach were quiet as they scanned the water around them. Kovach was familiar with the terrain and hid the skiff near the beginning of a popular hunting trail. "How did you get out here yesterday?"

Kovach asked, as they shoved the skiff behind some brush hanging over the water.

"Borrowed a friend's skiff," Gavan replied.

"You want to lead the way?"

"Where are you headed?"

"Same place as yesterday."

Gavan looked about slowly. "I'm not sure I remember," he said, with a scowl. "I just followed you."

Kovach set out deliberately—taking a roundabout way to a smaller valley and a larger stream, a good mile away from the area where they had met the previous day. The area was closer to Silver Bay than the larger valley, but had rougher terrain. Kovach kept checking the boy's face for some reaction. Sometimes he detected a worried look, but that was probably because most kids were awkward around adults.

For the most part, the boy followed without questions, neither sullen nor afraid. Kovach had hoped to hear more opinions from the boy about the previous day. "You know you're not in trouble anymore," Kovach said quietly.

"Thanks, I know," Gavan said. But the boy looked nervous, almost distracted. So Kovach led the way and the boy followed, keeping pace, without questions. They hiked slowly, with Kovach pausing occasionally to take some notes in a small book and mumbling explanations about grades, geological formations, vegetation—anything he could remember at all from long-ago readings about ecology. About two hours later they reached a large stream, one well-marked on topographical maps. Kovach threw down his pack.

"We'll finish up some work here, and then we'll have lunch," Kovach announced.

"Is this where we were the other day?" Gavan asked, looking around. "That little bit of rain made the water run faster."

"The water flow can change fast around here," Kovach replied. He removed some small bottles from the pack and explained how the nontoxic dye would help measure dispersion and water flow rates.

"Why does that matter for the road?" the boy asked.

"Streams meander around here. We have to decide the best path and avoid the flood plains. Otherwise, a heavy rain could wash the road out."

While Kovach talked, he studied the boy for any sign of distrust or doubt. But Gavan's eyes were glazed with boredom. He did not talk much, shrugging his shoulders at the engineer's lengthy explanations. He was good about following directions in taking water samples, watching without comment as Kovach ran a series of tests and took notes. The boy showed the most curiosity when he silently pointed toward a large fishing spider not far from Kovach's hand, then laughing heartily as the engineer jerked his hand away.

They did two hours of meticulous work that carried no resemblance to what the engineer had performed the day before. Kovach asked several times if Gavan had any questions, and the boy shrugged and shook his head. Shortly before noon, they stopped for lunch, sitting on a pair of large flat rocks near the waterway. Kovach unpacked four peanut butter sandwiches, two apples, grapes and ten large candy bars.

Kovach leaned back, bit into a crisp apple and felt a delicious relief. Without a doubt, the theft of his pack had been merely a stupid prank. The kid tried to be tough, but he lacked real curiosity about the project. Maybe Gavan had thought stealing the pack would halt the road. More likely the kid had made an impulsive decision to get even after Kovach had roughed him up. Scaring the boy had been a mistake. If only all mistakes were so easy to correct.

"You know, any road that goes through here won't be big," Kovach said, and took another large bite from the apple. "A little strip through here will make it easier for kids like you to access the wilderness."

"It's not supposed to be easy," Gavan replied. "Besides, I get around all right."

"But you could go on longer hikes, see different streams and caves. How many people in town come out this far? Not many. The forest won't change with the road. People will drive through, but very few will stop and step away from that road. If anything, a road will keep the tourists contained."

Gavan kept his head down.

Kovach tried again. "You went pretty far yesterday for being alone. You ever get lost?"

"No, but that's because I usually follow people," Gavan said. "They always know where they're going."

"You ever follow anyone besides me?" Kovach questioned sharply.

"Sure," Gavan replied.

"Anyone ever catch you?"

"No," Gavan admitted, in a less hostile voice. "You're the first."

Kovach slapped his knee and his laugh was full and free. Gavan slowly bit away at two candy bars, and then stuffed another two in his pocket. Suddenly, the boy began talking, asking a stream of questions. Kovach congratulated himself on thinking to bring along the candy—a cheap price to pay for friendship from a kid.

Unfortunately, the candy from the hotel vending machine loosened the kid's tongue and made him hyper. After lunch, Kovach methodically continued with his unnecessary fieldwork, the results of which would never be released or examined. All the while, Gavan followed and talked nonstop. Not only that, he behaved oddly, dawdling along the trail and shouting a string of stupid questions that had obvious answers. Bored, Kovach didn't reply half the time, hoping that the boy would stop talking. The nervous chatter put the engineer on edge. Kovach had long decided that Gavan was no threat; one more hour of work and he'd take the kid back to town. Then, he could return, finish the real job and forever end his connection with the cross-island road.

MORE THAN EVER BEFORE, Gavan was sure the cross-island road was wrong for Sitka. Frustrated, he stood less than five feet away from one of the road's instigators, and yet he could learn nothing. The engineer had something to hide, but Gavan still had no clue. He yearned to describe the ordeal to Tim. His friend would know what to ask. All Gavan wanted was to catch some glimpse of Tim.

Gavan had played the engineer carefully all morning— keeping the line loose, slowly, slowly testing the guy's trust. Early on, Gavan was careful to act the part of the surly teen, so as not to make the engineer suspicious. Only with lunch and the peace offering of candy could Gavan safely act friendly and loud.

But Gavan had trouble talking and thinking like a goofy kid, especially during lunch, when he kept wondering why Tim didn't make some kind of signal. Worry slowly turned to panic. He couldn't imagine that Tim had trouble following the pair, regardless of the new destination. From the very start that morning, all along the trail, Gavan had deliberately left broken branches and scuff marks.

Gavan scanned the surrounding forest, straining to hear some movement in the brush, any hint of Tim's presence at all. Every muscle was tense, and he rubbed his neck, trying to think. Damn, Tim was good, that is if he had managed to catch up and figure out the new location. As minutes passed, Gavan struggled to keep a conversation going with the engineer—if only to help Tim. They had been in the area for several hours, and Gavan had yet to hear a twig snap. Maybe Tim had given up and returned home.

Swift clouds the color of dull steel approached. Intense

winds whipped the treetops and then moved on, leaving an eerie silence that lasted only a moment or two, before more gusts took over.

A stubborn gust pushed down through the trees, and a large hemlock branch snapped and fell about twenty feet ahead. In seconds, the wind vanished, leaving a gloomy quiet. A distant scream pierced the silence and echoed against the hills. The scream could have come from any direction.

Gavan clutched Kovach's arm. "What was that?" he whispered.

Kovach looked around. Another gust swept through the overstory and toward the ground with a roar—muffling their voices. "The damn wind's playing tricks," he replied. "Or maybe the ravens. I've been coming out here for years, and they still give me the creeps sometimes."

"Ravens don't make noises like that," Gavan insisted. The large birds croaked notes with clarity or laughed maniacally. The scream mixed with the wind was full of fear or pain. Gavan looked around frantically and, ignoring Kovach, pulled a silver whistle from his pocket and blew three sharp bursts. Nothing. "Which way did that noise come from?" Panic gripped his throat. It hurt to breathe or talk.

"I don't know," Kovach said, frowning. "Maybe if we hear it again…"

Gavan had never felt so uncertain. With any luck, the noise was a trick of the wind or the cry of a wild animal. He wanted to do what was best for Tim. Maybe he should tell Kovach that another boy was following. The engineer might help, or he might get angry and immediately tell Tim's father. Or, maybe it would be faster if Gavan convinced the engineer to turn back. Tim had promised to follow and that meant he was somewhere between this stream and the cove along Silver Bay. If Tim needed help, he would hear them and call out. Possibly, Tim had never left home at all. Or maybe he watched from a few meters away, chuckling to himself about giving Gavan such a scare. Not funny, friend, Gavan thought. A bitter taste was in his mouth, as he spoke up.

"Haven't we done enough today?" Gavan asked. "The weather looks bad, and my mom will really worry."

"Sure," Kovach agreed. "No problem. Let's head back."

Gavan turned abruptly and headed for Silver Bay at a brisk pace, no longer hiding his fear or caring what Kovach thought. Outpacing Kovach, he stopped to blow the shrill whistle every hundred feet or so.

"That's driving me nuts," Kovach announced after the third stop.

"We don't want to run into a bear," Gavan explained. "Not in this wind."

"Cut the whistle," Kovach ordered. "With two of us, we're making plenty of noise just by walking along. Besides, remember I have that pistol in my pack."

Gavan unhappily returned the whistle to his pocket and picked up the pace. As they approached Silver Bay, Gavan removed the whistle and defied the engineer's request, blowing it hard, over and over. Kovach groaned and quickly pulled the skiff from its hiding place. He ordered Gavan into the boat and brought the engine to an angry roar. Aiming the boat for the center of Silver Bay, Kovach told the boy to move away from his seat next to Kovach and the wheel. "Do me a favor," Kovach shouted over the engine. "Straighten out those ropes down there and throw the gear into that crate."

Gavan stared at the engineer and then stood, kicking at the tangled rope in annoyance. He glanced back at the shoreline, hoping to see Tim's red boat. He clutched the side of the speeding boat and scanned the shoreline. "In a minute," he answered, in a distracted way.

Kovach reached out and shoved the boy's shoulder hard.

"Get down and clean that up now!" the engineer ordered. Then, pulling his own hat low, he put full attention to the wheel.

Gavan knelt and fooled around with the empty containers and odd fishing gear scattered about, slowly moving them to the bulkhead storage. The man had been pretty nice all afternoon. Gavan glanced at the engineer's face and saw that his eyes were locked on a skiff approaching from the other side of the bay. Suddenly, Gavan realized the man did not want to be seen, and Gavan swore to himself, mostly because the boat did not belong to Tim and because he still did not understand what the engineer was trying to hide.

Soon they were far from where Tim would have hidden his skiff—and Gavan gave up looking. Tim was practiced at hiding the red boat well. The deck was clear, but Kovach gruffly insisted that Gavan stay low. "The wind is rough," he shouted. "I don't want your mother blaming me if you catch a cold."

Kovach brought the skiff to full speed and Gavan realized they had passed the cove where the pickup and boat trailer were parked. Startled, the boy clung to the side of the skiff and looked at Kovach.

"Get back down for another minute," Kovach said. "I'm dropping you off at that dock close to your house."

Gavan took a deep breath, eager to get home and call Tim, hear his friend's voice. Kovach pulled the boat quickly to the dock and left the engine on idle. "Tell your mom that I'll call her. Maybe you can help the next time I'm in town."

"I won't have anything more to do with the cross-island road," Gavan said flatly. "And neither should you."

"It's too late for that, my friend," Kovach said wryly. "But I had fun once you started talking. I wouldn't mind another hike. Be sure to tell your mother that for me, and tell her that I'll give her a call."

The engineer held a post to steady the skiff, while Gavan

leaped nimbly onto the dock. Despite his wet shoes and pants, his entire body tingling with a chill, he felt better than he had in the forest. Only then did he notice the skiff was slightly larger than the one that he and Tim had followed the day before. He started to question the engineer, but Kovach immediately shoved the skiff away from the dock with one hand and hit the throttle.

Gavan called again, but he wasn't sure that the engineer heard as the man gave a friendly wave and directed the small boat back toward Silver Bay. Gavan regretted not confronting the man about what he was trying to hide. Playing dumb had not produced anything. Anxious and tired, Gavan ran home and immediately dialed Tim's number.

"But I thought he was with you, Gavan," Mrs. Bander said with alarm. "He's been gone all day."

Gavan ached with pure fear. "Are you sure?"

"Of course, I'm sure." Her voice went to a higher pitch. "He said he was headed for Silver Bay. With you. I lied to his father so he could spend time with you, and this is what Tim does?" She slammed the phone down.

Gavan gripped the receiver, fell against the wall and tried to think: He could take his parents' skiff and head to Silver Bay. He could ask his parents to help. Maybe the engineer would run into Tim. Instead, he called Mrs. Bander back and suggested that she call the police.

KOVACH WISHED HE understood why Gavan had been so frightened and in such a hurry to leave. Not that Kovach hadn't been ready to leave. Maybe the kid suddenly guessed that the engineer had not returned to the same stream. But no, the kid got upset only after hearing the strange noise. That scream alone could have tempted Kovach to never return to the forest surrounding Silver Bay. He shoved aside worry with the reminder that this was his last hike into the Tongass.

As Kovach hurried, he thought about Gavan. He regretted talking to the kid in the same menacing tone used by Kovach's own father, and cringed at how easy anger could take control of a voice. He wondered what Gavan would say to his mother, then shook his head. He was in a hurry to forget about a woman he couldn't have, and in a bigger hurry to finish this job and leave town. The engineer never wanted to see or think about the cross-island road again. Convinced that he had fooled any followers, Kovach landed his borrowed skiff near the most direct trail to his personal discovery, a small and remote stream in the desolate interior of Baranof Island.

This visit was his last and the hours of light were few, so the engineer retraced some of the easier steps from previous visits and combined only a few detours. Moving with caution, he couldn't risk being followed again. One curious kid had caused enough problems, let alone the nosy man who had watched Kovach with the kid's mother in the bar last night. Kovach walked faster, trying to forget the interruptions and delays of the last twenty-four hours.

He hiked several rough miles inland, where the dullness of once-emerald leaves signaled winter's approach. Kovach doubted that he'd see the stream again in any season. Besides, once the road crews arrived, this part of the forest would never look the same.

This visit was Kovach's fifth to the island's interior. Each time he had walked the length of the stream, searching for signs of human activity. He found none.

Not that he was surprised. Plenty of Sitkans knew Baranof Island's coastline in and out. Water teeming with herring, salmon, crab, whales and other sea life had dominated the town's culture for hundreds of years. But the tremendous bounty along the island's edges had left the center, with its rugged forest, treacherous cliffs of ice and rock, and desolate muskeg, relatively unexplored by most Sitkans. The stream, which began in a narrow valley nestled among the coast mountains and sprawled into the muskeg, was neither charming nor unusual for Alaska. Deer and bear rather than humans had forged the few trails crisscrossing the center of Baranof Island. Kovach had counted on privacy. For the scheme to work, the stream could present no sign of human contact.

Kovach kept looking about, hoping that he had this part of the forest to himself. He glanced at the sky and longed for rain, a cold and irritating downpour. Inclement weather not only obliterated traces of his own presence, but meant fewer interruptions from hikers and hunters. But only a few scraps of gray sky were visible to the west. Fragments of the offshore storm still swirled among the treetops. When the wind blew, someone could pass less than twenty feet away and Kovach would never know. He shook the thought. Why get spooked? No one would follow so late in the day—and he had just left Gavan off miles away.

He estimated needing two hours to finish. Pausing at the meandering creek, he removed the false bottom from his pack and a small bundle wrapped in brown paper. Kneeling, he went to work mixing the bag's contents with the pebbles along the inside curve of the bank. His gloved hands, numb from the icy water, moved steadily. Evergreen trees leaned over the rushing water, the branches intertwined like a long and beautiful braid.

He saved the bulk of the bag for the most difficult part of the job—climbing an eighty-foot unstable ridge. The source of the stream, a spring, originated about halfway up the ridge, where clinging vegetation masked the damp sheen. Kovach could not have found a more perfect location for an elaborate scam that would fool most geologists and mining engineers. Government maps did not show the stream. Possibly, military cartographers, who last examined the area in the 1940s, had missed it. Or perhaps recent earthquake activity had exposed an underground spring. Kovach pulled his way up the unsteady mess of dirt, moss, rock and exposed roots. The vertical cliff was patched with rock and soil, dooming trees and bushes to a tenuous life, and Kovach tested every hold.

Not far from the head of the spring, his foot loosened a smooth rock. Tightening his grip around a slender branch, Kovach gasped as his body slammed against the side of the cliff, shoving his face into brush and mud. The rock tumbled down the cliff, but the branch held. "Close," he whispered, refusing to look down. The sound of the rock thudding below played over and over in his head as he moved on.

Twenty minutes later, he reached his goal—a ledge halfway up the ridge. He huddled close to where warm spring water spurted from earth and rocks. Hurrying, twisting his torso to remove his pack, he accidentally knocked several rocks out of place. As they clattered down the hill, he swore. The plan would work only if the ridge appeared undisturbed. Once again, he was thankful for the heavy rains, which would eliminate any trace of Kovach in a few hours, let alone weeks.

Removing his gloves, Kovach extracted the bundle from his pack and compared the samples in his hand with the rocks embedded along the ridge. An excellent match. He swirled the contents in the warm water, burying a few and strewing others about. By the time any geologist investigated, the rocks would appear natural, exposed by the same geological disturbance that had created the stream.

Once the package was empty, Kovach lit a joint. He took a deep draw and held his breath for a long time. He didn't know the identity of his employer, but someone was willing to spend thousands to ensure that a road would be built across Baranof Island. A month ago, Kovach had admired the ingenious plan that would eliminate squabbling over an exact route. Yes, the road would attract tourists, whose sheer numbers Kovach detested. But he had more than enough money to escape to the remote corners of the state. Money. Thoughts of it triggered memories of his father, and Kovach automatically cursed the dead man.

"Mining engineering," insisted his father, after working for years as a salesman for a mine equipment firm. "You'll be set for life." The younger Kovach had hoped to study ecology, but instead, he attended engineering school with high grades and a higher tolerance for boredom. The profession offered none of the riches that his father had promised, not even stability. Engineers no longer amazed ordinary businessmen by manipulating numbers. Computers changed the status of the profession, and inexpensive software provided instant, precise calculations. Graduates of mining and civil engineering departments gratefully accepted positions once filled by experienced if uneducated shift foremen.

Kovach's early jobs had been along barren, dusty strip mines in Montana. An MBA would have been the ticket away from the mines and miserable crews. But executives wielded the power of rotating shifts and refused to rearrange schedules to allow ambitious engineers to attend even night classes.

The elder Kovach stopped bragging when Dennis couldn't afford a large home, a BMW or cruises to exotic locales. He accused his son of lacking motivation, integrity and other intangible qualities. Dennis silently agreed, accepting responsibility for allowing his father to set the direction of his life.

After four years, Dennis quit the mines of Montana and headed for Juneau, capital of development-happy Alaska, before the oil revenues began to decline. He created an exclusive statewide environmental consulting firm. Most clients were unnamed personnel of major corporations, who paid high fees, counting on Kovach to align results of any study with company desires. Selective about clients and tasks, Kovach lived frugally and attracted little attention. He hunted and fished eight months out of every year. He telephoned his father once a year at Christmas and refused to describe his life-style or comforts. He avoided other engineers, throwing away the dozen or so letters arriving each month at his post office box, pleas from desperate graduates in search of a job.

Kovach grabbed his water bottle and took a swallow, cleansing his mouth of the hot taste of marijuana. A move-ment about fifty yards to the east caught his eye. Kovach flat-tened his body against the ground, pressing his face against a boulder. A man in dark pants and a camouflage jacket crept out of sight.

"Damn, it's crowded around here," Kovach muttered to himself. He could not risk another witness, certainly not at the source of the stream. So he remained quite and waited, while spring water seeped into his pants. Only after a long fifteen minutes did Kovach resume working, rearranging dirt and clinging vines, eliminating any sign of his presence. He checked his handiwork and glanced downward at the thicket. Nothing moved below.

Mission accomplished, he thought, relieved and tired. Climbing up would be short, easy. He'd follow the top of the ridge and head for the easiest route back to the skiff. He'd avoid the hiker and leave the forest under the cover of dark-ness. Moving slowly, concentrating on every step, Kovach vowed to accept no more assignments connected with the cross-island road. His breathing came hard and he chided himself for not waiting to reach the top before smoking the dope. As he closed in on the upper edge, he smelled cigarette smoke. Startled, he looked up. In the twilight, the man in ca-mouflage leaned against a massive cedar tree.

"Hello, mate," said the man with a pinched smile, a base-ball cap pulled low over his eyes. "Looks like you could use a hand." The man did not move from the tree.

Kovach laughed aloud and swore to himself. The sudden intake of air hurt. The client had stressed the need for secrecy and knowing the names of anyone encountered by the engineer. Kovach had decided against mentioning the kid, but he'd have to report this jerk. An adult could form ideas about what Kovach was doing.

"No." He caught his breath. Kovach was in shape, but the constant dope took its toll on his lungs. "I just don't believe in taking the easy way on a trail." He almost groaned about the lame explanation and searched for handholds, determined to talk as little as possible. Six more feet. Four more…and then, the stranger sauntered to the edge of the cliff and leaned directly overhead. His voice was smooth, educated, rational, almost making up for a chin in need of a shave.

The stranger held out his left hand and slowly exhaled smoke toward Kovach's face. Annoyed, Kovach hesitated briefly before accepting. The man gripped hard and pulled, digging the heels of his heavy-duty boots into the dirt. He flung his cigarette away and reached underneath his jacket, producing a hunting knife with a lethal five-inch blade.

Kovach tried jerking his hand away, but the man had a powerful hold. Kovach yanked wildly again. The rock holding his left foot fell down the hill. As he lost his balance, he was forced to depend on the man's wrenching grip. "Is this a joke?" The man smiled, but didn't answer. "Look, I'm just a consultant for the city," Kovach protested, scrambling and then kicking hard for a temporary foothold.

"I know who you are, Mr. Kovach." The man's smile was eerie as he slowly eased his grip on Kovach's hand. Kovach clung to the dirt wall as soil and pebbles crumbled.

"Okay, then let me up," Kovach said. The fragile cliff would not sustain his weight for long. "Then we'll talk."

"Yes, let's talk." The strange fellows eyes glazed, his voice flattened. "Tell me what you saw this afternoon."

Kovach was confused. "What the hell are you talking about?" The man didn't answer, but stroked his thumb back and forth across Kovach's wrist, almost absentmindedly. Repulsed, Kovach had little choice but to hang on to the hand. He moved one foot a few inches, then his free hand, for better balance. He could not afford to make the nut angry. At least the stranger didn't ask about the road or what Kovach had been tossing around in the stream. But his limbs were in a precarious position and his pistol was unloaded and tucked away in his pack. Kovach's only weapon was his mouth.

"Why didn't you help the kid?" the man asked coldly, abruptly removing his hand.

"What?" Kovach's brain was in panic, a mess. "Today?" Damn the marijuana. He pressed every inch of his body against the wall of dirt and swore he'd throw the rest of the dope away. He'd never smoke again once he left the ridge. But dope or no dope, this guy made no sense.

"Why did you try to hide?" The man paced on his secure plateau, never moving far enough to give Kovach room to scramble to the top.

"I was working!"

"You're a lousy liar."

Kovach's old man had always accused his son of being a terrible liar, as if that were a major character flaw. "Damn it, let me up!" Kovach screamed in frustration, grasping for a root not far from the top of the ridge. More dirt sprinkled away from the cliff.

The man slowly extended his foot, pressing it against Kovach's shoulder. Kovach held tightly to the root. He was so close to the top, so close to walking away from the stupid road.

"Not so fast, Mr. Kovach. I don't know what you heard this afternoon. Maybe you're truthful, maybe not. Next week, you'll read the newspaper and understand my concern."

"I don't live in town," Dennis hissed. "I don't read the *Record*."

The foot pressed harder. Kovach's fingers felt raw against the bark. "No curiosity?" The man gave an odd chuckle.

"You're hiding something, Mr. Kovach. You didn't follow your usual routine today. You didn't bring your boat."

"So? Why are you watching me?"

The man shrugged. "You promised to work only on weekdays. I didn't expect you."

Kovach clutched his holds, adjusted his feet and wanted to groan, remembering his many precautions to avoid being seen, more on this day than ever before, all to protect Marcy James and Gavan. The man wasn't using names, and Kovach could not implicate them now. "Look," Kovach said, calmly. "I don't know your name. Your secret. Whatever. So let's forget we ever met." The man looked thoughtful, not answering. Kovach continued in exasperation. "I'm leaving town tomorrow. Anyone who's hired me can tell you that I can keep a secret."

"You watched me with that kid." The smile smoothed to a line.

"No," Kovach said, hoarsely, terrified. He only knew one boy and that was Marcy's boy. Surely Gavan had no time or reason to talk with this man. For the first time, Kovach forced himself to look downward, with the awful feeling that the direction offered his only escape.

"The kid told me you were here. I didn't believe him, but here you are."

"I don't know what you're talking about."

"The boy's dead, Mr. Kovach. Can you really keep that secret?"

"No!" Kovach screamed. "That's impossible!" He shoved his head against his shoulder, trying to push away the jerk's foot. "An accident..." Kovach said, breathing hard.

The man nodded and moved his foot. "Certainly. But the police won't see it that way."

Kovach swallowed. No escaping this guy, except down. If he could reach the rocks near the opening to the spring, he'd load the pistol. He'd have to move fast with no time to check his holds. But maybe he could get a head start, before the guy guessed. He had to be friendly and distract the guy. "You're joking, right?" Kovach kept his eyes on the man's face as he stretched his leg downward and swallowed, fighting the taste of vomit rising in his throat.

The man laughed. "No. The boy was real. Thirteen years old. Brown hair. Big eyes. Bigger imagination." The soft, wicked laugh bounced away. "I can't let you reach the top, Mr. Kovach. Or town, for that matter. But you can help me tremendously. I'll borrow some belonging of yours and deposit it near the body. Not your hat. Not subtle enough. Perhaps something from your pack…"

Angry, Kovach found a secure niche for his feet. He feigned weariness and leaned his head against his arm as he studied the cliff below, planning his next few steps. Taking a deep breath, Kovach abruptly forced his feet and hands into action.

The stranger caught on instantly, returning his knife to its holder. He picked up a rock, heaving it toward Kovach's head and missing by a centimeter. Then he clutched a branch and scrambled to follow. Kovach moved without hesitation, putting more distance between himself and the lunatic. At one point, he slid a few feet while hanging onto a long branch. Kovach was making progress and thought only about making it to the spring and loading the pistol.

Then his pack caught a snag. Kovach twisted, trying to break away. Precious seconds dwindled. He looked up and dirt fell into his eyes. His pursuer was directly above, eight feet away, close enough that Kovach could hear the man breathe.

Kovach wrenched his body hard. The pack would not jerk free. "There's no point in killing me," Kovach gasped, struggling to unbuckle the waist strap to the pack and extracting his left arm. The control in his voice amazed him and sounded as if it belonged to another man.

"I don't have to," the man laughed. "You're going to kill yourself."

"You're going to get caught," Kovach responded calmly.

"Not for killing you," the man taunted, inching closer, staying clear of Kovach's arm. "You're a loner. No one cares if you're dead. Why do you think you were hired?"

"But I wasn't alone," Kovach said.

The man paused in a comfortable perch. "Your friend from the bar. Marcy James. Is she out here?"

"No!" Kovach gasped, feeling cold. "She's nobody to me." He tugged the pack again and swore silently. He couldn't even reach the empty pistol.

"But why did she have your pack? What did you talk about for so long last night?"

"I tricked her," Kovach said. "She thought she could stop the road by intercepting my pack. But it didn't work, and there was nothing inside." Kovach stared upward, beyond the man, where the trees and branches cast graceful silhouettes against a lavender sky.

The stranger on the cliff pressed on with more questions about Marcy James. "Did she talk you out of finishing this job?"

Kovach tried to smile. "I'm a sucker for short women with long hair. She has no idea what I'm doing out here. If she knew, she'd hate me. Ask Ray. He knows."

"We don't pay Ray to think."

Kovach stared at his opponent, but shadows had overwhelmed details of his face. The impending darkness was on Kovach's side. All he needed was a bit of distance between himself and the maniac, then he could hide and wait out the night. Kovach decided to abandon the pack. He didn't need the gun once darkness fell.

"So, the client planned to kill me all along," Kovach said. "You don't think I'm smart enough to arrange protection?"

The stranger halted. "How so?" The voice lost its smooth monotone.

Confidence rolled through Kovach. Instead of answering,

he said, "If I don't return, my friend will lead people here." He tried to yank his right arm away from the frame. Nothing. He repeated the movement with more force and completely lost his footing. Scrambling, Kovach found no holds. Now, his safety depended on the pack staying caught. The branch bent in protest, slowly wrenching his arm from its socket.

"Prove to me that I can trust you," the man urged, lowering his hand toward Kovach. "Tell me who was with you."

Kovach refused to touch the hand, and instead clawed at the dirt, ignoring the pain as his fingernails bent backward. Only one person had a clue about Kovach's location, and that was Gavan James. No way would Kovach allow that name to pass his lips. But maybe, the mere possibility of another person would force the attacker to give up and walk away.

"And if you don't tell me, believe me, I'll find your friend," the man said, breathing hard, creeping closer. "I've got nothing to lose."

Kovach felt the muscles in his arm stretch and tear as he thought about Marcy's son. He prayed that the boy was at home with his mother and both were safe. The engineer kicked desperately to find some half-buried root or rock to support his weight. But all he found were velvety dirt, loose rocks and incredible pain in his arm.

The branch snapped. Kovach knew he had less than a few seconds before it broke away completely. He could take his chances falling, try and clutch some branch below, or... "All right," he gasped. "I'll tell you!" He lifted his right arm and reached for the other man's hand, grasping it firmly. Then with all his remaining strength, Dennis Kovach pulled.

Two bodies twisted and tumbled in the air. One fell fifteen feet, and a bush extending from the hillside stopped the worst of his fall. The other man fell the entire length of the cliff, his head bouncing against a boulder, his scream breaking off into silence. Pain vanished with the darkness, as his spirit soared and wept with the wind.

DETECTIVES WITH Sitka Police knocked at the door to 2216 Shore Road—a gray and white three-bedroom house nestled among conifers and spruce, with a porch open to a sweeping view of the sea. The home was the portrait of comfort and stability.

Marcy James, in blue flannel robe, her long blond hair loose, opened the door a crack. "Yes?" she asked tentatively.

"Sorry to bother you so late, Mrs. James," said Lieutenant Charles Dansby. "But Tim Bander's missing, and his mother suggested we talk to Gavan."

"Missing!" Marcy gasped, covering her mouth. "They're best friends. But Gavan didn't see him today."

"She explained that," Dansby said. "We still have questions."

Marcy nodded. "Come in. He's asleep, but I'll wake him." She ran lightly upstairs, and quietly let herself into her twelve-year-old son's room. He sat at his desk chair, near the window, his knees drawn to his chin.

"Gavan, the police are here," she whispered. "Tim's missing."

Gavan bent his head and made a choking noise.

"But you don't know anything, do you?" Marcy whispered, moving closer to him, putting her arm lightly on his shoulder.

He jerked his head back at her touch. "Because you made me go with the stupid engineer," he said bitterly. "I was supposed to be with Tim!"

She took him by the shoulders. "Don't tell them about taking the engineer's pack," she whispered urgently. "Unless they ask, of course. But they won't." He looked away from her, his face tight with fury. "I only want to protect you," she added softly.

DOWNSTAIRS, MARCY invited everyone toward the huddle of sofas in the living room. Charlie Dansby's gaze darted over the ceramic tile around the fireplace, the broad-plank wood floors, the original artwork, the large windows that framed Sitka Sound. "Nice house," he commented.

Marcy knew what he added to himself. For a fishermen. Over the years, she had learned to detect and ignore the snide observations. Instead, she politely offered coffee.

Lieutenant Stan Morris thanked her and declined. "We were hoping to find the kid here."

Her husband, Davy, in old clothes and bare feet, joined them. Marcy knew her family looked mismatched. With her blond hair, she didn't resemble her native husband and son. The detectives turned to Gavan, a miniature yet more defiant version of his father.

"We were hoping you could help us find Tim," Morris explained to Gavan.

"Maybe I can," Gavan said softly, rubbing his eyes.

Dansby leaned forward and shot questions, none of them written down. "Did you see Tim today?" Gavan shook his head. "Mrs. Bander is convinced that you know where he's at," the detective pressed.

"Maybe," Gavan said. "I called him this morning…"

"No maybe, son," Davy interrupted. "You know or you don't."

"Let Gavan answer!" Dansby snapped. Davy scowled and crossed his arms.

"I told him we couldn't spend the day together," Gavan said quietly, after a brief accusing glance at his parents. Marcy pinched her lips together as Dansby moved closer to the boy, preventing her and Davy's reactions from distracting Gavan. "Why's that?"

Gavan spoke up. "My father's right. We have to get out to the woods and start searching right away. I was hoping you had already started. I asked Mrs. Bander to call you a long time ago."

Marcy interrupted. "But Gavan hasn't seen Tim today. He spent the day with Mr. Kovach, the engineer who's consulting on the cross-island road."

Dansby glared at her and turned to Gavan. "I need to make sense of this. Did you see Tim today?"

Tears started to run down Gavan's face. "I was supposed to, but then plans changed. He decided to go out on his own, taking his boat to Silver Bay and then hiking."

"So you spoke to Tim this morning and that's when he told you his plan?" Gavan nodded. "How long did you talk with him?"

"Ten minutes."

"Was he upset about your change in plans?" Dansby asked.

"No, he understood," Gavan replied.

"Did Tim express any worry about anything?"

"He was afraid of his dad," Gavan said matter-of-factly. "He's always in trouble with his dad." Marcy pinched her lips to keep from smiling.

The detectives looked at each other and nodded. "Ellen Bander didn't want the father to know about Tim's plans with Gavan," Dansby confided to the family. "It's why she didn't call right away. But she insists that you are probably the only person who knows where Tim went."

Gavan swallowed. "Tim planned to follow us. Secretly."

The four adults stared at Gavan. Dansby took a deep breath. "Did you see Tim following?"

"No," Gavan said, hanging his head. Cassie, Davy's cat who was too old to stay on the boat anymore, wandered into the living room. Attracted to the center of attention, she curled around Gavan's legs, and the boy pulled her into his lap. "I wasn't surprised when he told me his plans on the phone this morning. Tim's quiet, and he knows his way in the Tongass better than most people."

"Whose idea was it?"

"His. And at first I tried to talk him out of it, but then I thought it might be a good idea."

"Did Kovach know that Tim might be following?" Dansby asked. Gavan shook his head.

"Why didn't you invite Tim?" Morris broke in. "Would Kovach have cared?"

"No, but that wasn't the idea." Gavan's face flushed. "Tim wanted to see if he could follow without getting caught. It's a game." The detectives waited and Gavan continued. "We do it a lot. We followed Boy Scouts, hunters. My dad." Davy took a sharp breath and sat on the sofa. Marcy joined him, feeling guilty and surprised by how much she did not know about her son.

"All right," said Dansby. "Do you know where Kovach is at now?"

"He dropped me off in a skiff at the dock down the hill. Then he headed back toward Silver Bay, to the woods I think. Maybe to the trail near the cross-island road."

"Why did he bring you home?"

"I got a weird feeling when we were out there and I didn't hear or see Tim. On the way back, I made lots of noise and tried to signal him. But I got no response. So, I talked Kovach into bringing me back home. I was hoping that Tim had never left his house. That he had changed his mind for some reason. I couldn't wait to get back and call him. Mr. Kovach dropped me off at the dock closest to my house, and all he said was that he had more work to do."

"The weird feeling—did the engineer made you nervous?" Dansby pressed.

"At first, yes," Gavan said, thoughtfully. "But later, I was glad he was around. The sky got dark, like a storm was coming. Then, I just got worried about Tim. I expected him to signal me at some point."

"Did you try calling his name?" Dansby questioned, eyebrows raised.

Gavan looked ashamed. "I wish I did. But no. I only made a lot of noise. I blew my whistle. But that was after we heard a horrible sound. Like a scream. It was awful. Mr. Kovach didn't like it either. He didn't argue when I said I wanted to go home. But I was really hoping to run into Tim on the way. Or, find out that he never went out." Gavan dropped his head into his hands, his voice breaking into a sob. "Please, can't we hurry and go look for him?"

Detective Morris paused and turned to Marcy. "Why don't we get him some water," he asked softly. She hurried to the kitchen for ice and water, and returned, handing the glass to Gavan. After Gavan took a few swallows, the questions resumed. "Could the noise have come from Tim?" Dansby asked.

"It didn't sound human." Gavan shuddered. "We couldn't even figure out what direction it had come from."

"Why didn't you tell Dennis Kovach about Tim?" Dansby asked.

"I figured the engineer wouldn't listen," Gavan said, his cheeks shining with tears. "And I was afraid he'd tell Tim's dad. And Tim would despise me for that. So, I just told Mr. Kovach that I wanted to go home."

"Did Kovach say anything else about his plans?"

"No," Gavan said. "He told me that I could work with him again, and to tell my mom that he'd be calling her soon." Marcy kept her gaze on her son, ignoring the curious glances from the two detectives and her husband. She lightly placed both hands on Gavan's shoulders as he softly cried and shook.

"Well, you heard what he knows," Davy said. "We should be out searching and not standing around talking. Did you talk to Kovach yet?"

"We can't find him." The detective kept his tone neutral. "You have any ideas?"

Marcy spoke up. "Gavan, do you think Mr. Kovach hurt Tim?"

Gavan shook his head. "Why hurt Tim and not me?"

"Crime doesn't always make sense," Dansby replied. Turning to Davy, he said, "A search party has already started, Mr. James. You're welcome to join us, and we could use Gavan, too. At least we'd have a better idea of where to look. Why did the engineer invite Gavan anyway?"

Marcy spoke up. "It's a long story. I arranged it."

"I guess that can hold," Dansby said. "Your husband's right, we want to start searching. Gavan, is there anything else that you remember that could help find Tim? We need everything. The truth."

Marcy held her breath as confusion spread across her son's face. "The truth is so big," the boy answered softly.

"We'll talk more later," Dansby promised. "For now, don't tell anyone about your hike with the engineer. Or Tim following. We'll handle all questions. That will keep reporters away." Dansby opened the door, allowing Morris to exit first. He looked back at Marc. "Nice house," he repeated.

FOUR

THE MASSIVE SEARCH began, focusing on Silver Bay and into the center of Baranof Island. A fisherman reported seeing a lone person in a small red skiff on Silver Bay early Saturday morning. State troopers found *Little Lucy,* Tim's skiff, in a secluded cove.

Ambulances stood idle not far from the end of Sawmill Creek Road, waiting to transport a boy who might still be alive. Davy and Gavan joined more than a hundred others searching around Bear and Glacier lakes. Gavan tearfully vowed not to return without Tim. Marcy stayed home by the phone, in case a call came in from Tim, and also made sandwiches for the search and rescue teams. Davy's cousin, Francesca Benoit, worked for the television station as a reporter, and stopped by Marcy's house for a quick cup of coffee. "The police expect foul play. They're sniffing around for people who don't like the Banders, and you're at the top of everyone's list."

"Only the father," Marcy corrected. "Everyone knows that I like the other Banders."

Francesca shrugged. "They have the transcript from Friday's special meeting. They're asking questions about the cross-island road."

"Who did they question?" Marcy asked.

"People at the meeting. Jeremy Bander's employees. Fishermen. Gavan's teacher..."

Marcy groaned, regretting her smugness. "Fenlow won't have anything good to say about me or Gavan, but maybe he's too timid to talk to the police," she said. "Did they talk to any of my friends?"

"Beth…"

"My lawyer," Marcy mused. "But she wouldn't have told them much."

Francesca nodded. "Don't worry, she didn't. I brought my copy of the transcript along to check out who spoke out against Bander. Unfortunately, the clerk didn't stop taking notes once the meeting ended. The outburst between you and Bander afterward? Every word's in there. Perni swears you're Bander's major opponent. He also insists that you wrote an anonymous note to the assembly members."

"What kind of note?" Marcy exclaimed.

"All the note said was 'Vote no.' It was attached to a document from forty years ago that makes any road sound cost-prohibitive."

"Did you bring a copy?"

Francesca handed the folder over. "I told Perni you'd proudly sign your name to any note protesting the road. But I'm not sure that helps you out."

"Should I call Beth? Do I need a lawyer?"

Francesca shook her head. "Not yet. Everyone agrees that you can't stand Bander, but that you'd never hurt his son."

"But what better way to get at a person?" Marcy murmured.

Francesca patted her shoulder before hurrying off, returning to cover the search. Marcy sighed, relieved that her husband's cousin hadn't asked about the engineer. Marcy wished that she could be certain that Tim's disappearance had nothing to do with the pack or the road.

Picking up the transcript, she found the copy of the anonymous note attached to a 1964 state Department of Transportation document. Francesca was right. Marcy would have happily waved the document in everyone's faces. Key phrases were underlined: "Any route across Baranof Island would traverse areas with high incidences of avalanches…motorists would not be permitted to stop… Almost any route across Baranof Island follows a major fault zone… The road would be impossible to maintain year-around…" Perni had scribbled on the copy, "Kovach to update?"

By ten o'clock Sunday night, Gavan and Davy returned, dirty and weary. Davy shook his head in defeat as Gavan refused his mother's offer of grilled-cheese sandwiches. The boy went to his room and, exhausted, fell into bed.

"He didn't want to leave," Davy said. "He's screamed out Tim's name over and over, until his throat sounded raw. Damn, it's rough out there. Hardly a trail. I never dreamed those two boys went so far! At one point, a volunteer came up and asked why I dragged a tired kid along." Davy raised his eyebrows. "The fire chief intervened. Then he talked Gavan into taking a break, said that he needed him to be fresh for another day."

"No sign at all?" Marcy asked.

Davy shook his head. "It doesn't look good."

"Where could he be? If he were lost, surely he'd have been found by now." She spoke in a low whisper, not wanting Gavan to hear.

Davy looked grim. "Gavan and Kovach hiked seven miles inland yesterday. Gavan never actually saw Tim, and we can only hope we're searching the right area. People keep asking questions and wanting to widen the search area. The police continue to operate on Gavan's claim that Tim insisted on following the engineer. And they're keeping quiet about Gavan."

Marcy placed a plate in front of her husband and sat at the table. "The only person who knows about Gavan is Ellen Bander. She hadn't even told her husband. She's so afraid of him. Maybe he…"

Davy interrupted. "Don't say it. I can't stand the guy, and he's wrong about Tim a lot. But he'd never hurt his own son."

Marcy watched him eat in silence and didn't ask whether Dennis Kovach had been located.

FIVE

Monday, September 21

MARCY WAS STARTLED AWAKE before dawn. Gavan, the first to rise, had gone to his parents' bedroom and touched his father's shoulder and then his mother's. The father and son left before dawn. The boy's face was pale. It was a school day, but the police requested Gavan's help.

Marcy stayed home, close to both radio and phone, helping to organize messages and tasks between the search team and town. She fielded no urgent calls, only occasional requests for more sandwiches and hot coffee for the searchers.

Silence smothered Shore Road. The only hint of movement came from waves rattling rocks on the beach and Marcy's rocking chair on the front porch. She checked her clock—2:43 p.m.—the quietest time of day. Older children were not home from school, younger children took naps. She stared, waiting for the mailman, the newspaper girl, the return of Davy and Gavan.

She rocked harder and felt wrong about sitting and doing little else. She could sew a patch on Gavan's favorite jeans, call Beth about transferring funds among her accounts, or catch up on records for Davy's boat. She could read a magazine or pack extra snacks for the search crews. She studied the dark shadows between the mountains, a peaceful scene that gave no hint that dozens of volunteers trudged through the wet forest, scanning every square yard for clues.

Marcy leaned her head against her hand. With every passing hour, hope of finding Tim alive dwindled. Official searches at sea stopped after seventy-two hours. Land searches were more flexible. The search for a child would never end. Not until a body was found.

Marcy wished the newspaper girl would hurry. The police had promised not to reveal Gavan's involvement, but cautioned that they could not prevent reporters from using any information they discovered on their own. Marcy closed her eyes until she heard light footsteps on her stairs. Leaping up, she opened the screen door and snatched the newspaper from the child.

The girl skipped away, out of sight in a matter of seconds. Marcy unfolded the slim paper and stared at the empty road, trying to remember the last time she had seen Tim walk away. The boy's sweet, familiar face smiled, a photo on the front page of the newspaper, and she returned to the rocker. Davy's cat tried to creep into her lap, and Marcy firmly moved her to the floor.

Tim's photo was large, the story brief. "SEARCH CONTINUES FOR THIRTEEN-YEAR-OLD," announced a bold headline. The article concluded without mention of Gavan. Marcy studied Tim's photo again. Though grainy, the photograph caught mischief in his smile, an intelligent gleam in his eye. "He planned to spend the day with a friend," the paper quoted Ellen Bander. "That's what he told me. He never lied. I know how that sounds, but it's true. Maybe the plans changed at the last minute." Tears came to Marcy's eyes as she remembered Gavan pleading. What would have happened if she had not made Gavan go with the engineer? Would both boys be safe or would two boys be missing? Marcy shut her eyes, wishing she had more answers for Ellen.

The mailman opened the gate and Marcy ran to meet him. Police had advised Marcy to check the mail for some note or postcard from Tim, even though Tim's parents had dismissed running away as impossible. A thirteen-year-old traveling alone could not slip away unnoticed. Sitka typically had two Alaska Air flights in and out each day and fewer scheduled ferry stops. Still, the boy's picture had been posted at airports and ferry terminals from Seattle to Anchorage.

She flipped through the dozen or so letters, mostly bills and statements from investment companies. No postcard. Nothing for Gavan at all. Going back through the mail, she paused at a small gray envelope addressed to her: typed, with her first name spelled wrong, no return address. Inside was one page, neatly typed:

Dear Marcey:
Leave town by Friday. Visit your family in Ohio, or convince Davy to take you to Europe. The choice is yours, anyplace but Alaska. Don't talk to the police. Don't contact anyone in Sitka. We'll find out. You can return in December. Follow this advice, and Gavan won't get hurt.

The letter had no signature, no reason for the strange order. The only clue was a Sitka postmark. She lifted her head and looked outside. Did someone watch, waiting for her reaction? A light breeze tickled the trees. A bird chattered. The school bus stopped at the corner and children laughed as little legs tumbled out onto the sidewalk and took off running. The noisy sounds of normality returned to Shore Road, everywhere except her home.

SIX

MARCY SLOWLY OPENED GAVAN'S bedroom door. The boy had not moved since searchers returned with the news that dogs first found Tim's clothes and then his body at the bottom of a treacherous ravine, under a makeshift pile of sticks and leaves. Scratches on the boy's face suggested that Tim may have been intercepted near shore and forced to hike to the secluded area less than a half mile from the shore. Severe head trauma was the official cause of death. The preliminary report from the medical examiner noted that the boy had been raped.

Night crept over Sitka Sound. Gavan sat on the edge of his chair in the dark, staring out his window, toward Tim's home. The boys had often signaled with a complicated system of blinking lights. Tonight Tim's home was in complete darkness. Moonlight revealed shiny dampness on Gavan's cheeks.

"Try to sleep," Marcy whispered. "You need it. We have to talk to the police again tomorrow." Her voice drifted off. She didn't like how the words tumbled out. Advice was never the essence of comfort.

"I should have been with him, Mom," Gavan said, dropping his face into his hands. "He went out there to keep an eye on me. And I did nothing for him."

"Honey," said Marcy, sitting as close to him as she could without touching. She hurt inside, yet she knew her pain was inconsequential compared with Gavan's. "You can't blame yourself."

"Mom, if I were dead, how would you feel?" Gavan said. "Would you have expected Tim to tell? Would you hate him for not ratting?"

She sighed. He deserved honesty. "I'd wish that…with all my heart. Tim's parents will go over hundreds of scenarios. But in the end, they won't blame you." They shouldn't, she thought. Tim was the older boy, she reminded herself. Tim's father had long castigated his son for preferring a younger playmate, a son of a fisherman. He disliked Tim's choices. That was why Tim had spent so much time away from home. That was why the boy had lied.

Gavan must have read her face. "I never liked them. But I feel so sorry."

Marcy nodded. "They won't want to see us for a while. Any reminder of Tim hurts. But Tim would want your life to go on. That's what you'd want for him."

Gavan wiped his face on his sleeve, before rolling into bed. He did not remove his clothes or pull down the bedspread. Marcy dared not interfere with that first step to sleep, the first step away from the sharp edge of pain and loss.

"He was the best friend a guy could ever have," Gavan murmured, without opening his eyes. "I feel like I'll never have a friend again. Maybe I didn't deserve him."

"Tim wouldn't agree." Gavan didn't answer. She bent over and lightly kissed his hot forehead, before slipping away and pausing by the window, staring into the darkness. A monster lurked out there, one who was so much more responsible than Gavan, one who could kill again.

MARCY RETURNED DOWNSTAIRS. Her husband leaned over a counter, distracted and despondent, as his cousin Francesca entered the back door, followed by Jane McBride. Francesca efficiently took the coats to the closet.

Marcy quickly scanned her comfortable family room, with

cedar wainscoting, a tan sofa with lots of plump red pillows, and shoved some newspapers under the sofa. The walls had cheery prints, including an old bakery scene featuring two plump girls. Sisters, Marcy had always assumed. Francesca and Beth were like her sisters, and Marcy was annoyed that Francesca brought along Jane McBride. Marcy didn't feel like talking with a stranger, whose professional working-woman polish made Marcy feel dull. She reached over Davy and retrieved an extra cup and plate. Davy must have sensed her irritation because he whispered softly, "We need ideas, and Francesca trusts her. We don't have to tell her about the money."

"I'm thinking about Gavan, not the money," Marcy muttered. "We don't need too many people involved." His cousin had long urged that Marcy and Davy hire another financial advisor in addition to Beth and had even recommended Jane. "I'd trust her with my life," Francesca had insisted. And Marcy had responded: "I'm keeping my finances simple, and Beth has kept the secret all these years."

Marcy moved closer to Davy, lowering her voice. "Letting anyone else know about our money is a huge mistake—especially now."

He nodded. "You're right."

As Davy followed Francesca and Jane into the family room, Marcy arranged crackers on a cobalt-blue platter, around hard cheddar and creamy goat cheese. With a quick tap, Beth entered the kitchen door. Marcy hurried to hug her friend. "You didn't know Tim, but we know this is a hard time for you," Marcy whispered. "The memories…" Long before Marcy had even heard of Sitka, Beth's younger brother had been molested and murdered. The killer had never been caught.

Beth's dark eyes sparkled with tears but she shook her head. "Please don't talk about it in front of the others," she murmured before turning quickly to hang her coat. Together, Marcy and Beth slowly joined the others, sitting on the sofa.

Cassie lifted her front paws to the table to investigate the snacks, wrinkling her nose at the goat cheese, then closing in on the cheddar. When Beth protested, the cat scampered behind Davy's legs. Marcy apologized as Beth swept cat hair from her ivory sweater and pants. "Davy treats that cat like a child! A spoiled one at that."

Davy lifted a pot of tea. "The cat doesn't like hot beverages," he countered. Beth smiled and accepted a cup.

Francesca moved her chair closer to Marcy and then yanked her long hair back tightly with an elastic cord. "How's Gavan holding up?" she asked, handing another elastic over to Marcy, known for losing such odds and ends.

"He blames himself," Marcy replied. "Those two boys were inseparable."

"It has affected the whole town," Beth said. "Everyone walks around, staring at one another, all thinking about the same thing, wondering if we could have done something differently."

"Gavan hasn't said much," Davy sighed. "He knows more than he's telling us."

Marcy flushed. "Surely, you're not suggesting…"

"I know when he's holding back," he insisted.

"Davy, give him time," Francesca said. "He'll talk to the police tomorrow. Remember, he's a child."

"Why do the police want to talk to him?" Beth asked.

"He was supposed to be with Tim," Davy began.

"But he wasn't," Marcy interrupted, remembering the stern warning from the police. "The boys spoke on the phone that morning. Gavan had planned on spending the day with Tim, but we punished him for skipping school on Friday."

"I could sit in on his interview," Beth offered. "As your attorney."

"We won't be there long," Marcy said, with less confidence

than the statement implied. In truth, she worried that an attorney would present Gavan as suspect rather than helpful witness. Too much television, she chided herself. "I'm not worried. But we didn't invite you over to talk about Tim."

"Something else came up." Davy opened a small drawer to the antique desk, pulled out the gray envelope and handed it to Francesca. "Should we mention this to the police?"

Beth leaned over and stared at the note, while Francesca read silently. "It doesn't make sense," Francesca said after reading the note a second time aloud. She passed it to Jane, who studied the envelope.

"Is it a prank?" Davy asked.

"Pranks don't include threats," Beth pointed out. "Do you have any ideas?"

Marcy and Davy looked at each other. "None," Marcy finally said. "You've known us since Davy and I first met." Marcy would never forget her initial apprehension at meeting Beth, a former girlfriend of her husband's. Ambitious, Beth had studied accounting and later law. Her first job was at Katmai Shee Corporation, organizing a small-business center for the corporation's shareholders, mostly fishermen and pulp mill employees who dreamed of owning their own businesses. Loans were repaid with low interest, along with the requirement that loan beneficiaries—regardless of failure or success—shared their experience with new borrowers. Davy had bought the *FV Day Lily* through Beth's program, and then hired a deckhand who promptly fell into the hold and broke his arm. Beth, representing Davy, had convinced the student's family to settle for seven thousand dollars. That might as well have been seven million back then. But Beth had arranged another loan. To everyone's surprise, Marcy became close to Beth. In fact, Francesca and Beth were the only people in Sitka who knew the extent of the family's wealth.

"Strange, they don't ask for money," Beth said softly.

"That would be easier, but not what this is about," Marcy cut her off with a small frown.

"Who's angry with you?" Jane asked.

Marcy waved her hand. "I have enemies, like anyone else has in a small town: Carl Abrams has never liked our cat and we've never liked his dog, but we talk. Paul Henrico's family was miffed about Gavan winning the science award last year. I wasn't happy when the Bogdens put up those obnoxious garden ornaments on their front yard. But that's everyday life. I say hello. I smile. I lend people a cup of sugar or would jump in front of a truck to save their kid." She leaned back and shook her head.

"The school can't stand Marcy since she refused to put Gavan on Ritalin," Davy added.

"But they have not been subtle," Marcy said. "The principal wouldn't send an anonymous note asking the three of us to leave!"

"Is Gavan angry with you?" Francesca bit her lip. "Could he have…"

"Francesca!" Marcy stood and snatched up an old cotton sweater of Davy's hanging from the kitchen chair and pulled it over her head.

"I'm covering all bases," Francesca said. "Sorry…."

"The obvious reason is the cross-island road," Jane commented.

"But I'm not alone," Marcy protested. "Everyone in this room despises Bander's road."

"Do you have an appointment book?" Jane pressed.

Marcy went to the desk and handed a book to Jane. "Birthday, dentist appointments—nothing important. All I can think about is what happened with Tim."

"The letter's postmarked Saturday," Beth pointed out. "Before he was missing." The room was quiet except for a hiss from the fireplace.

"Why do they want me gone so long?" Marcy nervously twisted her pale hair into an unruly braid.

"And what could Marcy know that I don't?" Davy asked fiercely.

"And that line about Davy taking me to Europe," Marcy said. "The state announced a special three-day opening!"

"It's someone who doesn't know about fishing," Beth said.

"Or, the person's pretending," Jane added.

"We might be overanalyzing a simple letter," Beth said, shrugging.

"That's what I think," Davy said. "I'm for tossing the note in the trash."

"Leave town," Beth said firmly. "You can't take a risk. Especially after what happened to Tim. Skip the opening and all three of you take a trip."

"Gavan can't miss school, and I'm not sure he'd do well with a move," Marcy said.

"It's never wise to give into threats," Francesca countered. "Stay in town, figure out who wrote the note and keep Gavan close to home."

"But do we show it to the police?" Davy asked.

"They'll ignore it," Beth advised. "They're busy with Tim."

Jane fingered the note. "I only hope this isn't a clue connected with Tim."

"But it doesn't mention Tim or Kovach," Francesca said. "Don't show it to the police. Not yet."

Marcy didn't want to talk about Kovach or the pack—not in front of Jane. The police had warned the family not to connect Gavan with the engineer, the only suspect. Marcy couldn't explain why, but was sure Kovach hadn't written the note.

"With any luck, we'll figure this out before Friday," Davy said. He offered more tea, but the women shook their heads.

"If this had happened a week ago, before Tim, we'd ignore it," Marcy said.

"Life was easy before," Davy said softly, heading for the kitchen. Francesca accompanied him and whispered something quickly in his ear. He flashed his cousin an apologetic smile.

"We're not telling Gavan about the note," Marcy cautioned.

Francesca nodded. "The kid has enough to worry about."

After the three women left, Marcy wrapped the cheese while Davy put the cups in the dishwasher.

"I'm glad we told other people," Marcy said. "The note seems less dangerous. But what did Francesca whisper to you?"

"She reminded me that Gavan could have died out there," Davy said. "And she's right. We have so much to be thankful for. Please, don't let me pressure him, Marcy."

Marcy leaned her head against his shoulder. "Don't worry. We will get through this. And I have a feeling that Gavan will help the police solve this."

SEVEN

MARCY WOKE UP HOPING THE note had been a wild dream. She started coffee, then checked the desk. But she didn't touch the folded gray paper still tucked in a drawer. She already had the words memorized.

"It's from a crank," Davy said, walking in with the cat.

"But why me?"

"Ask your buddy Kovach."

"He has nothing to do with this," Marcy said firmly. "Nothing happened that night. You know I'm not hiding anything from you."

He laughed. "I know that. You can't keep secrets."

"Oh?" Marcy said. "You forget how good I really am." Davy frowned, and Marcy didn't have to mention the family's money, millions in out-of-town mutual funds and accounts. She could tell he was thinking about it, too. They both kept trying to live as though that money did not exist.

She watched as Davy allowed the cat to leap to the floor and Cassie weaved between his legs, meowing, insisting on attention. Davy went to the refrigerator and poured a few drops of cream into a saucer. The cat daintily cleaned the plate. "That's not good for her," Marcy warned.

"She's so old," he said. "A little bit can't hurt. Gavan still in bed?"

She nodded.

"I wonder how long he'll be at the police department. Joe asked me to help him install some freezers…"

"Go," Marcy said. "One James parent will be confusing enough."

"I'll stay by the radio." Davy reached for his jacket. "Call if you need me." He shut the door, and Marcy shook the urge to turn the lock. Before leaving the night before, Jane urged Marcy to act normal. "Act" was the operative word. Tim was dead. School was canceled. Her child had stayed in his room since Tim's body had been found. Normality had vanished.

Marcy heard Gavan walk about upstairs and prepared a tray with granola, sliced pear and a glass of milk. She knocked gently. "Want to join me in the kitchen?" she asked.

"Not now, Mom," he said. As he mechanically reached for the glass, his eyes looked older. She stood a moment, wondering how the tragedy would shape the rest of his life. Lacking any words of comfort, she walked away and closed the door. Gavan was scheduled to meet detectives at the police station at eleven a.m. That gave her a few hours to feign normality. Don't show fear, don't do anything unusual, her friends had counseled. But Marcy could only pretend.

She gathered tools to work the garden, and wondered why she had to hide her fear. Maybe the writer would doubt whether the note had been delivered. Maybe the writer's anger would fade, along with the impulse to send a second threat. Marcy dropped her tools beside the rock wall that snaked around the house and looked over the Sound. The water resembled a soft, old quilt that morning, with hazy patches of blue, gray and lavender.

She donned garden gloves and dropped to her knees, reaching between strands of ivy and tugging at weeds and dead nasturtiums. She envied Davy, his certainty that the threat meant nothing. But he had always ignored problems. She wanted to talk and he'd evade her, heading for the docks and endless boat chores. She tugged at plants in rhythm to the waves caressing the shore. Her life before Gavan, before Davy, belonged to another woman, like a favorite story read a long, long time ago.

SHE HAD LEFT FLAT, suburban Ohio when she was twenty-two. Despite four dismal years earning a business degree from a community college, an effort to please her parents, she had no desire to work in an office. After reading an article about Alaska in the newspaper, she impulsively packed a bag and caught a bus to the West Coast, then a ferry to Ketchikan. She found temporary work on a troller, cooking and baiting lines in between meals. For the next year she drifted about the Northwest, from Kodiak to Oregon, working trollers when she could, or standing at the assembly line of seafood plants and waiting tables when no crew positions were open. While in Port Townsend, searching for a spot on any vessel headed north, she heard a group joke about an opening on *FV Day Lily.* "Where's it headed?" Marcy asked.

"Sitka, if the engine holds," said one man, laughing.

"He's offering twelve percent, I heard," another called out. "Sounds good, unless it's twelve percent of nothing."

"Don't even consider it," confided another woman, daintily sipping her third shot of bourbon. "Davy's a hell of a skipper and better looking than most. But he's unlucky and owes people up and down the coast. Why, you'll never eat, let alone get paid!"

Marcy picked up her bottle of beer and wandered the docks in search of the *Day Lily* and the man who had no luck.

The setting sun did not hide the flaws of the small, battered fishing vessel. Marcy slowed her pace and watched the man on board, who looked too young to be a captain. His black hair, tied with a leather cord, reached halfway down his back, gleaming like a raven's wing. Short, wiry and dressed in T-shirt and jeans, he moved quickly. Despite the cool ocean air, sweat beaded on his forehead. His cheekbones were high and his smooth skin had a gold tone. Native.

"I heard you're headed for Alaska," she called out. "Looking for help?"

His gaze paused at the beer in her hand. "I don't think so," he replied, without interrupting his task.

She put the bottle down on the dock. "I have references," she persisted.

He surprised her by leaping to the dock, landing less than a foot away. He was about three inches taller than her and she liked being that close to his eyes. Dark, alert, they didn't waver. A scar stretched two inches on the right side of his forehead. "Look, this is a small boat," he explained, wiping his brow. "I can't afford a girl looking for adventure between semesters, someone who only cooks and lays on deck between meals. I need a deckhand who can do it all."

She stared at the boat and all the miserable work it represented. He'd be lucky to have her. Plenty of captains had pleaded with her to remain a permanent part of their crew. But she had wanted to drift and see the coast in all seasons and moods. She pulled a pen from her pocket and jotted down names. "I've worked for these three captains. The last number—that's where you can leave a message." With that, she gracefully retrieved her bottle and walked away, not turning to check whether he pocketed the scrap of paper or tossed it into the water.

He called a few hours later. Together, they left at the hint of dawn.

A VEHICLE TRAVELING UP the hill interrupted her thoughts. Marcy could not help but stare, sighing as a neighbor's black Honda zipped by. She continued rearranging vines, waiting for the hum that announced other approaching vehicles. Four more cars and trucks passed by, and Marcy recognized the occupants of each. Two neighbors waved. The rest did not notice her crouched in the garden. At ten-thirty, she went inside and called Gavan.

"They'll ask about Mr. Kovach," the boy said, checking over apples in a bowl.

"We'll tell them what we know," she said.

The boy nodded, grabbed a Granny Smith apple and took a big bite. The simple sight, a boy eating an apple, soothed her worry like nothing else. Marcy went to start the truck and fingered her two keys, one for the truck and one for the house. She thought about running back and locking the door. But she was supposed to keep life normal, and the James family never locked the back door.

As Marcy and Gavan approached the glass door to the Sitka Police Department, Tim's father blocked the bulletproof window in the tiny lobby, arguing with a dispatcher. As Gavan hung back, Marcy stepped forward quickly, before she changed her mind. "We're so sorry, Jeremy," she began.

Bander tightened his lips. "You have your son."

"We loved Tim. The two boys loved each other."

"That friendship was temporary," Bander snapped. "That's the only reason I tolerated it."

Mortified, Marcy hurt inside too much to argue with Bander. A tall, gray-haired man in a gray suit and perfect white shirt interrupted, opening the door that led to the center of the station. "Come in, Gavan, Mrs. James." He shook hands with both of them. "I'm Lieutenant Philip Gallagher, with the state police in Juneau. Down the hall, second door on your left."

"Lieutenant Gallagher, I want to hear what that kid has to say for himself," Bander demanded. One hand pointed at Gavan, the other blocked the door.

The man's lips tightened. "I'm sorry, Mr. Bander, but not now."

"My son died! I have a right to hear. More than she does!"

"Gavan tried…" Marcy's voice broke.

Gavan spoke up. "It doesn't bother me if Mr. Bander sits in."

"That's considerate, Gavan," the state trooper said, putting his hand on the boy's shoulder and guiding him through the doorway. "But this is a homicide investigation. It's best that we talk alone. Jeremy, we intend to solve this, one witness at a time. We'll call when we have leads."

"It's not right," Bander said, bitterness seeping from his voice.

"We'll be in touch, Jeremy," Gallagher said, firmly shutting the door, the lock automatically clicking. Marcy took Gavan's hand as they followed Gallagher. He pointed to two chairs against the wall of the small, crowded office. Gallagher took a chair in the opposite corner, next to Stan Morris, the Sitka police detective. The other detective, Charlie Dansby, stood. "State police took over the case, Mrs. James," Detective Dansby began. "Rape and murder of a kid. Not supposed to happen around here."

Gallagher spoke more kindly. "Gavan, you're not a suspect. We do consider you a key witness. Because you're a juvenile, we want your mother to sit in on this interview. But we won't read any rights like you see on the television." Gavan nodded. "It's vital that everything we talk about in this room remain confidential. That's why I kept Mr. Bander out. Isolating information can go a long way if we get the chance to question the killer."

"I want to help," said Gavan, sitting straight in his chair, his voice high-pitched.

Gallagher twisted in his chair and picked up a computer printout. "Feel free to interrupt at any point. First, is there anything you want to add to what you already told the police?" Marcy frowned. The question was cryptic. She thought about the note, but couldn't blurt out that yet. Besides, he had directed the question to Gavan. Not knowing about the note, Gavan shook his head.

"Okay, let's go over what you told police Saturday night." Gavan gripped the arms of his chair as Gallagher went through a series of questions. Marcy admired her son's earnest, concise answers. Most questions centered on Kovach: Did Gavan remember what gear Kovach carried? Did he leave Gavan alone at any point? Did he talk about leaving town? Did he mention names or cities? Did he talk about Tim or other kids?

Gavan always caught trouble for talking too much at school, but with this audience he was a skillful persuader. After almost an hour, the lieutenant asked for five cans of soda. Everyone but Gallagher sipped in relief.

The detective quietly watched the boy with the soda. "Gavan, let's get one question out of the way. Tim was molested. Raped. Do you know what that means?" Gavan nodded.

"Be honest. Did Kovach try anything with you?"

"No," Gavan said, his eyes huge, unblinking.

"Did he touch you?"

"No," Gavan said. "Well, not the second day…" He looked nervously at his mother. Marcy caught her breath, afraid to listen.

Without a sound, Gallagher moved his chair closer and leaned closer. "Tell me what happened. How you met Kovach. How you came to spend the day with him."

"It's a long story," Gavan said. "I met Kovach the day before. In the forest." And he explained the whole story about the day the two boys skipped school, spying on the engineer and getting caught, Kovach and the pistol, stealing the backpack and even the sense of strange panic when they found the remains of the fawn. "That put us on edge," Gavan said. "I didn't want to go with Kovach the next day, and I didn't want Tim to go alone."

"A dead deer put you on edge?" Dansby asked cynically. "Not the fact that Kovach nearly choked you and held a pistol to your head." He directed a withering look toward Marcy. "How well did you know this guy, Mrs. James?"

Marcy squirmed and wondered if her son exaggerated. "Gavan, if you'd told me all this, I'd have never made you go with him the next day." She turned to the detectives. "I had no idea."

"I knew he wasn't going to shoot," Gavan spoke up, as confident as describing the outcome of a video game. Marcy was surprised at his urge to defend the engineer.

Gallagher held up his hands to quiet everyone, trying to restore some order to the questioning. Marcy realized that Gallagher had a suspect in mind, but the evidence didn't match the crime. "Gavan, we know it's embarrassing," the detective said gently. "If Kovach tried anything, you must tell us."

"No. I swear." Gavan was adamant.

The lieutenant sat back and stared at Gavan. He tapped his finger slowly and waited, as if hoping for a different answer, one that would offer an easy solution to Tim's murder. "So you had the pack. That's why Kovach was unprepared at the special meeting on the cross-island road. Did Kovach get his pack back?"

"Yes," Marcy and Gavan answered at once.

"Tell me how that happened," Gallagher directed.

Marcy undid her hair, then gathered it again to tie it more tightly. "I'm the one who should explain that," she began, hoping that she could match Gavan's clarity. She described her realization about Kovach's missing pack during the meeting on the cross-island road, and how she had hurried home and then back to the hotel. "I allowed Gavan to go with Dennis Kovach because he's an official for the city," Marcy concluded. "Besides, he was extremely gracious and understanding about Gavan taking the pack."

The lieutenant shook his head. "Believe me, Mrs. James, the men who commit these crimes don't look like monsters. They act like friends, uncles. They get close to families."

"Did you talk with Mr. Kovach?" Marcy asked. "Once you met him, maybe you'd understand."

"I'm sure he's a great guy, Mrs. James, but the police haven't had the opportunity to meet Mr. Kovach. He hasn't been seen since Saturday. He didn't pay his hotel bill. Other than some items left behind in the room, there's no sign of him. His office in Juneau's bare. He has a cabin up north—and troopers are checking that. But his disappearance, combined with Gavan's story, makes him a suspect."

"No!" Gavan said, sitting on the edge of his chair. "That's a waste of time. Mr. Kovach didn't hurt Tim!"

Gallagher shut his eyes and sighed deeply. "The man vanished. If he didn't kill Tim, his timing's unfortunate."

"But Gavan's still alive," Marcy protested, defensive about having her judgment as a mother questioned. She had looked Dennis Kovach in the eye and trusted him.

"Perhaps Kovach discovered that Tim had followed the second day and got angry," Gallagher countered. Marcy could see Gavan pondering that scenario. "Did Kovach give you anything, Gavan?" Gallagher asked.

"We had lunch, that's all," Gavan replied. Gallagher reached into a cabinet and extracted a plastic bag with six oversized candy bars—Reese's cups and Snickers. The packages were rumpled and dirty.

"Yes," Gavan whispered, staring at the familiar big packages. "Mr. Kovach brought a lot of candy along Saturday. I took all the ones without nuts."

"What about the ones with nuts?"

"He must have put them back inside his pack."

"And so you didn't give these to Tim?"

Gavan shook his head. "I didn't see Tim. Besides, he didn't like nuts either."

Gallagher rubbed his chin. "We haven't made it public, but these were found near Tim's body." Gavan stared at the candy, then at Marcy, and both were too stunned to respond. "Too bad we don't have Kovach's prints on file," Gallagher continued. "But we will. Soon. He can't stay hidden forever."

Marcy felt hollow inside, as Gavan leaned against her. "I should have stopped Tim somehow," Gavan said. "He would've been mad. But he'd be alive."

Gallagher shook his head and spoke earnestly. "Look at the facts, Gavan. Tim told you where he was going. You called his mother as soon you got back. Kids skip school, take walks alone every day, without getting murdered. You're not responsible for Tim's death. Someone else is." He paused before continuing with a professional, courteous tone. "We have a warrant for Kovach's arrest. Gavan's statement puts punch behind our warrant. The guy could be dangerous, and we ask that you let us know immediately if he contacts either of you."

Marcy reached out for Gavan's hand and nodded.

"And Gavan, thank you. You have been helpful. More than most adults."

"We'll call," Marcy said. "But I still don't think Kovach did it." She pressed her son's hand and thought about the gray note. Why would Kovach write a note like that? Unless he wanted to pursue Gavan. But he already had the chance on two separate days. "Don't you think there could be someone else?"

"Stan, take Gavan out and show him the computer." He closed the door. "Mrs. James, for now, I want you to keep your opinions to yourself," Gallagher said harshly. "Kovach may be a killer. At the very least, he's a witness. We have good reason to track him down and we don't need interference. Besides, we're checking other potential suspects."

Detective Dansby spoke up. "Mrs. James, you mind telling us where you and your husband were on Saturday?"

Marcy was startled. "Why, I was shopping, and stopped by a friend's house. Megan Cole. And Davy worked on the boat all day."

"Your husband's related to Francesca Benoit?" Dansby asked.

"They're cousins. You know that."

"The cross-island road," Dansby said, tapping a file. "Jeremy Bander's son gets killed out near the route that he wants, the route despised by you and Katmai Shee Corporation."

"And every other reasonable person who doesn't want to see this town drastically changed," Marcy said. "Tim Bander was my son's best friend. That's more valuable than any road."

"Where's your husband today?" Gallagher asked.

"On the boat. I can radio him."

"Why didn't he return the pack that night?"

Marcy didn't hesitate. "I'd just come from a meeting where the engineer spoke about losing the pack. I'm part of the committee fighting the road, and I owed the man an apology."

Gallagher tapped his pen against the desk. The interview was ending. Marcy touched the gray note inside her pocket. The note, postmarked before Tim's death, would confuse the investigation and frighten Gavan. She only wanted to escape the police station and the questions about Kovach. So, she remained silent as Gallagher led her to the computer where Morris and Gavan sat.

"Thank you both," Gallagher said. "Let me stress that you shouldn't talk to anyone. Remain quiet about your involvement with Kovach and the fact that he's the chief suspect. Advise your husband likewise. If anyone asks questions, please let us know… I'll handle Mr. Bander."

Before he opened the door, Gallagher pulled Marcy aside. "Mrs. James," he murmured. "If Kovach did hurt Gavan, let it come out. Denial, protecting someone like Kovach, never helps."

Marcy held her head up and stared at the detective's eyes. "Do you think Gavan is lying?"

Gallagher looked out the window. "No," he said finally. "But Kovach managed to get your kid alone. You both liked the man. Gavan could try to protect Kovach. I don't think Gavan's lying. But he knows more. It's just a feeling I have."

She didn't add that her husband had the same feeling. Marcy thanked him and hurried after Gavan, putting her arm around the boy's shoulder. "What did he show you on the computer?"

"How to look up records. Kovach didn't have one and neither did you!"

"Great," Marcy said wryly. Francesca had warned her not to leave Gavan alone with the police. "Did he ask other questions?"

Gavan shrugged. "He wanted to know if you and Dad had problems."

"What did you say?" Marcy tried to keep her tone calm.

"No more than anyone else."

Wrong answer, Marcy thought to herself. She had not expected Gavan's version of the truth to differ from hers. Sadly, she started the car and noticed Bander entering the police station. He had been waiting for her to leave, and she wondered how much the police would tell him.

EIGHT

Saturday, September 26

WITH EVERY PASSING DAY, the gray note seemed less ominous and more like an ordinary scrap of paper. Marcy stopped staring at passing cars, the telephone, the mailman.

Gavan had returned to school, but insisted that he would not attend a Saturday memorial service for Tim sponsored by the soccer league. The boys had played on the league's worst team—Tim playing to please his father, Gavan to keep Tim company. "You have to go," Davy ordered with a low, measured voice. "He was your friend." Gavan left the room distraught and close to tears.

"Does he have to go?" Marcy countered.

"How does it look if he doesn't?"

"Who cares?" Marcy asked. "I can't believe I'm hearing that from you."

"I care how people regard our son."

"If people think less of him because he can't bear a memorial service, that's their problem."

"Miss Buy Her Way Out of Trouble speaks."

"What's that supposed to mean?" Marcy snapped. "I'm not talking about money."

"But you will. Make donations to shut them all up. Look, we live in this town, and I play by the rules. Gavan has to face people, hear them talk about Tim's death."

"He hurts, Davy. Maybe he's not ready."

Davy closed his eyes. "Give this town more credit. The league's trying to help kids. Gavan should be there."

"Gavan doesn't need pressure from us on top of everything else."

"Life's pressure," Davy replied. "You can't protect him forever—especially from the problems he creates himself."

"He didn't cause Tim's death," she said bitterly.

"How do we know that?" Davy's soft tone did not make the words less harsh. "He needs self-control. Maybe the school's right. Maybe we should try the Ritalin."

"Damn you," she said, her voice low. "Gavan didn't coerce Tim into going, and Ritalin didn't protect Tim. Those two boys went together. I refuse to put a smart kid on some drug so he can be quiet at school! Let's talk later when we're…"

"When we're calm," Davy finished. "Except I wonder when our lives will ever be calm again."

BEFORE THE SERVICE, MARCY made a favorite of Gavan's, stacks of pancakes with maple syrup, sliced strawberries and sweet sausage. Gavan ate slowly, as if every bite hurt. Marcy didn't talk much either and reminded herself that she'd have more cause to worry if Gavan acted nonchalant about Tim's death. Gavan dropped his fork as Davy entered the kitchen. "Time to get ready, son," Davy said. The boy silently trudged upstairs.

As Marcy poured another cup of coffee, Davy moved close to her and folded his arms around her. "I don't want to argue. What happened with Tim and the note, we can't let it destroy our family."

"I know."

"Gavan has to face people. We could hide. But that would make only today easier."

"He's going," Marcy said.

"We'll go together," he said. "Damn, people won't have me

feeling guilty because my son's alive!" Marcy stepped away and poured them both more coffee.

SITKA SOCCER WENT ON RAIN or not, and the rule stood for the memorial service. People gathered at Crescent Harbor Park, overlooking the bay, mountains and solid gray blanket of a sky. The rain felt like tiny wet feathers against Gavan's face.

Families were out in force, and children outnumbered adults. At the edge of the crowd, the youngest children played. Mothers constantly admonished the children to stay in sight. Gavan was meek, and his parents hovered like sentinels at his side. Groups of people gathered, hugged Gavan, murmured support and stood nearby. Lieutenant Gallagher stood in the crowd. He nodded somberly, but did not approach.

Tim's soccer coach, the league president and a minister spoke. Tim's parents wore black and stood motionless. Ellen wept, and Bander's mouth was set. As simple words about Tim echoed across the field, an eagle circled overhead. Gavan stared toward the sky where the raptor drifted mile after mile without moving a wing. Candles were lit. A final prayer was read. The eagle pumped its wings with a few hard strokes and soared beyond Mount Verstovia, out of sight. Sunlight pierced the mottled clouds. Gavan hoped that Tim could somehow see his friends, the sky and a bird that looked as if it controlled the wind.

Afterward, the coach and team went to the Banders and shook their hands. Then the group approached Gavan. Jeremy Bander quickly left the field. Ellen Bander lifted her hand with a sad wave for Gavan. Grateful, the boy returned the gesture, before she turned to catch up with her husband.

After the ceremony, the crowd drifted slowly from the park. "I feel like walking," Gavan said abruptly. "I'll head home on my own."

"Why don't you—" his mother began.

Davy squeezed her hand. "Go ahead, Gavan."

"Be careful," she cautioned.

With mixed feelings, Gavan walked away. Groups of family and friends dispersed, and only Gavan walked alone.

PEOPLE STOPPED AND TALKED to Marcy and David, most murmuring words of sympathy and a few with questions. As Davy thanked everyone for their concern, Marcy was impatient. She clutched her husband's arm. "Let's get out of here," she said. "The killer could have been here. He could be watching Gavan."

"We need to talk with people," Davy said, frowning. "Rushing away will only make the conversations more difficult later on. Besides, Gavan needs space."

"I can't bear the idea that he'd get hurt."

Davy stared toward the top of Mount Verstovia. "He won't. Nobody's seen Kovach in a week."

"It's not Kovach," Marcy said, stubbornly. All week she had avoided conversation about the engineer, particularly since her husband still didn't know that Kovach had pointed a pistol at Gavan. "I just know."

"Nobody will dare go near a kid in this town for the next month," Davy said. "Look, I'll check with Ron on those supplies I'm waiting for. That gives Gavan some time and we'll pick him up on the way home."

"I'll wait in the truck." She hurried, hoping to avoid talking with anyone. She passed one woman scolding her toddler, another woman describing a recipe. The service was over, and everyday life resumed. She heard her name called. The school principal, Henrietta Cordola, approached. Her black silk dress, heels and swept-back hair belonged in a New York cocktail lounge.

"How's Gavan, Mrs. James?" she asked.

Marcy jammed her hands in the pockets of her old parka. "Not well," she answered.

"It's been a traumatic week," Cordola said. "School resumes Monday. This could be a good time to try the Ritalin."

"I don't want the ups and downs of life controlled for my son," Marcy said evenly. "It always takes Gavan a few weeks to adjust to a new grade and teacher."

"That adjustment won't be easy this year, according to Mr. Fenlow."

"That sounds like a threat," Marcy countered. "It proves that Mr. Fenlow's not willing to try. I suggest that you change Gavan's teacher."

"That's not an option," Cordola said. "You have one child. The school deals with dozens. Children must learn to cooperate with new people." She paused. "Mrs. James, we care about Gavan, too. His behavior makes finding new friends more difficult." The triumphant edge to Cordola's voice made Marcy ill. Before she could think of a response, the principal excused herself and hurried away.

GAVAN HEADED FOR THE historical park and its path along the sea. He had expected the regret and tears, but the ceremony had also soothed him. All week Gavan had felt obligated to find Tim and explain.

Gray clouds tumbled overhead. But on the horizon, the sun emerged, polishing the water like silver. Thinning clouds resembled a pile of satin ribbons, in coral, lavender and gray. Gavan deserted the trail, climbed down to rocks near the shore and found the flat rock, as long and comfortable as a sofa. When Tim and Gavan were younger, the rock marked the halfway point between school and home, a hiding place that could not be seen from the main path. Saving crackers from lunch, they stopped daily for a snack, occasionally flinging bits to the gulls.

Gavan sat and the roar of the persistent waves somehow made it easy to imagine Tim waited nearby. Choosing pebbles that had collected between the rocks, Gavan studied the handful, wondering if any had ever been held by Tim before. One by one, Gavan tossed the smooth rocks into the waves. One gull closed in to investigate, then another. The two birds bobbed on the waves like decoys, waiting for Gavan to throw something worthwhile.

"It makes sense," Gavan said aloud. "We should have known." He dropped his head to his knees. At last he understood why Tim had fretted so much about not meeting his spirit. According to Tlingit legends, boys went to the forest alone at some point during their twelfth spring and waited for a spirit that would direct them. Wind bending branches of a massive cedar might inspire the boy to carve. An eagle's flight could prompt writing songs that soared over the mountains. A floating leaf could lead to fishing. After the spirit appeared, the boy returned to his village, and his family arranged an apprenticeship. Boys who showed the least fear found success. Boys who returned without meeting a spirit performed the village's most unpleasant tasks. Tim could not find his spirit, but insisted that he had no fear.

Meanwhile, Gavan had met his spirit. Signs constantly emerged, urging him to protect the forest. Gavan was puzzled that Tim had never found similar clues. "I'm older than you," Tim had lamented.

"Someday it'll make sense," Gavan had always responded.

Wind wrinkled the surface of the water, and Gavan tasted its salt. "Why didn't you call out, Tim?" Gavan whispered. "If you had called, I would have come running." Gavan flung another pebble with all his might. One gull gave up and took off.

If only he and Kovach had heard something besides the one strange scream. Staring at the horizon clouds darkening to charcoal and violet, Gavan still wasn't sure if the noise had come from Tim. He had thought that every detail of those last two days with Tim and Kovach would remain etched in his memory forever. But the scream took over.

With little jumps, the seagull moved closer and Gavan wished he could feed the lonely bird. He slowly checked his pockets. No crackers or even hard candy. He only felt a piece of paper.

Kovach's map—another forgotten detail. Otherwise, Gavan would have shown it to Lieutenant Gallagher. He unfolded the small paper and admired the accuracy, defined by pinpoint pencil. Kovach's map focused on the area beyond Bear Mountain—and showed both streams, the one he had visited with Gavan and the first one where Kovach thought he had been alone. The last was marked with tiny A's and U's. The engineer knew the topography and could not have possibly confused the two streams. Gavan sadly touched the corner of the map where Tim's body had been found.

The police suspected the engineer, and Gavan wondered if the map would help or hurt Kovach. Carefully refolding the paper, Gavan returned it to his pocket. He could show his mother, but he didn't want to add to her worries. If the police wanted to talk to him again, then Gavan could hand it over then. But in the meantime, he had to save the map and hide it at home. More often than not, he left money, tissues, notes from school or homework in his pockets—and obliterated reminders returned with clean laundry. Gavan found a large smooth rock and added it to the pocket with the map, hoping the weight would remind him to remove the paper before tossing his clothes in the laundry.

The gull extended its wings, trying to regain Gavan's attention. "Sorry, fellow," Gavan said. The gull's dark eyes looked sad, and Gavan wondered if the bird remembered being fed by two boys. Gavan sat still and waited as the nervous bird paced a bit and then moved closer, cocking its head back and forth. Abruptly, the bird stretched its wings and flew away—leaving Gavan alone with his thoughts of Tim.

"I don't think Kovach killed you. But I'll find out, buddy.

I promise. I'll never forget you." Gavan flung one last handful of pebbles into the water and scrambled for the path that led to the highway and his home.

MARCY SEARCHED AS DAVY drove slowly along the road, rain snapping against the windshield. "There," she exclaimed with relief, after spotting the lone figure striding along the edge of Halibut Point Road. Davy pulled over. "Ready for a lift?"

Water dripped from Gavan's hair. Davy removed his jacket and passed it to the boy. "Thanks, Dad," Gavan said, shivering. "I mean, for making me go to the service." He leaned against the seat and closed his eyes.

Marcy wished that Davy could take off along some long road, so that the three of them could preserve this moment of peace, riding and talking in the warm truck, with fogged windows protecting them from nagging problems and memories. But long drives were not possible on Sitka's seventeen miles of road. The pickup could only travel a too-familiar route, back and forth, like a wild animal pacing in its cage. Moments later, the tires crunched against their gravel driveway. Heavy rain obscured their home and the surrounding trees into a blur of green, gray and white. "How about a fire and hot chocolate?" Marcy offered.

"Sounds good to me," Gavan said. He opened the door and immediately shed his outer layer of clothes. Marcy poured milk into a pan for scalding, then mixed dry cocoa, sugar, vanilla and some cream into a smooth paste. Gavan rubbed a towel through his hair, opened the pantry door and pushed boxes around.

"Hey, wait," Marcy chided, as Gavan stood poised on a kitchen chair, jamming one cookie into his mouth and grabbing another. "Get a plate for all of us."

Davy lit logs in the fireplace, Gavan arranged more cookies on a plate. As Marcy poured cocoa into three mugs, she thought about how Tim belonged at the table, too. She had not thought about the boy since the service. That was how grief played out—each period of forgetting would last a little longer until the memories became remote. Until the next tragedy hit. Annoyed, she shook her head.

"Let that cocoa cool while I change," Marcy said. She stopped in the bathroom and ran the comb quickly through her matted hair. Stripping her damp sweatshirt, she pushed the bedroom door open with her shoulder.

She stopped, in horror. Blood smeared her pastel patch-work quilt and closet door, the rag rug on the floor and even the book Davy had left propped open on the nightstand. Afraid to enter, Marcy backed away slowly. "Davy, come here," she called weakly. Waiting in the doorway, Marcy shivered in her T-shirt. She clutched her damp shirt, biting into the material hard as she tried to stop shaking.

Davy came around the corner. "What's up?"

She pointed into their bedroom. "Damn," he whispered. "What happened?"

She shook her head and stayed in the doorway, too terri-fied to follow him as he traced the sticky trail. Davy removed his shirt, using it to open the closet door. On the floor lay a bloodied mass of pale, yellow fur. Davy didn't speak. His hands shook as he took his shirt, gently covering the tiny bro-ken body and carrying it to the bed. Marcy tried to comfort him. But Davy shook his head and cried.

As Marcy backed away to call the police, she saw the two dripping, red letters on her dresser mirror, "GO," and a gray enveloped propped underneath. Marcy removed the letter from the unsealed envelope and read: "Marcey: Leave town. The cat was easy. Children are, too. Don't call the police. They can't protect you. A flight leaves this evening."

Marcy passed the letter to Davy.

Davy looked dazed. "You have to leave."

"Why me?" She went to the hallway, slumped to the floor and put her head into her hands. "Why now? This is the worst time for Gavan."

Davy gently covered the cat with a sheet. "Cassie... I had her so long. Why would someone hurt her?"

"Gavan should come with me. You, too."

"How would it look to the police if all three of us suddenly left town? We can't. You're getting on a plane tonight. Gavan will be safe with me. It's only two months. Maybe after I get the boat settled, after the police find Tim's killer, we can join you."

Marcy frowned. "What do we say to Gavan?"

"We can't let him see this." Davy turned and kicked a basket, scattering magazines across the room. He turned to Marcy. "I didn't tell you, but the police stopped by the boat. They had only one question for me." Marcy swallowed and waited. "They wanted to know if I thought you had an affair with Kovach."

She reached for his arm. "You know that's ridiculous. And what did you say to them?"

"I said what I thought was the truth. I said no."

"And that's true," she said.

"Think hard, Marcy. What do you know? Why is this happening to you?"

When she couldn't answer, he turned and walked away.

NINE

INSIDE ROOM TWENTY-TWO OF Alexander Baranof School, Gavan studied a fog bank, lumpy like an old gray quilt, creeping in from the bay and tucking itself around the base of the mountain group known as the Sisters. He leaned back in his chair, striking a pose that teachers often mistook for intense concentration. Normally, a lesson on early Civil War battles would intrigue him, if only because he'd catch Mr. Fenlow on inconsistencies and shallow generalizations.

But Gavan had better targets for his concentration. Why did Tim die? Why did his mother leave? He wrote "Tim" and "Mom" in his notebook and ripped the page out. Mr. Fenlow stopped his commentary on the Battle of Bull Run—and gazed about the room, stopping at Gavan. The boy kept his face blank, the offending paper curled in his palm.

Mr. Fenlow continued, and Gavan turned his attention back to the fog and the puzzles of his life. Before Tim's death, Fenlow would have demanded to see the paper. But Gavan's father had visited the school and briefly described the problems at home, his mother leaving town to care for an ill family member as well Gavan's grief over Tim, to the principal. Undoubtedly relieved to avoid Marcy, Mrs. Cordola had assured Davy and Gavan that the teachers would be supportive.

Gavan's parents rarely spoke about attention deficit disorder in front of him. They never understood that the flaw was his greatest strength. The family doctor who had delivered Gavan reviewed teacher comments and examined Gavan's schoolwork. He had asked the boy to wait in the lobby, but Gavan lingered by the door. "The boy might have a border-line case of what they call ADD," the doctor had said. "But then, don't most boys?"

"I remember it that way," Davy had said.

"He'll grow out of it," the doctor had assured Marcy and Davy. "Keep him busy though. That's the secret to raising a healthy boy." The man retrieved his file and went to the door. "Sure are a lot of referrals for ADD coming out of the school."

His parents had shoved a book, *Coping with Your ADD Child,* onto the top shelf of their bedroom closet and apparently forgot about it. Gavan pulled the book down and read it from cover to cover, surprised to learn that Ben Franklin, Winston Churchill and Thomas Edison had similar troubles. Even so, the book pointed out, few teachers could appreciate ADD.

No one, not even his parents, realized the intensity of his focus, and Gavan had his own label: SUBTRAC or Sublimi-nal-Ultra Brain-Triggering Rebel Attention Control.

What puzzled his parents most was his inconsistency: Gavan's classwork ranged from failure to brilliance. He con-stantly kept adults guessing at his intelligence. He longed to skip the rest of junior high and high school and start the courses described in the college catalogs at the public library. Instead of Fenlow's dreary list of statistics, Gavan preferred analyzing characters who fought on opposite sides of the Civil War, their philosophies and motivation.

But Gavan had to switch focus. He had to figure out why his mother left and find a way to reach her. He remembered a conversation with Tim last summer, after Ellen Bander vis-ited Juneau alone for three weeks. "They're getting a divorce," Tim had theorized. Gavan recalled how his friend had chiefly worried about leaving Sitka.

Was divorce possible for Gavan's parents? Sure, they fought, but his mother wouldn't lie or stop caring about Gavan overnight. He thought about her hair, remembering the gold strands tickling his face as she leaned over to kiss him in the middle of the night. How she tucked notes with lunches and constantly asked "what if" questions. That woman would never give up on her family.

He remembered the Saturday she left, his parents whispering with a troubled anger. They had locked their bedroom door and ignored the hot chocolate, which had long bubbled and burned over the stovetop. His mother had emerged with a suitcase, hastily packed, then wrote reminders for Davy, all the while pulling Gavan close for hugs. "This emergency has nothing to do with you, honey," she had said. "Do your best at school. Stay close to home. Never forget that I love you…" Her voice broke off.

"When will you come back?" Gavan had asked.

"Two months, sweetheart." The family had scurried back into the rain, piled into the pickup and headed for the airport, where they hugged one last time. Gavan heard his mother whisper to his father, "Promise, no Ritalin." And his father had promised.

The next day his father had called Gavan and showed him a shoe box. Crying, he only said that Cassie had died. Together, they buried her in a far corner of their yard, overlooking Sitka Sound.

"So wonderful when students are so deep in thought." Mr. Fenlow's voice rippled with sarcasm. "Would you mind sharing those thoughts with the class?" He tapped Gavan's desk with a pencil.

Students snickered, anticipating a snappy comeback. Gavan sighed. "My thoughts…"

"Yes, Gavan. We were talking about the South's resilience during the war."

"But the Confederates lost," Gavan replied, confused, not intending the comment as a joke. But the class laughed. Gavan groaned, wanting only some time to solve his own problems and not have to think about those from more than a hundred years ago. SUBTRAC. He nervously continued, trying not to annoy Fenlow. "They came to understand failure, sir. Failure's not nearly as frightening as success."

"The voice of experience," Fenlow snapped. Less students laughed. "That answer might fool other teachers, Gavan, but in this class, it's inadequate. If you pay attention, you'll have more to contribute. Krysta, your thoughts?"

Gavan sat up and kept eye contact with the teacher for at least four minutes. The man was an ass who had taught Civil War history for more than fifteen years. Rumor had it that Fenlow had not deviated from his first year of lesson plans. Each year, his history classes took the same tests, did the same role plays, and all the while Fenlow resented his seventh-grade discussion partners. For years, the teacher had boasted about writing a book, but the research was never quite complete.

The teacher's voice droned, a minor distinction compared with the empty desk two rows away. Tim. Gavan remembered the funeral, the irrational thought that Tim was not inside the coffin. Maybe Tim's spirit was still around, maybe moving with the swirling fog that obscured the Sisters. Sitting in class, Gavan imagined conversations with his friend. "My mom left," Gavan told him. "Maybe because of me?"

"Kids always think that about divorce," replied Tim, more practical than he had ever been in real life.

"She hurt when she said good-bye." Gavan didn't have to note how different his parents were from Tim's. "I'm sure that she didn't want to leave."

"Your dad. A strange guy."

"My aunt says I'm like him."

"No need to sound down about that."

"You sound better. Confident."

"It doesn't matter whether a life lasts thirteen years or seventy. It's something you find out when you're on the other side."

"If my mom had only told me more. Maybe I could help her."

"Adults think kids are useless. We can do more."

"We didn't stop the road, though, buddy. It's going through. My mom told me before she left town."

"You'll find a way." Gavan heard a voice that was so direct, so certain.

"Not without you."

"You have to, man." The voice faded away.

Gavan slammed his fist on the desk, and shouted: "Not alone, I can't!" The outburst startled the entire class, including Gavan. Fenlow stopped talking. Everyone stared as Gavan grabbed his books and ran out of the classroom. He could never explain how he felt to anyone.

CLASS BROKE MINUTES LATER. Thomas Fenlow could not stop his hands from shaking as he splashed cool water against his neck. Gavan James could make a fool of Fenlow only if the teacher let him. And that wouldn't happen. Water dripped to his pants. Fenlow swore, then took care to turn off the faucets with paper towels.

He glanced at the mirror and was startled by eyes unsteady with fear. The man in the mirror was not the man who existed inside his heart. The mirror showed a middle-aged man with thin hair and wary eyes, a man who never slept more than four hours a night.

Most people in Sitka thought of Fenlow as a teacher, and that disappointed him. A few knew him as an environmentalist, the point of reference he preferred most. To fit in and survive in a small town, he had to pretend to be a gentle environmentalist. He spoke about protecting whales and rain forests. He attended polite fund-raisers that served baked goods and organized campaigns for writing poignant notes to legislators. Only Fenlow knew what lengths he could go to to protect the little piece of Alaska that surrounded him.

The single, obvious cause behind every environmental problem was too many people. People crowded the world, tossing trash, building homes, cutting forests. Fenlow hated children. But he couldn't afford to leave. Environmental activism did not pay.

He thought about Tim, the little boy who was killed and smiled. A good deed as far as he was concerned. He wished a similar fate for Gavan James. Gavan, so annoying, should have been the one killed. Stupid doctors refused to diagnose him, but they didn't have to put up with twenty-five kids at once. Students like Gavan James made it impossible for anyone to learn—constant noise, disruption, arguments.

Fenlow remembered his own childhood, his ability to sit still and please the most demanding teachers. In public, his parents praised their son. At home, they were never satisfied. Late every night, he sat at the kitchen table doing extra work prepared by his mother.

As he got older, praise dwindled. Success in elementary school was college mediocrity. Fenlow was denied entrance to the finest graduate history programs and had to turn to teaching children to support himself. He thought bitterly about a boy similar to Gavan James from his own school days. The troublemaker became associate professor of agriculture at the University of Iowa. Agriculture, Fenlow sniffed. So practical. Yet jealousy seared his inside. Fenlow should be at a university, not the agriculture professor and certainly not Gavan James.

Fenlow smiled though. He could cultivate all of Gavan's worst bad habits, make the problems obvious to the other students and administrators, and maybe even drive him away from the classroom altogether. The man in the mirror liked the idea of targeting Gavan, and his laughter echoed weirdly against the bathroom walls.

TEN

Wednesday, September 30

MARCY WOULD NEVER FORGET the helpless feeling, landing at the Seattle airport, not knowing where to travel next. She waited at a ticket counter and asked about the next available flight. Less than an hour later, she set off for Florida.

She checked into a Palm Beach hotel. Taking long, slow walks, through parks and malls, she kept alert and detected no one paying any attention to her. Davy had warned her not to do anything rash, but she couldn't wait two months without trying to figure out who chased her out of town. Confident no one followed her, she headed for the library and found a book on hiring a detective. "Define your problem...set boundaries and time limits," Marcy read. "Former police or security experience is invaluable."

She went to a pay phone in the lobby and called a few names from the phone book. Receptionists and detectives brusquely demanded details.

"I can't solve a case in Alaska from Florida, lady," one man snapped, before hanging up.

"Save yourself money and wait the two months," was another's response. Marcy slammed the phone down. She picked up a free weekly paper in the library and flipped through the pages. A small ad caught her eye: "Private detective—Prefers odd cases; confidentiality guaranteed." She telephoned, and a man introduced himself as Mike Grogan. He listened patiently while she explained about Tim's death, the gray note, the cat, and the cross-island road. She didn't mention Alaska. "I'm not sure what I want," she admitted after rambling for several minutes. "Except to be home for Thanksgiving, and to prevent my family from getting hurt."

"It's a strange request," he said. "And it will be expensive."

"I understand," she replied quickly.

He gave her an address. "Come by this afternoon. We'll talk."

He was the first detective to consider her request, so she promptly doubted his ability. But she called a taxi anyway, which delivered her to an exquisite waterfront neighborhood. Standing in his secluded driveway, she told the taxi not to wait. The stucco home was small, but elegant. She followed a path to the door and rang the bell.

A huge man with tousled blond hair opened the door wide and said nothing. His face did not match his body: A set mouth and dark eyes were the picture of self-control; the rest of his body, the obesity, revealed despair. He obviously was accustomed to first reactions and probably expected her to make some excuse to walk away. Marcy stepped inside and shook his hand. "No one followed you," he noted. "I watched from upstairs. But that doesn't mean that they're not in contact with the cab company."

"I didn't call from my hotel."

She accepted a cool lime drink sat on a leather sofa and told him her story. "The place you describe is not around here," he commented. "Where's home?"

"Sitka," she admitted, anticipating an expletive and directions to the door. "In Alaska."

Grogan stood and refilled their glasses. "When do you want me to start?" he asked.

"As soon as possible," she replied, suddenly worried. His willingness to take on the task raised doubts about his skills and her own lack of plan. "But how?"

"We'll work on that together. But first, a caveat: Weird cases cost money. People with dough tend to have complicated lives. You say you have spare change, but I wouldn't know that passing you by on the street." He studied her. "How much money do you have and where did it come from?"

"The notes never mentioned money," Marcy said, repeating Beth's observation. "Hardly anyone knows how much I really have."

"I need to know everything about you," Grogan said, leaning back in the sofa.

IN THOSE EARLY DAYS, aboard the *Day Lily*, a comfortable life was always one season away. Davy had trouble keeping up with payments for the boat, insurance and permits that allowed him to fish for salmon and black cod. He was a skilled fisherman, but the *Day Lily* did not cooperate. Something always broke down at the most inopportune time.

Marcy tried to explain her new life in letters back home. Her family wrote back, pleading that she stop wasting time in Alaska, pointedly inquiring about Davy's background. Marcy stopped writing letters and sent postcards with short sentences about the scenery. Her family could never understand Davy's tenacity, how much one could learn from a man who kept hope alive, while working nonstop, inventing new meals from fish and seaweed, pleading for credit at docks along the coast.

When Marcy turned twenty-four, they were waiting desperately for checks from the seafood processor. The couple pulled into a small port, and Davy used the last of their money for cheese, bread and a cheap bottle of merlot. They hitched a ride to a nearby park and found a fallen tree in a field that overlooked the sea. Sprinkled through the grass were pale forget-me-nots. Marcy plucked the tiny stems and scattered the palest of blue flowers in his hair.

He handed her a birthday card. "I wish I could do more," he said.

She answered first with a kiss. "How could my birthday be better? I'm with you." She opened the card, and a lottery ticket from Seattle fell out.

"That's life with me," he said ruefully. "A one in a million chance."

"I feel awfully lucky," she warned. "What would you do if I won?"

He got up on his elbow. "Pay the bills. Never stop fishing. What about you?"

"I want a house by the sea, and forget-me-nots in my lawn," she said. "And you."

They watched the sun set over the Pacific, and returned to sea the next day. She transferred the card, with two dried forget-me-nots and ticket inside, to a box of mementos that she kept on the *Day Lily*. A few times she thought about visiting a library and checking the number on the lottery ticket, always when *Day Lily* was miles from shore.

Weeks later, they heard the fish ran strong not far to the south. On the way, *Day Lily's* engine broke down, and the vessel had to be towed to port. On the same day, Davy heard the bank had issued foreclosure notice on the *Day Lily*. "Damn, if we get the engine going, they'd have their damn payment in two weeks," Davy said, with desperation.

Marcy went to her box and fingered the ticket. She went to the library and signed up for fifteen minutes of time on the computer and checked the Web site for the Washington lottery. She clicked on the date of her ticket, and checked again. The numbers on the screen matched the number on the ticket in her hand—1-3-12-24-29-33. Marcy and Davy had worried for nothing for more than two months.

They borrowed money for the ferry and, once in Washington, they borrowed another fisherman's pickup to drive to

Olympia and pick up the first of twenty checks that would be distributed over the next twenty years—a total of $2,892,300. Driving away, Marcy felt breathless but couldn't stop talking. Davy was quiet, his knuckles white on the steering wheel.

"What's wrong?" Marcy asked. "Why did you insist on telling them that it's my money?"

"I don't need it," he said, not taking his eyes off the road.

"What do you mean? Our problems are over!"

"I don't want my life to change," he said, stubbornly.

"Do you still love me?" she whispered.

"Yes," he said, hitting the wheel. "But I'm afraid. That money will change the way you see me, Marcy. It might take a few weeks or years. But I'll know. And it will kill me."

"Stop, Davy," she said. "We have to talk."

He pulled the truck to the shoulder and dropped his head to the steering wheel. His hands were rough, stained and etched from hundreds of hard hours. He had never complained, he had never stopped dreaming. They sat quietly as cars sped by. Finally, she spoke. "This was your gift to me. Our lives don't have to change. We can go on the way we have."

He shook his head. "You make it sound so easy."

"It can be easier than this." She gestured to the holes in his jeans, the rusty borrowed pickup. "You aren't going to lose the boat."

He shrugged. "We'll have different problems People will never look at you the same. You'll wonder about me and what I want from you."

"No, damn you," she cried out, pushing his shoulder hard. "All I thought about was how we could pay off the *Day Lily,* buy some groceries and gas. No matter what you say, Davy, I'm the same woman who worked beside you last week."

"I want you to love me for what I am," he said.

"And I do," she said. "Davy, why did you buy the ticket?"

"That was long ago. It was garbage, and I wanted to give you the world."

"And you have," she said, smiling.

"I don't want to forget how to dream."

She put a finger to his mouth. That was the moment she came up with the plan. "So, we don't change. We still fish, and no one has to know about this."

He laughed. "Do you really think that's possible?"

"It is for me."

His eyes, like the color of the sea before a wild storm, locked on to hers, almost as if he could stare into her heart. She leaned against his shoulder. He was good. He was strong. He had made mistakes, but so had she, and they could admit them to each other. They had known each other long enough to know what the other person was thinking. They kissed, and he started the truck and they barely managed to merge into the traffic. A Lexus sped by and blasted its horn. They laughed.

For starters, they paid off the loan on *Day Lily*. Then they went to several banks and began accounts. Davy called a friend in Ketchikan who reported a hefty check had arrived from the processing plant. Davy took it as a good sign, and by the phone booth, he asked her to marry him. They chose plain gold bands. She wore an old favorite dress—pale yellow and blue. They got married alone. Davy's parents had died by the time he was fourteen, and he had run away from his first and only foster home, and Marcy's family was furious about the marriage. When she had called to tell her parents about her engagement, her father had snapped: "Now you're stuck. You can't afford to travel home for a decent wedding…not that any wedding could be proper with him as the groom."

Marcy had gently returned the receiver. Her family had never been pleased with her choices—first with clothes and books and later with men. She'd never forgive them for refusing to consider Davy's strengths. Sure, he didn't finish high school. He had spent some time in jail. And he thought nothing of spending his life chasing dwindling numbers of Alaska salmon on the high seas. Her parents would never understand that their rigid stability did not automatically make them better than her husband. Davy was not afraid to take chances. He was not afraid of failure. For the first time, she understood why he might fear the money.

Davy and Marcy settled in Sitka, Alaska's most beautiful port, and deliberately carried out the plan to allow no one in town to guess how rich they really were. Together, they bought equipment for *Day Lily,* a pickup and a house—in that order. Marcy invested the rest of the money, relying on advice from Beth. Marcy continued to trim Davy's long hair. She still cooked a lot of fish but added spices and wine. They drove a black pickup and wore comfortably faded jeans. Eating out at Sitka's best pizza restaurant was a once-a-month treat. Gradually, people on the docks noticed that Davy and Marcy looked different. Confidence had replaced the desperation.

Davy's luck at fishing turned that summer. He knew he had met success when he heard *Day Lily's* position announced over the radio, and fishermen with larger boats wanted to drop lines in his wake. By the end of the season, all bills were paid on Davy's money alone. A few years later, Marcy was pregnant.

The first year with Gavan, the baby, was delightful. When he was six, the couple discovered that they could not have more children. Disappointed, they focused energy on nurturing their only son. All the attention shaped Gavan into a child who had many ideas and little fear.

People could deliberately set out to change the way people thought about them. Marcy could not help but wonder at times what would have happened to her family without the money. But she always kept that thought to herself.

MARCY ENDED HER STORY, AND Grogan took a deep breath, then shrugged. "There's worse ways to get rich." He paused. "You and your husband having problems, Mrs. James?"

Marcy was startled. "Not at all!"

"But does your husband want you out of town for any reason? An affair?"

"No," Marcy said, adamant. "The person who did this killed his cat. This has nothing to do with Davy!"

"I'll reserve judgment," he said simply. "The worst crimes are committed by the person closest to the victim. If I'm working for you, you should expect me to consider every angle."

"If?" she asked. "I'm desperate to go back."

He paused and stared her in the eye. "I charge three thousand per week and require twenty thousand in advance. You pay all expenses. I expect absolute honesty. Dishonesty tends to make a case last longer. After a few weeks, I'll be looking forward to getting back to Florida."

She nodded slowly. "It's expensive. But if I'm home for Thanksgiving, it's worth it." She pulled out her checkbook.

"Wait," Grogan held up his hand. "Who has access to that account?"

"Only my husband. He thought it was best to open a new account before I left."

"Smart," he commented. "Except bank employees in town might talk. So, write the check out to cash and that way, no one knows that you're working with me. I'll drive you to the bank." He paused. "That was your husband's idea? Setting up this account so only he knows your whereabouts."

"Look—" Marcy protested.

"Yeah," Grogan stood and put his hands in the air. "He loves you as much as the day he married you. And he married you after you won the money, right?"

"You're wrong about Davy."

"Stay cool. No insult intended. But someone could watch him in ways that he doesn't know. Antagonize him the way I just antagonized you. How many times did these clowns waltz into your house? Once? Or maybe more. You're taking every cent out of that account. Checks and charge cards leave a paper trail. We want to control that trail."

He devised a plan for transferring cash from the account to a bank in Palm Beach. He asked her about charge cards, and she showed him three. "Wonderful," he said, smiling.

He also insisted that she call his references, and she liked what she heard: He was a loner who enjoyed travel and solving problems fast. Marcy signed the contract detailing services and conditions for the next ten weeks.

He asked her to describe Sitka and its tourism industry. "I can't stay in a hotel if there aren't a lot of tourists in town," he warned. "Do you have another place?"

She described the harbors and the fishing boats. "The quarters won't be deluxe," Marcy apologized. "But there's a man I can trust. He won't ask questions. So, you'll leave right away and stay in touch?" she asked.

"Not quite," Grogan said, with a smile. "I've got a better plan."

ELEVEN

DAVY MOVED HIS FAVORITE cooking utensil, a heavy frying pan, from sink to a burner set for high. He should have started dinner an hour earlier. He searched the pantry for a fast dinner. Pasta again, he decided, reaching for a jar of sauce. As he dumped it into the hot skillet, the sauce sizzled, scattering red dots across the stove. He swore.

"Dad, what's compound interest?" Gavan sat at the kitchen table. The boy was surrounded by open books and several ripped sheets of paper.

"That homework should have been done an hour ago," Davy noted, filling a large pot with water.

Gavan put his pencil down and spoke in a tone thick with patience. "I'm working extra hard on this last assignment. The teacher asked us to design five problems involving percentages."

"So why do you have to know about compound interest?" Davy asked, as he wiped the stove with paper towels and added a box of macaroni to the water. Too much macaroni, he thought too late. He didn't want to admit that he wasn't completely sure about compound interest himself.

"Mr. Hughes likes tough problems. How does this sound? 'Which will bring in more money over twenty years, five thousand dollars invested in a simple interest account at eight percent or one thousand dollars in an account with eight percent compounded daily?'"

"Sounds like a good problem," Davy said.

"But I need the answer. Maybe I could make one up. I bet Mr. Hughes doesn't know anything about compound interest either."

"Gavan, come up with problems that you can figure out. If I give you the answer, then I'm doing the homework."

"I'm just asking you how to do it."

"Beth's coming over. Ask her."

"Again?"

Davy didn't answer and stirred the sauce quickly.

"Why does Beth know more about money than you, Dad?" Gavan asked. "And Mom, too?"

"What gives you that idea?" Davy asked, frowning.

"She talks about it more, and you never do. Other kids, their dads handle the money."

"Nobody should talk about money in front of kids. You're too young to worry about compounding interest."

"Mortgages. They're percentages, too. Everyone will probably bring in a family mortgage problem. But we don't have one."

"It's nothing to be morose about," Davy said. "How do you know we don't have a mortgage anyway?"

"I watch the mail. I listen. You guys don't worry about that stuff."

"You're too nosy, Gavan."

"At least I don't blab at school. One kid said that people who don't have mortgages sell drugs. After that, I was too embarrassed to admit that we don't have one."

"Thanks for the discretion."

"Anytime," Gavan replied, twirling his pencil. "But Dad, do you?"

"Do I what?" Davy poured overdone macaroni into the strainer.

"Sell drugs?"

"No, damn it!" Hot water splashed onto Davy's hand, and

macaroni tumbled into the sink. He held his hand under cold tap water, then tried to retrieve most of the macaroni from the drain. "Please just finish the homework and let me concentrate on dinner!"

Gavan scribbled a few moments quietly, before letting out a large sigh. "I wish Mom were here. Did we do something wrong? Why doesn't she call?"

Davy abandoned the mushy macaroni to sit at the table next to Gavan. "There is nothing wrong with us. We don't sell drugs. We're not involved in anything illegal. Mom told you she'll be home in early December."

"After Thanksgiving!" Gavan countered. "But we've never been apart for Thanksgiving! Tell me why!"

Davy had no answers for his son, and any explanation sounded ridiculous. "Someone threatened us."

"Why don't you call the police?"

"Because of you, big guy. They killed Cassie. We're afraid of what they might do next."

"I'm not scared. You can't let people push you around. You always tell me that. Call the police."

"I'm not sure the police can help," Davy said. "What can they do, if we don't know why or who?"

"But you're working on that, right, Dad?"

Davy pushed his hair back from his eyes and felt guilty. He and Marcy had agreed to wait, an approach that could never be favored by Gavan.

"It has to be the road," the boy said matter-of-factly.

Davy shook his head. "I doubt it. Other people are against it."

"Do you think she's alone?" Gavan asked.

Davy nodded. But he could not help but wonder why Kovach had suddenly disappeared from town. Maybe Marcy was with the engineer. Maybe she had run away and forgotten all about the fight over the road as well as her family. Or, maybe there was a better reason.

"You know where she is," Gavan said. "And you don't want to tell me."

Davy sighed. "I wish."

"She won't last long out of town," Gavan said. "Like when she reads a book—she always goes back and peeks at the last few pages."

Davy laughed at Gavan's accurate description of Marcy. It was his first laugh since Marcy had left, since Tim had died, and it felt good. But his son didn't join him. "I'm worried about her," Gavan insisted. "How do we know someone didn't get her out of town to hurt her?"

Davy suddenly felt overwhelmed and couldn't answer. He stood and poked at the gummy macaroni, the paste-like sauce, then turned the stove off and scraped the meal into the trash. "Don't let your imagination run wild," he said, admonishing himself as much as his son. "She'll be home soon."

"You have a code," Gavan said, confidence in his voice, as he turned back to his homework. "And Beth is helping. I don't blame you for keeping it secret, but let me know if I can help. Now, what's another percentage, another money problem?"

"Percentages don't have to be about money," Davy chided his son. "Think about fish, people, probability, anything!"

"Fish?"

"Sure, the salmon population doesn't stay the same every year. Make a problem out of that."

"Hey, good idea! A cross-island road will decrease salmon by five percent every year. If a stream has a million salmon, how many years will it be before no salmon return?"

"That's a gloomy thought."

"Mr. Hughes loves when we apply math to everyday life." Gavan started sketching a table, with a column of numbers.

"You'll be the next person who gets run out of town," muttered Davy. "I'll call Beth quick and ask her to bring a pizza."

"We have to eat," Gavan agreed. "What's the percentage of Sitkans who like pepperoni?"

"Just finish the math homework. No more talking."

Davy telephoned Beth's number, wishing he could talk to his wife so easily. Like his son, Davy missed Marcy and longed to hear her voice. He had made a mistake by walking away from the airport without a code.

TWELVE

Thursday, October 15

THE ALASKA AIRLINES jet glided past sharp snowy peaks and skimmed over a bay shimmering in silver and emerald. Gordon Knowles was a twenty-nine-year-old reporter with the *Wall Street Journal* who had traveled about the world for feature stories, but even he felt awe as the plane landed in Sitka.

Knowles was in town to write a story about a proposed federal highway to cross Baranof Island. The road was totally unnecessary from his point of view. With less than ten thousand residents, Baranof Island could not even match the population of some blocks in New York City.

The news tip about a cross-island road had arrived by an anonymous phone message just after he had received a scolding from the assistant managing editor about two mistakes in an eight-inch article. The *Journal* ignored most of the thousands of anonymous calls, but Knowles regarded the tip as an omen. He lied to his editors, explaining that a college acquaintance had offered the idea. He explained that he needed a break from hectic New York assignments, and his editors agreed.

Knowles stepped into the tiny Sitka airport, and his feeling of awe vanished. Still, he didn't mind time away from his wife, Larissa. She had worked for the *Journal* before him and quit after the birth of their first child, now eight months old. He blamed his wife for the sudden rash of corrections, especially after she had refused to review his problem article over the telephone. "The baby's crying," she had snapped. "It's your job." She hung up. So he found a way to leave town.

Before he left, Rachel, the assistant managing editor and Larissa's friend, warned him that Alaska could be deceiving. He nodded politely—half listening and wondering if Larissa had told Rachel how often she had helped with his early stories. Lately, Larissa merely criticized and offered little specific guidance. "You look for too many experts," she contended. "Interview regular people. Make your stories real."

Maybe Larissa would read this story. But if she didn't, he'd handle a bunch of Alaska hicks. He'd prove to Larissa and Rachel that he could find his own stories. He looked about the miniature airport and groaned.

Nearby, a homely woman in shabby clothes and a duller perm leaned close against a man who was immensely overweight. The couple moved slowly, ignoring the crowd waiting to greet the other passengers and subsequently blocking Knowles' path to the baggage rack. Most passersby avoided the couple, with a few offering fast glances of pity.

Knowles had six weeks. He could only hope that most of the people in Sitka were not as fat and dull as the hideous couple leaving the plane.

MARCY NOTICED THE HANDSOME stranger's reaction and squeezed Grogan's hand. "It's working!" she whispered gleefully, while waiting for the luggage to appear and nervously patting her hair. She almost felt bald.

"Slow down," Grogan muttered. "Remember, you've never been here before. Stand close to me or other strangers. And absolutely no eye contact with anyone."

He called a cab, then they waited outside while other passengers collected their baggage. Marcy quickly noticed most people overlooked her and stared at her new companion with revulsion. Mounds of fat strained his clothes and swelled in large, soft lumps over his belt. At least six feet tall, he weighed more than four hundred pounds. Like a giant, every breath he took was audible. Marcy turned her back to the crowd near the door and puffed on the fourth cigarette of her life, all the while despising the soft paper between her lips, the foul aftertaste. Marcy stared at her reflection. She weighed less, but didn't look much better than Grogan.

Grogan protectively wrapped his arm about Marcy, keeping her close to his side, as if he had fallen in love. Like Grogan, Marcy loved her new persona. No one would ever recognize the plain, insecure woman as Marcy James.

MARCY HAD FOLLOWED ALL of Grogan's instructions.

"To figure out why you had to leave, you have to go back to Sitka and watch what's going on," Grogan had explained. "Change your appearance and add me. My weight will refocus attention."

Marcy gave the tiniest of nods, not wanting to hurt his feelings. She kept her Palm Beach hotel room, but prepared for the secret return to Sitka from Grogan's home. First, he urged her into new eating habits—plenty of fried seafood, desserts and milkshakes. At the same time, she booked passage for herself on a cruise to South America. Then she went shopping: With her charge cards, she purchased two dozen paperbacks and an array of clothes that could never be worn in Sitka—a black bathing suit, shorts and tops, a flowing silky skirt in teal and silver.

More than a week later, dressed in a white dress that hid her recent gain in weight, with her golden hair free and draped over her shoulders, Marcy boarded her ship—without a ticket. Grogan had already dropped the cruise ticket at a senior center near his home. "Maybe you can use this as a prize for your next bingo game," he suggested, and left before the woman with blue hair and papery skin could ask questions.

Marcy headed for the lowest deck, the area reserved for staff quarters, and slipped into Cabin B-16. Space was tight— room for bunk beds, a battered dresser, a tiny square of cracked linoleum. Grogan told Marcy little about the woman who lived in the sparse room, except that she cleaned and paid for her son's college tuition by transporting small packages between ports. Marcy quickly packed her white dress, and left her travel bag on the bed, wondering if she'd ever see or wear the dress again. Grogan had insisted that she leave all belongings in Florida. She'd got to Sitka without license, cell phone, keys, anything that could possibly reveal her identity.

Marcy opened her wallet for one last look at her photos of Davy and Gavan. Grogan then arranged for the bag to be mailed to his office. He also paid the purser to notify Grogan's secretary if any inquiries were made about Mrs. Marcy James. Finally, Marcy left two of her credit cards on the dresser for the cleaning woman, along with her Sitka address and a list of recommendations for purchases during the trip, all suitable for a middle-aged white woman, her Alaska native husband and twelve-year-old son.

Marcy stepped into the cabin's bathroom—more cramped than her shower stall at home—carrying a brown paper bag with scissors and other supplies from the drugstore.

Less than an hour later, a woman in dirty gray uniform with short brown hair stepped off the ship and jumped into the beige Taurus waiting in the parking area. Marcy tossed the plastic bag filled with locks of her once-glorious hair into the back seat. "How bad do I look?" she asked.

"Different," he said, smiling. "Even your husband won't recognize you. And from now on, you're Cindy Tumper." He zigzagged through the streets and took an exit on the highway north. He pointed out that no one followed. "Funny, I'm certain no one's tailed you all week long. You sure you had to leave town?"

"It seemed that way in Sitka."

"Nice change on the voice. Still, talk as little as possible when we hit Sitka."

They drove until after midnight. In Tampa they completed her new look, stopping at a thrift shop and purchasing worn jeans, T-shirts, a faded jacket, old boots and a beat-up duffel bag. In the hotel bathroom, she held her nose and added a cheap perm to the cheap dye job.

Marcy rubbed some dark eye shadow under her eyes and cocked her head before a mirror. By drinking several shakes a day, she had gained pounds that showed on her face. The puffiness and new hair emphasized her age. The new color actually highlighted green sparks in her hazel eyes, which Marcy hid with the glasses.

Grogan insisted on buying several cartons of cigarettes at a convenience store—Marlboros for Marcy and Merits for himself—before they caught a cheap flight to Portland, Oregon, where they connected with a regular Alaska Airline flight. Marcy grimaced. "Smoking gives you an excuse to light a match, look through your pockets, cover your mouth to cough," he cautioned. "Take advantage of all the possibilities."

MARCY GUIDED GROGAN TO Alaska Native Brotherhood Harbor and a shabby vessel tied at the end of the dock. The wooden boat, *Sal II,* belonged to Lance Willard, a fisherman with long gray hair and a longer list of strange friends from over the years. Lance didn't send *Sal II* out for fishing anymore—its hold was small, the engine rough. But fishermen could not help but be sentimental about the boats that had carried them through the most exciting years of their lives. Of course, the harbor master didn't appreciate retired boats like *Sal II* taking up dock space. At least one sunk every year, endangering neighboring boats. But when a fisherman had as many years and friends in Alaska as Willard, minor problems were overlooked.

The cabin was cramped but had two comfortable bunks and a tiny woodstove. Marcy had once fished with Lance and knew that he used the boat to put up the friends he had collected after more than forty years of fishing all over the state. Harbor dwellers—quiet by day, rowdy at night—got used to sponge baths, dirty hair, as well as layers of clothes purchased for a quarter apiece from thrift shops. The bankers, doctors, store clerks of Sitka did not know the names of wharf rats. Bartenders and police knew many of them well.

Alaska's harbors, including the four in Sitka, attracted drifters from all over the country, who dreamed of fast jobs that paid fast cash. Marcy was once one of the wanderers who heard tales of ten thousand dollars in earnings on herring fleet trips that lasted less than an hour or bonuses when a troller landed a hundred-pound king salmon.

The would-be fishermen quickly learned that the best crew jobs never went to strangers. A few rats found temporary work with onshore processing plants. Others landed jobs with struggling captains, not rich enough to hold the necessary state permits for most species. The permits, limited and regulated by the state, cost thousands of dollars. Young captains, like indentured servants of centuries gone by, eagerly promised away hefty shares of profits simply to fish with borrowed permits. Or they caught species without permits and sold the illegal fish to foreign buyers at sharp discounts.

The rats came and went like the tide. With every passing year, more transients arrived for fewer jobs. A few like Marcy matured and became stable members of town. But most lingered about the harbors and bars for a month or two and then disappeared, never to be seen again.

Marcy and Grogan were more quiet and sober than Willard's other friends. The two were never seen apart, with Marcy leaning against Grogan as if she were feeble. Other than a strange dependence on her companion, she was ordinary: short mousy hair, thick glasses with a black frame, dull clothes stretched across a stocky figure. She offered no reason for more than a passing glance.

Any stares lingered on Grogan. What startled people more than the weight, not unusual on the docks, were Grogan's angry eyes, vivid against the doughy face and wispy blond hair. The eyes did not match the man's soft, plodding style. Marcy could not have found anyone who contrasted more with her own husband, who at five feet, six inches, was wiry, with dark hair, gold skin and high cheekbones. Intense and energetic, Davy outworked men half his age.

Marcy waited quietly to the side, head down, as Grogan listened to the man's advice about the boat. She was relieved that Willard did not recognize her, though she was ashamed to admit that she had not seen him much in recent years. Still, fishermen clung to friendships regardless of distance and time. Willard had been kind and agreeable when she had called from Florida and asked if he would board two acquaintances. She had explained that both were awkward and shy, and asked that he remain quiet about doing the favor for her. "No need to explain more," Willard had interrupted. Then, he had offered to describe the two as old friends of his from Oregon and to dismiss any questions about why they didn't look for jobs or visit the bars.

Toward the end of the telephone conversation, Willard had changed the topic. "What are we going to do about that road, Marcy?" His question was plaintive. "Especially if you're out of town."

"Keep fighting, Willard," she said firmly.

So, Cindy Tumper and Mike Grogan came to town, but kept to themselves. Grogan did all the talking. The other liveaboards in ANB Harbor watched the couple disappear into *Sal II's* cabin and could only wonder about what went on inside.

THIRTEEN

Saturday, October 17

GAVAN WANTED TO FIND HIS mother, and he needed help. He could try with his father, his aunt or even Beth. But all three had known him since his birth and thought of him as a little kid who had a big imagination. He was highly annoyed with the adults' complacence, the lack of curiosity about his mother's whereabouts. So, he decided to find someone who was used to asking questions. If not the police, then maybe a reporter...and everyone knew where to find the *Daily Record* reporter, Bob Denson, on most mornings.

Denson, brash and not long out of college, was the nemesis of his aunt, the competition for every news story. Aunt Francesca had labeled him as immature, but also admired his knack for sniffing out news. Virtually every local story written by Denson hit front page of the *Daily Record,* and a few made it to the state wire. The news could be three inches on anything that made the town sound: a) quaint and country, b) stupid and country, c) mean and country.

His mother and other parents in Sitka warned their children to behave or Bob Denson would list their problems and address in the newspaper's police blotter. The most outrageous anecdotes hit the national wire, a mere inch or two, but that was enough to put Bob Denson in a state of ecstasy for a week before he began his relentless search all over again.

Bob sat with Jane McBride near the window, and Gavan decided to wait until the reporter was alone. Observing adults was almost as much fun as watching cavorting squirrels. Both exhibited anxiety and posturing. Gavan waited until Bob and Jane were engrossed in a conversation, then lowered his head and moved closer to their table, trying not to attract attention. He grunted toward an empty spot with two fishermen at a table for four, and they nodded politely. Gavan sat with his back to Bob and quietly ordered a bagel and a glass of water for the wait. Then he tucked his head into a book and pretended to read.

JANE HAD EXPECTED BOB'S attempts to pry information from her about the cross-island road, the town's top new story. "You don't have to be so loud," she cautioned.

"But what are the road opponents up to?" pressed Bob. "You know more than you let on."

"I don't," Jane countered. She glanced around Katlian Cafe on a typical Saturday morning. The diner was small, greasy and hot, with rough tables and chairs jammed together. No matter how many people packed into the diner, waitresses refused to turn a customer away. Instead, they dragged chairs from the back room and offered introductions.

A waitress slammed bacon and pancakes in front of Bob and toast for Jane. "No one keeps a secret better than you," he said, shaking his head.

"I don't intend to change," she said. "Does Lindsay know how you harass your sources?"

"Persistence pays off in this business."

"It pays off in every business," Jane said. "What's new?"

"A reporter from the *Wall Street Journal's* in town."

"I heard. What's he like?"

"A jerk."

"You're jealous," Jane said, with a smile.

Bob scowled. "He doesn't have to work. Everybody in

town's falling over to meet him and they forget about me! Did you know a guy in town makes jewelry out of salmon skin? Knowles interviewed him!"

"You can still write the story."

"Never!" Bob said. "Worse, Lindsay wants me to profile the reporter. She refuses to understand that he's the enemy."

"Lindsay's the boss. The guy is news. Do the profile."

Bob leaned over and whispered, "Do me a favor and don't talk to him."

Jane drank coffee and shook her head, explaining that brushing off an interview with the *Wall Street Journal* would be grounds for losing her job. Bob groaned and pushed his plate aside. Jane smiled at him. "Look at the bright side. He might write about you! Lord knows you've Alaska-nized enough people in town."

"Some friend you are."

She went to the counter for an extra coffeepot and poured more for them both. Holding the cup, she mused out loud: "Why's he here? The cross-island road isn't a sure thing."

"Maybe because Bander issues a new press release every day. I ignore most of them. I didn't realize he was sending them around the entire country. Do you plan to join his new coalition—Sitkans Who Adore Tourists?"

"We received our invitation. We're reviewing the request. That's all I can say. Oh, and we appreciate tourists whether or not we join. Not adore." She busied herself using a knife and jam and asked some questions, testing how much he knew about the internal conflicts at Katmai Shee. But Bob showed little interest in the technicalities of the cross-island road.

"Now that Marcy James skipped town, who should I contact on the opposition side?" Bob asked.

Jane frowned. "Beth Roberts is picking up while Marcy's out of town on a family emergency. Beth's working to convince the corporation and city to file an emergency injunction to stop SWAT's sale of bonds for a cross-island road. You might check the court records." Jane did not mention that she had annoyed road opponents by urging the Katmai board of directors to avoid antagonizing SWAT. The board of directors, bitter about Bander proposing a cross-island road so soon after the native corporation announced plans for its own small road, had decided to join the city for a court fight against Bander's road.

"Good for her," Bob said. "Thanks for the tip."

But Jane didn't respond. "Decide, Jane," Bob continued. "Either you like the road or you don't."

"The road's irrelevant," Jane said with a sigh.

"What do you mean?"

She opened his notebook and pointed to a blank page. "Get my quote right. With major public projects, you don't know the real answers until thirty years later. Bander could be right—the road could be the perfect way to boost Sitka's economy, while confining tourists and protecting the environment. Or, it could be the start of turning this island into a patch of pavement that resembles the rest of the United States. No one knows, and I'm not going to pretend.

"But Sitka needs answers soon. SWAT's on a roll. Their road proposal gets turned down with a close vote. They run to the Forest Service because forest rangers love any road that makes monitoring the Tongass easier. Before we know it, bonds are ready to be sold and construction's scheduled. No election, nothing! Bander discovered the beauty of industrial development bonds," Jane concluded. "Roads are not like schools or local projects. They don't go to voters. Minimal notice and virtually no public scrutiny."

Bob moved his chair close to Jane's. "Who makes the decision?"

"The Alaska Development Authority. A board of directors appointed to six-year terms by the governor. We're not the only state. Once appointed, these boards answer to no elected official."

"That sounds illegal!"

"They're absolutely legal, but not exactly accountable," Jane said ruefully. "Alaska has no limit on state debt and, of all the states, it has the highest amount of debt per capita." She played with her coffee cup. "Anything attracting dollars from outside of the state gets priority, and tourism represents outside money at its purest. A few Sitkans hate the road, but construction and tourist interests love it. And sadly enough, most people could care less."

"Of all times for the opposition to fall apart!" Denson said.

"They care," Jane said. "But going up against government bonding authorities is like tackling an invisible enemy. I don't understand why Bander bothered with the assembly."

"He's in a rush."

"He's also talking about putting the bonds on the stock market," Jane added. "Which could be why that reporter's in town."

"Who in their right mind would buy stock in an Alaskan road?"

"Risk can pay big, and Alaska means risk," she replied.

"Won't investors investigate the need for a road?"

She let out a laugh. "They don't care about the need, only the state's ability to pay. Bander might even convince the state or Forest Service to put up some land as collateral."

Bob dropped his pen and shook his head. "Too bad bonds are so boring."

"Boring?" Jane exclaimed. "It's terrifying for the people who understand."

"Maybe I'll write more next week when I have time…"

"You better hurry," Jane said, slyly. "Knowles will beat you to the story."

"I don't know about that." Denson leaned back in his chair.

"I've heard rumors about his interviews. My bet is that he could care less about bonds."

"No way. If Knowles works for the *Journal,* he cares."

Bob crumpled his napkin. "I don't trust the guy. Take my advice, start practicing the phrase, 'No comment.'"

"Get used to him, Bob. He's reserved a hotel room for six weeks."

"That's sightseeing, not reporting!" Bob slapped the table. "I better check out his paper at the library. See what he's up to."

"The *Journal* comes a day late here," Jane warned. "Use the Internet."

He checked his watch. "I'm late for a photo at the fire station." He stood and left a tip. "If you talk to Marcy James or Francesca, give them this advice. The mystery game attracts attention." He rushed out of the cafe. The early breakfast crowd had thinned, and Jane poured one last cup of coffee.

GAVAN STUDIED THE WOMAN'S face. He hardly knew Jane McBride, only that she had been to his family's home on a few occasions and his aunt respected her immensely. His mother was a bit envious of the woman, but that was another reason why Gavan should approach her. He added a dime to the tip left by the fishermen and turned around, quickly taking the chair vacated by the reporter. Gavan was blunt. "Do you know where my mom's at?" he asked softly.

Jane swallowed her coffee wrong. "No, I don't," she said, coughing.

"Neither do I," he said, with a sigh. "I don't think my dad does either. I thought I'd ask you because you were at our house that night, talking with my parents, right before she left. I miss her."

"The time will go by fast," Jane said gently. "That's hard to believe now, but a few months can go by quickly."

"I worry that she might not come home. Someone should start asking questions. Like that reporter."

"Asking questions could get her killed," Jane said ruefully.

"I can't just wait," Gavan said. "Please don't tell anyone, but I want to help her. Do you know Mr. Kovach?"

"No, I'm sorry." Jane explained how she had dialed the engineer's telephone number, an office in Juneau, repeatedly. "Early on, his answering machine up north accepted calls. But he didn't return any of them. Not mine, and not calls from the city. Last week, the phone company had a message that the line's been disconnected." Jane shook her head.

Gavan leaned closer to Jane and confided, "I think Mom left because of the road. Can you tell me more about what you were telling the reporter, about the road bonds?" They spoke for almost an hour. Jane explained to him how governments could borrow money for construction projects by selling bonds. Money borrowed and channeled through the government was tax-free and cost less than money borrowed from banks. Governments could loan money for longer periods than banks, up to fifty years.

Gavan asked questions and she answered each of them. But neither could figure out a reason why only his mother had to leave town.

FOURTEEN

Tuesday, October 20

INSIDE *SAL II'S* CABIN, Marcy studied her face in the small mirror. "I can't believe I'm doing this," she said, shaking her shorn head. "People stare. But they're not really seeing me!"

"People view couples as a unit, not two individuals," replied Michael Grogan. "You can't risk walking around town by yourself. Walking with a man completely different from your husband turns you into a different woman. I'm the essential part of your disguise."

"I hope you're right," Marcy said, following him on the deck. Winter and the holidays were approaching. At least she was in Sitka, close to her family, even if they had no idea.

Grogan donned his jacket. "Stay aboard. There's no reason for you to come along on this trip."

"I have to get off the boat once in a while," Marcy insisted. When on board, Grogan warned that they speak in low tones and keep all the curtains drawn. She smashed her frizzy hair with a cheap wool cap. "I'm going crazy. Besides it looks strange if I never leave the boat. I promise, I won't step out of the car."

"Let's go," he said wearily.

"I wish we didn't have to drive," Marcy hesitated by the Tercel.

"Walking's dangerous, get in the car," he ordered.

She slammed the rusty door shut and leaned her head back

against the worn seat. With Grogan driving, she scanned the streets, morose that her life was on hold. A former crew member of Davy's stepped out of Japonski Bar and stumbled off the curb, never looking her way. Rick had quit on Davy a few years earlier by not showing up for a black cod trip. The *Day Lily* left on schedule, and Rick's brother convinced his captain to squeeze another man on board the other boat. As the boat went down, not far from Sitka Harbor, the crew realized that they were short one survival suit. Rick refused to wear the suit his brother tossed, but that didn't save the brother.

"See anything?" Grogan interrupted her thoughts.

"Everyday people," she said softly. "Nothing to do with me." She glanced at the clock on the dashboard. "Hey, turn here, it's a shortcut."

"In Sitka?" Grogan snorted. "That's like taking a shortcut from the toilet to the sink on *Sal II*." But he turned down the narrow street.

School had been dismissed minutes earlier, and students strolled away in small groups. Marcy saw Gavan's dark green coat. He stood alone, waiting for a school bus, with his head down and cheeks glowing from the chilly air. His hair was too long, his mouth set too tight. She twisted in her seat and pressed her face against the window as they drove past. Grogan hit the gas, and the boy was out of sight.

"Damn," Grogan shouted, hitting the steering wheel. "You saw your kid!"

"He didn't see me," Marcy whispered. Grogan swung the car into the courthouse parking lot.

"You expressed more than mild interest back there."

"So what?" she snapped. "He's my son. Give me a break!"

"All we need—a report of two strangers cruising by the school eyeballing kids."

"Speeding through a school zone doesn't help," Marcy said, refusing to look at Grogan's face. "Nobody saw us."

"Yeah," Grogan replied. "Well, maybe I should think about heading back to Florida."

Her anger vanished as she tried to explain. "Look, I just wanted to see him. You can't imagine how hard school is for him. This has been a bad year in so many ways. He has trouble making friends and paying attention. His teacher pressures us to put him on Ritalin."

"They can't make you put your son on a drug."

"No, but they can suggest it over and over. This teacher complains that he disrupts the other students. But it's as if the teacher pushes Gavan into a state. I'm afraid that a drug would destroy the parts of my son that I love the most. Even worse, his best friend dies, and I leave town. I feel so trapped, and Gavan must feel even worse."

"You're not trapped," Grogan said flatly. "You have money. You're not supposed to be in town, but you are. You can do more than most people." He heaved himself from the car. "I'll be back in a moment."

Marcy watched the courthouse entrance. A few employees drifted in and out. Along came Fred Keger, leaning hard on his cane. Almost ninety, the man struggled with the door. A slip of the heavy glass door would easily snap the old bones. Marcy felt guilty about not running over to help, but the old man's struggle ended when Grogan exited and held the door.

Hurrying to the car, Grogan handed a pile of copied documents to Marcy. "I had them pull copies of the court calendars since the day you left town—criminal, civil, divorces, custody disputes."

"So much…" she murmured as she began to wade through the copies.

"Get used to it," Grogan warned.

"Here," Marcy pointed. "An emergency injunction hearing against the cross-island road bond sale! The plaintiffs are Katmai Shee and the city."

"That damn road," Grogan mused. "Maybe you know something that can stop the road."

"I should go to the hearing," she said.

"Too dangerous…"

"What's the matter?" she taunted. "No confidence in your disguise?"

FIFTEEN

Friday, October 30

MARCY CONVINCED GROGAN that she should attend the hearing under his careful supervision. Inside the building that housed the Superior Court, they avoided the elevator and took the stairs. Grogan paused on the landing for several deep breaths while Marcy waited without comment.

Traveling with Grogan changed the way she looked, the way she felt about herself. Alone, she'd take the steps two at a time, using them as an excuse to move as fast as the tomboy she had once been. Such pace was impossible with Grogan, and his heavy arm often kept a drag on her.

A tall woman with precision-clipped hair and a tweed suit stepped neatly down the stairs, her hand trailing gracefully along the rail. When she saw Grogan, disgust momentarily flashed in her eyes, followed by a glance of pity for Marcy. Some lawyer from Juneau, guessed Marcy, as her face flushed with embarrassment and the sudden desire to run away from Grogan and her own sloppy appearance. Grogan, leaning against the rail, didn't seem to notice. He couldn't always fail to notice, Marcy thought, staring at his massive stomach and flushed cheeks as she followed him to the courtroom.

He pushed open the heavy door to the somber room with pale wood and comfortable furnishings. They took seats in the last row. Grogan squeezed his frame into the chair and handed her the *Record*. Four men, two of whom Marcy recognized as Sitka lawyers, stood near a table with stacks of papers. All wore dark suits and white shirts, and ignored the newcomers. Marcy slumped in her seat. "Will anyone ask why we're here?" she whispered.

"They better not!" Grogan snorted. "The courtroom's open to the public. Everything except juvenile cases. You haven't been here before?"

"No. Why would I?"

"For starters, your kid."

She elbowed him. "Gavan's all right," she snapped.

"No names, Cindy," Grogan hissed. He glanced at the huddled lawyers. "Sorry, stupid joke."

"It helps to have a good lawyer, too," Marcy admitted, looking around. "She'll be here today. I wish there was a larger crowd of road opponents."

He checked his watch. "We're early. With luck, people will think we're two bums who came in for a seat out of the rain."

She sighed. "I'm tired of waiting. Damn it, Grogan, I fought the road for more than a year. Why did I have to leave now?" More people entered the courtroom, and their voices dropped to a whisper. Marcy recognized most of the faces.

"Lot of people hanging out in the hall," Grogan murmured. "I'll go hang out there for a few minutes. You read the newspaper while I'm gone. And don't get caught staring at anyone."

After Grogan walked away, she removed the hated glasses and placed them on his chair. She held the newspaper close to her face, but the eight flimsy pages did not feel much like a shield.

The front page photo showed a group of children, pointing to a pile of books they had read to raise money. She searched for Gavan, but no... Over the years, he had been the subject of several newspaper photos; her favorite was when the photographer captured Gavan's thrill of finding an Easter egg. The pleased two-year-old ignored the wild race for candy and sat down in the middle of the scrambling children to admire his treasure. Local articles and photos seemed corny, until they included one's own child. Marcy wondered if Gavan had read any books for the fund-raiser. Did Davy and Gavan read side by side near a fire? Crumpling the newspaper in her lap, she shut her eyes and missed her family.

The courtroom slowly filled, with half the crowd wearing suits, the other half wearing flannel and old denim. No one glanced her way. Marcy slouched, returned her attention to the paper and studied a front-page article on the injunction hearing. The article began with hostile comments from both sides, including some bitter criticism of her for abandoning the fight. "Cripes!" Marcy muttered.

Two men taking seats in front of her turned to stare, and Marcy dipped her head behind the newspaper, but not before she recognized one as Jeremy Bander. Her encounters with Bander had always been rare. Other than the children's friendship, the two families had shared few interests. The two homes were close enough for the boys to walk back and forth, and while Marcy ran into the tourism director at town meetings, the two adults typically sat on opposite sides of the room.

Tim's father stood so close, she could smell his pungent cologne. Her hands shaking, she reached for the glasses and returned them to her face, as she carefully peered around the side of the page. Bander had already returned his attention back to his conversation with his companions and Marcy felt dizzy with relief.

A lawyer approached Bander, and the two men eagerly shook hands. "We know this is a rough time," the lawyer said. "The judge knows about your recent tragedy and would agree to a continuance…"

"It's been rough," Jeremy said. "Nothing will bring him back. And nobody can say I wasn't there for him. He wouldn't let me get close!"

"Kids get to a certain age—" the lawyer murmured.

"I want to get this over as quickly as possible," Bander said, glancing around the room, his eyes lingering on Marcy and then nearby fishermen. "With every passing day, more people who have no stake in this project get involved."

"All right." The lawyer nodded and kept his face bland, apparently accustomed to a client's grief spinning in any direction. "It's our contention that any delays for a cross-island road are frivolous. That the state bonding authority is the most appropriate body to make a decision. That Southeast Alaska Tourism is a proper agent for administering such a project."

"Go for it," Bander said. Suddenly his head jerked, and he stared at the opposite side of the courtroom. Marcy immediately checked that direction, trying to see what infuriated him. Gavan was slouched in a seat across the aisle, about six feet away. Her breath caught.

Bander approached the boy. "What the hell are you doing here?"

Gavan stared straight ahead for long second or two. And then he looked sadly up at the older man.

Bander put his one hand on the back of Gavan's chair and the other on the seat in front of him, essentially locking the boy in place. "I always warned Tim to stay away from you. Why can't you stay away from me?" Gavan shrunk down in his seat and shook his head as if he could not speak. Bander continued: "Tim thought your family was better. I told him the only reason he admired your father, your mother, was because they have money. And the stupid kid laughed at me and insisted your parents don't care about money."

Like Gavan, Marcy cringed. She wondered if the man had any good memories of his son.

"Fishermen!" he spat the word with contempt. "So righteous—as if they had fished with Jesus. But I don't have to tell you that your father's money doesn't come from fish that cost less than two dollars a pound and are only legal a few months a year!"

Bander's voice grew louder, more angry. People in the courtroom stared in that direction and discontinued their own conversations to watch the exchange.

"Now, tourism's honest money. Anybody can do it. You don't need a license. You don't have to show a history of catching this fish or that. God forbid an old man comes up here for a vacation and hopes to catch a salmon. Fishermen howl if anyone takes one damn fish away from their quota. And your mother is the worst, talking about her way of life. Where is she? What is she scheming now with her engineer friend? Believe me, I'm going to get to the bottom of how your parents make their money…"

The entire courtroom had fallen silent. Grogan walked in and sat next to Marcy, but for once no one gave him a second glance. Bander's lawyer approached his client, and whispered in his ear.

"I don't give a damn who hears," Bander said. "That family caused my kid's death. This kid should be standing in this courtroom and answering questions! He knows more and I intend to find out."

"Don't worry about a kid," the lawyer spoke firmly.

"Hell, Gavan should have died, not Tim!" Bander pulled away from his attorney and broke down in tears.

The attorney hurried to one of his assistants. "See if you can get us a delay of an hour." A few people went up to comfort Bander, and Francesca crouched next to Gavan, rubbing his shoulder and softly questioning him—Marcy hoped Gavan's aunt asked about why he was skipping school.

Marcy gripped the newspaper, wishing she had something more substantial to hold. Grogan squeezed her upper arm tightly. "Stay calm," he admonished. "Responding to his insults will only shut us down."

Gavan stood, and Francesca guided him toward the court-room doors. Bander stormed away from his little group and blocked Gavan's exit. "Why did your mother vanish from town?" he challenged, a few feet from Grogan and Marcy. "Maybe your mother knows how guilty you are and ran away because she hates your guts. Or else she's with Kovach."

The lawyer hurried to Bander again. "The judge is not going to delay this hearing," he said. "Concentrate on what we're here for today. Or you'll be kicked out of this courtroom."

The bailiff called for order, that the hearing was about to begin. Francesca looked at Gavan and sighed. The two turned around and retook their seats.

Grogan moved his head close to Marcy. "Don't let it get to you."

She wiped a tear away. "I have to get out of here." She abruptly stood and headed for the door, unable to speak until they reached the downstairs lobby. Marcy leaned against the wall and covered her flushed face with her hands, feeling as if she had been slapped.

"I can't believe what he said. Bander blames Gavan and me for Tim's death. If Gavan had died, I wouldn't hate Tim!"

"Why do you care what he says? The man's distraught."

She rubbed her eyes and pushed herself away from the wall. "But Bander's right. My family's weird. Otherwise, I wouldn't be hiding."

"Do you think that he sent the letter?"

She wanted to say yes, but deep inside knew better. "He's too angry to send an anonymous letter," she admitted, sniffing.

Grogan handed her a handkerchief. "Did he seem happy that you had left town?"

"Not really." Marcy hurried for the door to the parking area. "He was more agitated about my sudden disappearance."

"Slow down," Grogan growled. "You're Cindy Tumper, remember?"

Marcy paused. "He was surprised that I had left. That means he didn't send that note, Grogan."

Grogan glanced back towards the stairs. "Maybe I should stay at that hearing."

"I heard enough," Marcy said. "I'll wait in the car. All I know is that Bander hates me. But he didn't write the note. So that means someone else hates me even more."

THE HEARING DID NOT LAST long. On the way back to ANB Harbor, Marcy suggested to Grogan that they needed help from someone else in town. Over takeout from the Chinese restaurant and a couple of beers, she convinced him that her friends could keep a secret. "Not your husband?" he queried.

"He'd be livid that I took a risk. Would you let me call him anyway?"

"No," Grogan admitted. "The phone could be bugged. Better not call his cousin either." Grogan reluctantly accompanied her to the pay phone at the ANB parking lot. Rain had sputtered all day. Traffic hit the puddles with a loud snapping noises. No one lingered near the phone. Marcy gave him Beth's number. He dialed and waited. When the message machine came on, he hung up. "We should wait," he said. "I have a bad feeling about contacting anyone in town."

"No," Marcy insisted, afraid that he'd change his mind. "Let's call Jane. She'll be in her office."

"How well do you know her?"

"Not as well as Francesca or Beth," Marcy admitted.

"Does this woman have any reason to want you out of town?"

"Not at all," Marcy said, rapidly dialing the number for Katmai Shee. "My cousin trusts her completely. Plus, she doesn't know anything about my money."

Grogan held up his hand. "Is Jane McBride in?" He used his most professional tone. "This is Ken Sevallo. The Permanent Fund." Put on hold, Grogan passed the phone to Marcy.

In less than a minute, Marcy heard Jane's crisp voice. "Hi, Ken, what's going on in Juneau?"

"Jane." Marcy held the phone tightly. "It's me. Marcy."

"Mar… Well, I can't say that we've had that much rain here. Excuse me a moment." She pushed the hold button and returned seconds later. "Sorry about that. Debby was here. Are you all right?"

"Everything's fine. Have you seen Davy or Gavan?"

"I spoke to Gavan once. He misses you. Are you going to come home?"

Marcy hesitated. "Not yet. And don't mention this call to Davy or anyone, all right? Not even Francesca."

"If you're sure that's what you want…" The bells of St. Michael's Cathedral tolled the hour, five o'clock. Grogan lunged to muffle the receiver.

"Marcy, did I hear…"

"Don't call me by that name." Marcy grimaced. "It's Cindy now. And yes, I'm in town. With a detective."

"In Sitka? Is that possible?"

"He gave me a good disguise. But we need help. Could we meet? When do you plan to go out on your skiff again?"

"I could take a day off…"

"No, don't do anything unusual," Marcy said. "We'll meet at sunrise, a week from Saturday. We'll send a note on the place."

"I can't wait to see you," Jane said.

Marcy glanced at a distorted reflection of her face in the phone booth. She looked haggard, almost demented with the glasses and dirty hair. Marcy wondered if she'd ever feel the energy she had before—playing soccer with Gavan, landing a king salmon, laughing with friends at a party. She turned away from the reflection. "Get ready for a surprise," she said, before saying farewell and hanging up. She turned to Grogan. "We'll meet out on the water. Two skiffs out fishing. It won't look unusual."

"Where?" Grogan said.

"Counterfeit Cove. It's secluded, not far from town. We'll have plenty of warning if anyone approaches."

"Sounds good. I'll mail the note now."

Marcy gave him Jane's address and watched him drive away. Then she glanced at the pay phone, wishing she could call home. She touched her hair, the short length feeling less strange every day. ANB Harbor was peaceful, dark, as she headed back for the boat. Fog and woodstove smoke drifted, despite a light rain, and pearl gray halos hovered over all the boat lights and streetlights.

A single truck roared up Katlian Street, its headlights momentarily exposing a group of ramshackle buildings across from the harbor, along with a person lingering near the boarded door to an abandoned home. After the truck passed, shadows returned, and the person in black was impossible to see against the wood that was gray with years of weather. Nervous, Marcy kept staring in that direction. People did not hang out on Sitka streets alone on rainy evenings. They sat at home. They sat in bars.

Panicked, Marcy abruptly turned away from the dock where *Sal II* was moored. Bending low, she ran past four boats and hid behind a brown boat that belonged to a friend of Davy's, one with no liveaboards. Cautiously, she climbed aboard and crawled across the deck. Slowly, she lifted her head to peer across the street and hoped that no one had seen. Fishermen kept an eye out for strangers on the docks. She dared not get caught on the wrong boat.

A car passed by slowly. The stranger had left the shelter of the doorway. Marcy waited a few more moments, then stood, ready to return to *Sal II*. Suddenly, from the corner of her eye, she caught another movement. She paused and watched as a black shape slowly moved toward *Sal II*. It was not her imagination; the figure moved far too deliberately for some ordinary drunk. Rather than walk down the center of the dock, he stayed close to the boats and shadows. His whole body was bent into a crouch and he wore a dark hooded sweatshirt.

A car splashed noisily down the street and slowed to turn into ANB parking. Grogan maneuvered the Toyota into its narrow space and finished a cigarette before leaving the car. The figure dressed in black casually reversed direction, jammed his hands in his pockets, and headed for the parking lot, boldly passing the Tercel and disappearing behind a truck, as Grogan opened the door. Marcy studied Grogan's face as he approached *Sal II*. He hadn't noticed the man in the hooded sweatshirt. Once *Sal II's* lights went on, the man emerged from the shadows on Katlian Street.

Grogan came out on deck suddenly, with a cigarette, obviously looking for Marcy. She slowly climbed down from her hiding place and watched the person waiting on the street until Grogan finished his cigarette and returned inside the cabin. Only then, the man in black sauntered away up Katlian Street.

Marcy climbed onboard and looked back. The intruder was gone, and Katlian Street resembled a scene from an old black-and-white photograph. With any luck, Grogan had thwarted the plans of a petty thief in search of easy cash. Troubled, she climbed aboard *Sal II*, and resolved to hide her fears from Grogan. He'd cancel the meeting with Jane and insist that Marcy leave town.

SIXTEEN

Monday, November 2

DAVY HURRIED TO ANSWER the phone, always hopeful to hear Marcy's voice. "Mr. James, this is Henrietta Cordola. The principal."

"Yes." Davy swore to himself.

"I'm afraid that Gavan hasn't been attending history class."

"History?" Davy knew he sounded defensive, as if to ask, "That's all?"

"It's a significant problem. He's actually doing well with other classwork. But history's important, too. It's the last class of the day." Davy tried to explain that he had seen some history homework. "Mr. James, that's not enough," the principal snapped. "We recognize that it's been a difficult year for Gavan. But the boy has all the characteristics of attention deficit disorder. Did your wife make you aware of our contention?"

"More than aware," Davy said, with frustration. "Look, my wife's out of town."

"Mr. James, let me be blunt. Are there problems in your home that could influence Gavan's schoolwork?"

"No, damn it! My wife had to visit her parents." He did not finish the lie. "I thought we had Gavan's attention problems under control."

"No," Cordola answered crisply. "If anything, the problems are more severe. As the classroom challenges increase, he has less control. He's withdrawing. We're worried for him. That he could hurt himself."

"Are you familiar with Gavan's work from previous years? Aren't you new this year?"

"I have his file in front of me."

"He's more than a pile of papers," Davy said. "He's a good kid who had a rough start this year."

Cordola paused, then her tone shifted abruptly to sweet cooperation. "Stress, a change in routine, can aggravate the condition and trigger an outburst of behavior problems. I imagine that's what we're seeing, especially with your wife away."

Davy remained stubborn. "Missing a few history classes hardly sounds like an outburst. My wife considered removing Gavan from school and having him accompany her. But we thought he'd feel more comfortable at home."

"I'm sure you both tried to decide what's best for Gavan," the principal responded smoothly. "But remember, as school officials, we handle dozens of children. Your wife rejected our suggestions. The file includes no mention of your feelings. Believe me, Mr. James, I've seen miracles. Many children take Ritalin. It improves behavior and test scores. Perhaps you'd consider—"

"For one class? No way." Davy kept his voice in control and repeated what he remembered of Marcy's arguments. "Last year, kids were kids. They didn't have to be perfect. This year, the classrooms are out of control. And the school blames the kids. I have a problem with putting kids on a drug."

"Mr. James, this is standard medical practice—"

"I support my wife's decision. Put that in your file. But, how long has he been missing history?"

"A few days. Teachers don't take attendance for each class, only in the morning. It's to Mr. Fenlow's credit that he noticed. We ask that you talk with Gavan about this."

"You can count on that." Davy rubbed his forehead, dreading the day when people could watch his reactions over the telephone.

"Please understand, if Gavan does not attend this class, if he refuses to do the work or be civil with Mr. Fenlow, then he'll fail. The situation is that serious. Gavan will have to repeat that class. We can't make exceptions."

"I'll speak with him," Davy promised. "He'll be grounded until he turns this history problem around."

Davy thought she would hang up. But Cordola controlled the conversation, playing a game where nothing Davy said was right. "Punishing a boy for behavior he can't control isn't a solution. Why don't you contact the social worker at school? She's a wonderful resource."

"Mrs. Cordola, my wife and I don't have problems controlling Gavan," Davy said calmly, refusing to accept the principal's assessment. "The school has a problem. I don't know if it's poor teaching, boring material, or a different standard of discipline. But I'll talk with him."

She kept her voice soft, as though she did not hear his criticisms. "Thank you for your support, Mr. James. Meanwhile, Mr. Fenlow generously offered to allow Gavan to make up the work. But he'll have to stay after school a few afternoons for the next two weeks. Acceptable, Mr. James?" He agreed and they exchanged polite good-byes.

"Gavan," Davy bellowed. "I want you down here now!"

GAVAN HUNG UP THE EXTENSION and swore. He had skipped history to attend the injunction hearing and look up bonds and road construction in the library. He ran downstairs, ready to apologize meekly.

His father's face was flushed. "The principal just called—" Davy began. The phone rang, and Davy scowled. "Hold on. That might be her again."

Gavan waited, wishing he could listen on the extension.

"Hello. Yes, Lieutenant Gallagher... No, she's out of town... I'm sorry. She can't be reached by telephone... Yes, but..." His father listened for a long time. "Of course, she's all right. I know it sounds strange that she can't be reached, Lieutenant. She'll return right after Thanksgiving. But regardless of what Mr. Bander claims, I know she's not with Kovach... Yes, good-bye."

Davy hung up the phone and sat at the kitchen table. "Damn, I shouldn't have let your mother leave." He picked up a placemat, rolling it tightly. "Gavan, where do you go when you're supposed to be in history?"

"The library, Dad," the boy replied. "Fenlow's a jerk, and I thought I'd use my time more wisely."

His dad closed his eyes. "A few missed history classes are the least of our problems. Look, I understand why you can't stand that class. But do me a favor. Go to class. Work with Fenlow. It's what your mother would want."

Gavan nodded.

"Everything will be all right if you turn this around," his father said. "Now let me call Beth." Gavan watched as his father picked up the telephone and wondered how he would find another way to get some extra time. He lingered in the kitchen, pouring a glass of milk and washing an apple, to listen.

"The police just called," Davy said. "They asked why Marcy's using her credit card in South America. How do I explain that? I didn't even get the bill yet... For all we know, it could've been stolen! What a mess. They think I'm evading their questions. Maybe I should call Gallagher. Tell him everything—the note and all... No, you're right, the police probably won't believe me. It sounds too strange. Beth, I'm frantic. How do I know that someone didn't kill her... Yes, I'll let you know if I hear anything from Marcy. And let me know if she gets in touch with you."

Gavan returned to the kitchen and asked his father about his mother and the charges in South America.

"I'd talk to you about this if you'd been going to class and doing your work," his father snapped.

"I just want to know if she's all right," Gavan said, turning away and dropping his head with deep disappointment. "South America is so far away."

"Look, all I know is that her credit card has been used in South America," he said. "I wish we knew more, but it does mean that she's okay. It doesn't matter who she's with or where she went. We know she's okay."

Gavan nodded and refrained from pointing out that the charge cards could have been stolen. His father probably knew that and worried, too. And Gavan didn't dare infuriate his father by asking about Kovach. "Let's not use the phone much at all," Gavan suggested, softly. "And maybe Mom will call soon."

SEVENTEEN

Thursday, November 5

MARCY STAYED ON THE BOAT, studying passersby on the harbor docks. Dozens of people wore dark sweatshirts, and none gave *Sal II* more than a passing glance. She was convinced that the man had been a petty thief and was thankful that she had kept the secret from Grogan. Unfortunately, the scare kept her onboard, and she lost valuable time before the meeting with Jane.

More than a month had passed, and Marcy was nowhere close to returning home. Instead, she voluntarily waited on the decrepit boat and read all day. Newspaper accounts on the cross-island road shed no clues and only infuriated her: The judge ruled against the emergency injunction. Board members and shareholders of Katmai Shee Corporation disagreed whether the injunction should have ever been filed. An anonymous source stated that Katmai Shee finance director Jane McBride had tried to convince the board of directors not to rush into court action. The source added that Katmai Shee board member Francesca Benoit and attorney Beth Roberts vowed to fight the tourism road.

Marcy and Grogan had run out of ideas. Everyday Grogan ate meals at different restaurants, took longer walks, waited in lines, trying to overhear more conversations. "This town's compact, and I hear plenty. But not enough about the road and nothing about you." He arranged smoked salmon on crackers with cream cheese. "Gavan's staying late at school a lot," he added.

"A school project," Marcy said. "Or he's in detention. Do you see him with other kids?" Grogan didn't answer right away. "You can tell me."

"Whenever I see him, he's alone," Grogan admitted. "He leans against the fence in that blacktop play area, and it's like he's separated by some invisible boundary that keeps other children away." He stood and looked out toward dozens of colorful fishing boats, nestled close together. "I remember standing alone like that, putting a lot of effort into trying not to mind. Then one day, I truly did not care."

Marcy wondered if Gavan had reached that point yet. "If you heard something, you wouldn't hold out on me, would you?" she asked. "I mean, I survived hearing Bander that day."

"Unfortunately, we want to hear more of that kind of talk."

"I'm so tired of waiting," she said. "Maybe it was stupid to come back."

"Why don't you take a break for a few days," Grogan offered. "Go to Seattle—"

"No. I won't quit."

"You could hire another detective."

"No way," she said with a grin. "No one else could have made me look like this."

"It's your money," Grogan said. "But I warn you. We might not ever find out."

Marcy sighed but didn't answer. She headed for the kitchen and started gathering ingredients for chocolate-chip cookies.

"I'm going out this afternoon," he said. "You feel like coming along?"

Marcy asked about where, and he listed the post office, the library, the grocery.

"I'll pass," she said slowly. "You can snoop around a lot more without me. Here, and take my books back." She packed three books into a bag, including the one she was reading. "I didn't like that one. Get something different, a biography. A story where I know from the start how it ends."

"Anyone in particular?"

"Surprise me." She scrawled a quick grocery list, only two items. He walked when he did not have much to carry or Marcy along. She did not want him taking the car.

"Sure you don't want to come?" he said.

"I don't feel like smoking today," she said, handing over the list.

He looked about the boat. "I feel like I'm forgetting something."

Marcy returned to mixing her cookie dough. "You have the library books, the card, money. Cigarettes?"

He stood in the doorway. "Nothing, I guess," he said. "See you later."

"Thank you, Mike," she called out. She went to the entrance and watched as Grogan approached the Tercel. He opened the door and reached for his baseball cap, then slammed the door and walked away. "Yes!" She crammed the bowl of partially-made dough into the small refrigerator. Checking that Grogan was out of sight, she snatched the Tercel's keys and hurried to the parking lot. Once inside the car, she removed the annoying glasses and glanced in the mirror, rubbing the red marks on her nose. Every feature looked older, except her eyes, which sparkled with excitement. She jammed a hat over her hair, slouched down in her seat and started the car.

She patted her pack of Marlboros—still plenty left from the Florida cartons. Grogan, on the other hand, smoked Merits constantly, almost three packs a day. He offered to buy her more cigarettes, claiming that her packs had gone stale. Marcy declined. For her, fresh cigarettes tasted no better than stale ones.

She headed for Crescent Harbor. The rain had cleared, and opal clouds lingered over the horizon. Marcy saw Davy's truck and pulled near the water's edge. His boat was in, but the deck was empty. She frowned and searched, at last spotting him on the deck of *FV Breezy Ann,* helping a friend arrange engine pieces on the deck. Her husband would not be home anytime soon.

Marcy blew a kiss in his direction and pulled the car out of the parking lot, checking behind her. No one followed.

She caught herself speeding on Lincoln Street and eased down to thirty. She carried no driver's license and could not risk getting stopped by police. Denson listed every infraction in the newspaper, including speeding tickets. The police would probably arrest a woman looking like Cindy Tumper who carried no identification. Grogan would never forgive her.

At the turnoff for Shore Road was a small convenience store. Marcy pulled into the parking lot and checked the clock—just after noon. Most neighbors would be at work, their children in school. Marcy jogged into the store, grabbed a root beer and at the last minute another pack of Marlboros. The young woman at the cash register tugged at overgrown bangs. Marcy asked if she could leave the car in the lot for about an hour, while she ran a small errand. The girl shrugged agreement and turned her attention back to the latest issue of *Vogue.*

Marcy lit a cigarette and walked toward a trail that wound up behind the properties along Shore Road. As vehicles passed, she made a point of blowing smoke and concentrated on the mild pigeon-toed shuffle that Grogan had made her practice. In less than ten minutes, she saw her home through the trees. Seeing no neighbors, she bent her head and headed briskly for the side door. Her heard pounded, as if she were trespassing on top-secret military property.

She tried the knob. Before Tim, before the letters, the family had never locked the door. But the door was locked, and she needed the key. She checked under a flowerpot, and the key hidden long ago was still there. Marcy slipped inside, leaned against the wall and listened.

The house felt silent, strange. The woodstove was cold, and the familiar fragrance from baking cookies or cakes was long gone. Other than the sink containing a few breakfast dishes, the kitchen seemed surprisingly clean. Did Gavan and Davy eat out a lot? Use paper plates? She tentatively opened a drawer where Davy tossed mail. Most had been opened. Bills had been paid. No gray notes. Not that Davy would have left them in a drawer accessible to Gavan.

The family room was a mess, scattered with graphs, pamphlets, and papers. Marcy examined the neon orange poster in the center: "Hypothesis: Do compost worms move faster than worms in ordinary dirt?" She opened a notebook with Gavan's crooked handwriting, a daily log of temperatures and distances covered by worms during daily two-minute races. She grimaced. A dirty box, containing a ruler and stopwatch, on her coffee table was undoubtedly the race track for the worms.

In the living room, Marcy paused at an embroidered pillow that she had made while pregnant with Gavan. Tiny stitches traced a lighthouse amid a raging sea, and three gulls. She gently touched the stitches to the fisherman's prayer: "Bless us, O Lord, our boats are so small, and the sea is so big." Checking her watch, she chided herself for wasting time. She had less than two hours. If only she knew where to start looking for answers…

Her most important papers were in her bedroom. She tiptoed upstairs, passed the antique mirror in the hall and avoided her image. Feeling sneaky, out of place, she opened her bedroom door with one finger.

Davy had removed the rug stained with Cassie's blood. The hardwood floor was bare. The bed was unmade. She examined Davy's dresser and its odd assortment of receipts, hooks, little tools and keys. She hoped to find some indication that he had tried to reach her and tell her to come home. But there were no unusual messages, nothing to suggest that he had discovered the reason behind the threat. Marcy stood before the closet, deciding to go through her pockets and bags.

Marcy was tempted to straighten her belongings as she searched, maybe carry some papers back to the boat. But Davy might notice, and he didn't need extra worries. She opened her navy bag and paused when she saw the zipper to the inner pocket half open with her gold hoops inside. Someone else had searched the purse. She often removed earrings and dropped them into purse pockets. After losing a favorite pearl, she had made a point to close the zippers tight.

She checked her other purse. The zipper was open. Thoughtfully, she pulled the zippers closed. Nothing was missing. Davy must have been searching, or even Gavan.

She reached back into one of her old shoes, and found the keys to her file cabinets. Out of habit, she kept them locked, to prevent anyone, particularly Gavan, learning about the lottery money. The boy had shown little interest in the files, only once mentioning that his mother kept far too many papers. He was right, she thought, slowly unlocking the cabinets.

The papers appeared untouched. More boxes waited upstairs, filled with annual reports, statements, letters, and some unopened envelopes. Marcy didn't know where to start. Beth knew more about the contents than anyone in the family, with most statements sent directly to the attorney, who then prepared a summary. Beth had an uncanny sense of the markets, and over the years had tripled Marcy's millions with shrewd investments.

But no one knew that. Marcy turned back to the closet, where she idly reached into pockets and found a ten-dollar bill. She stuffed it into the pocket of her jeans and decided to check Gavan's room and figure out why he was staying after school.

The boy's bed was unmade. No toys were strewn about. A stack of magazines and books waited next to the twin bed. Curious, Marcy checked the assortment: three science fiction, two books on civil engineering, three on public bond financing. Bookmarks peeked from the pages of every book. She opened one. Gavan was thinking about the road project.

She closed the book and went to the windowsill. The binoculars and flashlight that Gavan had used for communication with Tim had vanished. She suddenly wanted to leave Gavan a note. He might not tell anyone and might even think that she had written it before she left.

She opened his top drawer, where he often hid money, notes and other secrets among his underwear and socks. She guiltily patted the piles of money, cards, folded pieces of paper, nothing unusual—when she suddenly heard voices. She froze, glanced out the window. A van was outside, and the voices came from her kitchen. Marcy tiptoed to the doorway and listened.

"…home any minute."

"I don't give a damn," came a deeper voice. "You can take care of a kid."

"No one's supposed to know that we're here. Or we won't get paid."

"Stop griping…"

"We should've gotten here earlier," grumbled the other voice.

Marcy did not recognize the two men and started to cross the hallway, anxious to call the police from her bedroom telephone. But she paused as the men entered the hallway below. She couldn't dial and explain in time, not without being overheard. The men could grab her. Or worse, they'd take off before she heard their names. Either way, she'd blow her cover.

The two men talked about getting paid, and Marcy wanted to know who was paying. She slowly backed into Gavan's room, almost bumping into the open drawer. Searching for a hiding place, she stretched out on the floor and squirmed to maneuver her way under Gavan's bed, as close to the wall as possible. Marcy remembered crawling easily under her bed as a small girl, more than thirty years ago, dustballs tickling her nose. With her new extra pounds, she barely fit.

The position put her face to face with a smiling orange elephant, which Gavan had won long ago at small carnival traveling through town. Treasuring his prize, the boy had slept with the odd creature for months.

Heavy footsteps approached on the stairs, and she held her breath. Had they heard her squirming? She imagined the men storming in the room, yanking her from the hiding place. She cursed Gavan for not leaving some dirty laundry as a shield, and gently moved a sneaker and a book in front of her face. She hugged the elephant close to her neck.

A few feet away, one of the men laughed. "Don't have to worry about making the bed again. These people are slobs!"

"My wife wouldn't believe it."

"You searched her room last time," a hard voice called out. "Guess I should try. Did you check the pages of the books, shake out all the clothes?"

"You were here!" said the other in disgust. "Guess we have to start all over."

"As long as I get paid for the time!"

"Hey look! The file cabinets are unlocked." Marcy froze. "Our lucky day!"

"Plenty there. Wish the boss was more specific."

"It's not hard. Bills, checks, anything that ties her to Kovach." Marcy caught her breath and listened closely. "You know, when this woman left town, she probably took all that stuff with her."

"Shut up! That kind of thinking stops our cash flow. Do you feel like going back to standing at the seafood plant waiting for dead fish to slide down a ramp?"

"Or she tossed it into the garbage weeks ago. He'll send us to the town dump next!"

"Stop your griping! The guy who hires us thinks there's something here."

"That guy who hired us is weird."

"But he pays. I'll do anything to keep this job going." The two men went through the file cabinets in silence.

Marcy wondered what they thought she had from Kovach. She shook her head, unable to concentrate, except to keep wishing that she had a weapon. The nearest gun was in Gavan's room, a gift from Davy, one of the few possessions from Davy's father. The old rifle was strictly for bear-scare and target practice, and any ammunition was locked in the gun cabinet downstairs. Tempted to adjust her position, she squeezed the miniature elephant instead, while the men quietly searched through her files.

"Anything?" the whiner finally said.

"Not really. This is tough. He thought it would be in here."

"He could be watching us," the partner whispered. "Don't you feel it?"

"You're giving me the creeps, damn it! Shut up, and go poke around the attic."

"All those boxes!" he protested.

"Only the boxes with broken or new tape. Check the tops and reach down the sides. I want to stay on this guy's payroll. We have to find something."

Whiny paused at the doorway. "If he asked you to break the law, how far would you go?"

"What do you think this is, moron?"

"Hey, I know where to draw the line..." He climbed into the attic. The two worked in silence, and Marcy swallowed, trying not to gulp. Staying still was easier when the two argued. Time slipped by, and she worried about Gavan returning home from school, or worse, Grogan stepping aboard an empty *Sal II*. Maybe the boy had to stay late at school, or soon, he'd be walking in on the prowlers. She couldn't see her watch, but expected the school bus to roar uphill any moment, discharging a load of children. She would have to scramble from the hiding place, open the window and scream for Gavan to run.

The whining voice called from upstairs. "This is hopeless, Ray," he said. "Nothing up here." A name! The other guy didn't answer. Come on, Marcy thought, keep on talking. More names. Whiny climbed downstairs. "You hear me?"

"Yeah, I heard," Ray said, quietly. "Damn, these people have a lot of money. I found this at the bottom of the one cabinet She had crap jewelry, and then I find this!" The silence was followed by a long, low whistle. Marcy scowled. She suspected they found one of her many attempts at organization, a list she had printed off Beth's computer of all her accounts and totals.

"Who'd have thought they had this kind of dough," Whiny murmured. "Least of all a fisherman! I wonder if the boss knows."

"At least we found something. These people are no good. You don't hide money for no reason. She's involved with that engineer, and we know he's slime! We better get out of here."

"We didn't check the kid's room."

"Be my guest. Play with his toys. But I'm out of here." They noisily closed drawers and straightened papers. Finally, two pairs of heavy boots clumped downstairs. Marcy heard the door downstairs, the same one she had entered, shut softly. Gravel crunched outside the window. An engine started. Squirming out from under the bed, she banged her head and reached the window in time to see the white van pull out of sight.

"I can't believe this," Marcy said to the orange elephant. She shoved the toy into her pocket, feeling the need for a good luck charm. Gavan wouldn't miss an old stuffed animal.

She ran into her room, locked the files and tossed the keys back into her shoe. She had no reason to search because she had nothing from Kovach. If she only had a way to let Ray and Whiny know that someone had made a mistake. But they didn't want their money to stop. She had to figure out who was paying them.

The two men had not disturbed the house, and Davy would probably never guess that the house had been entered not by one, but two sets of prowlers. Somehow, she wanted to warn her family. A note? She heard the school bus in the distance. Her time was up. Keeping the house key, she left the door wide open, before running wildly out the back door, down the trail to the highway.

MARCY HAD NOT COUNTED ON Grogan deliberately leaving the bank card behind.

"Where the hell did you go?" Grogan roared. Marcy pleaded for understanding, explaining how she had carefully spied on her own home. "Please don't shout. People hear everything on these docks."

"Who cares? Certainly not you!" Angry, he paced, then pressed a button to the CD player. Slide guitar from the Allman brothers bounced against the walls. "There, I can yell all I want."

"Nobody saw me," Marcy insisted, putting her hands over her ears. "I was careful. I was the only one who could do it, and at least we have some direction."

"You don't trust me." He was red with fury.

"Are you angry because I took a chance or because it paid off?" she questioned, turning the stereo down. Immediately regretting the outburst, she reached for his shoulder.

He flinched. "Don't," he protested, not looking at her.

Marcy sat on the sofa, embarrassed and wondering if he mistook the gesture for pity. "We have to talk," she said softly. "Don't be angry."

"I'm worried," he replied, more calmly. "I remember how terrified you looked in Florida. We won't know whether anyone saw you until it's too late." He sat on the sofa. "This investigation isn't working out. I should quit."

"No, please. I can't afford to lose the best half of my disguise."

"That's all I am. A prop."

"No!" She sat next to him. "I couldn't have returned without you. I followed your advice on walking and talking. You've done a lot, but I'm convinced that something awful will happen if we don't figure this out soon."

Grogan straightened the pile of library books. He opened the refrigerator, pausing and shutting the door without removing anything. When he resumed talking, he was thoughtful. "All right. It's about Kovach. Did the two guys sound like they were friends with the guy?"

"Not at all. They found out about my money and assume that I'm involved in some scheme with him."

Grogan asked her to describe her time with Kovach once again. "I met him once, the night before Gavan went out with him. Then he left town suddenly, and the police suspect him in Tim's death. He was finishing his study on the road and—" Awareness hit her like an avalanche. She put her hand to her mouth, horrified. "Oh no."

"What is it?"

She swallowed and stood. "Maybe Gavan has what they want. Maybe he kept something after he stole the pack."

"Could these men work for Bander?"

"They didn't seem to know who was in control," Marcy noted.

"What would Gavan have kept?"

"I don't know. Kovach was so angry at first. But he calmed down after I returned the pack. I assumed that everything was intact."

"But he met your son the next day. His idea?" She nodded. "Did he ask Gavan a lot of questions?"

"Gavan didn't say."

Grogan frowned. "Who saw you with Kovach?"

"The waitress. A few people in the bar. No one I recognized."

"So Gavan spent more time with Kovach than you, and he knew what was in that pack. The newspaper mentioned that Katmai Shee and others want Kovach's paperwork on the road. Does anyone else know about Gavan and the pack?"

"Only the police, Davy and me. And now you."

"Gavan was one of the last people to see both Tim and Kovach. That's too big of a coincidence. Someone might have chased you out of town to get Gavan alone."

"No," Marcy felt her chest tighten.

"Cin—oh hell, Marcy," he lowered his voice. "I didn't mention it before, but I've watched your house. Davy and Gavan stay home alone a lot. No one else is watching them. His cousin stops by. And your friend, Beth Roberts. But I don't think anyone else cares." Marcy thanked him for keeping an eye on her family. "I can keep watching the house, but not the school," he warned. "People are paranoid about a child killer. Teachers are guarding that school better than a prison."

"If anything happened to him…" She couldn't finish.

"Nothing will. But from now on, we work together."

EIGHTEEN

Saturday, November 7

AN OLD RED BOAT TROLLED gently through the mist near one of the larger islands in Sitka Sound. Its single fishing line was slack. The only visible person on board was a massive figure who sat hunched on a stool, his hands wrapped around a Thermos. Marcy James waited in the shadows. A small Whaler passed, then returned and slowed for Counterfeit Cove. No other boats were in sight.

Minutes later, the boats waited side by side in a little cove, both engines silent. Marcy stayed below deck while Grogan welcomed Jane McBride aboard and led her into a rough homemade cabin of plywood. As Jane crouched to step into the dark space with benches and a tiny woodstove, Marcy remained hunched over in the corner with a lit cigarette, and could imagine Jane's thoughts, probably afraid and berating herself for not telling someone her destination. "Where's Marcy?" Jane asked, nervously.

Beaming, Marcy stood and extinguished the cigarette. "Call me Cindy," she said, removing the hated glasses. "Don't I look awful?"

"The weight and glasses. Your hair! You look completely different." Jane sank slowly into the other chair. "Cindy."

"I feel different. But I had to come back."

"Even Davy wouldn't recognize you!"

Marcy introduced Mike, and gave him all the credit for her transformation.

"Mike, you're a genius," Jane said.

Grogan turned water on to boil on a small cookstove, before heading to the tackle box for more bait. "You two shake out the gossip. Can you believe I've been here for a month and this is my first fishing trip?"

He headed back to his line, and Marcy leaned forward to hug Jane. "It's good to see you. Sitka isn't the same when you can't be with family and friends."

"Mike seems nice."

"He is, in a bossy big brother kind of a way. I'm not sure it's worth all this to come back." Marcy gestured at the shabby surroundings and her shabbier appearance. "But I couldn't wait and do nothing." Marcy placed tea bags in faded plastic mugs. "Have you seen Gavan and Davy?"

"They're fine, except for missing you. Francesca and I took a pizza over there one night. And Beth visits a lot."

"That's good. I tried to call her, but she didn't answer. So I called you. Grogan insisted that I tell only one person—and it couldn't be Francesca or Davy in case they're being watched. I was afraid if I waited that Grogan would change his mind." Marcy shrugged. "I hope you don't mind my unloading all of this on you. How's Gavan doing?"

Jane nodded. "He's grown at least an inch. He's quiet, and I'm sure he still hurts deeply inside. Nobody mentions Tim around him."

"Is he still working on his science project, the worms?" Marcy asked.

"He took over your family room!" Jane said, laughing. "Did he start before you left?"

Marcy hesitated. "No. I went home once. Grogan was furious. He's trying to protect me, but I have to find out more."

She looked away. "I walked around my own house and felt like my family doesn't need me anymore."

"Don't be annoyed that your family is so self-reliant," Jane said gently.

The tea kettle shrieked, and Marcy poured the water. "I'm uncertain about what to do next."

"What have you and Mike found out so far?" Jane asked.

"Not much, except that two men searched my house."

"Davy never said anything."

"They were careful about not getting caught," Marcy said. "I only know because I was there hiding under Gavan's bed." She held the warm tea cup to her cheek. "They're looking for something that belongs to Kovach."

Jane shook her head. "Who isn't? Everyone wants to see his report. He left town at an inopportune time."

"Maybe someone forced him to leave town, too," Marcy said.

"But why would you have Kovach's work?" Jane asked.

Marcy explained how Gavan went into the forest with Kovach.

"Gavan's trying to solve this, too," Jane said. "He stopped me a few Saturdays ago, and we talked about the road. He didn't mention Kovach at all."

"Kovach wasn't very nice to him, but Gavan doesn't think he's behind the threats or Tim's death. Only Davy and the investigators know about Gavan and Kovach. The wrong person can't find out."

"Could it be Jeremy Bander? He's pressuring the state to hire another consultant to replace Kovach."

"I wish, but I don't think so."

"A reporter from the *Wall Street Journal* is also in town asking questions."

"About the road? I'm surprised he'd bother with Sitka."

"Nice vacation," Jane noted. "Mountains, ocean, fishing,

the raptor center. Only a fraction of the country knows about this place, and it's more Alaskan than most of Alaska."

"It won't be if that road goes through," Marcy said.

The boat rocked as Mike entered the makeshift cabin. "Not a bite," he complained. "How does your husband make a living at this?"

"Tie something noisy on the line and join us," Marcy offered. "We'll hear if you get any action." When he returned, Marcy handed him a cup of steaming tea.

Jane sipped. "I'm surprised you two called me after that leak in the paper when I tried to discourage the injunction. Denson won't tell me who told him."

"The injunction didn't work anyway," Marcy said. "It didn't even delay the road all that much."

"Exactly. Even more amazing is Bander's next idea. He's offered to add a road that would circle Sitka and connect Katmai Shee land to his cross-island road."

"He wants to pave the island!" Marcy cried out.

"Politicians act like money from bonds is free money. And Bander has firm support from anyone who loves tourism. Environmentalists who normally oppose development don't mind tourism, which seems cleaner than manufacturing or logging. Increasing the number of tourists ultimately creates a larger constituency for protecting an unusual place. No question, this project looks viable on paper to an investor sitting behind a desk in New York."

"So we lost," Marcy said forlornly.

"Not necessarily," Jane said. "Something strange is going on. Bander's too open. He admits all the negatives, first brought up by you, now Beth. SWAT emphasizes the economic problems in town, like the short tourism season in Alaska. It's as if he doesn't want a decent bond rating!"

"Rating?"

"Lenders determine how much risk a public project poses

for investors. Projects endorsed by the Alaska Development Authority typically receive a decent rating. A higher rating, like an A, means less risk, less interest earned by investors. By releasing so much information, SWAT actually invites a low rating, which means a higher interest rate. The road will cost a lot more."

"Maybe no one will buy the stupid bonds."

"People will buy them. But a higher interest rate makes default more likely. And over time most major bond defaults have been highway projects. Developers overestimate traffic or underestimate competition. And that's what Katmai's road is—a competitor." Jane shook her head. "Meanwhile, Bander wants to list the bonds on the stock market."

"Isn't that unusual?"

"Unprecedented for a town the size of Sitka. Listing them for public trading means full disclosure before the Securities and Exchange Commission. Municipal bonds and other government bonds, like those for sewers and roads, typically don't get much scrutiny."

"Exactly how much will this road cost?"

"Bander counts on forty million in bonds, thirty million in federal highway funds and thirty million in subsidies from the U.S. Forest Service, which would sell timber rights to logging companies. They plan on cutting down plenty of trees along the road to create views."

"So much money wasted…"

"Typical road construction in Southeast Alaska costs about two million per mile. Estimates for Bander's cross-island road come in at a higher amount because of the terrain and the need for some tunnels and grading that will cost thousands of dollars per foot."

"How will they repay the debt?" Grogan asked.

"Tolls," Jane said. "At both ends of the road—fifty dollars

per axle. Conservative estimates anticipate about two-point-five million per year."

"One hundred dollars for a car to drive a road!" Marcy exclaimed.

"It's buried in his paperwork. And it's not that ludicrous when you consider that a cross-island road eliminates two days of ferry travel for northbound passengers. The number of ferry passengers disembarking in Sitka plummets. The ferry will eventually decrease service to Sitka, then eliminate stops altogether. Bander's road could eventually be the only way for cars, trucks, groceries, to come to Sitka.

"Meanwhile, the value of Katmai Shee property goes up overnight. So do our taxes. We barely know the potential of the land, and we're being rushed into a lot of decisions."

"I still don't see why tourists need a road," Marcy said, disgusted.

"Marcy, your group helped sell that road," Jane countered. "You made the middle of the island sound like a wilderness paradise."

"If I'm so helpful and Jeremy's so willing to release information, why did I have to leave town?"

"I have no idea." Jane finished her tea. "All I know is that this road's creepy. In more ways than one."

"You have to talk to Francesca." Marcy poured more tea all around. "It's time to convince Davy and Gavan to leave town."

NINETEEN

Tuesday, November 10

GAVAN FINGERED THE SMALL rock inside the pocket of his jeans and lingered outside Ken Jabard's classroom. He wished he could be in Mr. Jabard's class every year. A science resource teacher for the younger grades, the man was creative, the kind of teacher who remembered a kid's name years later.

Gavan peeked into the class. School had been dismissed, and most of the building was empty. Mr. Jabard sat at his desk, writing notes. Gavan glanced at the student projects lined along the wall—models of dinosaurs, volcanoes, the continental shelf in Legos, clay and papier-mâché. Each year, the teacher coordinated a geology science fair, asking students to focus on specific questions and learn as much as they could. Gavan remembered announcing that he had decided to study dirt. Other students tittered, anticipating another joke, but Mr. Jabard had responded eagerly. "Scientists take nothing for granted," he explained. "No subject is too mundane for the true scientist."

So, Gavan had set out to study how modern soil differed from the days of the dinosaurs. Mr. Jabard had explained how no flowering plants lived during the early periods when dinosaurs walked the earth. Gavan had set up two compost piles in his backyard. In one, he had arranged plant material from flowering plants and in the other, he arranged material from conifers. Mr. Jabard had arranged to have books on compost piles and agronomy sent from the University of Alaska library in Fairbanks. The teacher explained that he didn't expect Gavan to understand every sentence in the texts. Still, Gavan was impressed by how much there was to learn on any one topic.

Gavan hesitated, then knocked lightly on the door. "Come in," Mr. Jabard called out. "Hey, Gavan, how's it going? You stop by to see this year's science projects?"

"They look great," Gavan said, pointing to two bottles of murky water. "That looks cool."

Mr. Jabard nodded. "That student compared the effects of salt water and lake water on plants that grow around here. Comparing two samples is always more fascinating than a simple description of a single phenomenon. Like your project. That will always be one of my favorites."

"Thanks," Gavan mumbled, worried about how to bring up the topic of the rock with the teacher. "I'm doing another one this year. But I wanted to show you something. If you have time…"

"Certainly," Mr. Jabard said. Gavan nervously pulled the rock he had kept from Kovach's pack and handed it over. The man held it up to the light, then pulled out a magnifying lens, sliding his chair near the window. "This looks like gold." He pointed to a small strip along one side of the rock. "See the vein?"

"Really?" Gavan leaned over the magnifying glass.

"Did someone give it to you?"

"I found it," Gavan said, hoping to be vague.

"Where?"

"Laying around." Gavan hated the sound of his own obvious lies and tried to talk faster about picking up rocks every time he went for a walk, in town or in the forest. Mr. Jabard looked at the rock again and then stared at Gavan, waiting for more specifics. "Really, I'm not exactly sure where," Gavan said lamely.

"This is unusual," the teacher said. "You don't usually find gold laying around. Even in Alaska."

"Hmm," Gavan said, embarrassed. He wanted to back out of the door, avoid mentioning Kovach or Tim or the forest. But Mr. Jabard held on to the rock and stared. So, Gavan tried to think of questions that had nothing to do with where he had found the piece of gold. "Mr. Jabard, why was so much gold found in Juneau and none in Sitka?"

The teacher leaned back in his chair. "Miners searched for gold on Baranof Island. A couple of lines were found back along ledges in Silver Bay. Not much. A small railroad was built to transport the gold to Rodman Bay. The problem is the gold around here's embedded in rock. Thin veins, like this. Extraction and the railroad cost more than any gold actually found. That operation was abandoned after 1880, when everyone joined the gold rush in Juneau."

Jabard tapped the rock. "But there were some rumors about another group of men who found more gold on Baranof. They kept quiet about how much. After the big find in Juneau, that group claimed their gold came from the mainland and not from Baranof Island. But fishermen reported seeing flickering lights at night along Silver Bay. Maybe the men had a secret mine, but the rumors were never verified. Regardless, no gold's been found on this island since."

"Why does Juneau have so much?" Gavan asked.

"Natural occurrences jar it loose, creating nuggets. Those sources don't require expensive equipment. Anybody with a pan can pick up nuggets."

As the teacher continued to check the gold, Gavan hoped for more information rather than questions. "Do you think it's worth much?" Gavan asked, pretending excitement.

"Not a lot, not this piece alone. But I could find out the exact value for you."

Gavan shook his head. "Maybe some other time. I probably should talk to my parents first." Gavan held his hand out, and Jabard slowly placed the rock in the palm. Gavan shoved the gold into his pocket.

"Have you shown the rock to anyone else?" the teacher asked.

"No, I just found it the other day," Gavan lied.

"Then wait before showing your parents," Mr. Jabard said. "Your mom's not home anyway, right?"

Gavan nodded, embarrassed. Mr. Jabard continued. "Don't show anyone else for that matter. Please, do me a favor and give me a chance to check some books at home. It's terrible when a teacher doesn't do his homework, and I wouldn't want to look foolish."

"Sure," Gavan agreed. "Me neither." He was relieved that Jabard was just as intent about keeping the find a secret. Jabard offered to look at any other interesting rocks, and Gavan thanked the teacher and left. Walking slowly down the hallway, Gavan thought about Kovach, certain that the engineer had added the rock to the stream. But who in his right mind would throw away gold like that? Unless the engineer did not realize the rock contained gold. Gavan wanted to think about the whole scenario some more before he spoke to any other adult, including Mr. Jabard. There was no point in rushing off and telling anyone about the rock, and even Mr. Jabard was willing to wait.

Still, the teacher had sounded confident with his initial identification of the rock as gold, and the man knew plenty about geology. It was something Gavan had always wondered about, why the man didn't explore the island more in search of caves, glacial and volcanic rocks, the steep cliffs and other geological oddities of Southeast Alaska.

His mother once explained that Mr. Jabard had been near completing graduate research when he set out leading a group of young teenagers on a hike. One boy had wandered from the trail and got lost. Jabard and the others had searched, but the boy was found four days later, dead from hypothermia.

Jabard then dropped his plans to pursue a doctorate degree in geology. Even in the classroom, Gavan noticed how often the teacher's eyes strayed toward the window and the mountains beyond.

Gavan turned the corner and ran into his own teacher, Mr. Fenlow. "Staying after school for someone else, James?" Fenlow said.

"I'm doing some research on my own," Gavan replied.

"Spend less time on that, and more time on polishing your sloppy work habits," Fenlow scoffed. "Except it's too late in your case. Doing extra credit and sounding brilliant once a month isn't enough. Your mother did you a disservice by refusing to put you on Ritalin. Where is she anyway? I tried to call her about the cross-island road. A few problems develop, and she loses interest quick enough!"

Gavan bit his lip. He attended classes and managed to keep his father unaware of minor problems by switching the family's answering machine to announcement only. He didn't need an argument with Fenlow. "She has business out of town."

"Business! She couldn't stand you anymore!" Fenlow hissed. "They split over you, and you're running wild."

Gavan wanted to hit the teacher, shove him and escape from the school forever. But a sound, the sharp click of heels, approached from around the corner. Gavan rushed for the door, wanting to run away from thoughts of school, his parents and Tim. But Gavan could no longer bear the thought of walking through the forest without Tim at his side. Suddenly, Gavan could empathize with Mr. Jabard.

Gavan turned and watched as Fenlow listened politely to Miss Coyle, Gavan's one-time English teacher. Balancing a pile of books in one arm, she caught Gavan's eye and waved. Gavan smiled and waved back. Fenlow couldn't change the past. He couldn't control how others thought of Gavan. Fenlow was the mistake, and not teachers like Miss Coyle and Mr. Jabard.

TWENTY

Friday, November 13

DAVY WENT TO HIS SON'S room and looked around. Nothing was out of place. For a week, Gavan had kept insisting to his father that someone had entered his room and tampered with his belongings. "How can you be sure?" Davy had asked. "Your room's a mess."

"My books were moved. A bookmark fell out. My elephant's gone. And worst of all, someone was in my underwear drawer!"

"What kind of burglar heads for a kid's underwear drawer and leaves the television?" Davy had teased.

"I keep important stuff in that drawer," Gavan had said. "I'm telling you, someone was in this house."

Davy tried to subdue Gavan's fears, but was not surprised that the boy's imagination operated on full throttle. Francesca and even Jane McBride urged Davy to consider leaving town. Davy couldn't explain the missing key, and called a locksmith to change the locks. Gavan insisted on leaving lights on throughout the house. Following Gavan's advice, Davy memorized the placement of items on his dresser. After a week, nothing was touched. Still, Davy did not want the boy coming home to an empty house, and Gavan didn't complain when his father asked Cathy Wilson next door to keep an eye on Gavan more often. Davy also skipped the special salmon opening.

Like most afternoons that week, Davy waited for Gavan to come home from school by doing chores around the yard, chopping wood and raking. Only the day before a storm had swept through the island, and Davy walked idly about, collecting scattered branches and breaking them into neat pieces for the woodstove. He bent to retrieve one thick branch at the far end of the yard and uncovered a pile of cigarette butts. He crouched down to examine old Merits and Marlboros.

The road was about thirty feet away, so the pile had not been dumped by some driver cleaning out his ashtray. Gavan? The kid detested smoking and complained whenever he caught a whiff of tobacco from his parents' friends. Davy also noticed tiny broken branches strewn about, not snapped by the wind. Turning, Davy stood before a perfect view of his home. Someone had trimmed the brush to create an unobstructed view of his home.

Someone, maybe more than one person, had waited in this spot and stared into the windows of his home. Davy covered the cigarettes with the branch and waited for Gavan on the porch. Staring at the swirl of late afternoon color on Sitka Sound, Davy thought about Marcy so far away.

AFTER WALKING ALONG Halibut Point, Gavan and Davy stopped by the store to pick up enough groceries to get through dinner the next day. Davy's cooking skills had improved, and he managed to deliver three parts of any meal to the table at roughly the same time each night. His Friday night special consisted of grilled halibut with lemon and a box of Rice-a-Roni. He forgot salad and felt guilty about not heating up a can of green beans or peas. But Gavan knew his father detested vegetables, and only Marcy could convince Gavan to eat anything green. As Davy arranged grapes and a sliced pear on the two plates, he realized that they had adjusted to life without Marcy, a thought that made him feel empty inside.

After dinner, Gavan settled in front of the television, and Davy went through the house, switching on lights in the kitchen, living room and one bedroom. He stood in his own dark bedroom, gazing out at black patches of straggly trees and thinking about the pile of cigarettes. He waited by the window for at least a quarter of an hour. Nothing moved outside except the cold rain, falling like slivers of glass. The rain might keep the watchman away. Downstairs, Gavan bellowed about a good movie.

"Right there, Gavan!" Davy called out. Another minute and he'd give up and go sit with Gavan. He thought of Marcy and prayed that she was not in trouble. He couldn't imagine never talking to his wife again. He could almost feel her move next to him, curl her arms around his chest and lean her head against him. He longed to bury his face in the golden strands of her hair, touch his lips against the back of her neck. He could almost feel her breath against his ear and hear her whisper. But if he opened his eyes, turning to see her smile, the sweet memory would vanish.

Open his eyes! He shook his head and focused on the patch. A pinprick of orange flashed in the darkness and disappeared. A lit cigarette or a product of his weariness? Davy shoved his feet into an old pair of sneakers and took the stairs two at a time.

"Dad, this movie's about scientists who make a mistake with this eyeball and—"

"Gavan, I'll watch. I promise. Tape it, okay? I'll watch the beginning with you. But I have to run out right now."

"Where you going? Can you get popcorn?"

Davy kept silent. If he mentioned the intruder, the boy would refuse to stay inside. Davy had to fake an errand. "I forgot something on the boat. Sure, I'll get popcorn."

Davy called Cathy Wilson. In her fifties, she lived alone and never minded staying with Gavan. Marcy had always

provided Cathy's favorite brands of ice cream or crackers and
cheese. Invited to parties and holiday dinners at the James'
house, the woman was more like a member of the family than
a babysitter. She agreed to come right over. "And Cathy,
would you mind coming to the garage door? I'll leave it open."
That door couldn't be seen from the spot where Davy had
found the cigarettes.

Assuring Gavan that he would be right back, Davy glanced
toward the windows and the darkness beyond, resisting the
temptation to yank the cords to the wooden blinds or curtains.
Davy met Cathy at the garage door. "Thanks for coming on
such short notice," he rushed. "I'll be back, oh, in less than
thirty minutes."

"You have a number where you'll be at, Davy?"

"Ah, no. Just heading down the road to the store. Gavan's
watching a movie. About an eyeball." He inched his way out.

"How's Marcy's family?" Cathy asked. "When's she getting back?"

"Soon." He felt uncomfortable, knowing Cathy sensed the lie.

"Tell her how much I miss her. She's a good friend. My
best friend."

His face turned red, and he pushed his way out the door.
Better to leave abruptly before he said something stupid.
Marcy's long absence was getting suspicious. The person
who expected Marcy to leave town couldn't possibly have a
child and understand the constant demands from schools,
babysitters and friends. Not long ago, Gavan had come home,
complaining how his father had forgotten to send in two dozen
cupcakes promised by Marcy for a library bake sale. How
could Davy admit that he had no idea where his wife was?
Who would believe they were not having problems and separated? What if she didn't return? If she were dead, he'd be
the first suspect. Maybe someone planned to set Davy up for
her murder all along. He cursed and pulled up the collar of

his jacket. His imagination was more out of control than Gavan's. He had to focus on catching the prowler before he ran out of cigarettes or got bored.

Davy's eyes adjusted to the dark as he slipped behind his truck and crossed lawns. He thought about finding the smokers' vehicle, disabling it and forcing a confrontation. But no strange vehicle was in sight. Davy jogged lightly through a neighbor's back yard and connected with the skinny dirt path that ran behind his home. Waves churned and beat the shore.

The watchman would have his back to Davy and the beach. Ignoring the rain, Davy slowly crawled toward the clump of trees. His hand covered a smooth rock. Its hardness and the smell of salt comforted him.

He reached the stand of trees, where soft, brown needles packed the ground. He paused to control his breathing. Cautiously reaching out for the ragged bark of tress, he moved toward the patch of woods. As he slowly approached, in a low crouch, he detected the bitter aroma of cigarette smoke. Davy checked the gold light pouring from his home and was relieved to see Gavan slouched on the sofa out of sight. Suddenly the bedroom and bathroom lights flashed off, then the light in the family room, leaving only the eerie, bouncing light from the television. Cathy paused and stared out the window, before heading for the refrigerator. "Shit!" came a low voice less than ten feet away.

Davy froze. He dared not frighten the intruder until he saw a face. A foot scraped back and forth against the ground, extinguishing another cigarette. Davy regretted not bringing a knife or even a gun, but prepared to tackle the man and demand knowing why his wife had left town. Suddenly, a large figure shoved away brush, moving fast, passing less than six feet away and vanishing in seconds.

Davy paused in confusion, losing sight of his quarry and his only chance to find Marcy. His throat felt tight, until he spotted a man pausing near Davy's truck and ducking between houses.

About forty feet behind, Davy followed cautiously. He could learn a lot from a man who didn't realize that he was being followed. Davy crept slowly along the brush lining the road, not wanting to alert the prowler or run into an ambush.

Suddenly, a car roared to life from below. Davy scrambled downhill in time to see taillights pull out of the driveway next to the Ricci home. Posted with a for-sale sign, the overpriced two-bedroom house had been empty for months. The intruder had gotten away.

Davy thought about running to his pickup and continuing the chase, but he had not seen the color or make of the car. The rain released with a sudden burst as Davy trudged up Shore Road to his home. His chance to get some answers had vanished.

"You weren't gone long," Cathy said pleasantly. She sat on the sofa with Gavan's feet in her lap.

Davy ducked into the laundry room, changed his clothes and rubbed his hair with a towel. He couldn't sit. Not yet. He was furious at himself for losing track of the watchman. He could only hope that maybe he'd get another chance.

"This eye movie is creepy," Cathy noted, her eyes fixed on the screen. "Do you mind if I stay? I don't want to miss any of it."

"She's scared and doesn't want to go home alone," Gavan teased.

"Stay, please," Davy said, still breathing hard. He fell into an armchair, wishing that he could climb under the blanket with Gavan. "What's the eyeball up to?"

"It's from an experiment. Everything will go all right if the annelids get their eyes back! Where's the popcorn, Dad?"

"Oh, popcorn!" Davy said. "Damn, I forgot."

"Darn. The eyeball keeps growing. It makes me nervous and hungry." Gavan clutched a pillow.

"I'll call for some pizza instead." Davy reached for the phone book. Just then the phone rang. He was tempted not to answer, but he had promised Gavan to answer all phone calls, in case Marcy called.

"Hello?" He listened for a few moments. "You read our minds. We were just talking about getting one delivered. But to tell the truth, we're watching a movie, one about an eyeball. You might not like it."

"Beth?" Gavan asked flatly.

"That's handy," Davy said, hanging up the phone. "Beth offered to bring over a pizza."

Gavan groaned.

"Maybe I should head home," Cathy began.

"No," Davy said. "Stay, we'll watch the movie together." Cathy remained quiet, staring back and forth at her two neighbors, one full of nervous excitement and the other stiff with resentment. "Really, it will be like a party."

"You forgot to tell her a topping," Gavan griped. "And when she gets here, she'll ruin the movie."

"Gavan!" Davy warned.

"Then make her promise not to talk! Don't talk back!"

"Gavan, that's enough! Or you can head to bed." Gavan pulled the blanket to his chin and didn't reply. Cathy's face was troubled as she slowly rubbed Gavan's foot.

DAVY FORCED A SMILE AS Beth arrived with a small pizza—black olives and onions, an old favorite of Davy's before he married Marcy. "I would have brought a large if I'd known you were here, Cathy," Beth said.

With syrupy politeness, Gavan declined a piece. Cathy took a piece and carefully peeled away the onions. Beth made cheery jokes about the movie, which Gavan refused to acknowledge. He moved close to the television, less than four feet away, and increased the volume to an unbearable level.

"Okay, Gavan, we can take a hint," Davy said. He snatched the remote control, lowered the sound, and invited Beth to join him in the kitchen. They sat at the table, poured beer and talked softly. Distracted and irritated, Davy wished that he could stretch out on the sofa next to Gavan, watch the movie and forget the futile chase in the dark. After the movie, Gavan went to bed, and the two women said farewell not long afterward.

As Davy headed upstairs, Gavan called out softly. Davy stepped inside his son's bedroom and rearranged the covers on his bed, something he had not done in years. "Dad, do you still love Mom?" Gavan whispered. "Do you want her back home?"

"Of course," Davy said, taking in a deep breath. "More than ever!"

"You didn't go to the store, did you?"

"I had something on my mind."

"Dad. Do you like Beth better than Mom?"

"No," Davy laughed. "She's your mom's friend. Enough questions…you need sleep."

"All right." Gavan pulled the blanket around his ears. "But I hope you believe me the next time I tell you something outrageous."

TWENTY-ONE

Saturday, November 14

MARCY OFTEN HAD THE BOAT to herself while Grogan took walks late at night. Early on, she had tried to accompany him, telling him that she loved walking in the dark, catching glimpses of peaceful scenes in lighted windows. But he had shook his head firmly. "Fat men are feared, not scorned, late at night," he had said cryptically. "I want to be alone."

Marcy never asked again, and Grogan usually left late, after she went to her room for the night. He needs time alone, she thought. The boat gently dipped, out of sync with the waves, as Grogan walked away.

Wearing worn sweats, Marcy climbed into bed and turned her small lamp off. Outside, the wind was down and rain tapped a pleasant dance, as the *Sal II* moved slightly with the waves. Marcy clutched a pillow, bending it into two hard halves. At home, she did not sleep with a pillow, but alone, she liked holding something.

Thanksgiving was two weeks away. She'd return home soon, perhaps without answers. She wondered if Davy and Gavan would regard her as an intruder. She wondered if they would ever find out who wrote the notes and why she had to leave.

The boat dipped slightly, and not because of the lullaby rock of the water. She sat up to listen and heard only rain. With an empty hold, *Sal II* was as tipsy as an empty plastic soda bottle. Too soon for Grogan to return; besides, she always could tell when he stepped on board.

Her cabin was dark, cold. She pulled the blanket around her neck. She had never told Grogan, but she couldn't sleep until he returned. With any luck, the rain might chase him back early.

Whomph! came a noise from the main cabin. Someone stumbled into the piles of papers scattered on the cabin floor.

Marcy froze and clutched her blanket. A stranger was onboard. Grogan was used to stepping around the piles of court documents, newspapers, pages of notes and theories. The man who watched her from across the street—he had returned. With *Sal II's* lights out before nine, maybe he thought no one was on board. Marcy held her breath, and heard only silence.

Moments later, light footsteps treaded directly overhead. If she had fallen asleep, she might have never heard. She heard the refrigerator door open and then shut. An ordinary harbor thief was after an easy snack or cigarettes.

She sat up, shivering as her bare feet touched the cold wood floor. Annoyed, she wondered how to chase the thief. She dared not turn on a light to search for the socks and shoes she had tossed into the corner earlier. She inched away from her bed, wondering if the prowler would approach her bunk. Screaming would frighten him. But she wanted to see the creep, make sure it was the same one from the other night. And she certainly didn't want liveaboards from other boats rushing in for a rescue. Grogan would go ballistic about any attention. The tiny quarters had a bunk and shelves, leaving no place to hide.

She needed a weapon, but the gun that Lance Willard kept onboard was under the gallery sink and unloaded. All the knives were in the galley. Marcy eased herself along, pressing against the wall, to avoid making the old floorboards creak. After a moment, using her foot, she found her battery-powered Coleman lamp.

She picked it up. The solid lamp offered some protection. She felt around her shelf and along the floor, trying to remember other belongings. She fingered a hairbrush, a bottle of hand cream. She found a single sneaker and slipped it on her foot. Then she touched her hefty library book with its noisy plastic cover.

Upstairs, a cellophane bag, maybe pretzels, was ripped open, and Marcy almost jumped at the sudden noise. As the prowler crunched away, Marcy took a chance on removing the book's plastic cover. If he entered her bunk, she'd strike him with the book, then switch on the light. Only if he looked dangerous would she scream, then run and escape, before other fishermen came onboard. The liveaboards would call the police and she'd hide in the Tercel until Grogan returned. She shivered and felt foolish waiting in the dark. The plan was rough, but it was all she had.

She heard the plastic bag being shoved into the garbage, then drawers opened, one after another. A soda can popped. Silence again. Marcy leaned against the wall and imagined the guy sipping and thinking of where to search next. She couldn't decide which was more terrifying—everyday noise from an unwanted stranger or the intervening silences while he studied the meager contents of *Sal II*.

Footsteps moved to the short set of stairs leading to the bunks. Marcy's chest hurt. Did the prowler know that she was onboard? Did he deliberately bide his time to test her? Resting her finger on the light switch, she wished it were a trigger. The footsteps moved closer, cautiously, down the seven narrow steps.

The person paused outside the two doorways, before choosing the larger room, the one that Marcy had insisted Grogan take. A light flashed on, glowing underneath her doorway. Drawers opened. Suddenly, she worried that this was no ordinary harbor thief looking for a quick buck to spend at the nearest bar. The light went out and the prowler approached the door to her bunk. Marcy crouched, trembling, as a hand twisted the doorknob less than two feet away, and hoping the prowler did not shine a flashlight in her eyes.

As the hinge creaked, Marcy kept still, biting her lip. The sinister dark shape crept into the room, obviously not that of a drunk. He carefully reached about, searching for a light. The doorway was clear. Marcy could run. But she was sick of running, hiding, waiting.

While searching for a switch, his hand brushed against her shoulder and jerked away. Marcy aimed high and swung with all her might, using the book like an ax, for a solid hit. Then she picked up the lamp, and lunged for the door. Trying to swallow, she prepared to scream, though her mouth felt as dry as old newspaper. Her fingers fumbled against the switch, before the Coleman filled the small space with golden light.

The prowler, wiry and dressed in a black hooded sweatshirt, slumped to his knees, holding his head and groaning in an oddly familiar way. Marcy's throat was tight and all that came out was a small croak. It didn't matter. Her fear had vanished. She blocked the doorway and held the lamp high for protection, and tried again with a fierce tone: "Who are you?" she asked. "This boat doesn't belong to you!"

"Why'd you do that?" the prowler protested. "Mom, is that you?"

Marcy dropped the lamp and odd shadows jumped against the wall, as it rolled to the side. "Gavan, oh, Gavan," she gasped, falling to her knees and wrapping him in her arms.

"I knew it was you," he said. "I should have called out. Man, that hurts where you hit me." A edge of the book had left a red welt stretched across his cheek and a small cut near the cheekbone.

Marcy grabbed an old T-shirt and dabbed the wound. "Let me get ice," she said, standing.

He gripped her arm. "Wait," he murmured, leaning against her shoulder. "Don't go. Not yet. Oh, I knew you'd come back to town."

Marcy sat next to him and brushed the hair from his eyes. He had grown since she had left town, and was so much bigger in her arms. "How did you know?"

"Your hair's wild. So are the clothes. But you went to the library a couple weeks ago. You didn't see me studying at one of the desks. You leaned against the wall and stared out over the water. And I knew."

"No one was supposed to recognize me. But if you did..."

"The disguise was good, especially the glasses," he said. "But I was waiting for you. I knew you'd come back. Why'd you leave, Mom? And who's the creep you're with?"

She smiled. "He's not a creep. He's a detective who dreamed up this disguise. Did you say anything to your father?"

"He has no idea."

"That's good." She touched his chin and looked into his eyes. "You look well."

Gavan closed his eyes and tightened his hold on her. "I don't dwell on...Tim. I guess I don't blame myself so much, and I don't mind being by myself anymore. Does that make sense?" She nodded and they sat together silently for a few moments. "When can you come back home?" he whispered.

"Not yet. You can't tell anyone that I'm here."

"Not even Dad?"

Marcy paused. "Not yet. It would be twice as hard for the two of you to hide this secret together. Maybe this will end soon."

"Have you found any clues?"

She sighed. "It has something to do with Kovach. And the only reason I met Kovach was to return his pack." She lowered her voice. "What was in it, Gavan?"

He shrugged. "Not much. A camera, tools, some papers... Have you seen Kovach?" Marcy shook her head. "Me neither." Gavan reached into his pocket and showed her a rock. "I found this in the pack. Mr. Jabard said it has gold."

"You showed it to him?"

"I didn't say a word about Kovach."

Marcy felt nervous. So many secrets. Secrets led to lies. "Was Kovach looking for gold?"

"I don't know," Gavan said. "He didn't carry a pan or a pickax either day. And he was throwing stuff into the stream that first day and not the next, when I was with him. I don't know if he knew it was gold or not."

A chill went through Marcy and then annoyance. "Gavan, that pack has caused so much trouble. Some people think that I kept something from Kovach." She tossed the rock across the room. "You can't talk to anyone else," she said, sharply. "About the gold, about Kovach and about that pack. You can't get involved."

"But I am involved. My friend's dead." Gavan's voice was like steel.

"Gavan, don't argue with me about this."

"You're not around, but I'm supposed to guess what you want me to do." His voice was mean. "I have a right to answers—about Tim and about why I have the strangest parents in town."

Marcy couldn't control her fury, not only at Gavan but her inability to go home. She ran upstairs to the galley, grabbed a tray of ice, and smashed it onto a towel. She ignored the few pieces that scattered on the floor, ran downstairs and handed the bundle to Gavan. He held it to his face. Too late, Marcy thought. An ugly red stripe swelled from the corner of his eye to his jaw. "Gavan, I'm sorry," she said. "About the bruise. About leaving home. About everything."

He hung his head. "I just want you to come home. I'd do anything if you could just come home."

She hugged him close, but he squirmed away.

"I'm trying to help, Mom. I'm sorry, but I forgot about a map that I took from his pack. It was in my pocket and the only thing that I didn't return." She asked about what kind of map and Gavan explained. "A little map drawn by hand. It showed a stream by the cross-island road. I put it in my pocket the day we took the pack and then I forgot all about it."

She reached over and covered his hand that held the ice. "Maybe the map's our answer. Can you bring it to me?" He nodded. "Gavan, promise me that you won't prowl around at night anymore. The docks are no place for a kid at night. Your father will be livid."

"He won't know," Gavan said with disdain. "He's not at home, Mom. He went out tonight."

Marcy's muscles went tense. "He left you home alone?"

"He calls Cathy. And I leave through my window. They don't check me like you did."

Marcy let out a long sigh. "Promise to stay at home at night—and I promise we'll work together." He nodded and they kissed. She watched him run for his bike, his shadow bouncing under the harbor lights, and she wondered: where did Davy go at night?

TWENTY-TWO

Monday, November 16

ANB HARBOR WAS A SHORT walk from the drug store on Lincoln Street, about a block. Marcy started walking toward the street, but Grogan insisted they take the Tercel. "It will take more time to park than the walk back and forth," Marcy protested.

"Gavan recognized you," Grogan responded. "No more walks for you."

"People notice quirky behavior in Sitka—like driving two blocks," Marcy warned.

"Not with me," Grogan said. "I'm fat. That means lazy."

"Why?" she challenged.

"Why does fat mean lazy?"

"No, why are you overweight?" Marcy asked quietly. "I wouldn't ask, but you bring it up. Often."

He gave a short laugh, more mean than happy. "I could lose weight. But I don't want to. It's how I measure the character of the people I encounter. Some immediately detest me. Others take a chance on meeting the real person. I'd have no other way of discerning the difference."

"That's an excuse," she said. "Thought up after many years."

"True."

"You're not happy," she continued bluntly.

"Losing weight is not the answer. I'd still be a fat person inside a thin body." He stared rigidly at the windshield and drove around the block a second time, searching for a space.

"When did you gain the weight? Did your mother—"

"No!" he snapped. "My life was perfect with her. I remember her like an angel."

"What happened to her?" Marcy asked.

Grogan explained how his mother had died just before he started kindergarten. "Breast cancer. My father couldn't care for me. Several people offered to help, including my mother's best friend and my father's mother. My father asked me to decide. When I told him my choice, he frowned. I'd given the wrong answer.

"He took me aside and said we couldn't reject my grandmother's offer. I mumbled and lied and tried to hide my bitter disappointment. My grandmother lived in the next town, a ten-minute drive away. That might as well have been a hundred miles away for a five-year-old. They packed my clothes, and I moved that night. I never saw my best friend or my favorite toys again. My grandmother never wanted her son to marry. In the end, she won."

Marcy thought about her own parents and how distance had kept Gavan from meeting them. But she remained quiet, listening to Grogan, about how his grandmother decided that he should wait another year before attending kindergarten. "I cried, thinking of how my mother would have cried," Grogan admitted. "She had talked about school for so long and we used to take walks there, and she made the little brick school sound like the most heavenly place. I knew the alphabet and how to write my name. But my grandmother convinced my father that I needed to mature.

"That first year, she used food for discipline. When I was good or she wanted me out of the way, she plied me with sugary cookies and cakes. When I was bad, she refused to let me sit at the table. She never ate with her husband or my uncle, her youngest son. My grandmother hovered over the table, adding more to the plates before we had even finished the first helpings. While she cooked, she repeatedly stuck a spoon in. Never adding salt or spices, just tasting, testing.

"She grew up in the Depression. She admired cakes or pies for days before we'd eat them. I couldn't leave the table until every bite vanished. I'd try and hide mounds of mashed potatoes or hunks of bread spread thick with butter in the garbage pail. But she beat me and watched for weeks if I got caught. So, I got used to eating anything, no matter how bloated I felt."

Marcy thought about Grogan's mother, how upset she would have been about her son starting kindergarten, taller, heavier, more awkward than the other children. "I became a problem for the teacher," Grogan said. "Reading was my only escape, reminding me of my mother. I could hear her voice and it was almost like having her nearby.

"My father worked a lot and started dating. I was lucky if I saw him once a week by the time he decided to remarry. He asked whether I'd prefer to live with him and Lorna, or stay with my grandmother, for continuity in my life, as he put it.

"I knew the answer he expected. And I despise him to this day." Grogan backed the car neatly into a narrow space.

Marcy let out a long slow breath, thinking about her own husband and child. "It's a horrible story," she whispered. "I'm sorry. But your grandmother and father do not have to win in the end."

"You sound like—" He broke off. "You're right. But who says they won? I do what I want, when I want."

Marcy reached for his arm. "Remember, you're in Alaska. Almost everyone is thousands of miles away from screwy grandmothers and families."

"Is that why everyone comes?"

"Enough of them." Marcy tightened her grip on his arm. "Look. A white van. The one parked outside my house!" A short, scrawny dark-haired man climbed out. In his late twenties, he wore dirty work clothes and the resentful mask of a person who quit caring about school early, multiplying confusion and hardship in his life.

"Do you recognize him?"

"I'd have to hear his voice. I was under the bed."

Grogan copied the van's plate number before hurrying out of the car. "He just pulled up, but I don't think he's following us."

Marcy slammed her door and caught up. "Are we going to confront him?"

Grogan shook his head. "No way. He's the hired hand. Let's get close. We'll separate inside—I go to the lobby, you wait in line. That's your best chance to hear his voice. Don't look his way. If he comes my way, I'll get his box number." Grogan held the door for her. "When we're done, we meet in the car." He charged ahead, for the lobby and its walls lined with post office boxes.

Marcy turned right and waited in a line of six people, not including the man from the van. Maybe she should wait by the door. Maybe she could bump into him. She was about to turn and head back for the front door, when the man approached. So, she shuffled nervously back into line. The man, head down and reading his mail, stood in line directly behind her. Marcy faced the counter, pretending boredom, looking about as he tore at his envelopes. She smelled perspiration and stale cigarette smoke as he read his mail, and glanced again. He paid no attention to her and wore familiar black boots.

Suddenly, a crashing noise came from the lobby. Everyone in line, including Marcy, turned to stare as Grogan returned a metal garbage can to its standing position. She used the distraction to study the envelope in the man's hand, addressed to P.O. Box 689. The gray stationery matched the notes that had been sent to her. No return address, no name, no stamp. Unfortunately, the man clutched the actual letter in his hand, so she couldn't read a word. At the other side of the lobby, the commotion settled; Grogan lingered red-faced, mumbling apologies to no one in particular. Their eyes met and he winked at her. Marcy rubbed her nose, sore from the irksome glasses, and turned away.

Two clerks were on duty, but the line moved slowly. Rita patiently showed an earnest collector blocks of stamps. The young man studied each set, holding it to the light, then made a decision. Long an admirer of stamps and their collectors, Rita cheerfully complied and did not hurry the customer. Marcy could only assume that stamps' potential value made the job less ordinary, as if Rita were an art consultant. The collector hesitated over a block of stamps with birds. Behind Marcy, Van Man groaned. Rita glared, crossed her arms and scanned the line, as if to dare anyone to complain. Her gaze stopped at Marcy, and the clerk frowned. Panicked, Marcy bent over to rub an imaginary ache in her leg. She glanced up, but Rita still stared.

The collector spoke up. "I'm done," he announced. "Enough for this month." His order came to five hundred seventy-six dollars. He wrote a check, then pulled his wallet for identification.

"No need for that," Rita said briskly. "I remember all I need from last time." As the man paid, Marcy realized she'd be Rita's next customer. She dared not face Rita in person, yet wanted to hang around long enough until Van Man stepped forward to the counter. She reached into her pocket and fingered some coins. The collector carefully placed his envelopes in a briefcase. Rita smiled warmly at him, and briskly called: "Next please!"

Marcy jerked her hand deliberately. Coins clattered to the floor. She dropped to her knees, pushing her glasses on her nose and searching for the change. "Go ahead," she mumbled, refusing to look into Van Man's eyes.

He shoved his way in front of her. "Every moron in town showed up today," he muttered.

She recognized the whiny voice instantly. Scrambling about on the floor, she found two dimes and a penny. Then, another man in line politely handed over a nickel. Marcy stood and waited once more, listening and staring intently, hoping that Whiny might mention his name to Rita or maybe even toss the gray note away on his way out. The other clerk, Denver, waved Marcy over and did not look up as he rearranged stamps. "What can I do for you?"

"Um," she said, her eyes darting back to Van Man. "Two bird stamps, please." She clutched the coins as he tore two stamps away from a large block tucked away in a drawer.

At the next window, Van Man leaned over the counter, his voice getting louder. "But I have the key for that box!"

"You should hand the key over if you don't know who it belongs to!" Rita snapped.

He tucked the key back into his pocket. "The box belongs to me. I only want to know who paid for it!"

"We're not authorized to identify box holders," Rita said sternly.

"Here you go." Denver slid two stamps over to Marcy.

"Oh, not those," Marcy murmured. "I thought these were for postcards. I need that kind." Denver scowled and snatched the stamps back, returning them to a small container in his drawer.

"I'm expecting an envelope and it's not there," Van Man pleaded at the other end of the counter. "I have to know who to contact."

"I don't understand," Rita said, with exasperation. "You have the key, but you don't know who rents the box?"

As Denver gave her two more stamps, Marcy paused and studied the coins in her hand. "Sorry, I only have enough money for one," she said softly. She no longer had to hide her interest in the transaction at the next window. Denver and everyone in line listened to Rita's scolding.

Van Man looked about in helpless agitation. "I lost the name," he said with an angry hiss. "They sent me the keys. It's about a job. From out of town. You gotta help me out."

Rita stood her ground. "I'm sorry, sir. Postal regulations forbid us from releasing the names of box holders. You can talk to the postal supervisor, but I'm confident he'll repeat what I've explained." Rita smiled brightly. She knew more postal regulations than most of the postal service lawyers in Washington, D.C., and Marcy and everyone else in line knew that the Sitka postmaster would never contradict her.

The line had grown to nine people, and all of them stared and fidgeted. "Can I talk to the postmaster?" Van Man asked.

"He's at the main office on Sawmill Creek Road," she snapped. "Next please!" The dejected customer walked away. "That's the post office!" Rita said to her next customer. "Never a dull moment!"

"Anything else for you?" Denver said with a glare, calling Marcy's attention back to her own small purchase.

"No, thank you," Marcy said quickly. She pocketed her postcard stamp and change, and followed Van Man. From the top of the stairs, she watched him climb into the van and drive off in a hurry. Grogan waited in the car. "Let's go," she said. "He's headed to the other post office. He had a gray envelope that looked exactly like the notes sent to me, and he wants the name of the box holder!"

"We want that name, too," Grogan said.

Minutes later, they headed for the post office on Sawmill Creek Road. "Damn," she said. "I don't see that van." Grogan drove through the large lot and then parked. They waited ten minutes. "He's not coming," Marcy said. "He gave up."

"That's okay," Grogan said, turning the car back to downtown Sitka. "Let's make him come to us."

They stopped at the office supply store and found cheap gray paper and envelopes, not exactly like the stationery for

Marcy's gray note, but similar. "Should we wait?" Marcy asked. "They're using the same box to communicate. The wrong person could pick up our note."

"But that's the person we want," Grogan said. "I can keep an eye on the box to find out who picks up the mail."

They bought the paper, developed a plan and returned to the downtown post office. Marcy bent over and peered into Box 689. "The box is empty," she whispered.

"I know I saw him jam an envelope in there," Grogan murmured. "Someone already picked it up."

"That was fast," Marcy said, nervously looking around the empty lobby. "Could he have been watched?"

"Not while we were there," Grogan said. "So, should we send the note? We don't have a key, so we have to use a stamp. And our paper's different."

Marcy wanted to toy with her own tormentors and make them nervous. She wanted to find out who wanted her out of town. "As long as they don't connect a note with Marcy James, who cares?" Marcy urged. "And this guy wanted to know the name of the person who rented that post office box. We're not the only ones asking around. What do we have to lose?"

At the counter, Grogan penned the note: "Time to talk. Starrigavan. Camp site fourteen. Thursday afternoon at two."

TWENTY-THREE

Tuesday, November 17

JANE HURRIED DOWN LINCOLN Street toward the Katlian Cafe. She had been tempted to cancel her weekly breakfast with Bob. But the reporter always had plenty of gossip that he couldn't include in his articles. He was perceptive, a good judge of how the community would react on almost any issue. As she approached the door, she spotted Bob climbing out of his truck.

As usual, no tables were free. Doris, the waitress, handed over two steaming cups of coffee and asked them to give her a minute to pull some chairs from the back.

"Bob! Jane! Over here." The commanding voice came from a table for two tucked between the door and a large dead plant. Gordon Knowles sat across from his safari-style hat. "Please," he offered, pushing the hat and a copy of the *Wall Street Journal* aside.

"I'm not sitting with him," Bob muttered.

"There are no other tables," Jane murmured. "Come on."

"I'll wait. Look at him. He wants to brag."

"Let's find out why," Jane said quietly.

"He wants to talk to you," Bob said, reluctantly following her. "It took him long enough to figure out that you're a decent source. I was hoping he'd never find out."

Gordon jumped up and shifted an empty chair to the tiny table. As they sat, the three sets of knees bumped, and Jane smiled at Bob's discomfort. "I haven't seen you, Bob, since the profile in the *Record*," Gordon said. "Almost half a page! But I don't know why you called my wife."

"Sitka's a family town," Bob said, grinning. "She had great stories. I only wished I could have used more." Jane tapped her knee against Bob's, a reminder that antagonizing the reporter could shut down information.

Gordon leaned back in his chair. "You're lucky, Bob. Your stories are never done. They give you as much space as you want, and you can track the pettiest of details."

"That's not luck, it's called reporting."

Gordon laughed. "If you're ever in New York, stop by the office. Drop off a resume. The *Journal* editors would like you."

"I'm not their type," Bob said. "I like the rural life."

"Don't mention that in the interview. You could change your mind. I enjoyed my stay here, but I miss the city. I filed my story last night—and should be heading back to New York soon." He paused and smiled. "In fact, I'm surprised you're not busy writing this morning. Who would have thought a feature on some desolate road in Alaska would turn into serious front-page material?"

Jane raised her eyebrows.

Bob shrugged. "I'm working. Jane's my best source in town."

"Is your story in that issue?" Jane pointed to the *Journal* on the table.

Knowles' smile widened. "No, it's in today's paper, but that won't get here until tomorrow."

Doris came to the table. "The usual?" she asked. Bob and Jane nodded. Knowles was already working on his Danish and coffee. Doris returned with coffee and filled cups for Jane and Bob. She held the pot high, swirling the murky dark liquid. "I'll bring a fresh pot over, Mr. Knowles," she said, hurrying away.

"Wait 'til she sees my tip," Bob griped.

"She likes New York tips now," Knowles said.

"How much road does the *Journal* think Baranof should have?" Jane interjected.

"Anyone in Sitka who can add two plus two will be begging for a road after they read my story. And a dead body…that adds a mysterious touch, don't you agree?"

"Body?" Jane asked, glancing at Knowles, then Bob, who leaned back in his chair, his expression unchanged.

"So Bob didn't tell you?" Knowles was beaming.

"Not before breakfast," Bob said, playing with his napkin.

"Chauvinist," Jane accused, tapping his shoulder, fully aware that Denson had no idea what Knowles was talking about. "I can handle it. Tell me now."

Knowles obliged. "Yesterday afternoon, Dennis Kovach's body was found in a ravine in the center of the island. They found a partial report in his vest pocket. He had located gold… The poor guy probably got excited and had an accident on his way back to town. Broken neck. Head injury. He went quick."

"Just after my deadline," Bob said. "How'd you find out?"

"I was finishing a draft of my story and had a few final questions for the police chief. He invited me over to the station and told me everything. That made an easy lead for what would have been a boring road story—gold fever hits Alaska, again. No one knows how much gold yet. But those road bonds are sold."

"Where did he find the gold?" Jane asked.

"Get your pan ready. Close to the proposed route for Bander's road. But tell your shareholders not to worry. Gold will generate enough excitement and financing for two roads." Gordon drained his coffee.

Jane sat back in her chair with a frown. "But why didn't Kovach mention gold at the meeting that night? He must have known. By the way, who found Kovach?"

"Bander and some hikers." Gordon shrugged.

"So when do you take off?" Bob asked, crossing his arms and leaning over the table with a smile.

"Don't hurry me, Bob," Knowles said. "Maybe I'll try fishing. Find a charter captain who's a character—write another feature. You have any other suggestions for me?"

"Why don't you try the Miss Sitka Pageant on Friday night?" Bob said slyly.

Knowles laughed. "I'll leave that to you." He handed the waitress more than enough to pay for everyone's meal and sauntered out the door.

"The Miss Sitka Pageant?" Jane asked.

"Small town life at its best!" Bob protested. "This year, three overweight girls of questionable talent don swimsuits to compete for a ten-thousand-dollar scholarship and other prizes. Hey, Doris!" He pointed to Gordon's money. "Does his tip cover a fresh pot for us?" The waitress rolled her eyes but grudgingly delivered a fresh pot of coffee to the table.

"You didn't know about Kovach," Jane chastised him.

"No," Bob said, shortly, shoving a pancake into his mouth. "I have to catch up, get it in today's paper."

"Don't worry. You fooled Knowles."

"That's not hard," Bob scoffed. "He wouldn't have talked so much otherwise. Shoot me if I ever attend another Sitka police award banquet again. If they want coverage for their rinky-dink stuff, they can call Gordon at the *Wall Street Journal*. What an arrogant jerk. How did he get that job?"

"He knows who to annoy and who not to annoy," Jane said.

"Can I quote you?"

"Not about Gordon Knowles. But who owns that gold anyway?"

"Good question," said Bob, standing to finish his coffee. "Do me a favor and find out, will you?"

That afternoon's extra-run issue of the *Record* sold out by dinnertime.

GOLD FEVER STRIKES SITKA

The body of the engineer Dennis Kovach of Juneau, partially decayed and ravaged by animals, was discovered by three hikers late Tuesday in a desolate part of the Tongass National Forest, about two miles from the site of the proposed cross-island road and not far from where a thirteen-year-old boy was murdered.

Kovach claimed to have discovered a new gold vein in the center of the island, according to a report found on the engineer's body. He was the city's engineering consultant on the cross-island road and was last seen Sept. 19, the date of death for Tim Bander.

Police named Kovach as their chief suspect in the boy's death. A preliminary autopsy estimates that Kovach died not long after Bander. Because of the body's condition, an autopsy may not be able to determine whether the death was accidental or suicide. Police also announced that the discovery closes the investigation into the murder of Tim Bander. Police also report finding unopened candy bars, with the engineer's fingerprints on the wrappers, near Tim Bander's body.

Jeremy Bander, director of Southeast Alaska Tourism Council, had led two hikers from New York into the Tongass when they found the engineer's body. Bander described the two as venture capitalists from New York who may want to invest in road-related projects. The group radioed for help, and state police investigators responded to the scene.

A few rocks with traces of gold, said to be valued at about two hundred fifty dollars, along with a detailed map of gold deposits, were in the engineer's pockets.

Although authorities refused to release the exact location where Kovach's body was found, dozens of Sitkans trekked through the Tongass early today. The officials warned that the area is treacherous even for experienced hikers. Forest Service rangers have begun round-the-clock patrols of the forest, discouraging prospecting.

Earthquake disturbances during the past decade probably uncovered the gold, surmised a geologist with the University of Alaska.

The gold find is on Forest Service property. A validity exam, conducted by geologists and engineers, will begin in the spring for estimating amounts and locations. Once the study is complete, Forest Service and federal Bureau of Mining officials will decide who will extract the gold and how.

"Of course, if there's a lot of gold, the Forest Service would put any major mining contract out to competitive bid," said Paul Genalli, spokesman for U.S. Forest Service in Sitka. "If only trace amounts are involved, the Forest Services could open prospecting to individuals, possibly contracting the project out to a tourism group."

"Tourism groups could readily organize gold extraction after road construction," said Jeremy Bander, director of Southeast Alaska Tourism Council.

The discovery of trace amounts of gold will undoubtedly end opposition to the proposed cross-island highway. A major leader fighting road development across Baranof Island, Marcy James, has been out of town in recent weeks. She and other opponents could not be reached for comment.

The news of the gold find became national news this morning with a report in the *Wall Street Journal.* Brokers in New York report the bonds for financing the cross-Baranof road will be sold next week as scheduled.

Katmai Shee Corp., the Sitka Native corporation, had hoped to develop a cross-island road north of Sitka, between Katlian and Rodman bays. "We'll continue our plans," said Jane McBride, Katmai Shee finance director. "Our road offers access to valuable property and resources. The gold find is good news for the community, but will not force us to hurry our road or hamper our development plans."

Kovach's body was shipped to Anchorage for an autopsy, a routine procedure for unattended deaths.

"Dennis is dead," Marcy said, stunned as she stared at the newspaper. "So he wasn't driven out of town." She was distraught and could not even read beyond the first few paragraphs. "And no one has to worry about me stopping the road now that gold's been found." She slammed the newspaper down in disgust.

"I'd like to see an autopsy report," Grogan said. "Do you really think his death was an accident or suicide?"

"I'm worried, first Tim and now Kovach." She shuddered. "I wish Davy and Gavan would leave town."

"Your husband will be very careful after he reads this."

"Or, he'll assume that Gavan is safe. We should call. I want to see Gavan's map."

Grogan sighed, but hurried with her to the pay phone in the harbor's parking area. "You sure your husband won't be at home?" Grogan asked, as he dialed. She nodded. But Davy answered.

Grogan grimaced. 'I'm calling from the Youth Resource Center," he spoke quickly. "We're taking a survey and want to talk to Gavan James." Marcy huddled close to hear the other side of the conversation.

"Gavan's not home from school yet," she heard Davy say. "Who are you?"

Grogan hung up.

JANE TELEPHONED BOB DENSON. "Bob, why didn't you discuss the bonds in your article?"

"Jane, I appreciate your help, but I write the story," Bob said.

"But the financing's important. This gold changes the cost of the road."

"To the average reader in Sitka, those bonds are a bore."

"They've become a novelty investment. People are clamoring for them."

"Maybe when I do a follow-up. And there's plenty to follow. One of the Sitka detectives told me that the candy bars had more than one set of prints. But the state police won't identify them. Weird."

KEN JABARD HEARD OTHER teachers talk about the article as he left school. He asked to see the paper and read the entire article on the spot. "If you plan a field trip up there, my class wants to go along, Ken," said Mary Henry, an English teacher, with a laugh.

He gave a vague nod and glanced at the newspaper again. He remembered the rock in Gavan's hand, the boy's eyes shifting as he tried to think up fast lies.

Jabard thanked Mary and the other teacher. He climbed into his Jeep and slammed the steering wheel hard.

BY EIGHT, DAVY GOT AROUND to making a fire after Gavan went to bed early with a book, following a night of arguing over a poor grade on a math test. As Davy adjusted logs, the phone rang. Principal Henrietta Cordola identified herself and explained to Davy that she had been trying to call. "You're a difficult man to reach."

"Our message machine must be on the blink again," Davy said.

"I'm calling about two items, Mr. James." Her voice was

stern. "First, there's the bruise on Gavan's face. He told us it's a private matter and that he didn't want to discuss it."

"He told me he fell at school," Davy said.

"Hmm." The principal clearly did not believe him. "We have no record of that. Where? When?"

"I don't know...but boys get bruises."

"Not like that. Not on the face. Is your wife at home?"

"Not until after Thanksgiving."

"Mr. James, the social worker, the school counselor and I plan to speak to Gavan tomorrow about that bruise. You're welcome to join us. The school has an obligation to investigate such problems to prevent abuse. He's embarrassed and we must find out why."

"I didn't hit my son, if that's what you're implying," Davy said.

"No one blames you, Mr. James," she said smoothly. "We understand how difficult children with ADD can be. Maybe he was in a fight. ADD children are prone to fighting. But we must investigate. Second, we held a conference yesterday to discuss Gavan's problems. We sent a notice, but you never responded. The social worker has prepared a page of suggestions to improve Gavan's home life—"

"School is the problem, not home! What are you talking about?"

"Gavan's going through a rough period. His problems need to be addressed. If you ignore these issues at home, we must take action at school. We're suggesting counseling sessions. In school. We plan to proceed immediately."

"I never got a notice!" Davy protested.

"It was sent home with Gavan in a sealed envelope," she said. "I recommend that you talk with your son in a kindly manner and remain calm. Maybe then he won't feel compelled to keep these matters secret. And please feel free to stop by or call our office if you have any questions." She thanked him and Davy slammed the phone down.

He glanced at the woodstove and started to rekindle the fire when the phone rang again. He swore and prepared to argue more with someone else at the school. But to his relief, it was Beth. She offered to visit, and he agreed, longing to talk to another reasonable adult about Gavan. "Gavan's in bed," he told her. "I'll leave the door open."

DAVY WAITED ON THE SOFA and about twenty minutes later, the front door opened. Beth entered, carrying a bottle of sparkling wine and a newspaper. Davy was nervous around Beth, especially whenever he remembered how she had stopped talking to him before she took off for college so many years ago. Unlike his cousin Francesca, Davy had long ago forgiven her for the bitter words when he refused to finish high school. When she returned to Sitka from Seattle, she was kind and friendly again, but Davy always felt inferior to the attorney who had once been his high school girlfriend.

"Your paper was still outside," Beth said with a merry voice, handing the damp newspaper over. "Did you hear the news?"

Davy shook his head. "I've been arguing with Gavan all night, and I just got off the phone with the principal. If he weren't asleep, I'd have him down here letting him know that he's grounded for the next week. That won't help though. I wish I knew what to do."

"You need a break from all this." She smiled and gestured with her hand. "So, then, you didn't hear. They found gold on Baranof Island."

"Gold? Are you kidding me?"

"They also found Kovach. He's dead."

"God, no!" Davy turned and stared at her, stunned.

"You seem upset," Beth asked, puzzled. "I didn't think you knew him."

Davy spoke slowly. "No, but Marcy did. You know her, she tried to talk anyone and everyone out of the road, including the guys paid to work on it. What happened to him?"

Beth pointed to the newspaper. "He fell. Or committed suicide after killing Tim. Sad. But at least the mystery's all over." She retrieved his corkscrew from a drawer and adeptly plucked the cork from the bottle.

Davy grimaced, in no mood for wine. "It's not over until Marcy comes home."

"Soon...it's less than two weeks away from Thanksgiving."

"It's strange, though," Davy continued. "First Tim, now Kovach dead out there. Maybe Kovach didn't kill Tim."

Beth reached for wineglasses and poured. "It's not strange at all," she said. "The man was near the scene, and police found his fingerprints near Tim's body. The case is closed." She held his glass to the light as she handed it over. "You know, I love how Marcy mixes her dinnerware—the heavy pottery look with this crystal. It works."

"None of it is the same without her around." Davy placed his glass on the nearby table without taking a sip. "How can they be sure it's not murder, if they're not sure it was an accident or suicide?"

"The police have their ways," she said then retrieved his glass and handed it over once again, while lifting hers. "A toast, here's to gold and to Sitka..."

He lifted the glass for a halfhearted toast, pretended to sip and then returned it to the table. "That gold's not going to help Sitka," he scoffed. "Something's odd about Kovach finding gold and not telling anyone before his death. And thank God, Gavan's all right."

"What do you mean?"

He hesitated. The police had said not to discuss details. But Tim's death seemed so long ago. "Gavan was one of the last people to see Kovach alive. The police asked us not to talk about it. And now Gavan has this ugly bruise on his face—and it looks as though someone slugged him."

She frowned and didn't respond as she held the wineglass with both hands and sipped. Davy went to the refrigerator and found cheese. He placed the cheese, wrapper and all, along with a box of crackers, on the table. "I need advice about Gavan," he admitted slowly.

"What did Gavan say about Kovach?" Beth asked.

"Not much. At first, he had a million reasons why he's smarter than an engineer who had gone to college and started his own business. They hiked somewhere, and afterward, Kovach dropped him off at a dock and took off. The man probably couldn't wait to get rid of him. The police think Gavan was the last person to see the engineer."

"Gavan was out there with Kovach the day Tim died?" Beth asked, startled. "My God, he's so lucky. I mean…"

"We're not supposed to talk about it. But I know you'll keep this secret."

She nodded. "You don't have to worry with Kovach dead. And at least Tim's parents know what happened. Not like my brother…" Tears formed in her eyes. She looked so frail and vulnerable and Davy could not help but reach out and put his arms around her. Beth leaned her head against his shoulder and closed her eyes.

"How can the police be so sure that Kovach killed Tim?" he murmured. "And why not Gavan?"

Beth moved away to pour more wine. "They'll do an autopsy," she said. "Test DNA, I suppose. But I don't want to talk about this. It brings up old memories that hurt, Davy." Then, she chastised him for not enjoying the expensive bottle of wine.

He took one small sip, staring at his glass and feeling guilty. He needed her help, and he hoped that he was half as good of a friend to her. "Look, how much should I worry about this bruise and the call from the principal?"

She cut the cheese and arranged the crackers neatly in a circle on the plate. "Did Gavan say you hit him?" Beth asked. Davy shook his head. "Then you have nothing to worry about," she said, quickly dismissing the topic and turning attention back to the newspaper article. As she babbled about the details, Davy couldn't understand her excitement, especially considering that she had been one of the more vocal opponents to the road construction. Listening and nodding occasionally, he didn't offer much to say. Money always complicated matters, he thought to himself, and the gold find would be no different.

TWENTY-FOUR

Wednesday, November 18

LOW CLOUDS LINGERED ON the coast. The wind darted back and forth from the sea. Birds living in the forest did not chance flying and waited for the oncoming storm. Marcy sat in the Tercel as Grogan walked through Starrigavan campground twice, promising to look in all directions and check for any sign of a trap. About thirty minutes later, she followed him down a soggy path. "No one comes out here this time of year," Marcy whispered.

Grogan put a finger to his lips and paused at a fork between two campsites. He took the narrow path to site fourteen. Not far was the metal utility shed used by rangers for storing equipment. Grogan pulled a chisel and hammer from his pack. One swing and the lock was broken. He dropped to his knee, picked up the pieces, then deposited both pieces and tools into his backpack. He looked inside and then held the door open for Marcy. The shed was dark, musty, unkempt.

Grogan aimed his flashlight against shovels and racks leaning against the one wall. Nine grill tops were stacked in a corner next to several bags of fertilizer. He examined the floor. "No one's been in here for a while," he commented.

"Tourists stop coming in September, and Sitkans have better places to go."

Grogan pushed aside debris and arranged bags of fertilizer for them to sit out the wait. A mouse scurried through a rusted hole. "We can check the guy out before we talk. You stay quiet," Grogan warned. "We don't want them guessing who you are. If you sit still, they might not even realize that you're a woman."

"Gee, thanks," she drawled. "But I want answers, too." With that, she pulled a 9-mm pistol from her pocket.

"Where did that come from?" Grogan asked, frowning.

"On board *Sal II,* under the sink." She grinned and added, "Maybe you should clean more. By the way, it's loaded."

"I suggest you keep it hidden." Grogan unbuttoned his jacket. A small, serious Beretta rested inside a holster. "Unless you promise you're the better shot."

"We might find out," she said.

"Remember, shooting won't give us answers," he said. He turned the flashlight off and moved toward a cracked seam in the shed's wall. "I can see the path. We're set."

"I hope the right person got the note."

"The 'right' person is dangerous. He'd have been out here waiting."

"We're almost three hours early!"

Grogan lowered his voice. "Quiet. He could be around, watching, listening."

"Stop it!" she whispered, then put her hand inside her pocket and rubbed her finger back and forth against the smooth, cold barrel of her gun. "No other car was in sight."

His dark eyes flashed amusement. "We hid our car and walked. He could have done the same." Grogan put his hands on his knees and eased his way down onto the pile of bags. "Keep an eye out through that little hole. We don't want any surprises."

"Those guys in my house. They'd do anything for cash."

"Whatever happens, give them a chance to explain," Grogan reiterated. "I'll ask questions. We don't want them guessing that you're Marcy James. And remember, they could lie or say anything. They could name the mayor, the police chief, the candlestick maker. They could blame Davy. No matter what they say, don't let it get to you." He curled his hands around the back of his neck.

"Hmm." She leaned forward and peered through the small crack. Rain returned, and rattled the shed roof. Grogan found another crack in the wall; using a hammer, he bent the metal back for a better view of the nearby trail. Only then did he relax, pulling a bag of dried fruit from his pack and offering her some. She shook her head and closed her eyes as he ate.

Outside, rain pelted the roof. Nuthatches and sparrows made nervous noises in the canopy overhead. The indecisive wind drifted from the bay, swaying branches back and forth. The cold air went right down her neck, and Marcy pulled her coat around her tightly. What seemed like moments later, she was startled by Grogan sharply squeezing her upper arm.

"Huh?" she said, groggy and shaking her head. Before she could say more, Grogan covered her mouth. She tensed her muscles, remembered the plan and nodded. He moved his hand, as they heard a vehicle drive by, the engine slowing as it took the turn by site fourteen. He stood and peered outside. "White," Grogan said softly, more like breath than a word. "They'll be back."

"How long was I asleep?" Marcy whispered.

"Almost two hours. Shhh." He put his hands on the bags, and pushed hard to stand. Marcy stood, too, stretched her muscles and pulled the dark ski cap over her face. Grogan leaned close. Though his lips touched her ear, she could just barely hear his words: "Stay calm. Nothing rash."

He looked over the shovels and chose the heaviest and handed another one to Marcy. "Might come in handy," he whispered. "With the weather, they'll head right for this shed."

Marcy felt anxious peering outside and waiting, as the rain

drummed a sullen beat against the shed. Two men approached on the path, rain gear and hoods obscuring their faces, footsteps silent on the soft pine needles. "Why did we have to get here so early?" one complained loudly, as he circled the shed.

Grogan tapped Marcy's shoulder and gestured for her to wait on the other side of the doorway, close to the wall, but not touching the metal. She stood in a crouch, checking the gun in her pocket, before lifting her shovel high.

Outside, the pair moved closer. "This is a weird place to meet. Hell, he shoulda come to my trailer. We'd crack open some beers."

"Sounds good. Let's do that afterward."

"We'll have to stop for the beer. Do you have money?"

"We'll have it after this! Chips and dip, too. God, I'm hungry."

"Let's wait in the shed. We'll see this guy before he sees us!"

Marcy rolled her eyes. She remembered the bickering voices, the stupidity. The door shoved open, scraping against the gravel-strewn floor. A lumpy, wet shape hesitated in the doorway. "Can't see a damn thing," the one guy muttered. "I feel a web. Could be a big spider."

"Go on," the other guy complained and gave his partner a shove. "It's wet out here!"

Marcy pressed into the corner near an old wheelbarrow and held her shovel tight. The other man stepped inside, and Grogan immediately moved and kicked the door shut. Someone yelped in fear. Angry and intimidating, Grogan focused his flashlight on the two men. Marcy waited in the corner, staring and ready to attack.

"Hey!" The man from the post office put his arms out in defense. "You waiting for us?"

Grogan drawled, "You could say that."

"Okay, nice to meet you," Whiny interjected, his face paling. "Finally."

"We got the letter," said the man called Ray. "We've been ready for more work."

Disappointment struck at Marcy. The men had no idea who hired them. Grogan asked about how much they liked the work.

"We like the money," Ray said.

Grogan nodded. "But I'm a businessman. You have to convince me what you're worth."

Whiny swallowed. "Look, we went through the place three times!"

"And it never hit the police blotter, man!" Ray added.

Grogan paused, and leaned against the shed wall, blocking the exit. The shovel looked like a little stick in his arms.

"If you want, we'll look again," Ray said. "But it's getting dangerous." He nudged his friend.

"What exactly have you done?"

"Everything you asked." Ray spit defiantly.

"Including Tim Bander?" Grogan asked.

The men looked at each other and started to back away. "What the hell are you talking about?" Ray asked, his hand on the door. "We had nothing to do with that!"

Grogan nodded and paused. "Good. But maybe the person who hired you did?"

"If you didn't hire us, how would you know the box number?" Whiny shot back. He stepped back and stared at the pile of shovels and rakes in a hungry way, before glancing in Marcy's direction.

Ray shoved Whiny aside. "Shut up." He stepped close to Grogan. "Who the hell are you? We're not going to let you blow the best damn job we've had all year."

Grogan tossed the shovel to the side, and Marcy knew that Grogan had made a decision to work with the two. "How much did you get paid for breaking into the house on Shore Road?"

Whiny got nervous. "Why should we tell you? If you're not the guy who hired us, then you're the police."

"Shut up, Joe," Ray ordered. "Shore Road. We don't know about it."

"What's a job like that worth?"

"Five hundred." Joe gave a goofy grin when he lied.

"I don't even want you to break into a house," Grogan said. "This way you get paid twice. You get money from your mystery boss—and you get a bonus from me." Grogan paused, staring at them. He pulled out his wallet and extracted two hundred-dollar bills. "All you have to do is let me know when you get a gray note and what it says."

"That's all we have to do?" Joe pressed, staring. Grogan nodded and Ray snatched at the bills.

"I'll add two bills for every letter you hand over. Easy money."

"Do you work for the people who live in that house?" Joe asked.

"No," Grogan said. "They don't know, and I don't want them to know. We don't bother them." The truth, Marcy thought to herself ruefully. "How often do you get a note?"

"Once a week, sometimes more," Ray said, in a voice that was eager to please. The fast change in allegiance discomforted Marcy. She glanced out toward the path. Still empty. "We check the post office box every day."

"You ever ask for a meeting?"

"No..."

"Could you? Maybe ask for more money, or tell him that there's a complication."

"We're told not to ask questions." Joe fidgeted and Ray pulled out a pack of cigarettes. "To tell you the truth, we're afraid of the guy. You mind?"

Grogan shrugged. Joe scraped his boot in the debris on the shed floor as he waited for Ray to speak. Marcy could see him as a child, frightened and hungry, ready to do whatever he was told. She shook her head. That was either her imagination or thoughts of Gavan.

"The guy's starting to get into some crazy stuff," Ray said. "It's hard to back off now. We didn't mind searching the house. And the cat...hell, who likes cats? But this week we got a note to keep an eye on the kid who lives in that house."

"We don't want to get involved in that," said Whiny Joe quietly. "Nothing to do with a kid."

Marcy felt a rush of blood surge through her heart, creating a swelling sensation, as if it pressed against her back and chest. She felt like she was going to pass out. Somebody had found out about Gavan. Someone was out to destroy every part of her world. Grogan shot a hard look her way, an obvious warning to stay quiet. "Did the note say why?" Grogan asked, in a cool disinterested tone.

"No," Ray said. "But we kept an eye on the engineer and look what happened to him."

"I wanted to hate that kid," Joe added. "That family has everything. That kid doesn't know what it's like to have parents who think he's the biggest mistake of their entire life."

Ray nodded. "But we're not going after a kid. Especially after what happened to that other boy. We thought about going to the police after that last note, but we're both on probation."

"I only have two months left!" Joe exclaimed. "My wife would kill me!"

"We need money, but not that bad!" Ray concluded. "Maybe you can figure out how to keep us out of trouble."

"Are you with the police?" Joe asked, plaintively. "Or are you in trouble, too?"

"I'm not in trouble," Grogan said. "But I'm not with the police." Joe looked crestfallen. Grogan continued. "I have contacts. Maybe I can talk to the people who own the Shore Road house. If you call me right away about those damn notes, I can make sure that no charges will be pressed. And of course, the kid doesn't get hurt."

"Hell, no," said Joe. Ray shook his head.

"Stay in touch with this person," Grogan continued. "Act like you're going along. Don't argue. We don't want to give this guy any reason to go out and hire someone else."

"Christ, we're glad we met you." Joe looked ready to cry.

Grogan held out his hand and introduced himself, and Ray Roland and Joe Martiner gave names and shook hands with Grogan. Scowling, Marcy didn't move. The two men had invaded her home, killed her cat, pawed through her belongings. She'd never trust them. But she might as well have been a bag of fertilizer. Relying on a new friendship with Grogan, the two never looked her way. She clutched her pistol for comfort.

"How do we reach you?" Ray said.

Grogan reached into his pocket and handed Ray a pager. Pasted to the back were two telephone numbers. Grogan explained the first belonged to Ray's pager and the second belonged to Grogan's pager. "Ever use one?" Ray shook his head, and Grogan explained how the device worked. "After you page me, wait by the phone. I'll get back to you within ten minutes. Call the instant you hear anything."

Ray pocketed the card with instructions and clipped the pager to his belt. "I'd love to have my wife see me wear that," Joe said sadly.

"You two work it out," Grogan growled. "But someone wear it. All the time." He directed them to drive away first. As he opened the shed door, rain blew inside and the two men took off for the white van. Marcy wondered if they'd stop for the nachos and beer, to celebrate a new source of cash.

"I despise them," she said. Ignoring the dirt and rain, she sat on the floor and held her head with her hands.

"They're all we've got right now," Grogan said. He put one hand to her shoulder, then fastened the top button to her coat. "Let's get out of here." The path was muddy as they ran back about a quarter mile down the highway to the Tercel. Marcy's jeans were wet and heavy, scraping against her thighs.

"Gavan has to leave town," Marcy said. "Maybe we should all leave town together."

Grogan started the car and teased the accelerator, allowing the tires to ease out of the mud. "Removing the target won't eliminate the hunter."

"We can't use Gavan as bait!" Marcy cried. "Thanksgiving's next week. I can come back in two weeks. Why take a chance?"

Grogan kept his eyes on the road. "Someone willing to kill a kid is ruthless. He makes the rules to this game and changes them. He can hire other people, smarter ones than Ray and Joe. He could wait for you to return and finish the job. All it takes is patience and money. It's too late to run away. At last, we have an advantage. If the two bozos hand over the notes, then we're a step ahead."

Marcy stared out the window, furious about the two men. "How do we know we can trust them?"

Grogan checked the rearview mirror. "Well, they're not following us."

Marcy waved a hand in disgust. "They're too stupid. At least we should warn Gavan."

Grogan squeezed the Tercel into an illegal space three inches away from a Dumpster in ANB Harbor. Marcy was forced to squeeze past the steering wheel and climb out the driver's door. She had gained a fast twenty pounds and despised the bloated feeling. She vowed to return to her normal eating habits. The end of this adventure was near. She could feel it.

They went to the pay phone. A man held the phone with one hand and a dirty washcloth packed with ice against his mouth with the other. "Amm, ih hurhs," the man moaned. He struggled to explain something over the telephone about needing an appointment for "ho-hay." He waited and groaned. "Not Hur-hay. Ho-hay." He pointed out his broken tooth to Marcy.

Marcy couldn't take it anymore. She snatched the phone away. "Look, this gentleman's in pain. He needs to see a dentist now. Do you understand? It's an emergency."

"Oh, I didn't understand what he was asking," trilled the receptionist. She sounded like an eighteen-year-old, whose concept of pain was a boyfriend breaking a date. "Why, sure…"

Marcy hung up and kept the phone, shooing the man away. "Go! The dentist is waiting for you." She dialed her own number furiously and waited for the phone to ring as she watched the fisherman climb into a battered trick, with engine running. Marcy called out, "Good luck!" He waved his thanks.

ON THE EIGHTH RING, GAVAN answered the telephone.

"Honey, it's mom. How are you?"

"Fine, I guess…" He hesitated.

"Dad there?"

"Yes, my dad's here…" Gavan stared at his father and Beth. Both had stopped talking and watched Gavan on the telephone.

"He isn't alone," she said.

"No—"

"Be careful. Don't say anything. If he asks who called, I'm an annoying salesperson from Juneau, offering to clean carpets. You know what to say."

"Sure," Gavan agreed, cheerfully.

"Is it crew?"

"No."

"Business?"

"Close…"

"Well, it doesn't matter," she said. "Gavan, this isn't a game. You must be careful and stay close to Dad. You can't trust anyone."

Gavan couldn't think of a way to say how much he missed her, not with his father standing in the same room. And he had to end the call quickly or his father would get suspicious. His mother kept talking. "And no more wandering by yourself. But come see me tomorrow. Now, say something like, 'My parents will get back to you on that.'"

"My mom will get back to you on that," he said. "Hopefully soon!" Gavan slammed the phone down.

"Gavan, who was that?" his dad asked, pouring steaming tea into two hefty mugs.

Gavan looked at the cups and howled. "We only use those with Mom!"

"We ran out of cups, Gav," his father explained. "I forgot to run the dishwasher, okay?"

"You could have rinsed a few out. Mom wouldn't like that." He glared at Beth. His mother had bought the three mugs when Gavan was a baby—two rabbits at rest for the adults and a racing rabbit for the baby.

Beth bent her head with an amused smile, and proceeded to slowly add cream and sugar to her tea. She then raised her cup in a mock toast, antagonizing Gavan even more. "Perfect tea, Davy," she commented.

Gavan checked the jar for cookies. It was empty. "You forgot to buy stuff at the store," Gavan complained, hoping he could annoy Beth into leaving. "Mom always keeps this jar filled."

"Come to the store with me, and I won't forget," his dad said calmly. "Who called, Gavan?"

"Nobody important. A guy from Juneau who cleans carpets," Gavan replied. "He wanted to know if our rugs were dirty."

"You should have let me get rid of him."

"He wanted Mom, and so do I."

Gavan stared at the two adults, tempted to snatch his rabbit mug from Beth's hand. Damn, she'd probably ask for a second cup of tea and stay for dinner, too. Annoyed, he went upstairs and slammed the door to his bedroom.

Gavan stretched out on his bed and felt sorry for his father. Ever since Gavan had found his mother in ANB Harbor, he had felt less angry, less cheated, and his father didn't have that small bit of relief. Gavan toyed with the idea of giving his father a hint. If only Beth would leave… She wasn't helping at all. Gavan shook his head·and grabbed a library book on the history of gold in Alaska. Gavan decided his father didn't deserve knowing Marcy's secret, not if he expected ideas and help from Beth, while ignoring his own son.

DAVY WAITED A FEW MOMENTS until the door slammed upstairs and looked about in exasperation. The kitchen, with lots of windows, intricate white shelves and storage spaces, was large and country white. The sun highlighted the pottery and plates all in different shades of blue. The room was almost perfect without a complaining child.

"We miss Marcy," Davy apologized, sitting at the table. "It's been hard for Gavan."

"You hold your house together well," Beth teased. "Still the captain of the ship." He didn't laugh. Beth touched the rim of her cup. "Maybe you could try and join her."

His laugh was bitter. "But how? I would in a minute if I knew where she went."

"Surely she's been in touch?"

"No," Davy said. "All I know is what the police told me—she charged a few purchases in Venezuela and Brazil. She also withdrew a large amount of cash in Florida soon after she left here."

"Her other accounts have not been touched since," Beth said. Davy shook his head, not responding. He couldn't understand how his wife could possibly spend more than fifty thousand dollars. "Look, I remember the note," Beth said patiently. "You don't have to tell me anything."

"But I don't know anything," Davy said exasperated. "I

wish we'd ignored that note. She could be hurt. She could need me. And I wouldn't know. Beth, you'd tell me if you knew anything about her, wouldn't you?"

The woman set her rabbit mug down and nodded. "Of course."

"I'm worried." Davy stood and poured his tea down the sink. "Really worried. It's not like Marcy to follow orders." He glanced at the mug Beth was using. Gavan's comment had made him feel guilty, and he tried to think of a way to replace Beth's mug with another one.

"I know," Beth said wryly, picking it up and taking a long drink. "And Gavan takes after her. I can't believe she didn't get in touch with...someone."

"She must be scared," Davy said. "She didn't call you. And she didn't call Francesca, who's frantic and calls almost every day, asking if we heard anything. Who else would Marcy call?"

Beth raised her eyebrows and paused, before pointing upstairs.

"I doubt it." Davy shook his head, dismissing that idea with a laugh. "Gavan could never keep that secret."

"You said he's acting strange...surely he'd keep a secret for his mother."

"No," Davy said. "He'd burst if he knew where she was at. No, he's only acting strange because Marcy's not around."

"Did the school ever get back to you about the bruise on his face?"

"Gavan said the social worker asked him some questions at school," Davy said. "He insists he fell against a door jamb. We can only hope they believed him."

Beth held the mug, as if she studied the rabbit. "Marcy once told me they wanted to medicate him at school..." Davy did not reply, wondering where she was going. "Maybe you should try it while she's gone," Beth continued. "It could make your life easier. Especially if the school starts to investigate that bruise. Refusing to cooperate with them will not help your case."

"Marcy would never forgive me," Davy said. "Besides, I had the same problem as a kid."

"I remember," Beth said, nodding.

"Look, they didn't give me medicine, and I turned out all right," he insisted softly.

Beth held her empty teacup. "Only after Marcy won her money," she said. "Davy, hear me out before you get angry. That money gave you a big dose of confidence. It certainly didn't hurt your ability to fish. Maybe Gavan needs a dose of confidence right now. And this medicine does that. I'm your friend, and that's why I can be honest." She flipped her fine hair back.

"Not in this house, please," Davy said curtly, pointing upstairs. "I do not want to talk about the money in this house. Not around Gavan."

"Please, don't be angry with me," Beth pleaded.

"I'm not angry," Davy said, speaking low. "But you don't know how often I've worried that her money changes us in unknown ways. You don't know how often I wish I could go back in time and break up with Marcy."

Beth looked startled, and Davy continued quickly, trying to explain. "I just wish I had gone on fishing, and had some success before I asked her to marry me. The big catches might have happened anyway."

"Maybe, Davy." She stood and lightly placed her arms around his shoulders.

"But we'll never know. Anyhow, I've stopped caring about all that. I wish we had never told anyone about that money, not even you."

"You'd have had trouble investing it," Beth teased.

"Beth, you don't understand," Davy said. He stepped away

from her and went to the window to stare out at the Sound, it's colors sharp and brilliant in the sunshine. "I wouldn't care if that money disappeared tomorrow! All I know is how much I need Marcy now. I love her. I was silly to think that the money could have changed our feelings." He sighed and turned to face her again.

"You've been good, Beth." He continued to speak about his deepest fears aloud. "You never told anyone about Marcy and that money. I don't know if we'd have stayed together otherwise."

"I've always been good at keeping secrets," Beth agreed. "But who'd have thought Marcy could be this good?"

"It was her idea," Davy defended his wife. "I only wish that I could talk to her, find out that she's all right."

Beth bit her lip. "So, you're not angry with me?"

"Not at all," Davy said, gently. "And maybe you're right about Gavan. But I can't start anything while Marcy's gone."

"And if she doesn't come back? What if she likes whatever she's found?"

"How can you say that?" he asked, puzzled.

"She loves you, of course. But she's always wanted more…of something. Perhaps you should get prepared. In case…."

"Everyone wants more," Davy snapped. "Don't you?"

She smiled. "I upset you. I'm sorry." She carefully set her mug in the sink, donned her coat and slipped out the door, leaving Davy alone in the kitchen.

TWENTY-FIVE

Thursday, November 19

GAVAN SNEAKED ON BOARD *Sal II,* patiently timing every step with the rocking motion of the vessel. He stood at the cabin door to listen. In the galley, someone washed dishes and placed them in a rack to dry. The water went off—followed a moment later by the noise of someone sitting, as if the cushions had received a solid punch. Gavan crept inside, staring at the big man reading the newspaper. Slowly, Gavan slipped his hands over Grogan's eyes. "What the—" Grogan bellowed, shoving the hands away. "Christ, you scared me. How long have you been in here?" He wiped sweat from his forehead.

"Long enough to stab you in the back," Gavan said smugly. "Then wait and do the same to my mom."

Grogan shook his head and returned to his seat. "Pleasant thoughts for a kid."

"Don't make fun of my age. I could do a better job protecting my mother than you." Gavan pressed on as Grogan raised his eyebrows. "Detectives—the good ones—go all out for their clients. They don't eat all day."

"You read too many books, kid," Grogan replied. "And books always sound better than real life." He reached into the refrigerator for a beer and slammed a Pepsi in front of Gavan. Gavan let it sit unopened and asked about his mother. "Do you know how much trouble she's in?"

"That depends on how much you haven't told her."

Gavan looked away. "She had to leave town because some-one saw her with Kovach."

"Or because you have something that belonged to Kovach."

"They might want this." Gavan unfolded Kovach's map. "I found it in Kovach's pack. My mom told me to bring it by."

"Have you showed anyone else?"

"No…yes…well…."

"Which is it?" Grogan shot back. "Or have you forgotten which version is the truth?"

"I'll explain if you give me a chance, fat man."

Grogan surprised Gavan, moving swiftly despite his bulk and yanking Gavan to his feet by the ear. Gavan refused to flinch.

"You're an annoyance," Grogan said. "Is that how you got your bruise?" Gavan didn't answer. "You need to learn man-ners, son. If I thought pain would do the job, I'd try." He let the boy down and returned to the beer.

Gavan was about to speak, when he heard footsteps from the upper deck. His mother swung the door open. "Hi, honey," she said, happily kissing Gavan's cheek. "Have you been here long? I hurried, but I can see you two already met."

"Yeah," Gavan said. "We met." Gavan kept his tone neutral, and didn't go into detail. Grogan raised his eyebrows again, and Gavan smiled at the man's obvious surprise that a kid could re-frain from complaints over some rough treatment. Gavan pre-ferred handling his own problems, without help from his parents.

His mother didn't seem to notice the tension, speaking enough for all three of them. She handed the newspaper to Grogan and tapped the headline on the front page. Then she plucked six big chocolate-chip cookies from a wax-paper bag, arranging them on a plate. "I'll make hot chocolate…"

"Mom, this isn't home. Let's get on with business. I don't have much time, with Dad acting like the new director of homeland security."

She looked hurt. "I thought you might be hungry."

"Your friend will finish them off."

"Gavan!" she chided.

"Your mom will get home faster if we work as a team," Grogan said quietly, picking up a cookie. "This article is wild."

"Old Joe Frazier," Marcy said. "You can't believe a word he says."

Gavan leaned over the man's shoulder. The newspaper photo showed a grizzled man wearing a striped wool cap and holding a chunk of rock. His watery eyes and few remaining teeth gleamed.

Grogan read aloud: "'Sitkan Discovers Gold. Hundreds Head to Streams and Mountains. By Bob Denson. Joe Frazier emerged from the forest this weekend, displaying two large nuggets that he claimed to have panned from a stream near Cascade Creek—'"

"Note the 'claims,'" Marcy interrupted. "Denson doesn't believe him. Nobody does. He claims to sight more bears, whales, aliens, you name it, than all other Alaskans combined! Now gold!"

"Kovach was nowhere near Cascade Creek," Gavan noted.

"Any time there's a controversy in town, Frazier wants to be in the middle," Marcy explained. "He tells people that he's a retired physics professor. He confides to some that he was once nominated for a Nobel Prize. One week he claims native ancestry, and the next week another set of ancestors arrived on the Mayflower. One time he told a new reporter at the radio station that the governor from New York relied on him for economic forecasts! He constantly seeks attention."

Grogan continued reading for a few moments, then commented: "The state police never released the location where they found Kovach's body." He reached for another cookie. "I wonder if this guy has it right."

He continued to read the newspaper aloud: "'Historian and gold expert Larry Hanlo of Juneau, estimated the total value of Frazier's find at more than five hundred dollars. He added the size of the nuggets were unusual for an initial panning operation. Frazier refused to disclose the exact location of his find but demonstrated what he described as his own panning techniques for a crowd of one hundred at Oceanmart Grocery parking lot Wednesday afternoon. His fee was ten dollars.

"'Meanwhile, the Forest Service estimated that more than three hundred Sitkans and tourists ventured out into the forest yesterday with pans and maps in search of gold.

"'Most lack the necessary permits, according to Paul Genalli, spokesman for the Forest Service in Sitka. "Individuals can search and pan for gold in the Tongass National Forest, but a permit is required," Genalli advised. The permit fee is twenty dollars and comes with tips on panning and precautions for hiking in the Tongass National Forest. So far, more than fifty people have received warnings. Rangers will issue notices-of-violation beginning today.

"'Alaska Airlines, the Alaska Marine Highway and Southeast Alaska Tourism officials report record-breaking numbers of inquiries about Sitka from potential visitors....'"

"Fool's gold," Marcy scoffed. "I guarantee that Frazier discovered that gold in a Juneau shop. He'll more than make his money back with his workshops."

"Sitka will cash in on this gold either way," Grogan said.

Listening to the article, Gavan remembered Kovach aiming and tossing rocks into the stream, all the tiny little splashes. "Maybe Kovach's gold is fake, too," Gavan mused.

"The man's dead," Marcy snapped. "It's easy to blame him for everything."

"Hey, let's review all possibilities," Grogan said. "Not jump on one another's ideas. Gavan could have a point. And somebody is worried, about what you know."

"Are men really watching me and Dad?" Gavan asked, keeping his eyes down.

"That's what they said." His mother sounded nervous. "They promised to tell Grogan any plans."

A small alarm went through Gavan, and he hoped he managed to hide it from Grogan. He didn't like the idea of depending on a warning from the detective. He checked the man's expression. The big man did not smile. "What do the men look like?" Gavan asked.

"Don't even think about confronting them," Grogan said, sharply. "Your job is to stay close to school and your father."

"Dad's been crazed since they found Kovach," Gavan said, claiming a cookie. "He won't let me out of sight!"

"He's not doing a very good job if you're here," Marcy commented.

"I can trick him, especially when he's with Beth," Gavan said. "He could care less about me when she's around." His mother looked up with a frown, and Gavan immediately regretted the comment. Beth showed unusual concern for his father, but Gavan was sure the interest was not mutual. Still, he wanted to test for his mother's reaction. "She calls every day, and visits every other. I'm sick of her. I'm sick of you and Dad being apart."

"Are they—"

"Sleeping together?" he interrupted. "Not yet."

"That's not what I meant."

"Well, that's the bottom line. I'm a teenager, but I know about adults." He looked pointedly from Grogan to Marcy.

"Gavan!" his mother warned.

"Dad and Beth don't look right, and neither do the two of you!" Gavan insisted.

His mother looked relieved rather than angry. "Grogan and I work together. I'm sure that Dad and Beth are trying to get answers. More than you realize."

Gavan put his elbows on the table, hands under his chin and thought about that. "Mom, then why didn't you call Dad as soon as you came back? Don't you trust him?"

"Of course, I trust him," his mother said. "But men are watching the house, and any of us could be in danger. I must admit that I'm amazed you have kept a secret. It's big, and too much for me to expect of you."

"I'm older than you think, Mom," Gavan replied. "I feel old."

Grogan interrupted. "We need more ideas. If we figure this out, you'll be back together bickering in a week."

"That's not fair," Marcy protested.

"Enough!" Grogan bellowed. He dropped to a businesslike tone. "Gavan brought a map."

Gavan carefully pulled the map from his pocket, and watched as his mother and the detective studied the wrinkled piece of paper. "No names, no scale," Gavan explained, pointing. "This could be a trail anywhere. But I'm sure that this is the stream where Tim and I watched Kovach that day. Do you have a topographic map of that part of the island?"

Marcy rummaged through papers in the bookcase and found the topo. Gavan spread it out. "But see, the stream's not on these maps."

"Are you sure you didn't get mixed up somehow?" Marcy asked. "The Tongass is huge."

Gavan shook his head emphatically and pointed to lines on the wrinkled map. "The first day we saw Kovach at the small stream. The second day he took me to the larger stream. I'm sure he wanted me to think the two streams were the same."

"I need glasses," Grogan said. "This writing is minute."

"Engineers," Gavan added matter-of-factly.

"Don't generalize," his mother said.

"He smoked dope," Gavan added, in a helpful manner. "That's not like an engineer."

His mother didn't respond, and that annoyed Gavan. She

was getting better at ignoring his most aggravating comments, but he knew she wasn't happy.

"The map isn't labeled, almost as if he didn't finish," Grogan mused. "And see the little X's along the inside curves of this small stream. You said Kovach went to different streams on the two days. What else was different?"

"Everything," Gavan said. "He took a different boat each day. And when I was alone with him, we walked, and he took measurements and collected a lot of water in little bottles. When Tim and I spied on him, he didn't do any of that. All he did was pull stuff, maybe rocks, from a bag and toss them into the water. And then I found the one rock in his pack, the one that had gold. So either he found that one rock, or..."

"Do you have the rock?" Grogan asked.

"It's downstairs," Marcy said. Gavan and Grogan waited quietly, and a few moments later, she returned with the rock retrieved from her bunk below.

"My teacher at school told me it was gold," Gavan said, pointing and then handing the rock over to Gavan. "He knows geology around here."

Grogan examined it. "Could that stream be too small for an official map?" the man asked.

"No, there are other streams just as small," Gavan noted.

"Topographic maps are thorough," Marcy said. "But mistakes happen."

Grogan stood. "Kovach planting the gold, that's quite an accusation. How much did you see him throwing into the stream?"

"At least two bags, the size of a lunch bag," Gavan said. Grogan extracted a cigarette from his pocket. As the detective snapped the lighter, Gavan wrinkled his nose.

"Please, Mike, not in such a tight space," Marcy murmured. Grogan extinguished the cigarette. "Bander must have hired Kovach," she continued bitterly. "Bander knew exactly how to get his road through."

Grogan pointed to the newspaper. "The road might pay off for tourism. But how does Bander gain?"

Gavan had no answer, and neither did his mother.

"And even if Tim's dad paid for the gold, he didn't kill Tim," Gavan added.

"And we still don't know if the note has anything to do with Tim or the road," Grogan said. "Au is the symbol for gold on the periodic table." He picked up the map and stared at it.

"Should we call the police?" Marcy asked.

"All we can say is the gold's fake, and we can't prove that," Grogan said. "The police would pin it on Kovach, and that doesn't help much. We still have Ray and Joe. Maybe they'll learn more, and then we can go to the police." Grogan plucked a pager from a nearby drawer and handed it to Gavan. "Gavan, we need your help. Carry this. If we hear from Ray and Joe, I want to reach you immediately."

"Cool!" Gavan turned and admired the pager. "This is better than a cell phone."

"Be discreet," Marcy warned. "Don't show off at school."

"Mom," he said with a groan. "Stop worrying."

Grogan showed Gavan how the pager was set for vibrations rather than a loud noise. "If we page you, get to a phone fast. And stay close to your father or aunt or school. Somewhere safe." He also asked Gavan to check in with his mother twice a day by leaving a code of three zeroes on her beeper; for immediate help, he should leave a telephone number.

"I better get home," Gavan said. "Dad will start worrying."

"Do you want a ride?" Grogan offered.

"No. I'll stop by the library first and grab a book. That's where I told Dad I was going."

"Stay alert," his mother said.

Gavan stood and reached for the map, but Grogan covered the scrap with his thick hand. "Can we hang on to this?" Grogan asked.

"I found it," Gavan contended stubbornly.

"All right," Grogan said. He studied the map for a moment, before relinquishing it. "Don't lose it. It's evidence."

"I won't," Gavan said, carefully folding and returning the map to his pocket. He donned his coat, then paused in the doorway to hug his mother. "Do you still love Dad?" he whispered in her ear.

"Of course," she said.

The boy pulled up a hood over his head, leaped onto the dock and took off running.

MARCY STOOD ON THE DECK, watching Gavan leave the harbor and cross the street.

Grogan joined her. "Why does he do the opposite of whatever we ask? He's an okay kid. But he doesn't like me."

"It's not you," Marcy said, rubbing an ache in her shoulder. "That's how he acts with almost everyone. Everyone except Tim."

"He'll find another friend."

"Not if he doesn't give anyone a chance." Marcy frowned as Gavan paused to cross the street, then took a left on Katlian rather than a right toward the library. "He's not going to the library."

"Maybe he changed his mind," Grogan said.

"He changes his mind a lot," she said, with irritation. "He doesn't exactly lie, but he exaggerates. Fantasizes, like worrying about you and me having an affair. And Beth and Davy."

"I believe him about the gold," Grogan replied.

"I do, too," Marcy said. "But no one else will. Why did you let him take that map?"

"Why not? I'm tired of fighting. He intends to return to that stream. I memorized the map and he has, too. If we'd argued, he'd have left the pager and be on his way up there now. Why antagonize him?" With that, Grogan sat at the table with the topographic map. In less than ten minutes, he sketched out a rough version of Kovach's map. "If he checks in on the pager twice a day, he won't have time to go to the stream. If he doesn't check in, then we know where to look for him." Grogan tapped his map.

"Easier said than done," Marcy said, wryly. "Gavan moves like a wild animal in the woods." She stared out the window. "Why did he say he's going to the library and head up Katlian Street?"

"Look, I'll take the car in that direction and make sure he gets home," Grogan offered, going for his coat.

GAVAN KNEW THAT FEW people would believe his theory about Kovach and the gold. Sitka adults regarded him as the young version of old-man Frazier. And so Gavan had to prove that the gold had been deliberately sprinkled into the stream. He jogged to the parking lot, before realizing he'd left his bicycle at school.

He walked up Katlian Street, passing four dogs snarling over an empty McDonald's wrapper. Gavan passed the seafood plant and stared inside at a line or workers, draped in thick rubber aprons, as they trimmed fish and rinsed the stiff bodies of black cod. Refrigeration motors, fans and rushing water combined for a steady roar. Gavan leaned against the wall and focused on the noise, chasing all the worries from his mind.

He wished he had kept more from the engineer's pack. There had to be a clue. What happened to that pack anyway? The newspaper had never mentioned it.

That one day, his last with Tim, would remain more clear than any other yesterday for the rest of his life. But Gavan shoved aside all feelings for Tim to focus on the details of that day: kneeling in the soft moss and dirt, laughing as they extracted the camera, maps, papers, granola from Kovach's pack. But the memory always ended with the awful scream and offered no clues.

The noise from the plant equipment returned and Gavan resumed walking. He never had the chance to read over the papers in the pack. That had been a major mistake. He wondered if the police had found all the papers. If they had found the pack, they would have developed the film in the camera and called Gavan back for more questions. Or, maybe not…Kovach might have hidden the pack again somewhere along the trail. Gavan decided to call the police and ask specifically about the engineer's pack. As he hurried along, Grogan pulled alongside and rolled down the window.

"Your mom asked me to check on you," Grogan said. "She's wondering why you didn't head for the library."

"I forgot my bike at school," Gavan replied. "You two have better people to check on than me."

"I told her it was something like that," Grogan said calmly. Beth's brown Oldsmobile pulled up behind Grogan and a horn honked. "Someone you know?" Grogan asked.

"A friend of my mom's," Gavan replied.

"She'll ask about me," Grogan said quickly. "Stay cool. I only asked for directions." He casually waved and pulled away.

Beth rolled her window down and called out. "Hey, Gavan. Who's that?"

He stared after Grogan. "Guy who needed directions."

"In Sitka?" she said, raising her eyebrows.

"Another dumb tourist," Gavan said, with a shrug.

She watched the Tercel disappearing around the corner and then offered Gavan a ride. He had always refused. But November's sun went down early, and dark clouds smothered the mountains. His father would be furious, if Beth even mentioned that she had seen Gavan talking with some stranger. Gavan could not risk his father asking a lot of questions, not if Gavan wanted to hike to Silver Bay and find Kovach's pack or some other clue. The bike could wait.

Gavan kept his voice friendly. "Sure, I'd love a ride home." He opened the door and slid into the seat. The upholstery was worn, spotted. The square tank of an Oldsmobile with sagging fenders was more than ten years old and in tough shape. Somehow, it didn't fit Beth's personality. She was a perfectionist, from the precise haircut to the sharp pink-painted ovals of her fingernails. He thought about his mom's hands, the short no-nonsense nails, the skin lined but soft, and wished that he could hold that hand. He wouldn't care about feeling like a little kid. He could kick himself for not thanking her for the cookies. In the meantime, he had to work on being polite to her best friend.

"It's nice of you to stop and give me a ride, Beth," Gavan said.

She glanced over, obviously surprised. "No problem. What are you up to so late in the afternoon, Gavan?"

"Stuff at the library. Then I left my bike at school. But it'll be there tomorrow. Do me a favor and don't tell my dad? He doesn't like me walking alone. I told him I was with a friend," Gavan admitted. "It makes him happy to think I have friends."

She nodded. "Don't feel bad," she said. "Friends aren't easy to come by, and it only gets harder the older you get. People have their families, jobs, old friends. It's hard to make room in life for the new people who come along."

Gavan nodded. He understood why his parents liked Beth so much. Most adults asked children a series of questions and expected shallow answers about school or hobbies. Conversations with Beth were two-way. She constantly proved how much she listened to every word. But Gavan wondered how much of that was friendship and how much of that was her training as a lawyer.

"I worry, though, about you talking with strangers." She bit her bottom lip. "Even in Sitka."

"Yeah." Gavan focused on keeping his answers short and agreeable. He certainly didn't need a lawyer disrupting his plans. "But I'm careful."

"You can't ever be too careful," she agreed. "So what do you think about the gold fever in Sitka?" she asked, slowing for Sitka's only traffic light as it turned yellow. "Do the kids talk about it much?"

"Some," he said, scowling. "A few kids want to go out and start searching. All the ones who have never gone out hiking before. Nobody really knows where it's at, though."

"And you're not tempted?"

"I haven't been in the woods since Tim died," Gavan said, staring at the glass of the windshield.

"That's understandable," she said softly, pulling the Olds into his family's driveway, behind Davy's truck and his aunt Francesca's Honda.

She kept the car running, as Gavan opened the door. "You're not coming in?" he asked.

She flashed a smile. "I can't. I'm going to meet a client. Tell your father and aunt that I said hello. And Gavan," she paused. "Explore the places that you explored with Tim. Don't be afraid to remember." He looked down and paused, resisting the urge to slam the car door. He didn't want to talk about Tim. "But don't go out in the forest alone," she cautioned. "And hey, I enjoyed talking with you. We should try it more often."

Gavan mumbled his thanks and watched her drive away, relieved she did not come in. Somehow, Gavan knew she wouldn't tell his father about walking alone in town.

He removed his shoes outside and entered quietly, hoping that his aunt had distracted his father about the time. Davy had given permission for Gavan to visit the library after school, but Gavan carried no library books, and his father might ask about that. His father would ground Gavan if he knew the boy had been near the docks, and Gavan needed to be free to find answers about Tim and Kovach and the gold. Crossing the hallway, Gavan heard his father in the kitchen. "…called the police. She told me to expect a visit tomorrow."

Gavan paused to listen.

"You need a lawyer," Francesca said. "Call Beth."

"I don't want to involve her. She thinks Gavan should be on Ritalin, too. It's too embarrassing. Besides, calling my lawyer so quickly makes me look guilty."

"You can't fix this on your own."

"How do I explain my wife's disappearance?"

"That's not your fault. Call the detectives and explain everything. Show them the note." His father did not answer. "What did Gavan say about his face?" Francesca pressed.

Gavan wanted to scream in frustration. Fenlow had taunted him, then accompanied him to the principal's office, where the school nurse and a social worker asked dozens of questions, repeating themselves over and over. Gavan had given answers to protect his mother, but never intended to implicate his father. His aunt was right, his dad should call Beth. A lawyer would scare the principal.

"He told me he fell into a doorway. But I guess he refused to go into detail with the social worker at school."

"Kids," Francesca muttered. "Where is he?"

"He's supposed to be upstairs doing homework. But he's been working at the library a lot lately, on a project with some other kids."

"Davy, keep a close eye on him. He could get in trouble wandering around."

"I know. Francesca, what will happen if that social worker convinces the cops that I hurt Gavan?"

She looked down. "There's no proof. But with Marcy gone, who knows? The worst, they could put Gavan in a foster home while they investigated or until Marcy got back."

"They can't prove it because I didn't do it!"

"When it comes to protecting kids, they don't always wait until guilt is proven."

"Would they take him right away?"

"I don't know," Francesca said. "Call the police, Davy! You never called about the prowler, did you?"

"That was more than a week ago. I haven't seen anyone since."

"Are you waiting for a disaster?" Francesca asked. "Call about that prowler and the note! I worry about Gavan. I should be spending more time here."

"Damn it, I'm doing the best I can. The kid's making it to school on time. The homework's getting done. He's safe. I don't need these complications." Davy groaned. "I cannot stand dealing with the police and investigators about my son!"

Gavan sympathized with his father and remembered a story about his father as a child. Not long after reading about a classmate of Gavan's who had been caught shoplifting, both his parents had warned him against stealing and to stay away from other teens who might decide to shoplift. Then, his father had explained how he had once been accused of shoplifting as a child. The dark-haired native boy had made the mistake of standing in the drugstore and pulling out a pack of gum purchased from another convenience store. Davy had lacked a receipt and tried to point out that six pieces were missing from the pack and only one piece was in his mouth. But nobody listened. "Son, this man's a pharmacist," the officer had said. "Why would he lie?" At the police station, Davy had called his mother and explained. She then walked two miles to the other store, showed the man a photo of her son and pleaded with him to speak with the police. That store manager had immediately left his store and drove her back to the police station, to help defend Davy.

"Kids don't hang on to a pack of gum all day," the officer on duty had drawled. His father had described how Gavan's grandmother had responded with a long unblinking stare, while the convenience store manager had protested: "That kid's in my store almost every day," the man had exclaimed. "He's all right, I tell you!"

The police then released Davy. Apologies were exchanged between the pharmacist and the police. Gavan asked whether anyone had apologized to his father. Davy had shrugged and shook his head no. But he never left a store again without a receipt.

Gavan felt guilty about causing problems for his father. The man was always so quiet, so nervous about his reputation in town, so conscientious about his boat and all his belongings. Gavan had tried to explain the bruise, and never asked the school to call with questions. His father must feel like he needed a receipt, some proof, to keep his child. Gavan frowned, wondering why the social worker didn't believe Gavan's story about a door jamb.

"Be honest with the police and urge Gavan to do the same," she told Davy. "Maybe they can help us contact Marcy somehow, by tracing her credit card charges. Cops do that for people, Davy, but only for people who ask."

There was a pause and Gavan heard the refrigerator shut and close. "Maybe I'll send Gavan out of town, to cousin Ronny in Angoon," he said. "Just for a week or two."

"I don't know, Davy, sending him away now could make you look guilty."

"Too much weird stuff is happening. We can take the ferry."

"For how long?"

"Until Marcy returns," Davy said with a shrug.

Gavan wondered if he could refuse to leave Sitka? Why did his parents make decisions about him and tell other people first? And they wondered why he had to take matters into his own hands? He pressed his face against the wall. The bruise, faded to purple and yellow, still stung.

Davy continued: "Angoon's contained, safe. No stranger can step into the village without being noticed."

"If you're sure it's a stranger." Her silver bracelets made a ringing noise, moving against one another. "People assume it's easier to rob, hurt, kill strangers. But it's not. The best criminals get to know the victim. They find reasons for resentment. And it wouldn't take much to resent you and Marcy."

"Our money," Davy said, bitterly.

"Not the money!" Francesca snapped. "Your health. Love."

"Anybody can make that kind of life," Davy said.

"Really?" she asked. "You can say that with Marcy gone? If she didn't come back, you'd duplicate her?" He didn't answer. "Have you thought about what you'd do if Marcy didn't come back?"

"That's what Beth asked," Davy said. "Do you both know something that I don't?"

"No," Francesca spoke quickly. "But it's not like Marcy to leave and not contact us. She couldn't stand not knowing about Gavan. She's either talking with someone else in town or she's hurt. And we have no idea how to reach her."

"It's all I think about every day." His father returned to his chair and his voice was muffled and forlorn. "I hope he fits in. Angoon's a small village."

"He's your son. He'll do fine."

Gavan moved quietly upstairs and started his homework, ignoring the rest of the conversation. His father wanted to banish him to Angoon! Rarely in his short life had Gavan felt like he was the only one who could solve a problem. But that had changed. In his heart, Gavan hoped that Grogan and his mother planned to use him for bait. They could trap the killer by following Gavan. But if Gavan had to leave town for Angoon, Tim's killer could go undiscovered forever. Gavan shivered and reached for the quilt on his bed, draping it over his shoulders. Then, he hunched over the math. Gavan would work quietly, until his father came upstairs—and pretend that he had been home all along.

Gavan figured he only had a day or two. In the meantime, his father wouldn't let him out of his sight, and Gavan couldn't skip school the following day. He had a test in math, and the principal would call home if he missed that.

But school was getting out early before the Thanksgiving break. That might give him enough time to return to the Tongass. Somewhere in the center of the forest, he'd find Kovach's pack or some other clue. Something that would let everyone know the truth.

TWENTY-SIX

Friday, November 20

AS THE SCHOOL BUS TOOK A LAZY turn into the school's circular driveway, Gavan noticed the Tercel parked across the street. Gavan could see Grogan sitting in the driver's seat and staring, prepared to spy on Gavan. Gavan walked away from the bus, toward school and ignored the car. Once inside the school, he stood at a window and watched the Tercel roar away.

He went to the pay phone and called the police department. Detective Dansby paused and then admitted that the police had never located Kovach's pack. Gavan thanked the detective and worked efficiently throughout the day at his classwork. He wanted to walk out the moment the bell rang and could not afford any delays, such as a teacher demanding that he stay after school.

He finished the math test easily. During social studies, he caught himself reading the same paragraph over and over. Nothing could erase the image of the forest, the splash of water against rocks, leaves tickling his neck as he sat next to a friend and watched the engineer. Gavan couldn't wait to walk the forest and find that pack, discovering the reason why Tim and Dennis were dead. And if Gavan found out why his mother had to leave town, maybe he wouldn't have to go to Angoon.

After class, Gavan walked through the crowded hallway, tapping a pencil against the lockers and ignoring other kids, none of whom came close to Tim. At the end of the long hallway, the window revealed a brilliant sky for November, perfect for setting out on a long trek through the Tongass. He couldn't linger, though, with sunset before four p.m.

He had prepared for the hike that morning. His pack contained the map, food, water, fire starter, and his father's high-beam flashlight. No sleeping bag. He'd stay awake and work all night if necessary. He'd be in trouble for going into the Tongass alone, no matter how long he stayed, so he had to make the most of the trip.

The biggest problem was the fat man. Gavan had hoped to hop on the school bus that traveled the opposite direction from his own home, out Sawmill Creek Road. Then he had planned to hitch a ride the rest of the way, to where the trail began. But the trip was ruined if Grogan followed. Somehow Gavan had to get past the detective.

A hand touched his shoulder and startled Gavan. "How's it going, Gavan?" Mr. Jabard smiled. "You haven't been by to visit lately."

"I have a lot of homework and a test practically every day."

"It gets tougher every year. You know, Gavan, I want to ask..." His voice dropped low. "The gold you found. Is it connected to the gold they found on Baranof?"

Gavan nodded and looked around before speaking. "But I can't talk about it here."

"I agree," the teacher murmured.

"I'm going to the stream where it came from after school."

"What do you hope to find?"

"Proof that the gold's not real. Proof about who killed Tim."

Jabard looked impressed. "Do you need help?" he asked.

Gavan hesitated. He longed to solve this problem alone. If he involved anyone, the adult would get all the credit. But Gavan was running out of time. Mr. Jabard thought like a scientist, and he was one of the few teachers who was fair and saw potential in every kid. Gavan was a fool to hesitate. Nobody else cared.

"Have you talked with anyone else?" Jabard whispered.

"No," Gavan didn't mention his mother. She wasn't supposed to be in town. Besides, Gavan would sound like a little kid if he mentioned her.

"Do you want to work alone?" Jabard asked. "Or could you use some help?"

Gavan decided. "That would be great if you came with me. But we have to be careful. Someone's following me."

Jabard furrowed his brow. "Who?"

Gavan appreciated how the teacher believed him and didn't act patronizing. "A detective. Hired by my mother." Gavan looked about the hallway. Kids dispersed and headed to classes. "He followed me to school and he'll try to follow me home. He waits in an old car parked across the street."

"Does your father know?" Gavan shook his head. Jabard's hand lingered on Gavan's shoulder and he nodded. "We'll be all right. My Jeep's in the parking lot. It's maroon. If you want my help, meet me there after school. Wait in the back. And don't let anyone see you get inside."

THE BEEPER WENT OFF WHILE Marcy and Grogan pushed their shopping cart through the cookie aisle. Marcy grabbed the beeper from her pocket and checked—three zeroes, Gavan's signal for arriving home from school. The boy had paged them too early, just before school let out. "I don't like it," Grogan grumbled. "School lets out early today. He's going to make his move."

The school was less than a block away from the grocery store, and Marcy readily abandoned the cart. "Let's get over to the junior high," she said.

"If he doesn't get on that school bus, we know where he's headed," Grogan said, hurrying to the car.

Grogan's reaction increased her own anxiety. Since Ray and Joe agreed to share their information, Grogan no longer prevented her from walking about town. The detective didn't admit it, but he was ready to taunt the writer of the gray notes and force him into making a mistake. Marcy's pager vibrated again. She caught up with Grogan.

"Not Gavan," she said, disappointed and showing him the pager. At the pay phone, Grogan dialed, and Ray Roland answered on the first ring. Marcy pressed close to Grogan's shoulder.

"Yeah, what's up?" Grogan asked. He listened for a minute. "No, play along for now. We don't call the police yet. Not until we know who the writer is." Grogan hung up and turned to Marcy. "They got another note."

"What did it say?"

"Nothing about Gavan specifically," he said, checking his watch. "But I want to watch him climb on that bus and head home." Marcy started to open the car door, but Grogan stopped her. "I'm hanging on to the cell phone. You stay by this phone. The minute Gavan's due home, call and warn him that someone could make a move tonight. In the meantime, I'm going to follow his bus."

"Wait, Grogan," Marcy pressed. "What did the note say?"

"Ray and Joe are supposed to get a boat ready with weights," Grogan said quietly. "That could mean anything. But we have to be prepared for the worst."

Grogan climbed into the car and started the engine, heading toward the junior high where students would soon race out, eager to board waiting school buses. Impatient, Marcy stared at the pay phone—a block of heavy metal with greasy fingerprints, the short metal cord, rigid time limits and monotone recorded voices. The symbol of distrust and loneliness was her only link to Gavan, and she anxiously counted the minutes before she could call.

SCHOOL LET OUT WITH A SHRILL bell and the shrieks of happy students. Gavan, sticking close to a group of eighth graders, left by a different door than usual and hugged the building as he checked the parking lot. Spotting the Jeep immediately, he climbed into the back and stretched out along the seat. The vehicle smelled brand-new and was free of clutter. His heart pounded and he was ready to start the trek into the woods. The day was mild for Sitka in November, perfect for a hike.

Waiting, he checked the pager—making sure the alarm was still on vibration. He dared not let the pager go off at school or he'd have to answer questions, first from the principal and later from his father. He didn't want to answer questions from Jabard about his mother either, so he kept it on the vibration setting and jammed the small black box into his jeans. Soon, he'd be on his way, and maybe the next page to his mother would include an answer. He smiled at the thought of telling her that she could come home before Thanksgiving.

Minutes later, the teacher opened the driver's door and started the Jeep. Gavan sat up a bit, and caught Mr. Jabard smiling into the rear-view mirror. "Where's the man who's following you?" the teacher asked.

"Across the street," Gavan said, peering out the window, as Jabard slowly exited the school lot. "The little green Toyota. He's watching the buses."

Jabard laughed. "Some car! He can't be much of a detective. Is he following us?"

"No. But why are you turning left? Why aren't you headed toward Silver Bay?"

"I'm heading to my house first. We need decent food! You need a sleeping bag and warmer clothes. You don't have to hurry so much now that you have a ride." Jabard kept up an easygoing chatter in a low, protective voice.

Gavan reached for his small pack. He had saved most of a

large lunch that he had packed himself earlier in the morning. He had dressed comfortably, ready to work all night. Adults had access to cars and money, but they planned too much and were slow to start. For Gavan, no plans meant endless options. He had hoped that Jabard would understand the need for hurry. Deep inside, a feeling nagged Gavan that inviting the teacher was a mistake.

Driving away from the school, Gavan sat up and stared at the hazy mounds of island scattered throughout the Sound and frowned. He had lost control of finding Kovach's pack. That shouldn't matter, he told himself over and over. At least he was solving the problem without his parents, Beth and Grogan. And all he really cared about was finding the engineer's pack and getting his mother home.

ABOUT TWENTY MINUTES LATER, Jabard's Jeep bounced along a one-time logging road, rough and rarely used. "I didn't know this road was here," Gavan said, amazed.

"The government paid for the road, and the logging was stopped by a lawsuit—seems the road ran right over old Indian burial grounds."

"Should we be driving on it?"

"One car won't hurt," Jabard said. Gavan was about to argue when he was startled by the pager's vibration against his hip. He slipped his hand down his side and turned the beeper off, not bothering to check the number. He knew his mother. She'd continue paging all night long. Electronic nagging. He couldn't return the call out here. He wished he could reassure her and tell her that he was not alone.

MARCY STARED AT HER WATCH and slowly dialed her own telephone number. The school bus should have pulled away from Shore Road at least two minutes ago.

Davy picked up on the second ring, and Marcy quickly

hung up and swore. She then tried the number to Gavan's pager, waiting for the beeps and punching the number to the pay phone. She hung up, annoyed, wanting to call home again, but knowing that Davy would answer the phone again. So, she called Gavan's pager again and punched in Francesca's number. A group of high school girls stood waiting to use the phone, and Marcy reluctantly stepped aside. She leaned against the wall and lit a cigarette waiting for Grogan to return or Gavan to call. The cigarette was her timer. When it was done, she'd try Gavan again and Grogan. And then Francesca.

DAVY QUICKLY LET BETH IN the kitchen door and caught the ringing telephone. "Hello," he said. "Hello?" Then he slammed the phone down. "A hangup," he fumed. "Someone's checking on us."

"But who would do that?" Beth asked him. "Don't worry so."

Davy paced through the kitchen. "The social worker's due here at two-thirty. First, I don't know where Marcy's at, and now I don't know where my kid's at. But my lawyer's standing here ready to go. Damn it all!"

"Did Gavan call?"

"He left a message on the machine this morning that he's spending the night with a friend. He neglected to mention which one."

"At least he left a message. You can play it for the social worker."

Davy leaned over the counter and glared at the phone and then at Beth. "He should have talked with me. I have no idea where he's at."

"Let me talk when the social worker comes," Beth advised, removing her coat and shaking her hair free from the black velvet collar of her suit. "You're overwrought. Gavan will call later."

"He doesn't have a toothbrush. Nothing to wear. Besides, we have to get ready to leave for Angoon."

"Davy, stay calm with the school officials. No matter what the school officials suggest, remain agreeable."

"Damn it, Beth, you're not a parent. And believe me, you don't know how lucky you are!" He paced, then suddenly halted by the window overlooking the street. "Damn! Call the police, Beth. Get them here right away." He headed for the stairs, as Beth went to the window and checked the street. She called and asked Davy what was wrong.

Moments later, Davy returned with a small key. "That car outside. It's a man who's been casing our house. I'm getting to the bottom of this now." He unlocked his gun cabinet and pulled a pistol from the top shelf, then unlocked a small drawer below and removed bullets.

"The green car?" Beth asked, still standing by the window. Davy nodded. She gripped his arm. "Wait, that's the same car that stopped for Gavan this week, just before I gave him a ride. Gavan said the man asked for directions! I thought it was strange then, directions in Sitka." She stared out the window. "And now he's here. I'm sure it's the same car and man. Do you know who he is?"

"No idea," Davy said. "I only saw him once before."

"Let's wait a few minutes, Davy, and watch what he does before you go out. Why, he's not even looking at your house."

Davy checked the window again and pointed to the corner. "No, but he's staring at the school bus stop, and Gavan's due home any second. I'm not letting this guy get away a second time." Davy donned his jacket, put the loaded pistol into the side jacket and opened the kitchen door. "Just call the police, give this address and tell them it's an emergency outside," he ordered.

MARCY'S STOMACH TWISTED as she realized Grogan had ample time to watch Gavan get on the school bus and return a message to her pager. Worried, she checked the clock near the cash registers and her watch. She couldn't call her house again. The hangups would infuriate Davy. She dialed Gavan's pager number and after a series of short beeps, punched in Francesca's phone number once again. Surely, he'd call his favorite aunt.

She lowered her voice and suggested to the receptionist that she had a story for the television reporter. She stared at initials scratched into the metal of the telephone as she waited.

"Yes, sorry to keep you waiting," said Francesca, breathless. "Can I help you?"

"Hi, Francesca, it's me, Marcy!" Marcy could hear the gasp.

"Marcy! Thank goodness! Where are you?" Francesca's voice was jubilant, and Marcy cautioned the other woman not to use the name.

"Have you called Davy?" Francesca asked.

"Not yet," Marcy said, regretting that her first call to Francesca was so disorganized. "I can't."

"He's terrified that he might not see you again. Where are you?"

Marcy explained how she was in town, in disguise and getting close to finding out why she had to leave. "But Gavan could be in trouble. Has he called you today? In the last few minutes?"

"No," Francesca said.

"Could he have left a message? At the desk?"

"Everyone here knows to get me immediately if he calls."

"It's probably not a problem," Marcy said, gripping the phone. "But Francesca, could you call Davy and ask about Gavan?"

"Marcy, Davy's been going insane with worry about Gavan and you… You can call him… He's planning on taking Gavan to Angoon."

"I can't call him yet," Marcy said. "The threat's real and someone's after Gavan. Please, call and ask if he's all right?

I'll call you back in two minutes." Marcy hung up and waited and dialed. Francesca's line was busy. She punched the number again.

Francesca answered immediately, and her voice was somber. "He's not home. Neither's Davy, for that matter. Beth answered in a panic. But she also told me that Gavan called and left Davy a message. He's spending the night with a friend."

"What friend?"

Francesca sighed. "I asked that, but Gavan didn't say. He only left a message on the answering machine. Davy's pretty upset, according to Beth."

"I don't blame him. If Gavan calls, talk him into going home and staying close to Davy. Or you. It's urgent."

"Maybe everything will be all right," Francesca said. "Besides, maybe Davy is onto something, too. Beth said Davy just called the police about some man who's been following Gavan."

"Did she describe him?" Marcy asked warily, wondering if Grogan shouldn't be keeping an eye on Ray and Joe.

"All I know is that he's in an old green car."

"I don't believe this!" Marcy said, frantic. "That's my friend! And Davy called the police on him? Francesca, can I borrow your car?"

"Sure. Where are you?"

"Lakeside Grocery."

Francesca let out a low whistle. "That must be some disguise! Hey, I'm headed for the Katmai Shee office. You can walk there by the time I arrive. I'll leave the door open, the extra key's under the mat."

"Thanks for the car. I could be a while."

"I can always borrow a car from the station. But Marcy?"

"Yes?" Marcy held her breath, bracing herself for the advice.

"Think about going to Davy. He needs you. He's having problems with Gavan. The school's worried that Davy's neglecting him, and they're asking questions about a bruise on his face."

"Oh no," Marcy groaned.

"A social worker's stopping by your house today. That's why Beth is there. And now, Davy has no idea where Gavan's at. You could help each other."

"We'll be together soon. Maybe tonight. But I'm so close, Francesca, to finding out who wrote the notes to me. I think it's the same person who killed Kovach and maybe Tim. I can't blow my cover now. Please, promise me you won't tell anyone."

Marcy hung up after hearing Francesca's reluctant agreement to keep the secret, and then started jogging slowly toward the Katmai Shee building. With all the extra weight, she lost her breath quickly. Turning the corner, Marcy saw Francesca's red Honda waiting in the lot, standing out among the pickups. Marcy reached under the passenger-side mat for the key. As she started the car, she glanced up at the office window. Francesca stared out, with her arms crossed and one hand tugging her long braid. Marcy blinked the lights on and off and waved before pulling the car out of the parking lot.

GROGAN STARED AT THE approaching bus on Shore Road and smoked a cigarette. Surely he had missed Gavan climbing onboard back at the school. The kids pushed so much, and Gavan had a way of ducking his head and blending in with a crowd. Grogan would know in less than a minute. With any luck, the kid would run down the steps of the bus and run for his house and Gavan would not have go chasing after him in the woods.

The school bus slowed, flashing red lights. The doors opened. Three kids walked away, laughing and swinging backpacks. All girls. The bus pulled off. Grogan angrily shoved his cigarette into the ashtray. He could head back to school and check the building. Maybe the kid had to stay after.

If not, Grogan had to retrieve Marcy, and they'd immediately head to the forest and find that stream. Two backpacks were already waiting in the trunk, ready for when Gavan decided to follow the engineer's hand-drawn map.

As Grogan turned the ignition key, the back door to the Tercel suddenly popped open. Cool metal pressed against Grogan's neck. "Don't move," said the voice, low and male. Grogan complied except for a slow, careful shift of his eyes to the right. A hand had a steady grip on a pistol. Grogan shut his eyes and took a deep breath, wishing he had a cigarette lit. The gun pressed deeper against the thick fold of Grogan's neck. "Who the hell are you?" the voice asked.

"I'd like to ask the same," Grogan replied, leaning his head against the seat.

The man in the back seat went into a rage. "Why were you waiting for that school bus?"

"I'm parked on a public street," Grogan snapped. "That's not against any law."

The man swung his hand back and slapped the gun against Grogan's ear. Grogan didn't make a sound. Through the rearview mirror, Grogan got a glimpse of his attacker—Davy James, husband of his client. The detective put his hand to his aching ear and shut his eyes. "I'm not who you think I am," Grogan began. "I'm worried about your son, too." The gun slammed his ear again, harder. After a short gasp of pain, Grogan continued weakly. "He could be in danger."

"Where is he, you jerk?" Davy demanded. "And while you're at it, where's my wife?"

Grogan was confused. What did the husband know? Did he realize that Marcy was in town? Davy James pointed the gun at Grogan's head, wanting answers. Marcy had never mentioned a temper.

A siren whined. Flashing lights pulled close behind the Tercel. Grogan breathed a sigh of relief and wiped the sweat from his forehead as Davy leaped out of the car and ran toward the officers.

Grogan turned off his ignition and got out of the car, waiting for his chance to explain.

"Officer, this man's been prowling on my property before," Davy shouted. "This afternoon, I caught him waiting for the school bus, and now my son's missing!"

"All right, Mr. James. You can put your weapon away." The officer's hand covered the butt of his Glock, but kept his voice pleasant.

"I think he knows something about Tim Bander's death," Davy continued. "I know they found Kovach and all, but this guy is strange."

The officer called out to Grogan: "Sir, can you please back away from your car. I'd like to ask a few questions."

Grogan was tired and his head pounded, but he had enough sense to keep his hands in front of him and move slowly. Onlookers, whispering and pointing, already gathered across the street.

The officer raised his voice: "Sir, do you have a reason to be waiting at this bus stop?"

Grogan wanted to retort that he didn't need a reason, but he held his tongue. The officer called again. "Please answer. Do you live in this neighborhood?"

"No," Grogan replied, not liking the questions. "I didn't do anything wrong, and he assaulted me for no reason." Grogan pointed at Davy.

"Where's my kid?" Davy shouted.

"I don't know," Grogan said, in a low, calm voice.

"What's your name and address, sir?" The officer approached slowly, and Grogan could read the badge—Patrolman Dylan Michelson.

"Mike Grogan," he said, as he handed over his wallet. "I'm from Florida and staying at ANB Harbor for a while."

The officer checked the wallet, checking both the driver's license and Grogan's private investigator's license, then walked away to whisper back and forth with Davy.

Michelson returned, his right hand still tightened on the gun. "Mr. James claims you have been in his yard late at night. Is that true?"

"I haven't done anything wrong," Grogan said, firmly. "But I want to talk to a lawyer before I answer any questions."

"We can take care of that down in the station," Michelson said. "You're being arrested for one count of trespassing." Grogan protested, but the officer read him his rights and cuffed him, before leading him to the back of the police car.

Holding the patrol car's door open, the officer turned to Davy. "Thanks for calling us. We got a call from a teacher at the school about this same car. We'll call the troopers, and they'll probably fly on over in the morning. You might as well wait for them to arrive, before heading to the station and making a statement."

"But what about my son?" Davy said.

Michelson shrugged. "Well, at least this guy doesn't have him in the car. So, I wouldn't worry too much if I were you. Call the school first, then call your kids' friends." Grogan glared, as the two men continued back and forth. Meanwhile, more neighbors and cars gathered to watch the scene.

Only Grogan noticed the funny wool hat and Marcy's anxious face inside a red Honda across the street. She opened the door of the car, and tentatively approached the patrol car. But Grogan glared and firmly shook his head.

"Not on the bus," Grogan mouthed the words.

Marcy hesitated, and Grogan wasn't sure she understood. He wanted to tell her about Gavan, but she couldn't expose herself to Davy, not in front of the crowd. Somehow, he had to let her know about Gavan, so he started hollering, stressing certain words for Marcy. "Why *would I wait around here* if the kid's hurt!" Grogan looked at Marcy's direction, and the crowd muttered and backed away, afraid of the sudden outburst from a man who had stood by and waited meekly only a few moments before. "Why would I wait for the bus if I knew *he wasn't on it.* That doesn't make sense! If a kid's missing, *look for him and don't waste time on me!*"

"Hey you, cool it," Michelson said, and he slammed the door to the patrol car and ordered the crowd to disperse.

Grogan leaned back in the car and watched Marcy hurry back to the Honda and race away, not looking back. Scanning the group, he was immensely relieved that she hadn't made the mistake of stepping forward, shaking her husband's shoulders and shouting in front of the crowd. Ray's call had made Grogan nervous; the killer could be close and watching. With any luck, Marcy's presence in town was still a secret and she knew what to do. The kid had taken the map and planned to follow its delicate lines toward the stream. Alone. Grogan wanted Marcy to follow Gavan.

DAVY WATCHED THE PATROL CAR drive away, spoke briefly to a few neighbors and then returned to his home, where Beth waited. "I've been waiting for that jerk to show up."

Beth followed him to the gun cabinet in the family room. "Who is he?"

"I don't know. Michael Grogan. Gordon. I never heard of him. He has a Florida driver's license."

"My God, but why?" Beth said, sitting on the sofa. "Are you sure he watched the house before?"

"He's checking to make sure Marcy is out of town. Maybe she was right, this guy killed Tim and not Kovach. Maybe he's working for someone else!" Davy paced the room in frustration. "Damn! And where's Gavan? I'll have to lock the kid in a closet to keep him safe! The police told me to call the school."

"I already called the social worker," Beth said. "She agreed to delay the meeting until Monday."

"Maybe by then I'll know where my kid's at," Davy muttered. "I should call friends, but I don't know of any. Besides Tim."

"That man," Beth said. "Did he say anything about Gavan? Or Marcy?"

"No," Davy admitted. "But he gave me the creeps. I want Gavan home tonight. The police aren't worried, but I can't relax until I talk to him. Stay with me, Beth, and help me figure out where he's at."

She stood, looking dazed. Davy realized she was frightened, about the police and the strange man watching the house, as well as Gavan going missing, and he guided her back to the sofa. "Let me make us some tea," he spoke gently to her. "I'm sorry to be so snappish. But you know how much I love them both. Marcy would never forgive me if something happened to Gavan."

Beth nodded. "I didn't recognize that man," Beth said nervously. "But I'm sure it was him who stopped and spoke to Gavan the other day. And Gavan was so unfazed. He said the man had asked for directions."

"We have to tell the police," Davy urged her. "They want to talk to me in the morning."

"Yes, we'll tell them," she said. "But I wish I knew who he was." She took a breath and looked at Davy. "Gavan's probably fine, Davy, especially with that man in jail. I'll stay and we'll have dinner. If Gavan hasn't called by six, then…"

"Six! That's too late!"

She looked at him with sympathy. "Parents won't be home yet, Davy. And the kids are out fooling around, enjoying the time off. Trust me. I'm sure Gavan's fine."

MARCY TIGHTENED HER GRIP ON the steering wheel and accelerated. Grogan had been clear. He expected her to follow

Gavan rather than fight for the detective's release. And she couldn't let people know that she was in town until she found Gavan and figured out who exactly wrote those gray notes. If she had stepped forward and spoke to the police, in front of the neighbors, everyone in Sitka would know she was back in town before the end of the night, including the killer.

She could not let her son go alone into the forest, the place where Tim and Kovach had died. But she couldn't possibly search for the boy alone either. She whipped the car into the parking lot of the nearby convenience store, blocked the phone booth, and left the car running. She dialed, and Davy's cousin answered before the second ring. "Francesca, can you leave work?"

"Should I get someone to do the six o'clock show?"

"Yes…and dress for a long hike. Gavan needs us. I'll pick you up in twenty minutes and tell you everything. We might be out all night."

"Overnight?"

Marcy groaned. "You know Gavan."

"Stop by my house and grab my packs from the garage. They're ready for a hike. Just add some food and water. And Marcy, shouldn't we call Davy for help?"

Marcy hesitated. "I'm so afraid he's being watched."

"Okay, but we could use help." She paused, not sounding happy. "How about Jane McBride? She won't tell anyone."

"As long as she can keep up." Marcy smiled to herself, knowing that Jane had kept the secret. "Just hurry. Gavan is young and he has a head start."

GAVAN CLUTCHED THE DASHBOARD as Ken Jabard twisted the wheel and the Jeep crushed through the brush into a small clearing off the unpaved logging road. The boy checked the digital clock. The Jeep had made up for some of the lost time. But they only had a few hours left to head to the little stream and find Kovach's pack. Gavan was out of the car before Jabard turned off the ignition. "Hold on," Jabard said flatly. "You've been out here before. Tell me what we're looking for."

"See that ridge." Gavan pointed. "A few miles beyond that is the valley where Kovach worked."

"But I thought you wanted to look for clues about Tim, too." Jabard slammed the door, then paused, struggling to arrange his large orange frame pack over a bulky jacket.

Gavan shook his head. "There's no point looking around where Tim died. The police crawled over that area for days," he explained. "But they didn't look around where Kovach worked. His death wasn't an accident. I think that he was murdered, too, and we might find some answers if we look around there."

"The newspaper didn't say where his body was found."

"But I know where he worked and how he hid his pack. It's a basic hiking pack. Orange, just like yours. The newspaper never mentioned the pack, and so I called the police, and they admit that they never found the pack with his body or in his hotel room. So, it's out here. If we find it, maybe we'll figure out why Kovach was murdered. Maybe the same person killed Tim."

"When did you call the police?"

"This morning," Gavan said, impatiently.

Jabard frowned. "Why are you so sure that Kovach didn't murder Tim?"

"Believe me, I know." Gavan was firm. "I just know. I was with the guy. I have been thinking about this ever since. Kovach's killer made a mistake by chasing my mom out of town instead of me. But in truth, neither of us knows anything." Gavan adjusted his school backpack, and watched as Jabard studied a map. "If we hurry, that will change."

Jabard shoved the map into his pocket, not bothering to fold it. But still he did not hurry, instead walking back and forth along the logging road, not far from the Jeep. "We don't want anyone following us," he called out to Gavan. "Can you spot the Jeep?"

Gavan didn't see how that was necessary and gave a perfunctory check. "It's fine," he said, and with that, he headed for the ridge with long strides.

"Hold on!" Jabard called. Gavan turned, already thirty feet ahead.

"What is it now?" Gavan shouted, no longer hiding his irritation. "We're losing light fast!"

"Before we head too far, I want to check that gully over there." Jabard abruptly turned to the opposite direction of the ridge, a place not very far from where Tim's body had been found. Gavan shivered. He had hoped to never walk those trails again.

He swallowed hard and called out, his voice shaking. "Come on, Mr. Jabard! I think it's best we go to where Kovach was working."

But the teacher didn't pause, almost as if he had not heard. Gavan stood still, tempted to ignore the man and go his own way toward the ridge and Kovach's stream. "Mr. Jabard!" Gavan shouted again. But the man didn't look back, heading for a long gully with sloping sides. Almost out of sight, Jabard finally turned and waved his arm wildly, expecting Gavan to follow.

The boy sighed and wondered what the man could have possibly found by the gully. Uncrossing his arms, Gavan slowly trudged after his teacher. Spending the night alone, under the dark sky and darker forest, with odd sounds and shadows, not so far away from where both Tim and the engineer had died, lost its appeal. Gavan did not carry a rifle and wondered if Jabard had thought to bring a weapon. Bears attacked humans only if surprised; a pair of hikers, even unarmed, typically made too much noise to pose much of a surprise. At least that's what Gavan had always heard. He hurried to join his teacher, vowing to himself not to give in on every whim. "Mr. Jabard, I think you want to see the stream where Kovach was working…"

"Call me Ken, Gavan," the man interrupted, without turning around. Gavan grimaced and resolved to avoid calling the teacher by any name. Gavan remembered his mother once complaining about teachers who encouraged children to call them by their first names. He couldn't remember all her reasons or which teacher had made the suggestion. Maybe Mr. Jabard. At the time Gavan had argued vehemently, but now he understood. When they returned to school, Ken would turn back into Mr. Jabard.

The older man walked slowly, almost sauntering. "If we head this way, maybe we can find answers connecting Kovach with Tim," Jabard suggested. "Do you have any ideas about that?"

Gavan didn't answer, annoyed. Everyone assumed that the engineer had killed Tim. Anxious to reach the area worked by the engineer, Gavan had to humor the man and keep conversation to a minimum. He also had to resist making assumptions until he had more definite clues.

He checked his watch and realized that they were way behind schedule, even though the teacher had provided a ride. Mr. Jabard had a long stride, but stopped often to push aside branches or point out unimportant marks along the trail with a smile. Gavan sighed. Walking with the teacher was like walking with his parents on a Sunday afternoon nature hike. Gavan tried to keep an even pace, moving quickly around the tangles, often getting ahead. But every time Gavan moved ahead, out of sight, Jabard shouted.

Jabard's requests for him to slow down or wait turned to orders. Gavan swore under his breath and thought about the source of his annoyance. He had once admired Mr. Jabard.

Gavan wondered if he would always detest any adult who liked or helped him. The only person who had ever escaped Gavan's cynical scrutiny was Tim.

Jabard slowed his pace even more, even though the trail was not particularly steep. Gavan turned and noticed the teacher's eyes locked on him.

"After this, we head for the stream where Kovach worked," Gavan repeated, hoping to hurry the man. "Maybe we can still reach it before darkness falls."

"The stream that's not on the maps?" The man's voice was patronizing.

"It's on Kovach's map," Gavan said, darting among the trees. "And I saw the stream for myself."

Jabard smiled. "It would be a bonus if we found gold," he added.

Gavan didn't want to think about the gold. He had to keep focused on the stream and Kovach. "I don't think that Kovach found the gold," Gavan insisted sharply. "He deliberately spread it around. Maybe he was tricked."

"Kovach was a crook, ripping off the town, but you still like him?" Jabard asked.

"Sure," Gavan said with a shrug. "He wasn't perfect, but he also wasn't a murderer. What I want to find out more than anything is why Tim had to die. Who was out here that day besides Kovach..." Gavan stopped under a towering hemlock, its drooping limbs blocking the light. Gavan remembered the last time he had walked the woods and had an eerie feeling. He found himself wishing that his father walked beside him and not Jabard. The teacher came up close behind, his breath forced, maybe from exertion. "Finding that stream will be tough in the dark," Gavan murmured again.

"So let's not go," Jabard said, reaching for Gavan's shoulder. "How can you be so sure that Kovach did not kill Tim?"

Gavan shrugged. "I was alone with him, and he didn't kill me. So why would he kill Tim? It doesn't make sense."

Jabard looked puzzled. "When?"

"I'm not supposed to tell anyone, but Tim and I watched the engineer. We skipped school the Friday before Tim died. We followed Kovach." The boy slipped away. His hiking boots were sure, allowing him to skip over roots, loose rocks, along the rough path.

"But why?" Jabard asked.

Gavan looked about. Shadows expanded. Maybe he should have waited until morning. He definitely should have come by himself or someone like his father. Jabard only slowed him down. Too late to regret that now. Gavan was not sure about finding the pack, and the trip was not supposed to be fun anyway.

"The cross-island road," Gavan replied. "What else? Tim and I hated the idea of that road. But I don't care anymore. I'm out here for Tim. He was the only person I could trust. He was everything that I was not. He shouldn't be dead." Gavan walked on and realized that Jabard followed closely, eager to hear the story. Gavan walked faster. "It was my idea to follow the engineer that day. Kovach caught me, and my parents made me help him the next day. That's how I know he was hiding something. I was supposed to spend that Saturday with Tim, but instead, Tim followed us. He wanted to protect me. I should have stopped him. I should be dead. Not him." There, he said it. Gavan let out his breath, and it hurt. He no longer cared about Jabard or anyone else's reaction. Instead, Gavan looked up and thought about his best friend. Branches were etched against the afternoon sky, the light translucent.

"Don't say that, Gavan," Jabard snapped. "Tim didn't have to die."

Gavan's laugh was bitter. "People always say, 'Don't say

that, Gavan,' or 'You don't mean that.' I wish adults would stop telling me what to think. How to feel!" Gavan walked along the edge of some rocks. He leaped off an imposing granite rock, stranded by some glacier long ago, and landed smoothly.

Jabard stopped abruptly and dropped his pack. "We have to talk more about this," the man said. "We'll take a break."

"But we're not even close!" Gavan protested. He longed to reach the stream, to hear its distinctive rhythm against the rocks, what Tim had called perfect accompaniment for any Nirvana songs.

"It's a waste of time going that far," Jabard said, shaking his head. "You're not going to find clues from Kovach. Not after a month."

"I'm not stopping." Gavan was adamant. "I'll look all night if I have to."

"Let's stop and make some plans together." Jabard spoke patiently. With that, he unloaded his pack, removing the sleeping bag and the food.

Gavan kept his anger in check. Some daylight was left, and he didn't want to stop. Gavan tried to remember how much he had respected the man in the classroom, one of the few teachers who didn't resent him. Gavan owed him a chance. Still, it was a struggle to be polite. "I have to push on. I told you my plans before we left town."

"It's the engineer's fault," Jabard said, not looking up.

"No!" The word burst from Gavan's mouth. He knelt by Jabard, reached for the man's shoulder. "I only spent a day with him. But he didn't hurt Tim, and he didn't kill himself or have an accident. Kovach knew what he was doing."

"Maybe Tim wasn't hurt," Jabard said, strangely. He sat on a rock and idly picked at bits of moss from a rotting tree trunk. Gavan wanted to reach out, stop that hand from destroying what could be the miniature world for some microorganism. But he wanted to know Mr. Jabard's thoughts about Tim.

"What do you mean?" Gavan asked. "I read the newspaper. It was torture."

Jabard shrugged. "Sometimes people have connections and sometimes they don't. Maybe you and I connect." Jabard's hand crept over the rock and covered Gavan's hand. The skin was dry, smooth like snakeskin.

"And if we do?" Gavan asked, softly, wondering if the teacher could feel his pulse race. Gavan refused to move a muscle, refused to show fear.

"The connection starts emotionally, and then goes through a physical and spiritual process." An eager note crept into the strange, soft voice.

"You never planned to go to that stream with me," Gavan stated flatly.

Jabard laughed. "You want to find the engineer's pack? You're too late." He gripped Gavan's wrist. "I have it here." Gavan could not answer as fear sliced through him like a knife. He wanted to run, but was mesmerized by the man's pale gray eyes and deep wrinkles that made the thin face look sad. Suddenly, Gavan realized that this was Tim's last glimpse of the world.

Gavan looked down at his own wrist, as if it were a separate object, and tried to think. His hand looked tiny near the man's hand. His parents had warned him about men like this, but Gavan had always thought they exaggerated. He had always thought that he could recognize evil. But he had been wrong, and he felt vulnerable and stupid. Fear tried to claw its way out from every part of his body. He tried to relax his hand, so maybe Jabard would relax his grip and Gavan could jerk away.

Jabard smiled. "We're friends. You're at the age for experimentation. You like science and biology. Sex is only another part of science." Jabard's other hand moved to Gavan's knee and gently stroked. Gavan watched the hand like it was a hideous reptile. Funny, he could not feel it against his skin. He tried not to feel anything.

MARCY ASKED FRANCESCA TO slow her skiff, *Bluebird II,* and pointed to Grogan's pencil sketch. "Pull in anywhere along there," she said, pointing to the shore. "This could be where the map starts. We have to get around the ridge that leads to Bear Mountain."

"There's a cove up ahead," Francesca said. "But that's no easy hike, day or night."

"How did Gavan get out here?" Jane asked from the back of the skiff.

Marcy held out her hands and sighed. "Gavan is resourceful." She stared at the rocks and brush around the shoreline and the wilderness beyond.

"Marcy, are you sure he's out here?" Francesca asked.

"He's not at home. Not at the library or school. I don't know where else he could be. He's determined to figure out who killed Tim and Kovach. He showed us Kovach's map, and he knew Grogan thought the map was important."

"Gavan could be anywhere, and I'm not sure I trust this map," Francesca grumbled.

"We'll follow the trail," Jane said. "Start calling. It's all we can do. I certainly don't want to think about Gavan out here alone at night."

"He'll fare better than the three of us," Francesca said, shaking her head. "This is worse than looking for a needle in a haystack. It's a needle in the Tongass. We'll look for a bit and then we call the police. They'll organize a search-and-rescue team." She shoved her long braid into an oversized wool cap.

"Let's give this map a chance," Marcy agreed. "If we don't find him, then you can call the police."

"I'll look like a fool," Francesca said, easing her skiff into a protected area. The other women climbed onshore and secured the skiff, while she opened a case stashed underneath one of the seats. She removed a Magnum pistol and a box of bullets, loaded the gun and donned a holster and tossed packs to Marcy and Jane before pouncing out on shore. "Let's go. If we find that boy, I shake him. If he's back in town, I shake you, Marcy."

They set off in silence, stopping occasionally to listen. "He has such a head start," Marcy said, panting, the extra weight slowing her pace. She didn't have to tell Francesca that Gavan had studied the forest all his life. He could stalk and observe as well as his aunt and father. Maybe even better. It would be difficult to get close to the boy without him detecting the group of three women.

Francesca stopped and asked to see the map once again. As a fisherwoman, Marcy knew the waterways and islands around Sitka better than Francesca, but Francesca knew the Tongass and she shook her head with exasperation. "The map is so…bare. I don't recognize these streams. As far as I know, there's nothing out there but muskeg or ledges. And honestly, I don't see any sign that anyone's been around here."

"Should we try calling?" Jane asked.

"Save your breath," Francesca advised. "He had a jump on us. Wait until we find some sign that he's even out here."

"Let's head for the ridge," Marcy said. "It's on the map and maybe we can climb high enough to look around."

After twenty minutes, they crossed an old logging road, and Francesca crouched to study some tire tracks in the grass and mud. "It rained last night, so these are recent," she noted. "Let's follow them." She took out along the road, away from the ridge.

"But does this road go in the direction that we want?" Marcy called.

"Close enough," Francesca said. They continued for almost a mile, and the road narrowed considerably. Grass and seedlings flourished in the center of the road. Eventually, the tracks disappeared into large clumps of brush. Francesca pushed her way through, and the three women stumbled upon the maroon Jeep concealed behind some brush. "Do you think Gavan could have convinced someone to give him a ride?"

Marcy shrugged and sat wearily. "Or, he could have hitchhiked. I don't know."

"This is hunting season," Francesca said. "But most hunters give up by afternoon. Awfully clean for a hunter, but..." Marcy peered into the windows, but saw no sign that her son had been inside.

Jane tried the doors to the Jeep. They were locked except for one rear passenger door.

"Let's check it out," Marcy said, looking around.

Francesca climbed inside and found the registration clipped under the visor. "The Jeep belongs to Ken Jabard of Sitka," she called back, replacing the registration before crawling back out.

"That's a relief," Marcy said, walking around the vehicle. "Gavan must be out here with Ken."

"How well do you know this guy, Jabard?" Francesca asked.

Marcy slammed the door shut. "He was one of Gavan's teachers. One of the few Gavan has ever liked."

"I'm not sure if a twelve-year-old is the best judge of character." Francesca's scowl emphasized lines around her mouth. "How well do you know that guy, Marcy? How well do you know anyone? I couldn't believe that you let Gavan go out with Kovach."

"I trust other people." Marcy kept her voice calm. "I liked Kovach. And Jabard's lived in Sitka for years." She tightened her bootlaces.

"Maybe we can figure out which direction they went,"

Francesca said, staring at the ground and looking at the surrounding brush. "Marcy, use your head. Gavan told his father that he was with a friend. Teachers are not friends. What kind of adult male takes a kid out without asking the boy's parents? If they're out here together, I don't like it."

"You don't think…" Jane began.

"I don't know what to think!" Francesca snapped. "We don't know anything. We can't exactly inquire over the radio! 'Hey, anyone out there know if Ken Jabard likes little boys?'"

"I don't believe Jabard would…" Irritated, Marcy did not finish her thought. "He's a good teacher, and I trust him."

"That makes him more suspicious," Francesca said.

"Does my judgment rank with a twelve-year-old's?" Marcy protested. She had always understood why Davy had felt inferior to his cousin. The woman was as confident with her opinions as a goat on an icy ledge.

Francesca stopped and spoke gently. "No. But these guys aren't stupid. They lull parents and kids into a sense of safety." She checked the ground and looked up at Marcy. "You dragged me out here. And now I'm convinced that you were right and I was wrong. We're not returning until we find Gavan." She pointed to a space in the brush. "That way."

Marcy took off, and Jane had to almost run to keep up. Of the three, Francesca was in the best shape, frequently walking the trails around Sitka at least once a week. But Marcy carried the most anger and fear, and she reached the top of a little knoll ahead and had to wait for Francesca and Jane. Francesca stopped and signaled for everyone to listen, then fingered the broken tip to a branch.

"Someone passed through here," she murmured. "Not long ago."

"I'm surprised Gavan didn't follow the map," Marcy said. "This doesn't seem right."

"The teacher might have a different agenda," Francesca said pointedly.

"What could Gavan expect to find out here…" Marcy said, her voice drifting off. Dark shadows loomed, covering the entire trail. Walking was difficult. A damp coolness draped the forest. The sun would be completely down in less than an hour. Marcy shivered.

A large brown shape crashed from out of the brush, dodging crazily to avoid Francesca, then Jane. In seconds, the blur or an animal vanished. Marcy huddled close with the other two women, all startled. "What was that?" Jane gasped.

"A deer," Francesca murmured. "A doe. Something ahead on the trail must have frightened her."

The eerie silence returned. The forest was strange when there were no birds, no squirrel chatter, no sound of water. Marcy listened and looked around, before turning to Francesca. "That can't be Gavan," Marcy said, with disappointment. "He's way too quiet to frighten the wildlife like that."

"But he's not alone," Francesca whispered. The worry in her tone was contagious. "Let's keep moving on."

"Should we split up and call for him?" Jane suggested.

Marcy and Francesca considered that idea. "He might try to hide from us," Marcy warned. "He came out here to figure something out, and he won't quit. He'll assume we want to drag him home."

Francesca looked around a bit on the ground before nodding. "I lost their trail," she admitted. "So let's spread out a bit, but keep one another in sight. No shouting just yet."

"We'll find him," Marcy said.

"We'll use lights to signal," Francesca said. "That way, Gavan won't know it's us. Maybe he won't take off. And if we're lucky, we'll hear the two of them before they hear us and clam up. If any of us hears them or sees anything odd, flick your light on and off three times. The other two will head over and we'll meet. We make our approach together."

The three women spread out about forty feet apart, moving slow. It wasn't easy paying attention to roots, rocks and fallen logs in the twilight of the understory and the bobbing flashlights were not much help. Any sign of color or texture on the vegetation had blended with the dark shadows. Marcy and Jane both followed Francesca's pattern of dodging back and forth, managing to find the best way with clearings and obvious parts of animal trials. They had walked for at least a half hour when a strange noise interrupted the steady breeze of the evening forest. Despite her extra bulk and aching lungs and feet, Marcy was curious and wanted to hear the sound again, before signaling the other two women. She continued to tiptoe slowly, pointing her light down and listening.

A wood mouse scurried across her path, then another faint noise filtered through the trees. The bits of words gradually made sense: "...jer-r-r-k..." She took off in a frantic run, keeping the light pointed close to her feet, only using it as needed to check the few steps in front of her. Only as an afterthought did she remember to flash the light three times before taking o ff.

Panic swept through her and squeezed at every part of her chest and head. She ran hard, her legs thumping against the damp soil. She forgot fatigue and hunger, her extra weight and ugly hair. She dodged past trees and through brambles, not caring about anything other than reaching her son and holding him close.

A man's laugh came from the left and faded. Silence returned. The forest was so quiet Marcy could almost convince herself that she had imagined the laugh. She wasn't sure what direction she needed to move, and so turned off her light and walked slowly, carefully, toward the left, hoping to hear another sound. At one point, a branch snapped back against the soft skin underneath the eye. Marcy rubbed her finger against the stinging pain, smearing blood.

Still, her eyes had become accustomed to dark, and she checked each patch of ground before taking a step. The dampness of the ground and the softened pine needles helped control the noise. She wasn't sure where she was going, but she tried to hang on to the advantage of surprise.

She came across some huge boulders and sensed she was higher than the noise. Down below, in a gully, she heard clear words. "You're nothing but a jerk." Gavan's voice sounded strained. Marcy still could not see Gavan or the other person, but she could tell that her son was out of breath, possibly hurt or crying. She estimated that he was directly ahead, less than fifty feet away. She crouched and stepped slowly. At last, Marcy spotted a light twinkling through the shadows of the forest. Swallowing and unable to speak if she had wanted, Marcy edged closer. Then she saw him. On his knees, a man clutched Gavan's neck, twisting and shoving the boy's face into the dirt. The boy's hand flailed back and forth, helpless attempts to push away his larger attacker. Ken Jabard's back was to her as he struck Gavan's face hard. Her son's body went limp.

Marcy screamed and lunged, her one knee slamming into the attacker's lower left side. The man grunted in pain and stared at her, his face twisted in hatred, and she almost did not recognize Ken Jabard. Instinctively, she knew Jabard was not about to give up and walk away. Gavan squirmed and hit at Jabard with both fists.

Marcy's panic vanished. Gavan was alive and she focused only on getting her son away from Jabard, away from this gully and away from the Tongass. She tensed the fingers of her right hand into claws and with all her strength, swiped her fingernails across this face. He screamed and jerked away from Gavan.

"Run, Gavan," she said, firmly.

"You," Jabard spat out, slowly backing away, then circling away from the Coleman light. Marcy stood between Jabard and her son, and she wasn't about to give up the position. Jabard dodged to one side, and she wondered if he planned to escape or tackle Gavan. Instead, he lunged toward her, took careful aim with his fist and slammed her in the left temple with all his might.

Marcy landed hard on the ground, scraping her teeth and cheek against the dirt. Marcy couldn't think through the blur of pain, dearly tempted to close her eyes and let unconsciousness erase all senses. Trying to catch another ragged breath, she fought the black curtain coming down all around her.

Gavan stood. But to her horror, instead of running and escaping, the boy leaped toward Jabard and kicked the man's ribs. The man groaned, and Gavan quickly darted around to shield his mother from any more blows. He clutched her shoulder, and the firm grip helped clear Marcy's head.

"So Mommy comes along to spoil the fun," Jabard taunted, as he struggled for balance, preparing another attack, this time with a long hunting knife in hand. "You're not supposed to be in town."

Gavan moaned softly, but remained between his mother and Jabard. Marcy wished she could protest. She wanted to order Gavan to run away or scream for Francesca. But she could barely catch her breath through the pain. The man, the trees, the dim lantern light, circled around her slowly. Jabard moved closer and jabbed at Gavan with the knife, and Gavan dodged. Jabard smiled and, without taking his eyes from Gavan, kicked Marcy sharply in the ribs.

Her shriek pierced the air as she bent in pain and clutched her side. Gavan scrambled, ramming Jabard with his shoulder. Jabard slashed wildly and sliced through the boy's coat.

"This can go fast or slow," Jabard explained calmly, as if teaching a class. He turned his attention to Marcy, and her mind went blank. He meant to kill her. She reached out with her hand and tried to slide away, to stand. Her hand touched a round rock, hard and cold. She gripped it tightly and focused on remaining conscious. She took a deep breath. "Run, Gavan," gasped Marcy, hoping she was not imagining the sound of the voice pounding inside her head. "Get out of here."

"There's nowhere to run," Jabard muttered. As he swung his foot again, Gavan dived and used both arms to grab the leg in midair. The teacher grabbed at Gavan's hair, but also lost his balance and the two tumbled to the ground. The knife went flying out of Jabard's hand and he scrambled to retrieve it. Then he stood, ready to attack once again.

A gunshot blasted. Jabard screamed with fury and fell to the ground, only a few feet from Gavan. Francesca entered the clearing, her pistol pointed toward Jabard, sprawled on the ground and clutching his leg.

"I didn't do anything!" Jabard howled. "Gavan asked me to come out here with him and I hit his mother in self-defense!"

"I should kill you now," Francesca said. "Save your story for the police."

At last, Marcy could close her eyes. Time had stopped. Gavan was safe. Jabard was the killer and she could go home.

MARCY DIDN'T LOSE CONSCIOUSNESS, but she was exhausted and pain pierced the side of her head. Gavan cradled her in his arms, and Francesca walked about with her cell phone.

"Damn, I can't get a signal out here," Francesca said, joining Jane and staring at Marcy and Gavan. "Keep her talking, okay," Francesca asked. "We don't want her going out on us."

Gavan's hand gently smoothed her hair. "Mom, are you all right? Talk to me and tell me that you're all right."

Marcy opened her eyes and smiled. Her son's face was covered in dirt and tears. "Just a bad headache," she said.

"I'm sorry, Mom." Gavan's voice broke. "I'm really sorry."

Jane tapped his shoulder and crouched down. "Marcy, Gavan's fine. We got here in time."

"Mom, you saved my life." Gavan tried to fight his tears. Marcy smiled and opened her eyes, reaching for her son's hand, squeezing hard. She tried to keep her eyes open even as clouds of pain swirled in from the sky, pressing down on her head and neck. Suddenly, Jane returned to her side once again and poured some of her drinking water on cloth, someone's sweatshirt, and wordlessly handed it to Gavan. He rested the one sleeve on his mother's forehead and used the other to clean away some blood and dirt. Marcy could care less how Francesca took charge in the camp, keeping the gun aimed at Jabard while shouting orders about how Jane could reorganize the packs, carrying only water and other essentials.

A few seconds later, someone suddenly held a cup of water to her lips. "Sip slowly," Gavan advised. "You can come home tonight? Dad and I need you so much."

She took a deep breath and struggled to sit up. The water helped. "I'm…okay," Marcy said.

"We're going to have a tough time getting Marcy back," Jane said.

"I can make it," Marcy spoke up. "I want to get home."

"We can't trust him, Aunt Francesca," Gavan said, pointing at Jabard.

"I know," she said, nodding. "Let's tie him up."

Jabard started howling about his leg and needing immediate help. "Shut up!" Francesca snapped. "You're not going anywhere. Jane, do me a favor and search the packs for rope or anything like it."

"You can't do that!" Jabard protested. "I'm wounded."

"You better pray we find rope," Francesca said in a low voice. "We're not taking any chances that you'll get away."

Jane gathered the packs and moved them all in the center. Francesca backed away from Jabard and handed the gun to

Marcy. "Can you handle this?" she asked. "Keep this on him and I'll help Jane," Francesca said. "Don't give him any chances. If he makes one move to resist, shoot."

The heavy metal felt good in Marcy's hand and she readily curled her finger around the trigger. She crossed her legs and kept her eyes on Jabard while the other women went through the packs.

Francesca saved Jabard's pack for last. Acting as though she didn't want to touch the man's belongings, she dumped everything out—some clothes, a bottle of wine, pears and smoked salmon, more water and the keys to the Jeep. Francesca pocketed the keys. But going through the packs did not result in much in the way of restraints. Gavan handed over a ball of string and a rubber snake from his pack. Francesca had some hair ties, and Jane and Gavan donated the strings from their sweatshirt hoods.

"This with our belts should hold him," Francesca said about the selection. She turned to Jabard. "Get over against that tree."

"I can't," he growled.

Using two hands, Marcy raised the gun. "Move," Francesca warned, her voice like a hard edge. Jabard slowly inched his way to the small red alder, moaning with every movement. "Shoot him, if he moves one muscle," Francesca said again. Then she crouched down and pulled Jabard's hands tightly behind his back, wrapping the string around his wrist and tying a series of square knots. She doubled the sweatshirt strings and tied them around his ankles, then used her belt, along with Jabard's and Gavan's, to lash Jabard's arms and chest to the tree.

"You're tying me too tight," he protested.

Francesca ran her fingers along the smooth bark, then checked that each strand was secure before standing up. "No room for squirming," she announced. Francesca finally held out the snake, about two feet in length, before standing behind him and securing his neck to the tree with a firm knot toward the back.

"I can't breathe," he gasped.

"If you can talk, you can breathe," Francesca said, shortly. She quietly finished ripping a T-shirt to bandage his leg as the others watched in silence. Francesca stood. "Everyone ready to leave?" she asked.

"It's getting colder out," Jane commented. "And it might be a few hours before anyone gets him out of here." Francesca rolled her eyes, but picked up two of the sleeping bags and used them both to cover the restrained and injured man.

"If you try to escape, that cover will come off," Francesca warned. "It's going to be at least a few hours before the police arrive." She turned back to Marcy and Jane. "Hypothermia would be too good for him."

Marcy handed the gun back to Francesca. Then, with Jane and Gavan's help, she stood slowly. The piercing pain had become dull.

"Can you make it?" Francesca asked with concern. Marcy nodded. "Then let's get out of here," Francesca said softly. "I don't think he'll get loose, but if he does, we want a good head start back to town."

Marcy took a few steps and nausea swept through her. She leaned against Jane.

Francesca held up the keys to the Jeep. "It's not far, Marcy. Just back to the Jeep."

"I can do it," Marcy said doggedly, more to herself than any of the others.

Francesca left the one lantern by Jabard's side, grabbed the one pack holding the water and started out, ready to find the easiest and most direct route back to the Jeep. The climb out of the gully was the worst part of the hike. With Jane and Gavan at her side, Marcy took it slow.

As they approached the top, Jabard called out. "Marcy, call

your lawyer as soon as you get home. You're going to need her. I did absolutely nothing and you know it. You and Gavan are never going to get away with this."

Marcy caught her breath and could feel Gavan's arm tense at her side.

"Don't answer him," Jane murmured.

THE GROUP WAS QUIET UNTIL they were far from the clearing. The cloudy sky was as dark as the ground. Marcy had to focus to make every step secure and appreciated the steady support from Jane and Gavan. Both Jane and Gavan carried lights, and each supported Marcy with one arm. Francesca walked ahead, pointing out the smoothest ways for walking with the light.

Francesca spoke up. "Marcy, I'm sorry that I resisted coming out here tonight. No one else would have ever guessed."

"Hey, who else would have believed me and set out for a hike lasting into the middle of the night?" Marcy said. "I'm lucky to have you both as friends."

Gavan tightened the clutch on Marcy's arm. "I know I shouldn't have come out here without telling Dad," the boy apologized.

"Major rule when you take off anywhere around Sitka," Francesca called back in agreement. "Tell someone. You're incredibly lucky that your mother guessed where you went and brought us along. But we're not here to scold you."

"No," Marcy said. "We move on. And regardless of what Jabard says, you did nothing wrong. Neither did Tim. Adults should not take advantage of a kid's mistakes. You went out on a hike with a teacher and he attacked you."

"I feel like I should have guessed," Gavan said sadly. "Now I know what happened to Tim. I told Mr. Jabard that I was coming out here to search for Dennis Kovach's pack, and he offered to help. I knew Kovach didn't hurt Tim. So, we got out here, but Mr. Jabard didn't want to look for the stream or Kovach's pack. We argued some and he stopped here. It turns out he had the engineer's pack along. He got rid of the papers and the film. When he grabbed my hand, I got so scared. I tried to run, but he caught me and pushed me to the ground. I was sure he was going to do to me what he did to Tim. He was going to rape me."

Marcy felt a horrible chill and stopped. Hearing the word from the lips of her son was unbearable. She couldn't find the words to make him feel better, but she put both hands to her son's shoulders and hugged. Marcy was grateful she could touch her son and know that he was safe.

"You guys came in time," Gavan continued. "I was so scared." He started to sob.

Francesca came back and patted the boy lightly on the shoulder. "Let's rest here a minute." Gavan, Jane and Francesca all guided Marcy as she sank to the ground, exhausted. Marcy held her head, wishing she could walk away from the heavy throbbing.

"What will happen to Mr. Jabard?" Gavan asked, his voice small with fear.

"We'll call the police and he'll have a trial," Francesca spoke up with confidence. "For attacking you and for killing Tim."

"It's over for him, Gavan," Marcy said. "He can't hurt anyone else."

"I hope so, after what happened to Tim," Gavan murmured. "If only someone had been there for him. I was lucky." Everyone was silent. "After they found Tim, I wondered why he didn't call out. Scream. Fight back. Now I know. I was so terrified. I couldn't move or talk! But tonight I heard Tim's voice in my ear. He kept telling me not to make the same mistake. 'Holler, Gavan,' he said. 'Scream as loud as you can.' And so I did. And that's when Mom showed up."

Marcy wished she had words of comfort. But there were

none. And she would never stop being truthful with her son. She could only hold him close. Jane opened a bottle of water, and they passed it around, each taking sips, sitting quietly and listening to the wind mutter its strange noises in the treetops.

"We better get to that Jeep and get back to town," Francesca said after a few moments. "Marcy, can you stand to walk some more?"

Marcy nodded. "I want to get home."

The four of them moved slowly in the dark. The lights bounced eerily against the dark trees, and it was after eight o'clock when they made it back to the logging road. Jane started the Jeep, and quickly eased out of the hiding place. As the vehicle bounced along the rocks and overgrown logging road, Marcy started to gag. Jane pulled over twice to let Marcy vomit and then proceeded back to town, driving carefully.

FROM THE RIDGE, AN OLD BROWN bear watched the taillights leave her part of the island. Standing by was her last cub, whom she fed and guarded with her life. She grunted a mild warning, before disappearing among the trees. The cub understood. The group who crept along his mother's trail had posed no immediately danger, but his mother had taught him well. No human could ever be trusted.

PALE AND CLAMMY, MARCY stretched out in the back and leaned against Gavan. Jane kept her foot light on the accelerator, to avoid jostling Marcy or hitting a tree along the narrow road. On the way back to town, Francesca tried several times to call Davy by cell phone, but the phone rang on and on. "Your answering machine's not working," she complained. "I let it ring more than ten times."

"He must be there," Marcy said, feeling disappointed. Still, it would be fun to see her husband's surprise in person. "Unless he's searching for Gavan. If Davy's not there, he left some kind of note."

"Should we stop by the police station or call?" Jane asked as she neared the intersection of Sawmill Creek and Halibut Point roads, with town hall and the police station around the next corner.

Francesca twisted around the front seat and looked at Marcy. "I think we had better call the state police. This case is too big for locals, and we don't want them messing up the crime scene." She pointed toward the brilliant lights of the O'Connell Bridge. "Let's head to the hospital first."

"No!" Marcy said. "Davy must be frantic about Gavan. I want to get home now. Really, Francesca, I feel better after getting sick. And you know the doctors won't do anything about a little concussion. I didn't even black out! All I need is some rest at home."

Jane waited at the stop sign. "Well? She sounds feisty enough to me."

"All right," Francesca said reluctantly. "Head to Marcy's place and we'll call from there."

Jane turned the Jeep toward Halibut Point Road and drove north along the section of Sitka's shoreline most exposed to the Pacific. Even with the car windows closed, they could hear the crashing of the surf. Gavan had long since leaned against his mother's shoulder and slipped into sleep.

Marcy yawned. "It will be wonderful to sleep in my own bed," she said.

"We'll get you home, and you can head right into bed," Francesca said.

"Can I at least have a chance to say hello to Davy?" Marcy teased.

Jane eased the car into the driveway, and the gravel made only a slight crunching noise. Marcy gently moved her shoulder and shook Gavan awake. "The last thing you need tonight is company," Francesca snapped. Surprised, Marcy looked up and saw Beth's car ahead in the driveway. Francesca opened the back door, ready to help Jane guide Marcy into the house, but her mouth was set in an angry line.

"Maybe Beth will give us a ride home," Jane offered. "We can't keep driving this Jeep around all night."

"That's right," Marcy agreed. "There's no need for you to rush off. Beth probably came over to help Davy find Gavan. I'm surprised the police aren't already here! We have some explaining to do."

"I don't know why they didn't answer," Francesca muttered. "All right, Jane and I will stop in quick, call the police and tell Beth and Davy how you need rest. Beth can help by giving us a ride. Marcy, you've been through too much tonight."

"I'm tired, but I can't go right to sleep after all that happened," Marcy said. "Come in and have a hot drink. Gavan and I cannot explain this story all by ourselves." The weary group trudged toward the entrance and Marcy rang the doorbell.

"Really, Marcy," Francesca said. "It's your house."

"But I haven't been home in weeks," Marcy replied lamely. Francesca didn't wait, but twisted the doorknob and opened the door wide, inviting the others to follow her inside.

Beth was curled on the living room sofa. Dangling from her hand was a book. Her mouth dropped open in complete surprise at the sight of the straggly group. "Marcy, Gavan!" she said with a gasp. "Where have you been?"

"Where's Dad?" Gavan demanded impatiently. "We're all home!"

Beth looked at Gavan and then Marcy as if they were two ghosts. She approached Marcy and held out her hand. "Marcy, is that you? Your hair! Not even Davy would recognize you. Where on earth have you been?"

Gavan went into the kitchen, came out with two cookies and ran upstairs. Marcy gave Beth a long, warm hug and then moved slowly to the rocker in her family room, not even removing her coat. "Oh, how I missed my family and friends. And this home! Where's Davy? He'll be so happy that we found out everything."

Beth's eyes went round. "What are you talking about?"

"We found out who killed Tim. But wait, where's Davy?"

Beth sank slowly to the sofa, close to Marcy, and looked dazed, apparently fascinated with her friend's shorn hair and the extra weight. "He had a terrible night," she said. "He went to bed exhausted. There was a prowler here. The police charged the man. The school social worker was supposed to visit, but Davy couldn't find Gavan. Of course, Davy called me."

"Of course," Francesca interjected coldly, after draping both her coat and Jane's over a chair in the hallway. She unloaded her gun and placed the holster near the coat.

"Oh, poor Grogan!" Marcy said. "He's not a prowler! We have to call the police and get him out of jail!"

"Marcy, you sit!" Francesca ordered sternly.

"So you know that man?" Beth asked with a shudder. "He's dreadful. The police suspect that he may have helped Kovach kill Tim."

"That's nonsense!" Marcy said. "He wasn't even in town then. I went to Florida and found him. He's a detective who works for me."

"For you?" Beth asked, puzzled. "Are we talking about the same man? This man's hideous. Davy almost killed him!"

"Oh, we have to help him." As Marcy rushed for the phone, she swayed.

"Marcy, you must sit down!" Francesca ordered, leading her cousin to the sofa. "There's not a whole lot that can be done in the middle of the night to get someone out of jail. Even if he's innocent!"

Beth nodded and pointed to the mantel clock. "She's right. As soon as we get you settled, I promise, I'll call the station and explain. But it will take time for the police to drop the charges. And I can't even bail him out until the morning."

"We still have to call the police though," Jane insisted. "We left Ken Jabard out in the woods."

"What happened to him?" Beth asked. She stared at Jane, then Francesca.

"He attacked Gavan," Francesca said shortly. "It's a crime scene and I want the state police out there first before anyone else."

"But is he still alive?" Beth asked.

Francesca shrugged. "I shot him, but he's still alive. We tied him to a tree, and he won't be going anywhere too soon."

"I'm surprised you didn't kill him," Beth murmured.

"I want Jabard to face a judge and jury, and hear what society thinks about his sort of crime. An arrest and a long trial will do more to educate parents and kids than a quick killing by me. That would have been in the news and forgotten a month later."

"Can you absolutely be sure about Ken's intentions?" Beth pressed. "Why, he's lived in town for so long with no problems. You're sure it's not a misunderstanding?"

Marcy cringed and was grateful that Francesca was blunt. "We walked up on him as he was trying to rape Gavan in the woods," Francesca said. "There was no misunderstanding. We got there just in time."

"What did Jabard say to you before you left?" Beth asked, full of curiosity. "Could he talk?"

"He whined, claimed we had no proof." Francesca yawned. "He'll try to find some way to blame Gavan. But it's not going to work."

"All right, then." Beth folded her hands and then unfolded them. "Francesca's right. Get the state police there first. It won't take long to get here by helicopter from Juneau. Not more than two hours. Where exactly is Jabard?"

Francesca plucked her topographic map from a pocket and threw it on the coffee table. "About a mile in from an old logging road, more like a path. One Last Chance Road. Not far away from the end of Green Lake Road."

Gavan returned to the family room and leaned against the counter. "I couldn't wake up Dad. I shook him and tried to tell him that you were back, Mom. But he just groaned."

"Leave him go!" Beth scolded, and her harsh tone startled everyone, stopping the conversation. Then her voice melted into gentle concern. "He's been sick with worry about you, Gavan. He made calls all evening and then crashed after dinner. He said he hasn't been sleeping well lately."

"Maybe we can try again before we go to bed, Gavan," Marcy suggested.

"I would have thought that he would be leaping about at the sound of Gavan's and Marcy's voices," Francesca said, with a frown. She extracted her cell phone. "Let me make that call to the police."

Marcy felt bile rise in her throat. "Oh my God, I feel so sick," she said, moaning. Holding her stomach, she stumbled for the bathroom.

MARCY SAT ON THE FLOOR by the toilet while Francesca stroked her back. "It's the concussion," said Francesca. "Damn, we should have stopped by the hospital…"

"I was in such a hurry to come home and see Davy," Marcy said wistfully. "But really, I do feel better now."

Francesca turned on the shower and tested the steamy water. "Get inside," she said gently. "Rinsing off will feel good."

As Marcy washed away the grime and blood, she felt clean and stronger. Francesca returned to the bathroom with a thick towel and some clean sweats. "You okay in there?" she asked.

"This will go down as one of the best showers ever," Marcy said, with a laugh.

After Marcy dried off, Francesca insisted on checking that her pupils were the same size. "I'm sure you have a concussion, but the eyes look fine. A few days rest should do the trick. If you vomit tomorrow or the headache gets worse, you'll have to go in and see a doctor."

"I'm feeling much better," Marcy insisted. "But I wish Davy was up."

"I just tried to rouse him, too," Francesca admitted. "He's really out. I told you that he hasn't been the same without you. Or maybe he's coming down with something. Tomorrow." Marcy nodded sadly, and together they returned to the living room.

Beth had arranged a platter of hot cocoa on the coffee table. Jane already sipped on a mug and was already trying to blink away the sleep from her eyes.

"I called the police for you," Beth added, handing mugs over to Francesca and Marcy. "A team is on their way from Juneau. They're going to call the local police and just ask them to remove Jabard and secure the area."

"And they were okay with that?" Francesca asked, surprised. "I mean, you weren't even there. They didn't want to talk with us?"

"I'm a lawyer," Beth said smugly. "They'll go out tonight and ask questions in the morning."

"I don't like the idea of Jabard talking to the investigators before we do," Francesca said.

"He's one person and there are four of you," Beth said calmly. "Don't worry. You can explain in the morning."

Gavan stood in the kitchen with his steaming mug and Marcy called to him. "It's been a long night, honey. Maybe you should go to bed."

"Let him drink his cocoa first," Beth urged.

"Mom's right," Gavan said quietly. "I'm tired. I think I'll take this upstairs and go to bed. Mom, do you think the three of us can stay at home tomorrow and play some games?"

Marcy sighed. "Probably not. We'll be busy all day with the police."

The boy nodded. "I'm glad it's over and we know what happened to Tim. Good night, everyone, and thank you again." He kissed his mother and aunt. The other women called good night and watched him climb the stairs.

Beth went back to the stove, refilled the pitcher with more hot cocoa and then moved about the room, refilling the mugs. Francesca put her hand over Marcy's mug. "Go easy, you don't want to get sick again."

Marcy nodded, leaned back and closed her eyes. "I can't believe Ken Jabard. He helped Gavan so much last year—and all along he was the one who killed Tim. He would have killed Gavan if we hadn't stopped him."

"Well, I was staying tonight anyway to help Davy," Beth said, hovering near the sofa. "So, I can stay and help you tonight. And I'll also be here in the morning to sit in when the police ask their questions."

Francesca turned to Beth. "Do you know what to do for a concussion?"

"Sure," Beth said. "I'll let her sleep. Lots of sleep. Maybe I'll call the police and ask them if they can hold off until the afternoon."

"Not quite," Francesca said. "I'm staying tonight, too."

"All of you stay," Marcy invited. "Francesca and Jane don't have any way to get home except for Davy's truck or Jabard's Jeep. There's plenty of room and, look, poor Jane's already drifting off." Francesca yawned. "You need sleep more than me," Marcy teased.

"Then it's settled," Beth said. "We can all stay. Marcy won't have to do a thing."

"How's Davy?" Marcy asked.

"He missed you," Beth replied. "He's a different person without you around, I must say."

"I'm so happy to be at home before Thanksgiving," Marcy said softly. "Beth, thanks for helping him out so much. I can't wait to see him in the morning."

Beth smiled. "Maybe you should stay in the guest room to-night. He was exhausted, and it might alarm him if he does get up in the middle of the night and finds another person in bed!"

"Maybe you're right," Marcy nodded sadly. Then, she went to the hall closet and found two blankets and covered Jane who was fast asleep. Beth carried the empty mugs and pitcher to the kitchen and started loading the dishwasher.

Marcy nudged Francesca and told her it was time to head upstairs. "I'm tired," Francesca admitted. "I'm going to have to set an alarm to get you up every three hours or so."

"But why?" Beth asked.

"That's what you do for someone with a concussion. Make sure she doesn't actually pass out from a small bleed in the brain."

Marcy put her arms around Francesca and guided her to-ward the stairs. "I'm in better shape than you," she said. She turned back to Beth still cleaning in the kitchen. "Beth, that can wait until the morning. Will you find everything you need for bed?"

"I'm fine," Beth promised. "Don't you worry about a thing."

Frances and Marcy went straight to bed. As Marcy drifted off to sleep, she heard the churning from the dishwasher.

ON HIS WAY TO HIS ROOM, Gavan paused outside his father's room and left his cup on the floor. He could not understand why his father didn't wake, elated at the sound of his mother's voice. The house was supposed to be back to normal, but the night did not seem complete without a triangle of kisses and smiles. Gavan slipped inside the room where his father slept and slowly approached the lump under the covers. Placing his hand on his father's shoulder, Gavan gently shook, but his father's head wobbled back and forth, mouth hanging open. Gavan noticed dark circles around his eyes and his breathing sounded broken. Gavan opened the window wide, letting in lots of moist November air and shook his father's shoulder harder. "Come on, Dad, wake up," Gavan whispered, pinching his father's arm. "Please."

But nothing worked. So still, not even twitching his eyes, Davy resembled the drunks Gavan had seen a few times, although his parents always had tried to distract him whenever they passed one. His father looked miserable, and Gavan backed out of the room, worried. To think he had imagined inviting his father along on the mission he was about to undertake.

Gavan shook his head. His father had missed so much. Tomorrow, the jubilant feelings of his mother's return would not be the same. Sadly, Gavan headed into the hallway and retrieved his mug, still brimming with cocoa. He slipped into the bathroom, ditched the hot chocolate down the toilet and flushed. He entered his bedroom, left the mug on the dresser and fell into bed with his clothes on, after making sure to leave the door open a few inches.

Typically the soft glow of lights from downstairs, his parents' murmuring talk, lulled him to sleep. But not tonight. The night was not over for Gavan. He waited until the adults finished their drinks and the conversation drifted toward yawns, followed by silence and more yawns. He heard the footsteps of his mother and aunt on the stairway. He listened to the sounds of the kitchen being cleaned. Except for the noise of the dishwasher, the house was quiet. But still, the lights did not go out. Gavan anxiously checked his alarm clock. He could not take a chance on leaving the house, as long as anyone else was awake. He could not afford to get caught.

He almost drifted off and pinched himself, forcing himself to keep his eyes open. Less than an hour later, he heard footsteps in the hallway. The doorway to each room opened and closed. Someone wandered about, checking on everyone. Probably his mother. Before she had left, his mother had always entered his room late to tuck the covers about his neck. She closed the windows if rain had started and kissed him on the forehead. He had never thought much about the midnight checks, but after she had left town, he had missed them dearly. Still, he did not expect her to roam throughout the house tonight. They had been through so much. Gavan closed his eyes and waited, wondering if she felt all right.

His door inched open. Gavan opened an eye, waiting for the familiar routine. A dark figure crept into the room and headed directly for the window. He heard the scraping noise of the window being closed and locked. Against the night sky, he saw a profile with smooth hair. Damn, he thought, bossy Beth was in his room, shutting the cracked window and opening the vent! His family always turned the furnace off at night, preferring cool ocean air, bedroom temperatures no higher than fifty-five degrees, and piles of flannel sheets, quilts and blankets.

He held his tongue though. He had plans for the rest of the night and could afford no delays. He breathed slowly and feigned sleep—hoping Beth would simply leave and go to bed.

Her dark shape crossed the room and switched on Gavan's desk lamp. He felt a hand on his chest, a blanket tugged. Gavan felt a strange fear, remembering Jabard's hand and his inability to scream. He centered all his focus on breathing steady and slow, even though his pulse raced and he felt the need to gasp or jerk away. But if he moved at all, if he started talking with Beth, he'd never escape the house.

Gavan stayed still by remembering Tim. Along with all the help from his mother and aunt and Jane, Tim also had protected Gavan, by reminding him to scream, and Gavan had made a promise in return. He intended to keep the promise.

A small pack waited on the desk, and inside was another flashlight and the longest and sharpest knife from the kitchen, which he had hid under his sweatshirt when he first came upstairs to wake his father. No one was going to stop him from returning to the Tongass and finding the logging road at night.

But he couldn't think about that yet. Instead, he relaxed and took a slow smooth breath, thinking about his friend, a blue sky, bursting with brilliant white clouds, an eagle gliding away.

Only a few seconds, but at last, Beth moved to the desk, retrieving the empty mug and turned out the light. She walked away, shutting the door firmly, with a click.

He heard the woman go downstairs, and then he heard more water running, followed by silence. Oddly, the lights did not go out and he groaned, wondering if Beth planned on going to bed at all. A sudden clanging noise came from a distant part of the house, followed by some silence. Annoyed, Gavan slipped out of bed, opened his window and shut the vent. He tiptoed to the hallway and listened. He heard another noise of metal, like a small tool falling and hitting the top of the washing machine. Beth was in the utility room. He wondered if something was wrong with the furnace.

Gavan scowled. Soon, she would wake everyone in the house. He slipped back inside his room, looking out the window, wondering if he could dare leave the house with Beth still up. If she came back to his room and found him missing, would she care, immediately waking his mother and father? Or, would she wait until the morning to raise the alarm?

A noise reverberated through the vent. In the hall, he heard another door open. Gavan peeked out. His mother stumbled in the hallway, her hand rubbing the side of her head. From the bathroom, he heard a cabinet open, a bottle of pills shake and water run. He climbed back in bed, closed his eyes and waited, in case she decided to enter his room and check. Another loud clang came from the utility room.

"What now?" his mother grumbled, not far from Gavan's door. She went downstairs, heading straight for the utility room. Gavan tiptoed and followed. The sound of conversation replaced the loud noises. Thank goodness, his mother was probably explaining that the family did not care for the furnace pumping away at night. He remembered playing with the thermostat a few times and making the house swelter. He half wished his mother would scold Beth and send her to a room.

The women spoke softly. Gavan entered the kitchen and decided to hide, in case the two women came upstairs suddenly. He opened the door to the pantry, feeling relief for the first time since his mother left that it was not well stocked. Curling up tight, he sat on two cartons of soda and pulled the door closed, settling in and hearing scraps of conversation.

"...MAKING SOUNDS," BETH EXPLAINED. "I've done this before, you know."

"I don't know why you bother." Marcy was tired and annoyed, but Beth followed her upstairs.

"I couldn't sleep," Beth explained, her voice was low and sweet. "Really, Marcy, back to bed. You've had a rough night."

"God knows I'm tired," said Marcy wearily. She paused in the kitchen for another drink of water.

"Here. Let's take your water upstairs," Beth suggested. "We can count this as a check and turn off your alarm! You need sleep."

Marcy turned and noticed the financial documents spread all over the kitchen table. She checked and saw statements from some of her largest accounts. "Beth, why are these papers here?" she asked, curious and no longer tired.

After some long seconds of silence, Beth responded. "Davy asked me to check them," she said, defensively. "He was worried whether you were coming back."

"But I am back. So, you certainly don't have to look at these tonight."

"No problem." Beth's voice was annoyed, high-pitched. "Tell you the truth, I'm bored to tears helping you with this stuff, Marcy. You've done well over the years. All thanks to my advice. But I guess you don't need me anymore."

"What are you talking about?" Marcy asked.

"Look, why don't you go to bed," Beth snapped. "I'm tired, too. We'll talk in the morning."

"But I can tell you're angry. What's wrong?"

"Marcy, have you ever thought about me?" Beth said harshly. "I researched investments for you. I gave you good advice. You made lots of money. Sure, you give me a percentage. But what do I have?"

"Beth, I felt like I had to force you to take money. If you want more…."

Beth slammed the glass to the table, sloshing water over the papers. "Let's talk later," she said, her voice low and firm.

"What happened while I was gone?" Marcy pressed, gathering the papers into a single pile, not wanting them out in case Gavan woke up early in the morning. "I can take these up to my bedroom."

"Stop that!" Beth said. "Francesca said you need rest!"

"Beth, I can't sleep without knowing what's bothering you."

Beth slipped into the other room and then moments later returned, pointing one of Davy's pistols. "My God, what are you doing?" Marcy asked, horrified. "Put that down now!"

Beth's voice was high and hysterical. "You ask too damn many questions. I tried to keep this simple. But you had to persist. What are you going to learn by going through those papers? You always came to me! I did everything for you! But you have the nerve to patronize me, tell me what I can look at and when!"

"I only wanted you to rest tonight, too," Marcy said.

"No, you're telling me what to do. You're spoiled rotten. Like Gavan! Get back downstairs."

"Not while you're holding that gun," Marcy snapped. "Put it away." She couldn't imagine Beth, her sweet-natured and sensible friend, shooing her.

Beth approached and slapped Marcy in the face. "You asked for that," Beth spoke sharply, her voice full of contempt. "Not another word, or I'll shoot. I didn't do all this work to get stopped at this point. Especially by you. Get downstairs. And if you don't listen, I'll go in and shoot your stupid kid. This is Davy's gun, and it'll look like he did it. Or you. And everyone in town will believe it. You walked out on your family for two months, and your son's the biggest pain in the schools!"

"Beth, we're friends!" Marcy said with a gasp. "How can you say this to me?"

"You're so stupid," Beth hissed. "Marcy, I warned you to stay out of town. If only you had listened." Marcy had no choice but follow Beth's orders and move slowly downstairs. The woman pointed the gun directly at Marcy's chest. "You have money," Beth said, furious. "You had your chance to live and do what you want. Now it's my turn—and I'm not going to let anyone stop me. I warned you to stay away until December. I didn't want to hurt anyone."

Marcy thought about lunging for the gun. But Beth was a few steps out of reach, giving her plenty of time to shoot.

"Listen to me and Gavan does not get hurt," Beth promised. Marcy thought she heard a measure of self-control and took that as a sign of hope. Beth then tossed Marcy a pillowcase from the laundry and ordered her to stand in the corner, between the furnace and the wall. "Hold still, put the pillowcase over your head and hold your hands together behind your back."

"You won't hurt Gavan?" Marcy asked.

"Just listen and no one has to get hurt," Beth promised. "You see, I have this gun, and the only way you can help Gavan is by letting me tie you up."

Marcy complied and in a few moments Beth had tied rope tightly, first around Marcy's arms, and then around her legs. Beth spoke in a soothing tone as she guided Marcy to the floor. Beth then removed the pillowcase from Marcy's head and started to shove a sock in Marcy's mouth. "Wait," Marcy pleaded. "Don't gag me yet. At least tell me why. I deserve that from you."

"All right, but don't bother screaming," Beth said. "Everyone who drank the hot chocolate is out. And I have some work to do here." Marcy watched as the petite woman placed the gun on the furnace and then used a wrench and crowbar to disconnect the vent from the back of the furnace.

Beth spoke calmly as she worked in the tight space behind the furnace. "I used your money to purchase bonds for Bander's version of the cross-island road. Before that, I used your money to buy rocks streaked with gold, and I hired Kovach to ditch them somewhere along the proposed road and include the 'discovery' in his final report."

"He worked for you?" Marcy asked, in disbelief.

"Kovach had no idea it was me. Or you, Marcy. It was your money that paid for his work. I contacted him through the mail, and used Ken Jabard as a go-between."

"You and Ken? But why?"

Beth laughed. "We hooked up after my brother's...accident. I was watching my brother that afternoon he died. School was out and he wouldn't stop whining. So, I pushed him outside, locked the door, and turned the television up loud. He knocked for a while, and I turned up the television louder. After a while, he wandered away. I didn't realize that he had wandered over to a neighbor's.

"Jabard was living in an apartment then. After a while, I

unlocked the door and called my brother. I got a little worried, and went out to look. I saw Jabard emerge from the forest behind our houses. When he saw me, he looked afraid. I asked him if had seen my brother, and he must have heard the fear in my voice. Everyone knew how my father punished us."

Beth paused, and her hand lingered on Marcy's shoulder. "But no one ever stepped in to help. I still remember how Jabard stared at me. He told me that my brother had been sobbing about my locking him out of the house. He told me how he understood and promised not to tell anyone what I had done. As long as I didn't mention running into him on the trail. He told me to return home and not to worry. That my brother would return soon." She laughed. "But of course, my brother didn't return. Dogs found his body a few days later. Everyone believed me when I explained how he had run outside and how I had called and tried to find him. The police assumed the killer had taken the clothes. I only guessed about what happened months later."

"Beth, kids fight." Marcy's voice shook. "You could have told someone. You should have never protected Jabard."

"But Marcy, you don't understand. He was good to me. So kind. Even when I was older, I couldn't be absolutely sure. I didn't want to believe that Jabard had hurt my brother. Besides, my life was so much better after my brother died. I didn't have to come home and baby-sit every day after school. My parents loved me more. My father was angry, but never with me. No one ever mentioned my brother around me, and it was easy to forget." Beth smiled, as she returned to work on the furnace, standing back and checking the exhaust vent.

"So who came up with the idea about putting gold near the cross-island road?"

"Jabard did," Beth said. "I told him that I had a source of money. I never told him it was yours, but he might have guessed. He recommended hiring Kovach, who found a wonderful stream not on any of the maps. Everything went perfectly until Francesca started trying to talk you into letting Jane McBride help with your finances. I couldn't take the chance that she'd discover what I'd done with your money before the hearings about the road began. I had already made arrangements to transfer your money and keep it in a local account, then I used those funds to purchase Sitka municipal funds and Bander's road bonds. Then, I sent that note for you to leave town. You should have listened. The bonds soared after the news about gold hit the newspapers. I made enough to get out of this town and find my own freedom—enough to return money to your accounts so no one will ever guess. I don't have to stay in a little town and work for little people. Believe me, I deserve this after what I've done for you."

"Who wrote the gray notes?" Marcy could not stop asking questions. She wanted to hear the truth, even though every answer from Beth meant that the woman had no intention of letting her go.

"I did," Beth replied briskly.

"How could I have been so wrong about you?" Marcy said, with disgust. "Beth, the police will never believe that this is an accident."

"The police in this town are fools. Jabard proved that during my brother's investigation, and we did it again with the investigation into Tim's death and Kovach's disappearance."

"Please don't hurt Davy and Gavan and the others," Marcy begged. "They don't know about any of this."

"I promised that I wouldn't hurt you, Marcy," Beth said with a laugh as she picked up the sock again. "Time for you to shut up."

She used two fingers to insert the sock, and Marcy used all her strength, lunging and catching Beth's index finger in her mouth, biting with all her might. Beth screamed, then pushed her other fist against Marcy's head. Marcy cried out and Beth shoved the sock inside.

Marcy gagged, twisting to loosen the ropes.

"Damn you, Marcy James," Beth said, her eyes sparkling like those of an angry hawk. "You all deserve to die. And no one's going to miss you." She left the furnace room for a few moments and returned with Gavan's hockey stick, placing it near the vent. "Perfect," Beth said, with pride. "Time to turn the temperature up. The furnace will release carbon monoxide into the whole house. All the windows are shut. Everyone's asleep. Carbon monoxide's heavy, so you will definitely go first. The others may or may not wake up in time."

Marcy growled and tried to wiggle her tongue, but it was jammed against the bottom of her mouth.

"Don't fight this, Marcy," Beth said, waving the gun and wrench triumphantly. "I promised that I wouldn't hurt you, Marcy, and that was the truth. You're lucky, Marcy, it's a nice way to go. Be careful, I wedged that sock in very tightly. Relax, or otherwise you will choke…

"I'll be back before morning. In the meantime, I plan to finish off what Francesca started. I'll use her gun on Jabard, leave it there and head back here. You'll be dead by then and I'll untie you and turn down the thermostat. Then I'll report the tragedy. It will be interesting to see how this plays out in the paper. Suicide? Accident? Most likely an unhappy teenager who found an opportunity to murder his family. The cops and Denson are imaginative. But they'll never suspect me."

Beth looked about, and then turned off the light to the utility room, leaving Marcy in darkness. "Good-bye, Marcy," Beth whispered.

GAVAN HELD HIS CROUCHED position in the dark cupboard, though his legs had gone numb, and struggled to listen, trying to figure out what to do. Should he follow them? Try to fight with Beth?

Another thump came from downstairs, near the furnace

room in the back. He opened the pantry door and went to the basement door, hearing enough to know that Beth had no immediate plans to kill his mother. Beth didn't want to shoot anyone and wake the family. So, he went to his bedroom and gently shut the door. Gavan could turn off that thermostat. But first he wanted Beth to leave, assuming that only Marcy knew her plans. If Beth caught him awake, he was sure that she'd use the gun. Especially on him. He collected his stuffed animals from under the bed, along with a hefty pile of dirty laundry, and bunched them under his sheets and quilts. He examined the lump and pushed at its middle. In the dark, the setup would pass for a sleeping boy. Not that he ever slept with covers over his head, but Beth didn't know that.

He crept to the vent and opened it. Warm air blasted at him. He sniffed and felt silly. He knew from science that carbon monoxide was odorless. But the dry, hot air did smell stale, almost poisonous. He had no idea how quickly the gas would take effect. He moved quickly about in the dark, familiar bedroom and found his sneakers. Then, he opened his window and straddled the window sill.

A small tree was nearby. Gavan leaped and grabbed the thickest branch. He had left his room once that way when he was eight years old. His father had threatened to chop the tree down and Gavan pleaded for the birch, promising never to exit the house that way again. Eventually his parents forgot, but Gavan still occasionally tested the branches, and knew they could hold his weight. The only problem was that he could not reach back and close the window. Refusing to worry, he scrambled down the maze of branches, leaping to the ground and running to the nearest stand of conifers at the edge of his family's property.

Drops of rain hit his face, as he leaned against a cedar and clenched his teeth. He hated the idea of leaving his mother behind, tired and terrified. But he had to wait for Beth to leave. The house was quiet, the lights were out. Not far away, on Shore Road, the headlights of a car flashed and sped on by. Gavan studied his home. No passerby would suspect anything unusual with the house, least of all a mass murder in slow-motion.

Only Gavan could stop Beth's plan. He waited for her to leave, crouching under the cover and crossing his arms tight. He wore two sweatshirts, not enough for a damp November night. The sprinkles turned to real rain, bouncing against the trees with a pleasant sound and making the air smell clean.

He shut his eyes, and shivered. A vision of Jabard's arms flashed before him. He saw a gnarled vein and Gavan's mouth suddenly went sour. He'd never forget the slippery hand stroking his hands and then his hair, all the while Gavan's throat was tight with fear. Gavan had fought his hardest and couldn't stop the man. Tim must have fought the same way.

Gavan started to cry, hurting as he thought of his friend, about how they would never talk again. Cold rain ran down his skin and mixed with tears.

The door to his house opened. Gavan sniffed and wiped away the tears, and then focused on standing still in the shadows. Beth ran out, dressed in an old hiking coat and pants that belonged to his mother.

Gavan held his breath, hoping she would not circle the house, searching for him. But she didn't glance his way. Instead, she started the Jeep and moved it from the driveway. Then, she ran to her car and pulled it to the road. Quickly, she returned the Jeep back to its place in the driveway and turned it off.

With a little skip, she ran back to the Oldsmobile. The car, its headlights still dark, moved slowly down the road. When she reached the lower road, she switched the lights on and picked up speed.

Gavan had no idea how quickly it took for carbon monoxide to work. Still, he took a moment to run to the road and look. No sign of Beth's or any other car. Keeping low, he ran back to his house and tried the doors to the kitchen and utility room. Both were locked. He groaned and ran around to the front, turned the doorknob. Beth had locked them all.

He heard tires on the slick street and dropped flat on the porch. A pickup, not an Oldsmobile, drove on by. Gavan thought about breaking a window, but he didn't dare attract attention and a neighbor's call to the police. Not yet, he thought.

Beth had locked the doors, but surely she did not take time to lock every window in the house. He raced to the nearby shed and searched for anything to help him reach the first-floor windows. He grabbed four of the biggest flower pots and ran back to the largest living room window that faced Sitka Sound, rather than the street or neighbors. The bottom of the window was about five feet off the ground—and Gavan alternated the pots and their plates, upside down underneath, creating a stack about three feet high. He carefully stepped on top and the pots held.

Keeping his balance, he pushed up against the window, but his hands slipped against the wet glass. Swearing, he removed a sweatshirt and wiped his hands and the glass thoroughly. Then he pushed again. The window opened a crack. He wedged his fingers inside, gritted his teeth and lifted.

As the window opened, one of the pots slipped and broke, and Gavan tumbled to the ground.

Gavan raced to the shed, grabbed another pot, one still filled with dirt, and ran back, adding it to the stack. Again, he grasped the ledge, and pushed his hardest to move the window up. Then, he hefted his whole body up to the sill, crawling through the space and tumbling inside. His feet knocked against a case, breaking a vase and a glass bird that was a favorite of his mother's. Pausing, Gavan listened, hoping no one upstairs would mistake him for an intruder. But the house remained dark and silent and too warm.

Gavan rubbed his shoulder and ran for the hallway. Beth had set to thermostat to ninety, and he turned it off. The furnace immediately paused. Without hesitation, Gavan ran to his father's room and closed the vent. He paused only a second to check and make sure his father was still breathing. He ran to his aunt's room and repeated the procedure. Sweat dotted her brow and neck, even though she had shaken off the blankets. Her breathing sounded fine, and he flung open a window, then arranged a blanket over her shoulders.

The wind blew a cold blast of rainy air into the room, and Gavan felt sharply awake, completely intent on what he was about to do. Passing through the family room, Gavan noticed that Jane's face looked flushed. He threw all the nearby windows open wide—and covered her with a comforter. Finally, he scrambled downstairs to the basement and the furnace room, opening every window he passed, fumbling in the dark. He could not turn on lights, afraid about Beth or anyone else passing by. He did not want to wake up the other adults. Not yet.

The basement air was hot. "It's okay, Mom, it's me!" Gavan called out softly. He didn't stop, but immediately unlocked and swung open a window and then the door to the outside. As moist air rushed in, his mother's weary face gleamed with tears of joy and relief. Gavan stood by the door and swung it open and shut, hard, like a giant fan, cooling and clearing the air. The dismantled furnace remained quiet.

As the room cooled, Gavan moved close to his mother. "Mom, are you okay?" he whispered. She nodded, as he gently removed the sock from her mouth.

"Oh, Gavan, thank God you woke up."

"I never went to sleep," he said softly. "I was in the kitchen and heard everything."

"I'm horrified about Beth," Marcy sobbed. "She must have hated me for a long time."

Gavan loosened some of his mother's ties and looked about. "I'm afraid to turn the lights on. She could come back."

"Let me go and we can call the police. We have to let them know, so they can catch her."

Gavan responded with a quick hug, then went to the door that led outside. He looked out toward the dark shapes of mountains in the night. Leaves twitched in the rain, pearly clouds hung low, and the rain resembled tiny pieces of silver thread. Hiking would be rough on a night like this, and he knew Beth had not made it very far. He needed a moment to think about what to say to his mother.

"Gavan, honey, don't be afraid. She's not coming back now."

He turned toward her, his face hidden in the shadows. "The police. You'd call, Mom, if I untied you?"

"Of course! Quick, get a knife in the kitchen and cut me free. Then we wake your father. She probably drugged him, too."

"That's what I thought," he murmured. He did not move from his post by the door and thought about Beth. She'd be nearing One Last Chance Road by now. It would be rough in the woods at night, moving all alone. But once on the logging road, she'd find Jabard in no time. Long before dawn. She'd call out and he'd assume that she was there to help him. Gavan stared off in the direction of the mountains invisible in the rain and darkness. But he could hear Tim's voice from the last day they had spent together. "Gavan, other people talk, but you act. You get things done." The voice was a memory, one of many good memories of Tim, and Gavan smiled.

The good memories could overtake the terrifying ones. Gavan probably would never forget the pure fear when he realized that he could not talk Jabard into letting him walk away, when he realized he could not escape. He remembered his shame, pleading with Jabard to let him go, promising that he'd tell no one, relaying the wordless message that Jabard did not have to worry, that he could go and find another boy. Anything to let Gavan live. All the same and more had happened to Tim.

Gavan had made a decision. He could never live with himself if Jabard had the opportunity to hurt someone else.

"Get a knife," his mother repeated gently. "I know you're tired, but please get the knife and let me go."

Gavan moved closer to his mother. "No," he said. "I can't do that."

"Why not?" she asked, puzzled.

"I'm sorry, but I can't let you go."

"But…"

He shook his head firmly. "We can't call the police tonight. We'll call in the morning, after Beth has had time to get into the woods." He let the words drift, but not from a lack of conviction. Somehow, he hoped that his mother would agree. He'd give Beth until dawn, time to reach Jabard. Tim's killer would never go free.

"Gavan," Marcy said. "Please listen to me. Jabard will be punished. He's not going to get away with Tim's death. Or what happened tonight. People will believe you."

Gavan shook his head bitterly. "No one could ever know what I felt tonight. What Tim must have felt. If they understood, then they wouldn't let that happen to kids. One way or the other, I'm making sure that man never touches anyone else ever again." With that, Gavan went to a shelf for an old blanket that the family used for picnics. He wrapped it around his mother, tucking it around her shoulders and arms. "How's your head, Mom?"

"Better. But, Gav…"

"You can't convince me," he warned. "Don't try. I'm sorry, but I'm not going to change my mind."

"Gavan, what about your father and aunt upstairs? They could wake up."

"Don't think about it. If you yell, I'll gag you again myself. But trust me, Aunt Francesca and Dad are out from the cocoa. I threw mine in the toilet."

"How could Beth do this?" his mother moaned.

"She's not happy, Mom. She never will be." With that, he grabbed another blanket, and found some towels, propping them under his mother's head for pillows. Then he sat close to her, with the other blanket. "We'll give her some more time, and only then will we call the police."

"Gavan, think about what you're saying," his mother said. "About Beth not being happy. Happiness is all I want for you. And if you let Beth kill Jabard, you might regret it someday."

Gavan laughed and gave her a kiss. "That argument works the other way, too, Mom. I'll regret it more if he ever has the chance to hurt another kid again. It's only a few hours. Whatever happens to Mr. Jabard is my responsibility. I was all ready to go out tonight and do it myself. But Beth took over."

Marcy shivered and did not respond. Gavan wondered what she saw in his eyes—he liked to think that he felt more hope and conviction than vengeance or pain.

"If he doesn't die tonight, I'll never forgive myself," Gavan said. "But Beth is good at getting jobs done—when she really wants them done." With that, he tucked the blanket around her once again, and waited nearby like a sentry to her heart.

TWENTY-SEVEN

Thanksgiving Day, November 28

MARCY WOKE UP IN THE DARK and chilly silence, welcoming that first moment of anticipation and alertness before memory kicks in. She pulled the covers to her chin and then remembered that it was Thanksgiving and that she was home with her family. She crept out of bed to steal some time alone to think about the day ahead, a holiday so rich with expectation and offering a glorious break from the past.

Once downstairs, she started the coffee, making it extra strong. Then, she quickly moved through the kitchen and family room, gathering newspapers that only partly explained the complicated events of the past week—Jabard found tied to a tree and shot dead; Beth's car abandoned along One Last Chance Road and the lawyer missing, presumed dead; an elaborate scam about a gold find in the Tongass; Gavan abducted, but then found safe and alive by his mother and friends.

Marcy crumpled the newspapers, knelt before the woodstove and stuffed them quickly inside. Once she would have carefully clipped the articles, carefully placed them in a box in the attic, attempts to preserve family history. But the words were sterile, strange, and could never come close to her most vivid memories—the pain of leaving for Florida, the hurt of walking through town with Grogan and noticing the glances of disgust, the frustration of waiting and finally that one precious moment of relief, running through the forest and hearing Gavan's voice.

Marcy added dry twigs and two small cedar logs, lit a match and watched the papers twist and burn away.

The house was peaceful, her husband and son still asleep, and so she poured her coffee and sat on the chair closest to the fire, checking over her list for Thanksgiving dinner. Initially, Marcy had planned on spending the day alone with her immediate family. But Davy and Francesca had protested, urged her to join with friends and family, to talk and laugh and forget. Francesca volunteered to host the large Thanksgiving dinner, but Marcy was firm. "No, all I thought about the last few months was spending Thanksgiving at home, and so let us have it here, and everyone can help."

And the list of guests grew. The police immediately dropped the assault charges against Grogan, but he was in no hurry to leave town. Marcy wanted him to experience a Sitka Thanksgiving, potluck style with friends. Francesca and her husband had offered to come early with salmon appetizers and help with the last-minute preparations, mashing potatoes and making gravy. Bob Denson and his girlfriend were making cranberry and pumpkin breads. Lance Willard and other fishermen offered to bring wine and beer. Marcy had even invited Ellen Bander, after she had stopped by with flowers and expressed gratitude for finding her son's killer. "Not yet," Ellen had said sadly. "I'm not ready yet. But please invite me again someday." Then, she looked around the hallway and smiled. "Tim loved your home and was always bursting with funny stories about spending time with your family. Don't ever change." She hugged Marcy and said good-bye.

No one could image how hard it was for the three family members to adjust to living with one another again after the separation, the awkward questions and long periods of silence. Indeed, the toughest part of the week was explaining to Davy why she had not contacted him, especially before setting out on the search for Gavan. "I wanted to protect you," Marcy said simply. Her husband had agreed that he probably would have confided in Beth about Marcy's return, and Beth would have reacted quickly to kill the family.

"It's over," Davy said, with relief, holding her in his arms. "We have to get back to a normal life. No more secrets. No more denying what we think. We say and argue for what we want—all three of us—but then we go on and never forget what's most important to us." As Davy wrapped his arms around his wife and son, Marcy glanced at her son. The boy smiled quickly and then looked away.

Marcy didn't have the heart to tell her husband that every person carried secrets that could never fully be explained. She simply could not explain all her feelings about the night that she had rescued Gavan. In the basement that night, Gavan and Marcy had resolved to answer all questions from the police and tell the truth. But the next day, the investigators' questions were few and pointed. Gavan had described how he could not sleep and got up from bed to turn off the furnace. Marcy had started to explain how she and Gavan debated over calling the police to chase Beth. But Detective Gallagher had raised his hand and stopped the explanations. "The case is closed," he had said firmly.

A few other people guessed about the timing that night— Davy, Francesca, Grogan. But they didn't ask many questions, with most assuming that Marcy had somehow delayed the police, either deliberately or not. And she didn't rush to defend herself or deny responsibility. Without a doubt, she could have argued more with Gavan. She could have screamed.

Marcy added another log to the roaring fire, then checked the clock. She had another three hours before she had to pop the turkey in the oven. The pumpkin pies were ready, the cranberry sauce was made. She only had to peel potatoes and prepare some vegetables, cream corn and green bean bundles wrapped in bacon. Dawn was just breaking over Sitka's mountaintops. Marcy sipped her coffee slowly and stared at the red coals.

Ironically, few in town cared about the details of Marcy or Gavan's decision that night. Most were satisfied that Jabard was dead and could no longer hurt other children. Few worried about Beth Roberts, who had never returned to town after hiking out to kill Jabard. A rescue team of volunteers, police and firefighters searched for three days, by foot and by helicopter. But they only found the abandoned car, along with the gun borrowed from Francesca and Marcy's hat, more than four miles inland from Jabard's body. Police theorized that Beth had killed Jabard, then panicked in the night, losing her way in the forest and possibly falling to her death in some remote ravine.

The story caught national attention, but the murders were only a small part of the story. Most pundits crowed because the powerful *Wall Street Journal* had to explain how one of its reporters had been fooled into promoting a development scan. The bond prices crashed and bondholders sued the newspaper. The *Journal's* editors fired Knowles, and the state canceled all road construction for the Tongass. Meanwhile, requests for information about Sitka as a tourism destination skyrocketed. Reports that gold, natural or not, dotted a stream in the middle of Tongass National Forest had ignited gold fever throughout the world, and tourists were eager to try a hand at panning for the novelty.

From upstairs came creaking noises from Gavan's bedroom and Marcy smiled, imagining her son stretching and waking to a new day. Her child had always claimed that Thanksgiving was his favorite holiday, and this year, the James family had so many reasons to give thanks. But most of the reasons would go unspoken. Marcy had learned that love could exist, even flourish, amid doubt and disagreement.

She could accept differences in others, even those whom she loved most.

She closed her eyes and thought of Gavan. They had only spoken once about the decision not to call the police and stop Beth and that was when the boy had untied his mother's arms. The basement had been cold and dark, and a blanket was not enough to prevent the shivering and aches. So, well before dawn, Gavan had slowly untied his mother's arms and legs.

But she did not hurry away to call the police, instead rubbing her arms and then pulling the pair of blankets around them both.

"Something tells me that we can't let him go," Gavan had said, leaning against Marcy and closing his eyes. "Trust me about this."

And Marcy didn't move except to nod. "I understand," she replied. She had to trust her son or he would forever become a distant stranger who didn't matter. She had loved him completely without knowing him, on the day he was born, and more than twelve years later, she had discovered that those feelings had not changed. Still, Marcy and Gavan were curious enough to try and understand their differences.

"Thanks, Mom," he whispered gruffly. He wrapped his arm around her and she could feel the warmth of his body, much like when he used to climb in bed with her every morning as an eager toddler. But she also could feel his strength. So many years ago, she had carried a little baby boy about in her arms. She had taught him silly songs, and wiped away countless tears and smudges of dirt. They had read books for hours and talked about what was right and wrong with the world. And somewhere along the way, he had learned how to make his own choices.

Marcy expected they would both move on and accept the memories of that night. Gavan could control what and how he would remember.

As children grow up, the memories and stories of childhood become myths. The details shape a child's life, providing motivation, hope and comfort as life grows more complicated. Every person shares some of the stories, allowing others brief glimpses into the transformation of one individual. And other stories, the most important ones, are withheld, pushed into the dark passages of the mind and kept a secret from the rest of the world.